Stephen Wilkins was born

Between 1998 and 2001 he ⌐ubai as a
University Lecturer. He has had several articles on
education, training and human resource development
in Dubai published in international journals. Stephen
now lives in East Anglia, where he works as a teacher.
Dubai Creek is his first novel.

Stephen Wilkins

Dubai Creek

Matador
9 De Montfort Mews
Leicester LE1 7FW, UK
Tel: (+44) 116 255 9311 / 9312
Email: books@troubador.co.uk
Web: www.troubador.co.uk/matador

This novel is a work of fiction. The names, characters and incidents portrayed in it are the work
of the author's imagination. Any similarity to real persons, living or dead, is coincidental and
not intended by the author. Some of the places and locations featured are real, and their
descriptions and details accurate, whilst others are imaginary.

ISBN 1 905237 47 2

Typeset in 11pt Stempel Garamond by Troubador Publishing Ltd, Leicester, UK
Printed by The Cromwell Press Ltd, Trowbridge, Wilts, UK

Matador is an imprint of Troubador Publishing Ltd

For
Marina, Andrew,
my Mother, my Father,
Julia and Ray

Preface

I am very pleased that the first print run of *Dubai Creek* was well received and that it sold out within two months of publication. I am saddened, however, that some readers thought I'd portrayed Dubai in an overly negative way. This was never my intention. This is a work of fiction but, as it covers several real-life issues, I thought it would be useful if I give readers an idea of where the boundary lies between fact and fiction.

My novel represents one western expatriate's individual view of Dubai in the light of his fictional experiences. Most of the everyday routine events that Nick was involved in were typical of those facing expatriates five years ago. But some no longer apply today. Furthermore, the narrator's viewpoint expresses just his own, often biased, view of a situation. For example, Nick found the car ownership transfer process complex and cumbersome. In reality, however, it is a very effective process that actually works. In the UAE, it would be impossible for anyone to buy a second-hand car and 'inherit' loan debts or outstanding traffic fines.

Much of the book is pure fiction. Storylines have been exaggerated or rendered shocking for greater effect. I carried out a significant amount of research before and during the writing of my manuscript. At no time did I find any evidence of police unfairness or mistreatment of prisoners or any general anti-western sentiment after 9/11.

One of my aims in writing this novel was to help the expatriates and the indigenous population to understand each other better in order to promote increased tolerance. I greatly enjoyed living in Dubai and hope that I have succeeded in conveying my admiration for the nation's rulers and how successfully they have established what is certain to be one of the leading cities in the world in the very near future.

Stephen Wilkins
April 2006

Dubai Creek

*D*ubai Creek flows from the Arabian Gulf into the heart of Dubai. About the same width as the River Thames at Tower Bridge, its clear, blue water is usually bustling with activity. The creek is the first thing that most people see when arriving in Dubai by air. First they see the old, traditional areas of narrow alleys surrounded by white buildings with flat roofs and souks selling spices, gold and textiles. Then they will see the tall, modern and distinctive tower blocks that provide offices for several government departments and many of the country's leading companies. Dubai Creek became one of my favourite places in Dubai. I enjoyed walking down the promenade on the Bur Dubai side of the creek and admiring the spectacular city landscape or resting in one of the many gardens from where I could watch others strolling, jogging, participating in group keep-fit exercises, sleeping, or in the case of children, playing. I also found it fun to explore the dark alleyways in which traders displayed their wares and to ride across the creek on one of the abras, the small wooden boats that operated as water buses.

Before I went to Dubai, I had, of course, heard of it, but I didn't really know where exactly it was and I couldn't recall having ever met anyone who had been there. However, since returning to the UK from Dubai I keep coming across people who have also been there. My new boss worked in Dubai for a couple of years, one of my major clients is an Arab from Dubai, my new next-door neighbour was brought up there as a child as his father had a job there, and I must have come across at least a dozen or so people who have been there on holiday. It's not surprising really, as Dubai has become one of the UK's most popular long-haul tourist destinations. Much in Dubai will impress the visitor. It has a hot, dry climate, some of the best hotels in the world and long, clean, golden sandy beaches that line clear blue seas that rarely feel cold. The city's architecture is unique, imaginative and truly impressive. All types of shopping opportunity exist from modern shopping malls selling designer goods at cheap prices to exotic souks selling spices and gold. The range of sporting and recreational activities

1

available is incredible and includes diving, sailing, fishing, shooting, swimming, tennis, squash, camel or horse riding and flying. There are many impressive golf courses, which are among the best in the world. The large areas of desert provide many opportunities for fun including dune or quad biking, sand boarding or skiing and wadi or dune bashing in 4x4s. It is possible to go climbing, caving or hiking in the mountainous regions, and in the city there are several large parks so lush and green you wouldn't believe you were in a desert region.

Everyone I've met who's been to Dubai loved it. No one has had a bad thing to say about the place. However, visitors base their view of Dubai only on superficial observations made over a number of days. To know and understand Dubai one has to live there for months, or perhaps even years, and even then one might not experience every side of that unique place. Maybe that's the same with every city; I'm not sure. Anyway, I have lived and worked in Dubai, and I will tell you about it. I won't leave anything out. I will tell you about my highs, my lows, my triumphs and my secrets.

My adventure started one cold, wet and grey October morning when I got to work and was greeted by the receptionist who said, 'Good morning Nick. Mr. Anderson would like to see you at ten, and don't forget you've got Mr. Clarkson at eleven thirty and the Smithco presentation at two.' As I walked along the corridor towards my office I wondered what Mr. Anderson, head of my division, wanted to talk to me about. I had worked for JBNC for just over five years and I'd only come into contact with Mr. Anderson on a handful of occasions. I'd attended a couple of meetings that he had addressed and I'd had a few brief conversations with him at office functions like the Christmas party. I wasn't senior enough to interact with Mr. Anderson on a regular basis. It was my boss's boss who reported to Mr. Anderson. I found it hard to concentrate on my work that morning as I kept wondering what Mr. Anderson wanted to talk to me about, which was very unfortunate as I had plenty to do that day. I sat looking out of the window and tried to recall if I had done anything wrong. I did have a minor disagreement with a client the week before; had they complained, I wondered? Perhaps it would be good news, a promotion or a pay rise? Rather unlikely, I reflected. More likely to be bad news, perhaps redundancy. Staff were being laid off in yet another round of cost cutting intended to stop the decline in group profitability.

That was the slowest two hours I'd experienced in a long while. I could not take my eyes off the clock fixed on the wall by my office door. I don't know why I was feeling so anxious and nervous, just like a naughty schoolboy waiting outside their headmaster's office shortly before receiving a good caning. After all, I was generally considered good at my job and I had recently won some very profitable contracts. At five to ten I got up and made my way towards Mr. Anderson's office. When I got there, I found Jasper Harrington sitting on a chair in the corridor right outside Mr. Anderson's office. I guess that Jasper Harrington was about the same age as me (I was 27 at that time) but he

3

was well known in the company as a high flier, an achiever who was expected to go all the way at JBNC, maybe even to director level. I didn't know Jasper, or Jas as he liked to be known, well. We'd worked in the same teams for a couple of projects but not together on a one-to-one basis. He was typical of young men who had been to a good public school, or at least what I perceive to be typical: an overly confident personality, a smart appearance with never a hair out of place, shoes that were well polished every day and a voice which pronounced each syllable with great care, but which had that nasal sound that some people think posh.

'Hello Nick, good to see you again,' Jas said.

'Likewise,' I replied.

'Are you here to see Mr. Anderson as well?' Jas continued.

'Yes, he asked to see me at ten,' I answered. Jas told me that he had also been asked to see Mr. Anderson at ten and that he too was wondering what it was about. Just then, the door to Mr. Anderson's office opened and out came Mr. Anderson. He invited both Jas and me into his office at the same time. We all sat around Mr. Anderson's large oak table that smelt heavily of furniture polish. 'Well I guess you're both wondering what I wanted to speak to you about,' Mr. Anderson began. 'Well, you see, an opportunity has come up at short notice which I thought you may be interested in. You would essentially each be doing the same jobs that you're doing now but the financial reward would be much higher because you would get an accommodation allowance and you wouldn't have to pay any tax.'

'It's overseas then?' Jasper interrupted excitedly.

'That's right,' replied Mr. Anderson. 'Last year we set up an office in Dubai, which has become very successful and they now require two more high quality consultants like yourselves. I think it's a good opportunity for both of you. If you do well there you will be well placed to return as a section head or you may decide to develop an international career.' Mr. Anderson continued explaining at length why the offer was too good to turn down but I wasn't really taking in what he was saying. My mind had started wandering. Where exactly was Dubai? Would I like living there? What would I do with my flat in London, which I only bought two years ago? What if I was going to get back together with Jenny, my girlfriend with whom I split up only last month?

For a while I thought pleasantly about Jenny, who I was missing, but then I remembered our last evening together when she said that we weren't right for each other. Perhaps she was right. She was a nice girl but we really had nothing in common. My problem was that I hadn't met many girls in London with whom I seemed to have much in common. I did have a good social life and I had a string of girlfriends, but they tended to come and go rather quickly. Perhaps I expected too much, but I'm not sure that I did. All that I wanted was a girl who was reasonably attractive, who had a good personality and who was easy to get along with, and who had a bit of a brain. I'd had enough of the airheads who hang around in the city bars hoping to hook a rich guy like myself. Not that I was rich exactly, but I guess that the average man in the street would have considered me well off.

After we left Mr. Anderson's office Jas asked me if I wanted to meet up for a drink later that day to discuss the offer made to us. By this time I already had other plans formed in my mind for when I finished work that day, and to be honest the decision of whether or not to go Dubai was one that I wanted to come to on my own without any influence from Jasper. I knew he was eager to go from the moment he realised he was being offered an overseas posting. Anyway, I could tell he was disappointed that I turned down his offer to go out together after work. 'Shame you can't make it,' he said. 'It might have been mutually beneficial to talk things through. Another time maybe?' I agreed to meet up with him at some other time during the week.

When I finished work at six, I emerged from the warmth and comfort of my office into a dark and wet street. I wondered if I could get to Foyles, the bookshop, before it closed. Wanting to get to Foyles as quickly as possible, and not wanting to get too wet, I hailed a passing cab and asked to be taken to Charing Cross Road. When I got to Foyles at six thirty I was relieved to find it still open and relatively busy, and I went straight to the travel section. I found the books on Cyprus, the Czech Republic, Denmark, the Dominican Republic and Egypt, but could not see any on Dubai. I went over to the service counter and asked the assistant, 'Don't you have any books on Dubai?'

'Try looking under the United Arab Emirates,' she replied. I went back to the display of books and then found several on the United Arab Emirates, or the UAE as it is more commonly known. I then remembered that Dubai was one of the seven emirates that made up the UAE. Abu Dhabi and Sharjah were two of the others. There were some books aimed at tourists but also a couple aimed at expatriates living and working there. I began flicking through the pages of the various books reading with great interest everything written about the UAE, and Dubai in particular. I became so engrossed in those books that I completely lost track of time. The next thing I became aware of was hearing the shop assistant calling out, 'We're closing in five minutes. Please bring all purchases to the counter now.' I looked at my watch; it was eight o' clock so I must have been stood there reading for a good hour and a half. I made my way to the service counter and bought three books. I then caught the tube back home.

After I finished my dinner, I sat down on my settee and gazed out of the window. I didn't draw the blinds so that I could admire the beautiful river view from my lounge. At that time I lived in an apartment overlooking the Thames. From my balcony I had a spectacular view of Tower Bridge and behind it you could just get a glimpse of the Tower of London. The city lights lit up the night sky magnificently and down below on the water a pleasure boat quietly passed, obviously doing one of those evening dinner cruises. Whenever friends or family visited my home they always admired the view from my lounge. Everyone seemed to love it. I was proud of my home and of what I had achieved in my life. What I achieved hadn't come easily, however; I had to get a first class honours degree from the London School of Economics, an MBA from a less reputable university that I shan't name and then I had to work long and hard at JBNC to get where I was. JBNC is one of the world's top five accountancy firms. I was well aware that many young men envied what I had: a beautiful, stylish home, a good job with a large salary, a new 5 series BMW, an extensive wardrobe and usually a lovely girl in tow. Most of the men who lived on the nearby council estates had none of these things. I sat and wondered if I was really prepared to give up my comfortable and quite exciting life in London for a place halfway around the world that I really knew nothing about. I eagerly started reading my newly acquired books on the UAE, and to be honest, what I read I found greatly interesting.

Mr. Anderson had given us a week to decide whether or not we wanted to go to Dubai, but three days after the offer was made I had already made up my mind to accept it. I had made my mind up before meeting up with Jas and a group of his friends at Shelley's on the night of that third day. I think that Jas had also already made up his mind to go, but neither of us openly admitted it. Instead, we discussed as a group the pros and cons of going. About six of us sat drinking cocktails in a quiet corner of the trendy bar. One of Jas's friends, Jim, started the conversation off, 'I'm sure Dubai's an exciting place to live and work but I think you'll miss the things you take for granted in this country, like democracy, culture and alcohol.'

'Dubai's not dry,' Jas quickly interrupted. 'Alcohol is freely available to the expats and according to Mr. Anderson the nightlife is rather lively.'

'And your Mr. Anderson is a good judge of that is he?' replied Jas's friend a little sarcastically. I guessed that this friend was probably just jealous that we had the opportunity to go and live in the sun and make big bucks while having a lot of fun, whereas he would be stuck in some boring office job in London. Then another female friend chipped in, 'Well you'll certainly have to be on your best behaviour. You can get a good whipping if you get caught spitting in the street or if you get caught chewing gum.'

Again, Jas was quick to reply. 'I think it's Singapore you're thinking of Laura,' he said. 'You can't buy chewing gum there but you can in Dubai. And I'm sure things are not as strict as some people believe.' That provoked a response from Jim. 'I wouldn't be so sure you know. I watched a programme a couple of nights ago about corruption and torture in Saudi Arabia.' That comment encouraged me to participate in the discussion. 'But the UAE is not Saudi Arabia,' I said. 'It's like comparing England with Northern Ireland or even France or Spain.'

'Yes, but you can't lose your head in England, Ireland, France or Spain if you say something which the ruler or government doesn't agree with,' Laura replied, hoping to have the last say on the subject.

'But you can lose your knee caps in Northern Ireland if you cross the IRA,' was Jas's response.

The evening seemed to drag towards the end. It seemed that all of Jas's friends were constantly attacking Dubai and stating only its problems or disadvantages, or what they thought were its problems and disadvantages, while Jas and I ended up staunchly defending the country. It seemed clear to me that none of Jas's friends wanted him to go. Maybe they were just jealous or maybe they didn't want to lose him as a friend. What was even clearer to me by the end of the night, however, was that both Jas and I were on our way to Dubai.

The trip

*J*as and I were booked economy class seats on a flight with the *Emirates* airline. Jas was disappointed that we weren't given business class seats. So was I, but I didn't admit it to Jas, as I generally don't like others to see me as a whinger. I prefer to take a positive outlook on life, as I believe it's healthier for myself and because, lets face it, no one really likes a moaner. Jas and I are both about six feet tall so the legroom was a bit cramped, but after an hour into the flight, after we'd both had a few drinks, we seemed to notice the discomfort less. The *Emirates* staff were all very attentive, giving passengers plenty to eat and drink, and maintaining a pleasant manner despite having to work in challenging conditions. The plane was rocking about a bit and there were several groups of Arab men who persisted in standing in the aisles despite obviously hindering the progress of the stewards with their food and drinks trolleys. I wondered if this was typical behaviour of the local Arabs, to be selfish, inconsiderate and oblivious to the world around them. Eventually, I got to tuck in to my chicken dinner and although it was tasty enough it didn't seem to be that hot. I wanted to blame those Arabs blocking the aisles for that but I suspected that perhaps all the meals were the same temperature, even those given to the passengers right at the back of the plane next to the galley.

Jas was a guy who liked to be constantly talking. I was in the mood for a bit of quiet but I did my best to keep the conversation going. We talked about Dubai, about politics and current affairs, about assignments we'd recently completed at JBNC, about people we both knew and about ourselves, our backgrounds, families, likes and dislikes and of course we compared work résumés. Jas and I both did the same job: we were business consultants. Basically, we went into companies that were having problems or that wanted advice and we sorted the problems or gave the advice. To be honest, if I were the Managing Director or Chief Executive of one of our client companies, I doubt that I would have been willing to pay £1500 a day for my services. I sometimes wonder how helpful to companies I really was. How useful can a twenty seven year old armed only with an MBA and relatively no experience in the real business world really be? But the companies always seem pleased with my work and each assignment I tackled was for a bigger company paying a bigger fee. Consequently, my earnings went up substantially. I made about fifty thousand pounds that year. I wouldn't have been surprised if Jas had made sixty or seventy thousand, but that was not something we discussed. I'm sure Jas would have loved to compare earnings so that he could have confirmed his superiority, but I would have considered such comparison bad taste, and Jas realised that.

After all the passengers had completed their meals, the feature film began on those little screens fixed into the backs of every seat. I was disappointed that the film was *Free Willy 2*, a 'wildlife adventure' about an orca whale. I wasn't really watching the film but I still managed to follow the rather weak plot and I was mildly amused by the model whales. Jas advised me that the sequel used model whales because there was a bit of a scandal about how the real whale was treated in the original film. I did notice, however, that all of the children in my view seemed to be engrossed in the film. When *Free Willy 2* finished we were treated to some vintage BBC comedy: early episodes of *Absolutely Fabulous* and *Only Fools and Horses*. They were a little more entertaining but I wasn't really able to watch those either as Jas ensured that my attention was focused on the conversation topics he chose.

Seven hours after we took off from London, the captain announced on the speaker that we would shortly be arriving in Dubai. I wondered what the airport would be like. Would we go straight from the plane into the terminal or would we have to take a bus from the runway? If the latter, what would the temperature be like at two o' clock in the afternoon in mid November? Was I wearing the right clothes? From the guidebooks I was expecting about twenty degrees, but the books also said that the winter months could be cooler with strong winds. Then, I caught my first glimpse of Dubai. I could see the entrance to the creek and many buildings built closely together. From the air, Dubai looked just like any other city, but a rush of excitement passed through my body. Before I knew it, we were touching down on the runway. We did have to take a bus from the runway to reach the terminal building, but it was somehow a pleasant experience. The sun was shining, there was a gentle breeze and the temperature must have been somewhere close to twenty degrees. I couldn't help smiling to myself when I briefly remembered the cold air and grey skies I had just left behind in London.

Within thirty minutes I had passed through passport control and customs, and had collected my cases from the luggage hall. I had never got out of any airport so quickly. I was impressed. Jas, however, was held up in the customs hall. I saw him being led away by an official but didn't get the chance to speak to him to find out what was happening. I didn't know if it was a routine stop and search or if Jas had brought something with him that he wasn't supposed to. I continued into the arrivals hall to meet up with the driver who was meeting us so that I could advise him that Jas had been held up. The hall was very busy. People were bustling around in every direction, many calling out in loud voices. I was surprised that most of the people looked South Asian rather than Arab. Was I really in Dubai and not in Bombay or Karachi? In Dubai, the term 'Asian' is commonly used to refer to people originating from the Indian subcontinent, which includes countries such as India, Pakistan, Bangladesh and Sri Lanka. The term is not generally applied to UAE citizens.

Eventually, I saw a slim Asian man holding a board saying 'Mr. Harrington and Mr. Williams, JBNC'. I approached him extending my arm for a handshake and introduced myself. 'Nicholas Williams,' I said. 'Pleased to meet you.'

'Welcome to Dubai sir,' replied the man. 'I'm Mohammed and I'll take you to your accommodation.' I explained that Jas had been detained in the customs hall. Mohammed said that it was a common thing, as new workers often brought with them things that they shouldn't, or things, like videos, that needed checking. When eventually Jas appeared some thirty minutes later he explained that his entire video collection was retained for inspection and that he had to collect it from a police station in seven days time. Mohammed led us to the car park and we got into a rather old looking Toyota Corolla. As we left the airport behind us we sped off down a long straight road lined by large retail outlets, but somehow these shops looked like they did little business.

'Where will we be staying initially?' I asked Mohammed.

'You have been booked into the Al Kareema apartments in Bur Dubai,' he replied. 'You will each have your own self-catering apartment. They are a bit basic but rather reasonable. As you have been booked in for two weeks and the expense is being deducted from your annual housing allowance it was decided not to put you in more expensive accommodation. Anyway, in two week's time you can move into any accommodation you wish.'

'What will we get for fifty five thousand dirhams?' asked Jas.

'You will have a big choice,' answered Mohammed. 'You could have a good one bedroom apartment on the Sheikh Zayed highway, where your office is, or you could have a two bedroom apartment in Bur Dubai or Deira, although I don't think most Europeans like to stay in Deira. You could even have a small villa in Mirdif, out by the airport. That area is becoming quite popular. But if you two wanted to share, then you could have a nice villa in somewhere like Satwa, or even possibly in some parts of Jumeirah, which is up by the coast, where all the largest tourist hotels are. Don't worry sir, you will have plenty of choice for your budget. It is a very generous allowance.'

'That's good to hear,' replied Jas, very pleased with himself.

'Just contact any of the real estate agents,' Mohammed continued, 'and they will sort you out. Also, you can buy a newspaper to get an idea of prices and regions.' None of the places that Mohammed had mentioned meant anything to me.

I noticed that the streets were quiet with very few people walking around. 'Is it always so quiet on the streets?' I asked Mohammed.

'It's Friday,' he replied. 'Our weekend is a Thursday and Friday, so no one is working today. Well, not in the offices anyway.' I then remembered reading this in one of my books, but such details hadn't stuck in my mind at this time. There was so much new information to take in. Most of my effort in London had gone into arranging my visa, which required a considerable amount of time and effort (not only visits to the UAE consulate, but also to my solicitor and the Foreign and Commonwealth Office to get my academic certificates testified), and rushing around buying a few things I thought I'd need in Dubai which perhaps I wouldn't be able to get there.

As we went around a roundabout with a clock perched high on tall, curved concrete legs Mohammed commented, 'Clock Tower roundabout.'

'Appropriate name,' replied Jas. He often came out with pointless or inappropriate comments I noted. Then, as we crossed over the Al Maktoum Bridge from the Deira side of the creek to Bur Dubai we got a marvellous view of the creek and the city. I felt in a real holiday mood, relaxed and excited at the same time. A minute later we came to a big crossroads. 'That's Bur Juman shopping mall,' Mohammed said pointing out to his left. 'It's one of the biggest in Dubai. It's good for designer goods, perfumes, watches and those kinds of things, but not for food or everyday items. And ahead of you is Bank Street.'

11

'I suppose that's where all the banks are,' said Jas, trying to sound clever.

'Yes,' replied Mohammed. Jas looked a little surprised.

'And behind you is the embassy district,' continued Mohammed who was then interrupted by Jas again, 'Because that's where the embassies are.'

'You've got it!' returned Mohammed. 'At least quite a few of them. The embassies of Pakistan, India, Yemen, Oman and Egypt are all there, but many others too. And the British one is across the road down by the creek. You see, the government likes to have the same types of business in the same district. Then everyone knows where to go. Simple and lovely!' I was inclined at that time to agree that it sounded like a logical idea. After all, we have industrial zones and green belts in the UK. Isn't that the same kind of thinking?

We then turned off the main road and into a district full of high-rise apartment blocks. Some looked quite nice, others not so nice. The 'not so nice ones' looked older, less well maintained and they had air conditioning boxes on their balconies. I remembered that one of my books advised against renting homes with those, as they were unable to cope with the summer heat as well as central air conditioning systems. We turned left and right a few times and then Mohammed pulled up outside a building, which looked neither particularly new nor old. 'Al Kareema apartments, gentlemen,' he said. 'Your home for the next two weeks.' As I got out from the car I saw that the building was not very impressive. It was about ten stories high and had no balconies. Its white walls were broken only by rows of small square windows. It looked the equivalent of a two star hotel that might be found in Eastbourne or Blackpool, or somewhere like that. I glanced at Jas. He too didn't look too thrilled by what he saw. As Jas and I went to take our cases from the boot of the car, Mohammed told us to leave them, as the porter would bring them in. So, we went up the few steps outside the apartments and into the small lobby. It was clean and basic, but reinforced the impression of being a smaller, family run hotel.

Mohammed spoke to the Indian girl at the reception desk, who then informed Jas and I that she needed to take photocopies of our passports and credit cards. Mohammed explained that while our rooms had already been prepaid and the rate included electricity and air conditioning, our credit card details were held to settle extras like the telephone. While the receptionist disappeared into a back room with our passports and credit cards, the porter came alongside us with our

First night in Dubai

*A*fter an hour or so, there was a knock on my door. It was Jas. 'Just wondering if you had any plans for tonight?' he asked. He suggested we could go for a walk to explore the locality and then find somewhere to eat out. I said that it sounded like a good idea. He had already been to the supermarket and asked if I wanted a drink in his room before we left. I was rather thirsty so asked what he had to offer. 'Tea, the old yellow Liptons tea that they used to sell in England, coffee or Diet Coke,' Jas replied. I asked for a cup of tea, but emphasized that only if it wasn't too much hassle to prepare. Jas, gracious as ever, said that as it happened he quite fancied a cup of tea too. So we went to his room for tea, and shortly after ventured into the big unknown world outside.

Jas led the way confidently. 'I don't really know where we're going,' he said, 'but the receptionist said there's nothing in that direction, so we'd better go this way.' He led us across the open, sandy space that I could see from my room. I wasn't too thrilled about this, as I feared that sand would get into my shoes and then be uncomfortable to walk on. 'Reminds you we're really in a desert doesn't it?' Jas said chirpily. I grunted unenthusiastically and retorted, 'Well so long as there are no snakes.'

'Not very likely right here in the city,' Jas replied, 'but I wouldn't be so surprised if there were some big, fat rats around with all these big open bins everywhere.' As we approached the road behind our apartment block the kerb was lined by three big steel bins, which did each have a lid, but which were all left open. They were each filled to the top with rotten food and household waste, and stunk awfully. In fact I could smell the bins some time before Jas mentioned them, while we were still ten metres or so away. I don't know why, but I peered into one of the bins, and as I did so, a cat jumped out so quickly I thought it was going for my face. But it scurried hurriedly away.

A stream of car headlights in the distance indicated a main road, so

Jas suggested that we head off in that direction. I looked at my watch. It was a quarter to seven. The sun was close to setting and the sky was a deep orange colour. The air was still warm. As we passed tower block after tower block I was conscious that we were the only ones walking in the streets. It was so pleasant out that I wondered why everyone would want to stay in their apartments. I made a remark along these lines to Jas. 'They're probably at the beach, or at a park, or somewhere else that we do not yet know about,' was his reply.

'Probably,' I agreed, although I wasn't very convinced by his explanation for the empty streets.

When we reached the main road, there were more signs of life. There were a few groups of men around. Each group was huddled together busily chatting, some sitting on a wall alongside the road, others standing on street corners or outside what looked like some offices. All the men looked South Asian. They probably came from places like India, Pakistan, Bangladesh and Sri Lanka. There were no women to be seen anywhere. Cars, and many Jeep-style vehicles, sped past us on what was actually a dual carriageway. Some seemed to be going faster than seemed prudent. But the road was pleasant, well landscaped, with an abundance of palm trees and exotic plants lining both sides of the street. Then, ahead of us I saw the Ramada Hotel. It didn't look like a very new hotel. 'Looks like the hotel has a nightclub,' said Jas eagerly, pointing at a side door with a canopy at the top of a stairway. 'That could be handy,' he continued.

'I wonder if it is any good. Wonder what music they play and all,' was my response, but I was then cut off by Jas again. 'And whether there are any ladies,' he said. 'And if there are, what they are like. We will certainly have to investigate one evening, Mr. Williams.'

On the other side of the road was a shopping mall, complete with a McDonalds on the ground floor. 'Well, at least we'll be able to survive on Big Macs if we can't find anything else decent to eat,' Jas commented as we both looked across the road smiling. Not that I am a big fan of fast food or anything. I might have had the odd pizza or kebab, but I rarely ate burgers back at home. On our right hand side we passed a branch of *Spinneys*, a large, European-looking supermarket. I suggested that we take a quick look inside the store, as it might be where we'd be doing our shopping for the next two weeks. It was bright and clean, and much like any other supermarket. By the entrance door were cash dispenser machines, and then there was an in-store café on the left and the row of checkouts to the right. Most of the customers looked like westerners. My eyes also fell on the customer notice board. There were flats for rent, cars for sale, furniture for sale, and notices from numerous people offering themselves for numerous different things—cleaning, tutoring children for GCSEs, teaching guitar, teaching English language, teaching Russian language, you name it, it seemed to be there. The majority of advertisers seemed to have western names.

When we left Spinneys, we continued walking down Al Mankhool Road until we reached the junction with 'Bank Street'. Bank Street was busy with both cars and pedestrians. The majority of pedestrians were walking from right to left, away from Bank Street and towards the heart of Bur Dubai, so we followed them. We passed a few nice looking restaurants, which included a couple offering Indian and Chinese cuisine. I was pleased that it looked like eating out in Dubai would not be that different from eating out in London. As we studied the menu outside the Chinese restaurant I wondered if the restaurant's customers would include the local Arabs, or whether they were there solely to serve the international workers and tourists. All of the restaurants were still empty. I was soon to find that eating out in Dubai followed the Mediterranean tradition of a late start. It's not surprising, given that many workers in Dubai work a 'split shift' with a break between one and four in the afternoon. Many office workers don't finish work until eight or eight-thirty each day. But as today was a Friday, the office workers wouldn't have been working anyway. Jas suggested that we ate at about eight-thirty, and he asked if I had any preference regarding type of food. I replied that I'd be happy with some Chinese cuisine, unless we saw anything better in the meantime.

We then turned off the main road, and ended up on Al Faheidi Street. This street was as busy as Oxford Street in London and, with the great number of neon lights on the shop fronts and at the top of buildings, the street was also as bright and colourful as the Las Vegas strip. There were a lot of shops selling electronic items, things like cameras, televisions, music systems and computers. Others sold watches, jewellery or Indian confectionery. There were also several rather grubby looking small restaurants and take-aways in between the shops, but they seemed to be catering solely for the needs of lower-class workers, and by this term I mean the lowly paid labourers from the Indian subcontinent. Many of the shops in the side streets seemed to specialise in textiles. Their window displays were filled with cloths that had a wide variety of designs and textures, including silks, cotton and lace.

Many of the side streets were pedestrianised, but on any road that did take traffic, the traffic had slowed to a snail's pace. I noticed that there were not many westerners walking about in this district, not like the great many we had just seen in Spinneys. There were only a few tourists, mainly Germans I think, who were trying to take a quiet evening stroll, or perhaps casually looking for a bargain in one of the electronics shops, while around them everyone seemed to be frantically rushing about. There were more women to be seen around now, and children also. As I stood still for a moment to soak in the atmosphere I really thought I was in India, not Arabia. The whole street scene looked Indian. It wasn't just that most of the people looked 'Indian', but shops displayed Asian writing, not Arabic characters, and the atmosphere of the whole place was one of neglect and squalor. A pleasant sort of squalor however.

I watched another group of men excitedly exchanging conversation on a street corner. One was spitting into the road, another dropping some cigarette packaging onto the street. My preconceived idea of a strict and clean Dubai was fast fading. So, people did abuse their environment in Dubai just like in any western city. For a moment, I was quite disappointed. We eventually got back to the Chinese restaurant on the main road and had a pleasant enough meal. The food did not quite live up to the quality of the restaurant's fixtures, fittings and decoration, and even the excellent service of the staff. The food was closer to that served in Chinese restaurants in London than the Chinese food served in China or Hong Kong, but something about it reminded me of canteen food. It might have been the type of noodles used or the rather bland flavours, I'm not really sure, but Jas agreed that something was not quite right in order to regard our meal as a 'quality meal'.

First day at work

When I got down to the lobby of our apartment block at five to eight the next morning, Jas and Mohammed were already waiting for me. Jas teasingly looked at his watch and declared, 'Three minutes to spare, so no worries.' I really wanted to tell the pompous twat to shut up, but I just smiled and exchanged greetings and a handshake with Mohammed. Five minutes after we had left our apartments, we came to the eight-lane highway known as the Sheikh Zayed Road. Both carriageways were very busy, with the vehicles in all lanes travelling at or above the 120 kilometre per hour speed limit. As we hit 130 kph, a buzzer, rather like that of an electronic alarm clock, started in the car. 'Don't be concerned,' said Mohammed. 'All cars in the UAE have alarms that go off when they go faster than 120 kph. And everyone does, so you just have to get used to the rather irritating buzzing.'

'Is this the road that takes you straight to Abu Dhabi?' Jas enquired.

'Yes,' replied Mohammed. 'And it's also the place you'll be spending many of your days.' Both sides of the highway were lined with skyscrapers, which included offices, shops, hotels and residential apartments. The buildings all looked new, and they were somehow quite impressive. Then, Mohammed suddenly cut across two lanes, causing a number of vehicles to brake violently to avoid hitting us, and onto the slip road running alongside the main highway. 'And that is your office,' said Mohammed, pointing to the right before driving into the underground car park.

Mohammed led us into a large open plan office, with about twenty desks. As we passed a couple of empty desks, Mohammed said, 'That one will be yours, Mr. Harrington, and that one yours, Mr. Williams.' Between us was an occupied desk. 'And that is Sheba, your admin support assistant,' Mohammed continued casually waving in Sheba's direction, but not stopping to do a proper introduction. Sheba

19

pretended not to hear Mohammed and continued typing on her keyboard. Our work area led directly to our new boss's office. A wall of glass separated the two offices, but Mr. Tomlinson, our new boss, also got the panoramic view of the Sheikh Zayed Road. When Mr. Tomlinson saw us being led by Mohammed into his office, he rose immediately to his feet and extended his arm for a vigorous handshake. 'Ah, Mr. Harrington and Mr. Williams I presume,' he said. 'Mike Tomlinson, General Manager of the Dubai branch. Pleased to meet you. Did you have a good trip? And I hope everything is alright with your apartments.' He spoke so quickly, he gave us no chance to answer his questions. Jas and I simply nodded as cheerily as possible.

We spent about thirty minutes with Mike, who tried in that time to tell us every interesting fact about Dubai. He made it all sound very exciting, as he described the places he recommended us to visit, including some different beaches, many clubs and restaurants, and even some sports and leisure clubs. He also gave us some advice as to where we might like to live, and which areas to avoid. We found out that Mike was a keen golfer. We told him about our walk down to Al Faheidi Street the previous evening, and his response was, 'Don't be tempted to buy any electronic goods at Al Faheidi Street if you go back down there. Especially things like cameras and computers. A lot of them are counterfeit. No point in wasting your money. You might as well go to one of the big chains in the malls, and the prices will be pretty similar there anyway.' I wondered if Mike's warning was based on fact or gossip. If on fact, and if it was common knowledge, then why didn't the government put an end to the sale of counterfeit goods?

Mike was an American, and he lived up to the British stereotype of Americans: bold and brash and 'in yer face', outspoken, with a personal view on everything, but friendly and lively, always happy and positive in mind and spirit, just the sort of person one would like to meet at a party or, perhaps, to have for a boss. Actually, at the time I was wondering about the last point; I'd never actually had an American boss before, so it was to be a new experience to look forward to. It looked as if Mike might be the sort of boss who mixed business and pleasure as he'd already invited Jas and me to a barbecue at his villa the coming Thursday night, which would correspond to a Saturday night in the western week.

After our thirty minutes with Mike, Jas and I were given a guided tour around the office by Inga, Mike's tall, blonde, could-be-a-model Danish personal assistant. We were introduced to at least twenty different people, all of whose names I failed to remember by the end of the tour. Except for one or two of the ladies, of course. Though I don't normally fraternize with members of staff of the opposite sex, it was interesting to see what opportunities might exist should I get desperate. Eventually, Jas and I were left at our desks to make sure our computers were working okay, and to start 'sorting ourselves out' (Inga's phrase).

Two days later, Jas and I had a 'day out' at the Hyatt Regency Hotel, located close to the beach but also right in the heart of the city, down by the mouth of the creek that splits Dubai in two. We were sent on a one-day course entitled "Overcoming the culture shock—A guide for expatriates new to the UAE". It was delivered by an American psychologist called Maureen. She had lived in Dubai for fifteen years, and claimed during that time to have seen numerous expatriate workers come and go. Some could not last six months, some just saw out their first contract of one, two or perhaps three years, while others, like herself, became semi-permanent. Not permanent, she explained, because it was not possible to get residency permits for an indefinite period, and it was not possible for foreigners to buy property, although there were rumours that it might be permitted in a few year's time.

The course took the form mainly of Maureen talking, and the twenty or so participants listening, or occasionally asking questions. I guess a lot of what was covered was interesting and useful, both for our business and private lives, but, in fact, over ninety per cent of what she told us, I had already read in the books I bought at Foyles. Wouldn't any person with just half an ounce of common sense seek out and read such books if they were contemplating uprooting themselves from their safe and predictable lives back home for one completely different in an alien culture half-way around the globe? Maybe other people didn't have my foresight and genuine interest to find out all about the place where they might end up living for several years. Nevertheless, I was impressed that JBNC had booked us onto this programme of 'cultural awareness', but the highlight of the day was definitely lunch in the revolving restaurant twenty-five storeys high.

The food was great. It was a 'help yourself to as much as you like' international buffet, with Arabic, Iranian, continental, Indian and Chinese dishes. The views of the city were truly amazing and ever changing as the restaurant revolved. At one moment I could see the rooftops of Deira, the area in which the hotel was located, the creek, busy with numerous dhows entering and leaving, the offices and apartments of Bur Dubai on other side of the creek, the Port Rashid docks and beyond the shimmering blue sea. In the far distance I could even just about make out the Sheikh Zayed Road with its two rows of skyscrapers on either side of the street. Fifteen minutes later I was looking in completely the opposite direction, along the coast in the direction of Sharjah, Dubai's neighbouring emirate to the North East.

I did pick up a few useful hints from Maureen however. Her main message was that expatriates shouldn't expect things in the UAE to be the same as back home. We should avoid constant comparisons between what we experience in the UAE and what we were used to experiencing in our home country; it would not achieve anything, and it would not make us happy, if we kept criticising things in the UAE. Maureen warned us, for example, that the term 'inshallah' would be one that we would hear many times, especially in business. It actually means 'by the will of God'. The locals say it after everything: 'I will complete your report tomorrow, inshallah,' or 'you will get your delivery on Monday, inshallah.' Many westerners interpret the use of the word 'inshallah' as a casual excuse that something might not actually occur as planned or expected. However, most emiratis are religious and do believe in the power of God. They, in fact, use the term whenever they want to express an intended action. If a westerner questions their use of the word 'inshallah', or worse still, mocks them for using it, he or she is most likely going to cause considerable offence to the local.

That first week Jas and I didn't do any 'real' work. We were expected to show our faces briefly at the office each day, but we were given a lot of time to see to the many tasks that needed to be completed, like finding a home, buying a car, getting a UAE driving licence and opening a bank account. The company saw to other things, like our labour cards and medical insurance.

Home-hunting

From the moment I arrived in Dubai, I had been wondering whether or not I wanted to rent a home with Jas. He had made it perfectly clear that he wanted to home-share with me but I had a few reservations. Firstly, I believe that it is wise to keep professional and private lives separate so that one can forget about all work-related things when not at work. How else can one relax and enjoy one's leisure time? But secondly, I do enjoy having time on my own when I can just please myself, watch whatever TV channel I want, adjust the heating or air conditioning just as I like, that type of thing. And thirdly, and perhaps most importantly, I wasn't sure that I wanted to share a home with Jas. I wasn't sure that we had all that much in common and I did find him a bit pompous and annoying at times. But he asked me at least twice a day whether we should look for a home together. I always answered, 'Yeah, whatever' trying to sound as casual and disinterested as possible, but he never got the message, and due to my lack of decisive action I ended up going to look at villas with him. Jas had decided that we needed a three-bedroom villa so that we would always have a spare room in which we could put up friends and relatives from the UK.

In the end, I volunteered to phone around some property agencies. Jas was keen to move to a district called Jumeirah, which had been mentioned by Mike as being one of the nicest regions for Europeans 'like ourselves' to live in. The problem was that we could not get a three-bedroom villa for 110,000 dirhams a year, the amount of our joint accommodation allowance. The average price seemed to be anything between 120,000 and 250,000 dirhams. Jas persuaded me that it was better for us to 'pay a bit extra from our own pockets' to live somewhere safe, and where we would really enjoy our time in Dubai. I called an agent called Al Zakheel Real Estate. I was invited to go to their office where I could look at the details of their extensive property list and then an agent would drive us to a selection of properties. I wasn't sure exactly where the office was; all that the secretary on the phone kept saying was, 'Behind beebee shop in Al Karama, behind beebee shop!' When I asked for a street name, she replied, 'No street name. Just come to beebee shop.'

Jas and I stopped one of the state-controlled cream coloured taxis outside our apartment block. When I asked the driver for the 'beebee shop at Al Karama' he looked at me a bit puzzled and repeated, 'Beebee shop? You want beebee shop in Al Karama?' When I nodded, he just sped off. Five minutes later he stopped outside a shop called *The Baby Shop*. 'Ah,' said Jas. 'It was baby shop, not beebee shop'. I wondered whether the driver had brought us to the right place, and if so, how he understood where we wanted to go. The journey had cost only twelve dirhams, about two pounds in UK currency. I wondered how much I was supposed to tip, but realised from the driver's big smile that I had probably been over-generous when I offered fifteen dirhams and indicated that no change was required. I asked the driver if he knew where the Al Zakheel Real Estate office was, but he didn't know.

When we stepped into the street, there was no obvious sign of the office. We walked back and forth up the road but there was no sign of the office, and there was no one on the street to ask. Eventually, Jas suggested we ask in the baby shop. The shop assistant was very helpful; she directed us down a little alleyway between the buildings that we hadn't even noticed. The property agent was in the same building as the baby shop, but on the third floor, and the office was accessed from the rear of the building. The back of the building wasn't very pleasant. The ground was covered in sand and rubbish, gently swirling around in the light breeze, and the stench of refuse wafted out from half a dozen or so of the big communal steel bins that seemed to line so many streets.

At least we were not disappointed by the selection of properties when we eventually got to the office. Some of the villas were on small compounds, mostly on the edges of Jumeirah, but most were on streets that looked pretty similar to what one might find in Spain, and virtually all had the use of a communal swimming pool. Some of the compounds also had communal gyms or fitness rooms and/or saunas, and the more expensive villas even had private swimming pools. We set our budget at 130,000 dirhams and made up a shortlist of three properties. Sunil, the senior rentals negotiator, offered to take us to view each of the properties. He drove us in a Nissan Sunny that had definitely seen better days. I wondered whether the car was roadworthy and whether it had to pass any sort of test, like our MOT at home. Worse still was Sunil's driving. He drove far too fast and far too close to the vehicle in front, and he never had more than one hand on the steering wheel. Most of the time his left hand dangled out of the window. I realised that Sunil's driving was only typical for Dubai. Virtually every day since our arrival I had witnessed a car accident. The most common problem seemed to be one vehicle hitting the bumper of the vehicle in front. But even in the city centre, where the cars couldn't have been going that fast, many got quite crushed and battered.

All of the villas were pleasant enough but one stood out. It was, perhaps, a bit older than the others, but it was by far the most spacious. It had a nice sized plot of land, nicely landscaped and not overlooked by any other property. It didn't, however, have a swimming pool. Advantages of the property highlighted by Sunil were that it was only a 10-15 minutes' walk to the beach and to the local shopping centre, which had three small malls and a Spinneys supermarket. Jas and I both knew it was the one for us, so we went straight back to the real estate office to pay our deposit and complete the required paperwork.

Mike's barbecue

On our first Thursday night, Jas and I took, at about 7 pm, a taxi to Mike's villa. He lived in Umm Suqeim, a few miles up the coast from Jumeirah. He had explained previously at the office that with three children he could get a much bigger property in Umm Suqeim than elsewhere, and the region had a similar cosmopolitan atmosphere to Jumeirah and it was also conveniently close to the Emirates International School, which all of his three children attended. He had three girls, all blonde and very pretty as I was soon to find out: Haley, aged eighteen, who was going to university in the States the following summer, Nichola, aged sixteen, and Hannah, aged thirteen. He also had a wife, Stella.

Mike's directions for the taxi driver must have been good because the driver had no difficulty in taking us straight to the villa. As we drove up his road there was no mistaking which villa was Mike's. Parked in the street outside were at least a dozen vehicles, mostly expensive saloons and 4x4 Jeep-type vehicles, all double-parked. A wall surrounded his villa, perhaps 8-10 feet high, but it had a gate that was wide open. From behind the wall we could hear many voices in conversation and much laughter. Jas and I entered through the gate and tried to see if we could see Mike or anyone else we knew. The garden was large. There was a barbecue going on the patio close to the house and under a huge gazebo towards the bottom of the garden at least a dozen people sat chatting. Children of all ages were running around and happily playing with each other. Most of the accents I heard sounded American or European, but there were also a few Asians, probably from India and the Philippines. It was obvious, however, that the Asian men were professionals, probably Mike's business contacts or chums from his golf club.

Suddenly, I heard Mike's voice from behind me. 'Welcome gentlemen, glad you got here all right,' he said. 'Come, let me get you a drink and introduce you to a few people.' We were introduced to

Mike's family, and Jas and I were each given a nicely chilled bottle of Budweiser. 'Have you applied for your alcohol permits yet?' Mike enquired. 'You'll need those if you want to drink at home.' With all the other things we had to do, we hadn't, of course, had time to apply for our alcohol licences. 'Are there any unattached ladies here tonight?' asked Jas cheekily.

'What a guy. What a guy,' was Mike's first response, then he continued. 'Now let me see. Well, there's Stella's friend Monica. Don't worry, she's close to your age. She's quite nice and she recently split with her boyfriend. And there's a German lady called Ursula. She's from a client company. Quite attractive to look at, depending on your taste in women, but she's a bit scary. You know those Germans! You'll see what I mean when you meet her. And, now let me think, oh yes, there's Ani, who's a Filipino girl. I'm afraid that's about it tonight; the rest are all here with their partners or are too young for you two.'

'No harm in asking, was there?' replied Jas cheerfully. However, I wondered if it really was the most suitable of opening topics of conversation to have with our boss. What would Mike think of us? That we only came to his barbecue to get pissed and laid. But he seemed not to have minded Jas's question, and after a bit of pleasant chitchat he left us to circulate. I was pleased to soon find myself separated from Jas, who ended up talking to a couple from Kentucky. That left me free to track down each of the three single ladies. Jas, I concluded, was all mouth and no action. It looked like he would be talking to the couple from Kentucky for quite a while. In that time I would meet each of the single ladies and then I would have first pick. Hopefully, one of them would be worth going for. The first I met was Ursula, and she was as scary as Mike had said. She was a good six-feet tall, and rather well built, but a bit butch actually. She looked fit, however, like she worked out regularly in a gym. She had a nice head of long brunette hair and she was well tanned all over. She wore a tight little white dress that showed off her figure to best advantage, and she wore lots of gold: several chains around her neck and one around an ankle, rings on most fingers and at least five or six bangles on her right wrist. All in all, she sparkled more than a Christmas tree dressed up with lights and tinsel. Her strong German accent and very loud voice pierced my eardrums and got on my nerves a bit, so I got away from her as quickly as I could.

I was much happier when I bumped into Ani. Although, in my opinion, Filipino girls are not as obviously attractive as, say, Thai girls, Ani was a very pretty girl. She had a child-like face with quite big eyes, a small nose and delicious looking lips. She had smooth golden skin that glowed in the light provided by lanterns scattered around the garden, and black hair cut in a modern 'bob' style, which made her look more western and less Asian. Like most Asian girls, Ani was quite short, coming up to about my shoulders, but she was fit and well toned. I soon found out why: she was a fitness instructor at the health and leisure club that Mike went to. I was surprised that Stella didn't mind Mike inviting his pretty little gym instructor to his home. Maybe Americans were more relaxed about these things, or perhaps she had complete faith in Mike's fidelity, or perhaps she just didn't care! As Ani told me about her job and her hometown in the Philippines I couldn't stop myself wondering whether or not Mike had bonked her. Maybe that's why Mike hadn't offered any additional information about Ani, as he had about Monica and Ursula, when Jas had asked about the presence of single ladies at the party.

Some time after I had decided that I did quite fancy Ani and wouldn't mind bonking her myself, I realised that she was a little vain and quite full of herself. She paid attention to every male who passed where we stood and she talked at length about how men tried to pick her up at the club. Eventually, I decided she wasn't right for me and that it was time to track down Monica. I thought the best way to do this was to go and talk to Stella. This proved easy to do as I found her standing momentarily alone on the patio. She seemed pleased to meet someone new. As she talked about how wonderful life was in Dubai, I noticed that Jas was still standing in the same spot he had been two hours earlier, still talking to the same couple from Kentucky. The well-built man with a long and thick blonde moustache was now waving his hands about animatedly as he spoke.

I, perhaps unsubtly, asked Stella about Monica. Apparently, she had not been feeling well and had gone home early. Well that was the end of my fun for the night I thought, but it was not quite to be so. Stella asked if I had had anything to eat, and when I said that I hadn't, she insisted that I did so immediately. She had put on an impressive spread. On a big table was laid out a selection of meats that had been cooked on the barbecue, three large bowls with different salads, jacket potatoes, pizza slices, Arabic pitta bread and numerous small bowls with various sauces and dips, including hummus, my favourite. Upon learning this, Stella proudly declared that the hummus was home made and that the chickpeas had been prepared over five full days. All the food was very tasty. I always thought that one can't beat a good barbecue, and I hadn't been to one for several years. That's because I lived in a flat in London, and so too did all of my friends. None of us had a garden, as far as I could remember. Yuppies were not supposed to like having gardens as grass had to be cut and weeds pulled. People like my friends and me, were supposed to be either busy at work or out enjoying ourselves around town, and we certainly didn't have time for gardening.

As I looked around, I really did feel like I was in some kind of paradise. The air was warm, there was only a gentle, very pleasant breeze, the garden was romantically lit with numerous little lanterns, the food was great and everybody looked happy; there were no miserable faces at all like one sees at parties back home in London. I felt that this feeling of happiness must be the real reason people come to live and work in Dubai. And as a pleasant, sweet aroma of strawberries wafted through the air, I noticed a group of people under the gazebo smoking shisha from two 'Arabian' water pipes. The pipes consisted of a hollow glass base filled with water and a vertical pipe section, together standing a total of some two and a half feet tall. On top of the vertical pipe, coal burnt in a little bowl. Also connected to the vertical pipe was a colourful hose on which the smokers sucked to draw the shisha (the mix of tobacco, molasses and fruit flavourings) through the water. The water acts as a coolant and filter. Each smoker, sitting in a circle around one of the pipes, took three or four long, slow puffs before passing the mouthpiece to the next person for their turn.

As I was tucking into my food, Stella and Mike's eldest daughter, Haley, approached Stella and me. 'So, you're one of the new big shots from London I presume,' she said playfully.

'Yes, from London,' I replied, 'but I'm not a big shot. Well, not yet anyway.' Stella decided to help out with the cooking on the barbecue and I was left to entertain, or be entertained by, Haley. She was a very mature eighteen year old. She could easily have passed as twenty-three or twenty-four I thought. She looked like she was straight out of *Baywatch*. Tall, blonde and tanned she wore what looked like a two-piece swimsuit with a see-through patterned wrap over, which was tied with a knot around her waist. According to what she told me, it seemed that she had brains as well as beauty. She was expecting to graduate from her school top of her class and she had already secured a place at Yale. I acted suitably impressed and Haley glowed with pride as I told her how proud her father must be of her. For the next twenty minutes or so I did a lot of listening as Haley told me about her active social life in Dubai. I lost my concentration towards the end when I realised that I needed the toilet. I asked for directions, but Haley said she would take me there.

We entered the house and passed through a very big kitchen before coming to a corridor, which led to at least another three or four rooms. 'There you go,' Haley said. 'It's at the end of the corridor.' I went into the bathroom and locked the door. I put up the toilet seat and started to urinate in the bowl. Suddenly, I heard a voice coming from behind me. It was Haley. 'Can I help you?' she asked.

'I think I can manage, thank you,' I replied as I wondered how exactly she thought she could help me. 'I thought I locked the door,' I continued.

'It often comes unlocked again,' was Haley's reply. Then, as I continued to piss in the toilet, she asked if I was enjoying the party. I said that I was, and she replied, 'Good. Then I'll probably see you again soon, as Mum and Dad do a barbie nearly every month. So long as you stay in Dad's good books you're bound to be invited again.' I finished urinating, did up my zip, and turned to wash my hands in the sink. I was conscious of Haley standing very close to me. I could feel her breath on my neck, and a rather large breast brushed briefly against my upper arm. This began to turn me on a bit and I felt a twitching in my pants, but at the same time I wanted Haley to leave me alone. It was wholly inappropriate for her to flirt with one of her father's staff, and I was nearly ten years older than her. Far too old for her! 'Would you like a tour of the house?' Haley then asked.

'Your Mother has already promised to do that,' I lied, as I pushed past her hurriedly.

In the end, I did get a tour of the house, but Mike did it, and Jas came too. I think that Mike was keen for us to see all of his home. It was more like a palace really. There was whitish-grey marble flooring throughout the ground floor, which was covered intermittently with expensive Persian rugs, and there were big marble pillars in the hallway by the stairs leading to the upper floor. The decoration of the house had an Arabian feel throughout, from the style of the lampshades and the artwork hanging on the walls to the coffee table in the lounge, which was actually a wooden antique door from Oman. The tour left out no room, including Mike and Stella's own bedroom and Haley's also, the walls of which were plastered with posters of stars from the pop and movie worlds.

A week later when I was preparing my wash to be sent to the laundry, I checked, as usual, all pockets in my clothes to ensure that nothing was left in them. In my shirt pocket I found the end of a cigarette packet. On the back of it was written, 'My mobile number is 0508825427. You can call me anytime. Haley'.

A morning at the beach

*O*n our way back home from Mike's barbecue in the taxi, I agreed to meet Jas at ten the next morning to go for a swim at Jumeirah. Mike had told us that if we wanted to go to a beach we should go to one of the beach parks, either at Jumeirah or Mamzar, as 'the sand is a bit cleaner and one gets a better class of person there'. But Jas and I knew there was also a public beach in Jumeirah, the one that was quite close to our new home. 'That will do us, won't it?' Jas had said.

'We're not snobs are we?' I agreed. The next morning, we got into one of the cream taxis and asked for 'Jumeriah beach'. The driver asked if we wanted the park, but we confirmed that we wanted the beach and not the park. Minutes later we were speeding up the Sheikh Zayed Road, past our office. The road was quieter than usual being a Friday morning, the religious day of rest. The driver kept on the highway for what seemed like ages. The journey was taking far longer than when Sunil from the property agency had driven us a few days earlier. 'This is the way for Jumeirah beach?' I eventually asked the driver.

'Yes, yes,' he replied. 'We're nearly there. Not much further to go'. The fare meter was showing 24 dirhams. No journey we had done so far had cost more than 15 or 16 dirhams. I thought that this driver was trying to rip us off and just as I was about to say so to Jas the driver pulled up to the curb and stopped. 'Here, Jumeirah beach,' he said cheerily pointing ahead to a narrow strip of beach. 'And there, the Jumeirah Beach hotel,' he continued, now pointing to our right.

I was sitting in the front and paid the fare of 28 dirhams, waiting for my change from 30 dirhams. I knew something wasn't right. As Jas and I got out of the car, Jas asked, 'Where are the shops?'

'No shops here,' replied the driver as he sped away.

'The bastard, he's ripped us off,' I said turning to Jas. The beach was not a pretty sight. The side adjoining the hotel had a tall concrete wall, the other side a fence with barbed wire at the top. In the distance to our left we could see the chimneys of the big aluminium plant.

'Never mind,' said Jas. 'We're here now. Let's make the most of it. Let's get some sun and have a swim.' The beach was almost deserted. On it there were only two Land Cruisers, big Toyota 4x4s, and what looked like a group of young, local Arab men. They were fully dressed in their long white dishdashas. As we walked down the beach in the direction of the sea one of the young Arabs approached us. 'Did you come for swim?' he asked.

'Yes we did,' Jas replied.

'No good here,' continued the young man. 'My friend, he bite by sea snake. No safe in water.' He then walked off returning to his friends.

'What was he talking about?' Jas asked. 'I haven't read about sea snakes in any of my books on Dubai.'

'Well, either he's a kind soul warning us of some kind of danger or perhaps they just want the beach for themselves,' I replied.

'Well I bet it's the latter, so they can fuck right off. I'm going for a swim. That's what we came here for isn't it?' was Jas's response. We put towels down on the sand, stripped down to our swimwear and then lay on our towels. Within minutes of doing this I realised that it wasn't very warm at all. Sure, it was sunny and there was a clear blue sky, but it was very, very windy. The waves crashed ferociously onto the beach a good three or four feet high. I turned to Jas and said, 'I think I might give that swim a miss. The sea doesn't look very warm or inviting to me.' Though Jas spent considerable time trying to persuade me to go ahead with a swim, neither of us did go in the end.

Within thirty minutes we'd both had enough. 'Let's head back home,' I suggested. 'We can go out somewhere else this afternoon.' We got up, got dressed and put our towels back in our sports bags. As we passed the group of young Arab men, they waved to us and we waved back. Jas, however, was looking at their Land Cruisers, one white and one black, rather than at the men as he waved. 'Those Land Cruisers seem to be the in thing out here, don't they?' he said. 'Rather smart I'd say. Nice and solid. Think I might get one of those.' Two weeks later, and 135,000 dirhams poorer, Jas did indeed have a new, white Land Cruiser of his own. The vehicle seemed to be expensive to me, roughly what it would have cost in the UK. I pointed this out to Jas reminding him that the UAE was supposed to be tax free, and therefore things should be cheaper than back home, where most goods have $17^1/_2$ per cent Value Added Tax added to their price. Jas's explanation was that while there was no tax to pay on purchases in the UAE the higher costs of getting things to the country often meant that things would not be cheaper than at home. I did wonder anyway why Jas needed such a large vehicle. Why on earth would one person with no close friends or relations nearby need a vehicle that could comfortably carry eight people?

We continued walking back up towards the road. When we got there we found that a car passed only every three or four minutes, and none of them were taxis. We waited for about twenty minutes and then I began to lose my rag a bit. 'Bloody brilliant,' I shouted as I threw my bag to the ground. 'Now we're stuck out here. No bloody taxis and I bet they don't have any buses out here either.' No sooner did I say this, we could see a bus approaching from the distance. 'Look!' said Jas pointing across the road. 'There's a bus stop over there. It must be in the right direction for the city centre.' The bus stop was on the other side of the road some hundred metres or so away. We both sprinted towards it, but realised that we wouldn't get there before the bus, so we held out our arms as we ran, hoping that the bus would stop anyway. But it didn't. As the bus passed us, the driver's head turned towards us, but he looked right through us, as if we didn't exist. 'Bastard! Bastard!' was the only response I could come up with.

Jas suggested that we walk down to the Jumeirah Beach hotel, which we did. That turned out to be a good idea. Outside the hotel was a queue of taxis waiting for business, but we decided to go into the hotel. I was familiar with this hotel as it was mentioned, and highly recommended, in my tourist guides, and it had a very distinctive design: the whole building was in the shape of a breaking wave. Inside, the hotel was very impressive. It certainly deserved every one of its five stars. We just wandered around a bit. The lobby was large and interesting, and the lifts, with walls of glass moving up and down facing out from the building offered panoramic views up the coast. We went up and down in the lifts a few times and wandered along numerous vast corridors, and as we passed each of the hotel's eight restaurants we stopped to study the menus. 'We'll have to come here again,' Jas exclaimed. I nodded in agreement. The only disappointment was the way we were treated by a member of staff when we were walking along the ground floor of the hotel in the direction of the swimming pools and beach. A short, stout Indian man dressed all in white, including a white turban wrapped around his head, approached us and enquired whether we were guests at the hotel. When we said that we were not, he asked us rather rudely, 'Then what are you doing here?' Though I didn't like the way we were spoken to, we still went to one of the hotel's bars for a beer before taking a taxi back to our apartments.

In the evening, we took another taxi down to Al Faheidi Street, with the intention that from there we could walk down to the creek. We walked down a series of narrow alleys and lanes, where only people on foot could pass. Most of the shops were selling textiles, and their windows displayed colourful cottons and silks with varied designs. In between the textile shops was the odd spice merchant, travel agent or small food store. Merchants passed down the alleys pulling carts loaded with produce. The atmosphere of times past was easily imagined, as everything looked as it might have fifty years before. We eventually came to the abra landing stage. The abras are the wooden boats that ferry people between various points on opposite sides of the creek. The landing stage was busy with people both arriving and departing. The boats seemed to leave as soon as they were full, and they carried about twenty to twenty-five people.

'Let's go over,' said Jas. 'Look, there's a map on the wall over there that shows where they go to. It seems that the boats from here only go to two points on Beniyas Road, on the Deira side of the creek. They don't seem to be all that far apart, so it doesn't really matter which one we go to.'

'Do we need to get a ticket or anything?' I asked.

'Everyone else just seems to be paying the driver on board,' replied Jas. 'Come on, let's jump on.' Getting onto the abra was not that easy. First, we had to walk down the stone steps, which were wet and slippery, and then we had to jump onto the boat, which was violently bobbing up and down amongst the spray that was splashing up from water hitting the steps. The boat's deck was also wet and slippery, and there was nothing to grab hold of when jumping on. It took an elderly couple, German tourists I think, several minutes to build up the courage to take the final leap on board. There was no member of staff to help them, and the boatmen only shouted at each other in languages of the Indian subcontinent. The seating was arranged back to back up the middle of the boat. There was no railing to stop you from falling overboard, should by chance you fall forward off your seat. I would not have liked travelling on the abras with a young child. There was a canopy overhead, however, which would offer some protection from the sun during the day.

The boatman collected fifty fils from each passenger, which was equivalent to less than ten UK pence. Once the boat was full and he had collected all the fares, he set off. He steered the boat from its stern using a tiller, similar to those found on canal boats or smaller sailing boats. The engine, which had been running continuously, even before we had got onto the boat, was loud and sounded rough, but it moved us across the creek surprisingly quickly. There was, however, a powerful smell of fuel coming from the engine. As the boat cut through the water, it created a lot of spray, which wet some passengers sitting towards the front of the boat. A dhow passed us, going in the opposite direction. A dhow is a traditionally made wooden boat that is commonly used to transport cargo between countries around the Arabian Gulf, the Indian subcontinent and East Africa. This really was quite an adventure!

When we got to the Deira side of the creek, we just walked around for a bit. We each ate a couple of shawarmas, which we bought from a snack bar. The sharwarmas were made of slices of roasted lamb carved from a spit and served with pickles and spicy sauce in Arabic bread. It was a tasty little snack. Then we returned to the Bur Dubai side of the creek on another abra. From the landing stage in Bur Dubai we walked all the way back to our apartments.

Helping a neighbour

Two days later, I travelled back to my apartment from work without Jas, as he had decided to work a couple of extra hours at the office. As I entered the building's lobby, my eye caught a beautiful figure waiting by the lifts. I walked over to the lifts as slowly as possible so that I could enjoy the view. The view was a tall, slim but shapely woman with long black hair. I couldn't see her face, but what was most exciting for me were her very tight fitting leather trousers. They left nothing to the imagination and, to be honest, she had the tastiest arse I'd seen since arriving in Dubai. The lift arrived and the woman struggled to lift a huge sack that had been sitting on the floor. I offered to carry the sack into the lift, which she gratefully accepted. The top of the sack was open and inside I could see lots of clothes: trousers, jumpers, tee shirts, shoes, even underwear, all apparently thrown into the sack without any care. The woman had narrow eyes, yet she didn't look like she was Chinese, Filipino or Thai. For one thing she was far too tall, but also her facial features were somewhat different to women from the countries just mentioned.

'What floor would you like?' I asked.

'Eighth please,' she replied. I pressed the button for the eighth floor and the lift started moving upwards very slowly. The lift seemed old and was squeaking quite a bit. 'Where are you from?' asked the woman.

'I'm from the UK,' I replied. 'From London to be precise. And you?'

'From Kazakhstan,' was her answer. She then asked if I was working in Dubai, and I told her that I had only arrived in Dubai nine days before and that I worked for JBNC. She responded as if she was familiar with the company name. The lift stopped moving and its doors opened. I offered to carry the sack to her apartment and again she accepted. She said that she had the last apartment in the corridor. She walked some way ahead of me, as I was unable to walk very fast, the sack being very heavy indeed. When she got to her apartment she didn't take out a key, but knocked loudly on the door. From inside I could hear a baby crying. No one came to the door and she knocked again, even more loudly this time. Eventually a young boy, who looked like a small male version of the woman, opened the door. As the woman took her sack and entered her apartment, she turned to me and said, 'Thanks for your help. It was very kind of you to bring my bag right to my apartment. What room are you in?'

'614,' I replied as I turned to go back down the corridor.

I entered my room and went straight to the fridge for a coke. I opened a window, as it was a little stuffy in the apartment. A pleasant breeze blew in. I flicked off my shoes, jumped onto my bed, used the remote control to switch on the television and drank my nice cold coke straight from the can. I hadn't up until that time really had a chance to see what the television programmes were like. I flicked through the dozen or so channels. Only two were showing programmes in the English language: Channel 33, the local station based in Dubai, and CNN. The CNN reception was not very good; the picture had white streaks flickering across it constantly and the sound was rather muffled. Channel 33 was showing some American cop show, something at least twenty years old. I was grateful not to be a telly addict, given that the choice didn't look too promising. I knew, however, that most expats subscribed to a satellite service, and that I would too eventually, if only to get the Bloomberg business channel, some sports and some films. My plan for the evening was to cook myself some pasta, and then to take a little walk to clear my head before going to bed early. Both Jas and I had been doing a lot of rushing around since we arrived in Dubai and frankly I was exhausted. I don't know where Jas got his energy from to be able to continue working into the evening.

I browned some beef mince and then added a ready-made Bolognese sauce. And then in a second pan I cooked some pasta shells. I love pasta meals. They are tasty and very quick and easy to make. I remember that when I was a student at university, many students seemed to survive only on pasta. It was the only thing that everyone knew how to cook, it was hard to mess up, and it was also very affordable. Sometimes I'm surprised that I never grow tired of eating the same old thing over and over. Maybe one day I will. When I finished making the meal, I sat at my breakfast bar and ate it. The television was still on but I wasn't really paying any attention to it. I think that single people often leave their TVs on just to provide some background noise, thus helping them to avoid the silence that would remind them they were alone, and perhaps lonely. Suddenly the cop show came to an abrupt end, while the lead character was halfway through a sentence. It was replaced by a picture of a mosque, which was accompanied by some Arabic speech, more sung than spoken really. I looked at my watch. It was 7.49 pm. Would the programme eventually continue I wondered, or was this the way TV programmes ended in Dubai? And if so, wouldn't the timing schedules be messed up?

I had a few old copies of the *Gulf News* lying around my flat. That is one of the two largest English language daily newspapers published in the United Arab Emirates. Colleagues advised me that the *Gulf News* was better than the *Khaleej Times* as it had a better coverage of European and international news. The *Khaleej Times* was better for news from Asia. Anyhow, I'd bought the newspapers mainly to get the contact details of property agents when Jas and I had been home hunting. I hadn't noticed any television listings when I had previously flicked through the papers, so I gathered three different papers from around the room to find them. I was curious to see the range of programmes available on Channel 33 on a typical day. Fifteen minutes passed and I still hadn't found any TV schedules. I was a little flustered by now, bothered by having to scan every page of three newspapers, and quite disappointed also. This was the first daily newspaper I had ever come across in any country that did not have a TV guide.

I turned off the television and glanced around the floor looking for my shoes. I caught a glimpse of myself in a mirror that hung on the wall behind the TV. I was quite pleased with what I saw. I wondered what the sexy woman from Kazakhstan had thought of me. Were we in the same league I wondered, or was she a little too good for me? I thought about what her husband might be like and what he might do for a living. What do people from Kazakhstan do? I realised that I knew nothing about the country. I only had a vague idea of where the country lay geographically, and to my knowledge I had never met anyone from Kazakhstan before. I wondered if I would meet the foxy woman again. After all, she had asked my room number as we parted. Thinking about that for a minute or two, I decided that that was a slightly strange thing to do. A woman wouldn't do a thing like that back home in England, certainly not!

Guest in my room

I put my shoes on, grabbed a light jacket, picked up my wallet and keys, then headed for the door to have my little walk before bedtime. As I shut the door behind me and started to set off along the corridor, I heard my phone start ringing. I briefly debated in my head whether I should continue walking and pretend I didn't hear it or whether I should go back to answer it. Who could it be? Probably Jas, wanting to know whether I had already eaten or not, or possibly my mother. I decided to return to my room to answer the phone. It continued ringing and ringing, so the caller was very patient, or at least very persistent. I entered my apartment and lifted the receiver. 'Hello,' I said.

'Hello, its Alira from apartment 802,' was the reply. 'You know, the one you helped with the heavy bag a little earlier. I was just calling to thank you for your help.'

'It was no trouble, no trouble at all. Only what any decent gentleman would have done,' was my response. No sooner had I said it, I realised how pompous I sounded. There was a brief pause, then Alira continued, 'I was just wondering, if you were free tonight, whether you would like to go out?' There was a moment of clumsy silence. I was having difficulty taking everything in. Was the foxy woman asking me out on a date, or what? What about her husband, what would he think about that? What about the children?

'Hello, are you still there?' Alira asked.

'Yes, yes. I'm sorry, I was going to have an early night tonight and I still have a few things to do,' I replied.

'It's only just gone eight o' clock. We needn't go out for long if that's what you wish,' was Alira's response. Tempting though the offer was I really wasn't in the mood for socialising so I said, 'Thank you very much for your very kind offer but I really do think I'll have to pass on it tonight. Maybe we can get together another night, I'm really rather tired tonight.'

'If you are too tired to go out maybe I can visit you briefly in your apartment so that I can thank you properly for your help earlier this evening.' She was persistent this woman. How could I possibly turn down this offer? Why would I want to turn down this offer? After all, it wasn't every day that a beautiful young woman invited herself into my home. However, I had an uneasy feeling in my stomach. Something didn't seem right. This seemed an awful lot of fuss for the little help I had given her earlier in the evening. But maybe that's the way people were in Kazakhstan, or maybe this woman was just friendly or just keen to meet a new person from a new country. Maybe she did just want to say 'thank you' and maybe even give me a little gift. I couldn't think of any polite way to not accept Alira's suggestion to visit me, so I offered to make her a cup of English tea.

Ten minutes later there was a gentle knock on my door. I opened it to see Alira smiling. She had changed her clothes. She was now wearing a skimpy red dress, which revealed two very nice, juicy tits and a pair of long, slim, smooth and golden coloured legs. 'Come in, come in,' was all I could say with a big grin on my face. I must have looked pretty gormless, but then I guess that a babe like this would have been quite used to men staring at her in amazement. But then, she was a bit overdressed, or should I say underdressed, for a home visit to a strange man who she had only just met a little over an hour earlier. I was finding it difficult putting all the pieces of the puzzle together. What was this woman doing alone with me in my apartment? She had two children after all. Or....or....maybe they weren't her children. Maybe they were her sister's, and she was not even married. Maybe she was single and fancied me. This was more maybes than I could bear. I would find out everything there was to know about this woman, but I would be very subtle, very subtle indeed; she wouldn't even notice that I was giving her a thorough interrogation.

Alira sat on the one proper chair in my room while I put the kettle on to make the tea. It turned out that Alira did all the initial interrogating, not me. She wanted to know my age, my weight, whether I was married or single, whether I smoked, whether I drank alcohol, whether I had a good job or not, whether I enjoyed my job, about my home in London, about my family, about my past loves. An hour or so later I realised that Alira knew an awful lot about me, but I had learned nothing about her. So, I decided to begin my interrogation. Within a short time I had found out that she was thirty-two years old, she had been in Dubai for just over two years, she was originally from Alma Ata, the old capital of Kazakhstan, she had been married but left her husband because he was a drunk who beat her, she had no other close relatives apart from one sister who lived in Moscow and she loved, really loved Dubai. She was very dismissive of her own country; 'It's cold, really cold in winter and everyone always looks so miserable,' she said. 'And most people are so poor, our homes are old and cold, many of us don't have things that you probably take for granted, like telephones and computers, and many of us live on bread, potatoes and vegetable stews. It's a sad and depressing country. I just had to get away. But the weather in Dubai is lovely and people here treat me with respect.' I found it fascinating to hear stories about people Amira knew back in Kazakhstan, and about the country's culture, history and geography.

Alira drank my tea and said how much she liked English tea, especially Liptons. I told her that Liptons had been a big brand in England many years ago but now was not really available anymore in the UK. I was conscious that Alira was incredibly sexy without having to try at all. She sat on my chair with one leg crossed over the other, causing her dress to ride right up her smooth golden thigh. Her revealed cleavage was equally exciting. Just looking at her began to turn me on, but then I remembered the children in her room. 'So, do you have a partner now?' I asked.

'No,' she replied. 'I've decided to take a break from men. In fact, I did live in the UK for nearly a year. The last time I was in Dubai I met a charming man from Wales. He swept me off my feet and begged me to go back with him to Wales. But it was awful, everything was awful. He lived in Blaenavon, what a dump! Do you know it? I was shocked when I first arrived. It was no better than Kazakhstan! The same miserable faces everywhere. And I was so bored at home every day with nowhere to go and no one to talk to. Here in Dubai I have many friends, from Kazakhstan and from many other countries too. And Tom, he was no better than my first husband. When we were in Dubai, he said my son was not a problem, that he would treat him like his own, but in his country he completed ignored him and was, at times, quite cruel to him.'

'And you have other children?' I interrupted, trying to gather all the relevant facts about the lovely Alira.

'Yes, I have one son aged twelve and a daughter two years old.'

'And they live with you here in Dubai? Does your son go to school here then?' I continued.

'Yes they live with me, but no, Toni does not go to school. He looks after his little sister.'

'So he doesn't go to school at all,' I persisted. 'Is that a good thing?'

'I can't afford to pay for a school here, and anyway, he is needed at home to care for his sister when I go to work. Toni enjoys looking after his little sister. He really adores her.' I was having difficulty taking this information in. How on earth could a twelve-year-old cope everyday cooped up in one small room with a baby that he would have to feed, clean and comfort when it cried? My body language must have portrayed how I felt.

'I'm not a bad mother,' Alira said. 'I'm caring for my family the best I can. I have no one else to turn to for help, and of course the government here gives nothing to foreigners.'

I thought for a moment. Maybe it was unfair of me to be so judgemental. After all, I didn't really know anything about Alira, her life or situation. For all I knew, maybe it was common for twelve year olds not to go to school in Kazakhstan. Maybe they worked on farms, or cleaned cars, or even worked in shops. I realised that I knew nothing of Alira's country or culture, and therefore it was unreasonable of me to judge her. Trying to mend bridges I tried to continue in a more supportive and comforting tone. 'I can see how much you love your children,' I said, 'and I'm sure that you are doing everything you are able to give them a good life.'

'I'm doing my best,' was Alira's reply.

'So you are able to survive here okay?' I continued. 'You can make enough money to pay the rent, and feed and clothe your family, and pay all the bills?'

'You know what I do, don't you?' Alira then asked, giving me a cheeky smile. To be honest, I had been wondering, and I had noticed that Alira hadn't offered the information earlier.

'You do know?' Alira asked again. Was she implying that she was a prostitute, I wondered? There was an awkward silence in the room for a moment.

'You....er.....you......how should I put it?' I began, but I was promptly interrupted by Alira who said, 'Yes, I'm a prostitute. And what do you think about that?'

'As you said, you've got to do what you've got to do to take care of your family.'

Then, I was surprised by Alira's reply. 'But I love it. I love the thrill of it. I go into a bar, I pick out my target, make sexy eyes at him then reel him in like a fisherman reels in a fish! It's like a game for me. Can I or can't I get the man as a customer? But I am a good judge. I usually score with the men I target. When I go into a bar I know straight away who will go with me and who will not.'

I was somewhat surprised to discover that a woman could walk into a bar in Dubai and proposition men for business so openly. What would happen if someone complained? What would happen if a man or the management of the bar called the police? Would she be sent to prison, immediately deported or even stoned to death? I have to admit, I was intrigued by Alira's revelation, so I continued to ask questions. 'So, which bar do you usually go to?' I asked.

'I go to most of the hotels around the Al Mankhool Road, but not the Ramada, because I don't really like going to nightclubs, and the bars there are too risky.'

'And who are your customers?' I continued.

'All sorts. All nationalities. All ages. But I prefer Europeans or other westerners. I don't go with Arabs anymore. They are unpredictable and can be quite dangerous. I had a friend from Azerbaijan. A sweet young girl, so nice and innocent. I saw her go off with two local men one night about a month ago. I haven't seen her since, and neither have any of her other friends. She rented a studio apartment a few streets from here. The rent was not paid, so the landlord put all her things in the street in a bin, and now someone else lives there. We think the men took her off into the dessert. Either they keep her there locked up as a prisoner or maybe they killed her and buried her somewhere.'

'Did anyone report it to the police?' I asked.

'Of course not. How could we? All the girl's friends are in the same business. How could we tell that to the police? We would be locked up in prison and then sent back to our home countries.' There was then a little pause. I really wanted to know what positions or acts different men asked for and what prices they were prepared to pay, but I didn't have the courage to ask. Then, suddenly, Alira asked, 'So, are you up for it?' This sudden question caught me by surprise. Sure, Alira was a babe, and sure, I wouldn't have minded bonking her, but no, I was not prepared to pay to bonk her. So, my response was, 'No thank you, I don't think so.'

'Why not? I'll guarantee you'll really enjoy yourself. I've never had a complaint yet.'

'It's very tempting, but I think I'll pass,' I replied.

'Go on, treat yourself! You won't regret it!'

'No, really, no thanks,' I insisted.

'But I'm very open-minded. I do most things. Whatever you want,

I can do it.'

'No, I don't think so.'

'Do you have a problem?'

'Like what?'

'You have a limp dick, or maybe you are gay. Is that it? You're a homosexual?'

'No, I am just an English gentleman and I'm not in the habit of paying for sex. Look at me. Do I look like I am the kind of man who has to pay for sex?'

'It's not a case of *having* to pay. But why not pay? Men pay for everything else. If I were your girlfriend you would buy me presents, you would take me to restaurants and maybe even take me on holidays. Wouldn't that cost you a whole lot more?'

'It's not the cost. I'm just tired and not really in the mood.'

'So all my time here tonight has been a waste of time, has it?' Alira then asked in a more aggressive tone.

'I'm sorry if you did not enjoy yourself here tonight, but I did, and if all you wanted from me was business, then you should have said so straight away. I think you should better leave now.'

'It's your loss. Believe me. You don't know what you've missed,' was Alira's reply as she got up and moved towards my door. And then she was gone. I was immediately relieved when she had left. I decided not to take the walk I had earlier planned. Instead, I went to bed. I did not tell Jas or anyone else about Alira. I guess I felt a bit gullible having invited her to my apartment for tea.

Settling in chores

*T*he next week was long and hard. I spent all day at work, and several hours most evenings reading everything I could about the new stock exchange in Dubai in preparation for my first assignment. Our two weeks at the Al Kareema apartments were almost complete. Jas and I had agreed to move into our new villa on the date on which our tenancy agreement began, the coming Thursday, as this was also the day we were due to leave the Al Kareema apartments. I checked each day whether my furniture and personal possessions had arrived at the Jebel Ali port, as I was not keen to move into the villa with no bed to sleep on, seats to sit on and wardrobes in which to hang my clothes. But each day I was told that my container had not yet arrived, and neither had Jas's, even though he had used a different shipping agent who charged him considerably more per kilo shipped than I had paid. As each day passed, it seemed increasingly likely that we would either have to stay in the villa with no furniture or make arrangements to stay somewhere else. I had already enquired with the attractive green-eyed, pale-skinned Indian girl at reception whether we could extend our stay at the Al Kareema apartments, but she had advised me that it would be impossible since they were already fully booked. Jas was keen to move into our villa whatever the circumstances, so I felt obliged to move in with him. However, I'd rather have found a hotel somewhere for a few days.

At 8 am on the Thursday morning Jas and I set off by taxi to the property agent to collect the keys to our villa. By 8.45 am, we were inside our villa with just a couple of suitcases each. We hadn't previously agreed which bedroom each of us would take. One room was obviously the master bedroom. It was the largest and it had big French windows, which offered a very pleasing view of the garden as well as direct access into it. Jas suggested we tossed a coin to decide who would get the room. He threw a coin in the air and I called out 'tails'. The coin landed on the floor revealing the picture of a falcon so

I immediately declared, 'I've won. The room's mine!' As I passed the coin back to Jas I noticed that the other side of the coin didn't have a 'head' either, but I decided to stay quiet on the grounds that Jas had suggested a silly way to decide who got the best room. He was obviously disappointed with the result. I felt a little sorry for him because I wasn't really that bothered which room I took, but I did get some perverse sense of satisfaction from depriving him of the room. Sometimes I think that I am not a very nice person; I certainly do have a little mean streak.

Jas and I agreed to buy a new television, video, cooker, fridge-freezer, washing machine and various other items for the kitchen, bathroom and other shared areas of our home. We agreed to add together the total spent on all items and then to split the cost equally between us. We bought all our electrical goods that same day at a large store on the main Dubai to Sharjah road. Sharjah is another of the seven emirates that make up the UAE. The salesman promised that everything would be delivered two days later, on the Saturday, some time during the evening, as deliveries weren't done on Fridays. Our visits to the telephone and electricity/water companies had obviously been successful as all utilities were working satisfactorily. The temperature was just right inside the villa so we didn't have to worry about using our air conditioning units. These were rather unsightly boxes placed in the walls or windows of most rooms. Sunil, the senior rentals negotiator, had assured us that they would be perfectly adequate, even on the hottest summer days. I remained somewhat sceptical about this, given that my guidebooks for expats in the UAE advised against renting accommodation without central air conditioning. Sunil's strong negotiating skills won us over, however, plus we did love almost everything else about the villa.

On the Saturday afternoon both Jas and I left work at 5.30 pm so that we could be at home when our electrical appliances were delivered. We waited for the delivery sitting on the ground at the front of our villa. The air got cooler and cooler, and the sky got darker and darker as the evening went on. Eventually the sun disappeared. 8 pm passed, then 8.30 pm, then 9 pm with no sign of our delivery. 'I don't think they're coming,' Jas finally declared. I offered to phone the shop to find out what was going on. After being passed to a third person on the phone I was finally speaking to the deliveries supervisor who told me that we were definitely down for a delivery that evening. He asked if I could be patient and wait for just a bit longer. 9.30 came and went, then 10, then 10.30, then 11. By now I was pacing up and down our driveway. 'This is bloody ridiculous,' I shouted. 'They surely can't be coming now.' The situation was made worse by the fact that we had no furniture and were uncomfortable, and we were also a bit cold now after sitting outside for too long. Then, at about 11.40 pm, just as we were going to our separate rooms for the night, a lorry pulled up outside our villa. 'Mr. Williams or Mr Harrington?' one of the deliverymen called out cheerily.

'What kind of fucking time do you call this?' was my reply, but I said it softly so that only Jas heard. He gave a tug at my arm as I went out towards the lorry and said, 'Nick, take it easy. Let's just get the stuff indoors.'

We now had a television but we didn't watch it because we were tired of sitting on the floor, and Channel 33, BBC World and CNN did not offer us the kind of entertainment we wanted. Instead we went for walks or to the bar at the Marine Beach Club, the nearest place to us that served alcohol. We now had a cooker, but nothing to cook with or eat off. For one week we slept on the hard tiled floors of our villa, and for one week we ate out every night. Then, our shipments from the U.K. arrived, and after seeing to the customs bureaucracy, which for me involved three trips to the port on three consecutive days, our lives finally improved. We had comfortable settees to sit on, comfortable beds to sleep on, and all our personal necessities to hand.

Jas had already placed the order for his new Land Cruiser at the Toyota showroom. I decided to buy a second-hand Nissan Patrol 4x4 from an Aussie expat returning home. I had seen the car advertised in the *Gulf News* and the price seemed reasonable for a vehicle only two and a half years old in excellent condition. I didn't originally want to buy such a large vehicle but was eventually coerced into it by Jas, Mike and all the other males at the office. They unanimously agreed that a 4x4 was a 'must have' in the Emirates. I had opened a bank account with *Mashreq Bank*, one of the local banks in the UAE, and decided to get a loan from them for the car rather than changing British money. It seemed silly to use my savings, which were earning good interest in a British bank account, to buy dirhams when I would probably be changing dirhams from my pay each month to buy pounds. At first, the loan application and approval procedure seemed simple, just as it usually is in the UK nowadays, but in the end it was a lot of hassle. They wanted to see many pieces of documentation, including my passport and residence visa, my driving licence, my contract of employment, a letter from my employer giving permission for me to take a loan and my tenancy contract for the villa. But they didn't tell me this at the start. They insisted on doing everything face to face. One day I would go to the bank with certain pieces of documentation, only to be told I also needed something else. I would return the next day with that item only to be told that I was now missing another thing. On one occasion I even had to get Mr. Aussie to meet me at the bank so that the bank officials could inspect his vehicle registration documents.

Registering my Nissan Patrol

*T*o transfer the ownership of the Nissan Patrol from Mr. Aussie to myself required both of us to visit the Traffic Police Department together. Luckily, Mr. Aussie knew where it was, though he had never had to go there before. It was located just past the airport, some ten minutes drive from the city centre. We parked up at about 8.30 am and followed signs saying 'vehicle registrations'. There were many different buildings, quite spread out in green, landscaped grounds. When we got to the vehicle registrations department we came to a huge hall with many different counters and queues. There were dozens of people scurrying about while others stood looking hot and bothered in long queues. It was not clear where to go or what to do. We decided to queue at the information desk. It took twenty minutes to get to the front of the queue and we were then simply told, 'Go to Mr. Sharma at the last counter,' as the man in a dishdasha vaguely pointed to one corner of the hall. We queued at the last counter in a row of counters for another fifteen minutes before being told that Mr. Sharma was on the other side of the hall. We began queuing again, this time for twenty-five minutes. We had to jostle about as people, probably locals, jumped the queue in order to get immediate attention. Everyone else looked like they were from the Indian subcontinent. There were not many westerners in the whole hall. I remarked upon this to Mr. Aussie, who told me that it was usual for westerners to send someone else to see to the necessary tasks.

Mr. Sharma looked at all of our documents and then snapped, 'Mortgage paper not complete. Go and complete first.' I was confused. 'What's not correct?' I asked. 'The bank said I was finished.'

'Vehicle details not entered. Driving licence details not entered. Go and complete properly.'

'I need to go to my bank and return tomorrow?' I asked.

'No, man outside can do,' was Mr. Sharma's reply. The mortgage papers were completed in Arabic so neither Mr. Aussie nor I could read anything. Outside the building, many people were hanging around. On either side of the main path we saw one man sitting behind a little table. 'I think those are the translators,' said Mr. Aussie as we approached one of the seated men.

'Excuse me,' I began, but I was immediately cut short.

'Please wait,' said the seated man. Then another man approached and said, 'There is queue. You fifth in queue.'

'But this man will complete my mortgage papers?' I asked in order to confirm that we were in the right place. The man nodded. Eventually the translator completed my forms. I paid ten dirhams, less than two British pounds, to the translator, which was okay, but as it took him only around five minutes to complete the job I thought that it wasn't a bad little money earner. We then went to the 'open new files' counter. After another wait of fifteen minutes we got to the front of the queue and handed over all of our papers. 'Where is your application form?' asked the young lady. 'You must submit a completed application form.'

'Where do I get that from?' I asked.

'You can get one from the information counter,' she replied.

'Why the fuck did the bastard not give us one when we were there?' snapped Mr. Aussie as we headed back towards the information desk. 'I am expected at work by ten thirty,' he continued. It was already a quarter past ten. When back at the 'open new files' counter with our transfer application completed (thankfully we were allowed to complete that in English) I was told that I had to pay ninety dirhams for new vehicle number plates. I asked if I was getting a new number but was told, 'No, its only because there's a new design for the plates.' I was given a little slip with a number on it. 'Go to the cashier's desk and wait until your number is called. Then bring your receipt back to me with your "no plate certificate".' This was the document needed by Mr. Aussie to declare that he would own no vehicle in the UAE after transferring the ownership of the Nissan Patrol to me. Mr. Aussie had to go to one counter for his 'no plate certificate' and to another to cancel his insurance. At the 'no plate certificate' counter, the man sitting behind the desk told Mr. Aussie that he still had three outstanding traffic fines. 'Traffic fines?' Mr. Aussie repeated.

'You have three tickets for speeding,' repeated the man. 'A "No plate certificate" will not be issued until your fines have been paid.'

'I was not expecting *three* tickets. Where can I get the details?'

'Back outside, turn left, in next building. Pay fines there too.'

'That's another thing over here,' said Mr. Aussie to me. 'You only find out about your fines once a year when you come to do your annual car re-registration, or if you try to transfer ownership of your vehicle.'

The man at the insurance counter was not happy either. 'Your certificate is no good,' he declared. 'It does not specifically say "cancel insurance", it only says that your car is sold.' The young man could see that Mr. Aussie was growing impatient, so then asked, 'Do you have the new buyer's registration card?'

'Not yet,' replied Mr. Aussie.

'Bring it to me when you have it and that will do I suppose.' I then had to queue to pay the fifty dirhams for my new registration card, and we queued yet again to collect the new number plates. Then we went outside again, and paid again, five dirhams this time, for one of a number of scruffy men hanging around with a screwdriver to take off the old number plates and put on the new ones. None of them would come to where we had parked the car however, despite it being only a two-minute walk away. Instead, we had to go to where they stood, where there were no spare parking places, stop in the middle of the road, let one of them do the job, and then return to another parking space close to where we had originally been. Finally, we had to wait for my new registration card. We were told that it would take 'twenty or thirty minutes', but in the end we waited one and a quarter hours.

For the record, Mr. Aussie and I finally left the Traffic Police office just after one o' clock. The whole thing had taken four and a half hours, and I had to pay out good money no fewer than four times for something or the other. Mr. Aussie dropped me off at my office at JBNC before driving himself to his place of work. I didn't have the use of the car for another few days because I still needed to give Mr. Aussie the money for it. Before I could get the cheque for this from the bank I had to show them my new registration card. Unfortunately, I was having a busy little period at work and couldn't get to the bank for a few days. I think that Mr. Aussie was grateful to have a few extra days use of his Nissan Patrol, but I prayed each day that he didn't have an accident or do anything to damage the vehicle.

The bureaucracy involved with getting settled into Dubai nearly killed me. During my first month in Dubai, I must have spent a total of two or three whole days in queues or simply waiting for something to happen. I spent many of these hours at the bank in order to open a bank account, and later for the car loan, at the telephone company and water/electricity company to get utility connections for the villa I shared with Jas, at the docks trying to get possession of my shipment from England, at the driving licence office to get a UAE driving licence (luckily that was straight forward, as local licences were issued automatically to people holding a UK driving licence), at the car registration office to get the Nissan Patrol registered in my name, and at the Department of Health, where I gave blood for an HIV test, a requirement for all expats wanting work permits. And this long list excludes things like waiting for my electrical goods that chilly Saturday night. In addition to all the queuing and waiting, I must have completed twenty forms or more and made as many payments. I had to pay deposits to the utility companies and I had to make a payment at the docks for processing the 'importation' of my personal belongings, and further payments for my driving licence and car registration card, and to get my HIV test processed. I know that the bureaucracy and time wasting I had to endure is not something unique to Dubai. I've had friends who emigrated to America and Australia, and they too reported that the first few weeks were hell. I was glad, however, when everything had been done and I could settle into some kind of routine.

First job

*M*y first proper job in Dubai was working for the Al Saadha-Wasel Trading Company. This was a medium sized manufacturing business that made socks, tee shirts and underwear, that kind of thing. They even supplied Marks and Spencer and BHS in the UK. The business was owned by two local families: the Al Saadha family and the Al Wasel family. The owners wanted to float the business on the new Dubai stock exchange, and I was the adviser who would ensure that everything went off smoothly. I spent much of my first three weeks in Dubai doing all my homework. By the time I made my first visit to Al Saadha-Wasel's head office, I considered myself an expert on Dubai's financial markets and the new stock exchange.

As I still didn't have the use of my own car, I had to go to Al Saadha-Wasel's head office by taxi. I wasn't sure that the taxi driver took the most direct route to the office, but he got me there eventually, just in time for my 8.00 am appointment. If the driver had taken an indirect route I could not tell whether it was due to his lack of familiarity with the city or whether he was trying to get a higher fare from me. I had discovered by then that virtually all taxi drivers were from overseas, and a great proportion seemed to be newly arrived in Dubai, and therefore they didn't really know their way around the city to a standard that may reasonably be expected of a taxi driver. In fact, on one occasion, a driver in a cream state-controlled taxi had got a little lost. He added at least fifteen minutes to my relatively short journey and at least ten dirhams to my fare. He offered to pay my complete fare from his own pay, and begged me not to complain about him, or else he would probably be dismissed and sent back to Pakistan.

Al Saadha-Wasel's head office was relatively modest by Dubai's standards. Most firms of its size had prestigious offices in the heart of the city or along the fashionable highways, like the Sheikh Zayed Road, where my own office was located. Instead, Al Saadha-Wasel's offices were adjoining its factory on an industrial estate on the outskirts of Rashidiya. Ali, the firm's Chief Executive Officer, later told me that this was so management could keep a tighter control on things to maintain high product quality and operating performance. He said that other local families ran their businesses far too casually. That's why his firm was the most profitable textiles company in Dubai and why he was able to supply Marks and Spencer, the UK's largest clothing retailer, which demanded the highest quality standards, standards which other local competitors could not achieve.

The entrance foyer to the Al Saadha-Wasel head office was large and cool. The walls were painted white and the floor was made of white marble with light grey speckles. When I announced my arrival to the receptionist, I was asked to take a seat on a settee on the other side of the hall. I sat beneath a large framed picture of Sheikh Maktoum Bin Rashid al-Maktoum, the Emir, or ruler, of Dubai. His portrait was to be found in a prominent position in most commercial offices and in other places, such as shops, banks and government offices. It is a custom throughout the Gulf region for organisations such as these to hang portraits of their local ruler for employees, customers and visitors to their premises to see. As I looked over my shoulder to admire the portrait I wondered if I would ever have the opportunity to meet the Sheikh in person.

On the coffee table in front of me were some of the firm's promotional brochures. I flicked through a few. The minutes ticked by very slowly. Not many people passed through the foyer but the phone rang constantly. I glanced at my watch; it was 8.20 am. I waited, and waited. Eventually it was 8.30 am, then 8.40. I was growing more and more anxious, and a bit pissed off. Had the owners forgotten about me coming, were they really so busy to keep me waiting this long, or were they just playing with me? I started to pace up and down the foyer. Eventually I went over to the receptionist. 'Mr. Saadha knows I'm here, does he?' I asked.

'Mr. Saadha not here yet,' was the reply. 'He shouldn't be much longer now. This is usual arrival time for him'. I went and sat on the settee again. If Mr. Saadha came to work at 9 am why make an appointment for me to come at 8 am I was asking myself. I told myself to stay calm. It would not do if I fell out with my client on the first day. But the air conditioning in the foyer was on full blast, and I was now beginning to feel somewhat chilled. I was not happy being treated this way. I had never been treated so badly, and with such little respect, in the UK. At least someone could have offered me a coffee or something to stop me freezing altogether.

At about ten minutes past nine Mr. Saadha's personal assistant, a slim Indian man, came to collect me. We went in the lift to the third floor and then passed through an open plan office with about 15-20 people before coming to Mr. Saadha's office. Ali Al Saadha, the C.E.O., and Sadiq Al Wasel, the Managing Director, were about the first two locals I had actually spoken to since arriving in Dubai, except for a handful of officials at places such as the airport, the driving licence office and the offices of the phone and electricity companies. 'Assalam aleikoum' (Peace be to you), said each of my hosts as I shook their hands. 'Wa'aleikoum ussalam' (And on you be peace), I replied. They seemed pleased that I knew the basics of local etiquette. I also did my best not to break any of the 'rules' that had been taught to me by my colleagues at JBNC and by Maureen at the cultural awareness course at the Hyatt hotel; things like using only my right hand for shaking hands or eating, because the left hand is regarded as 'unclean' (not a problem for me as I'm right-handed anyway) and not showing the soles of my feet when sitting. I did not, however, get any apology or explanation as to why I was made to wait for over an hour.

Both Ali and Sadiq were wearing dishdashas, the traditional white robes worn in this part of the world, complete with white guttrahs (headdresses) held in place by the twisted 'agal'. The dishdasha of each man was pristine, a brilliant white that looked as if the garment had just come from the wash before being perfectly pressed. They both wore leather sandals in which they were barefooted. I couldn't help noticing that their toenails were as well cared for as their perfectly manicured fingernails. Ali was about fifty, he had large shifty eyes, and with his thick grey beard he did not look like the sort of man you would immediately trust. Sadiq looked at least fifteen years younger. He was keen to be seen as the more dynamic of the two, equipped as he was with an American MBA, which he mentioned quite frequently. He too had the obligatory beard worn by most of the locals, but his was cut short. Sadiq spoke good English, but Ali was not fluent. He did not seem comfortable conversing in English at all, but it was clear that he had a strong and forceful character. I felt a little sorry for the old chap; after all, why should he have to speak a foreign language with me in his own country?

The day of our first meeting, Ali, Sadiq and I did not talk business at all; not about their plans for the business, not about their expectations of me, and not about any of my ideas. Instead, we concentrated on building a personal relationship, something required in their eyes before a successful business relationship could be established. Ali and Sadiq told me all about the business, about their personal work histories, and in the case of Sadiq, also about his education, about their families, about their hobbies, like horse and camel racing and about the wonders of Dubai. They were as good as listeners as they were as talkers. While talking or listening they looked me straight in the eye with a seemingly genuine interest in everything we spoke about. It was clear that they liked conversation, even if Ali did find it a little tiring doing so in English. They wanted to know all about my education, my work history, my life in London and my first impressions of Dubai. When the conversation turned to the topic of my family, Ali expressed great surprise that I was not yet married. 'A man your age should be married,' he said. 'Marriage makes a man complete. Do you not get lonely living all alone?' Before I could answer, Sadiq interrupted on my behalf, 'I am sure that Mr. Nick wants to be married, he just hasn't met the right girl yet. You know, western families are not as helpful in these matters as ours.' I wasn't sure what to say so I simply smiled and nodded in agreement. Ali did not leave the topic alone immediately. In fact before he moved the conversation onto another subject he said that he would be keeping an eye out for me to find a suitable wife. He seemed most genuine in his offer, and I wondered if he had it in mind to marry me off to a distant relation, or whether he also mixed with suitable westerners.

Throughout our conversation we drank endless cups of tea and glasses of water. The tea was served in little glass cups, without milk, but with sugar and mint leaves. I had never drunk tea without milk before, but served in the way it was, it was a tasty and most refreshing beverage. The drinks were served with locally made biscuits and pastries, which were also tasty, though a little on the sweet side. Ali's assistant returned to us almost every thirty minutes with fresh supplies. Ali and Sadiq ate and drank continuously, and encouraged me to do so also. Around lunchtime, Ali suddenly stood up and announced that he was going to pray, and he suggested that his assistant take me to the room that would be my office for the next four months.

I left with Ali's assistant, feeling that I had given a good impression of myself to my new clients. The room allocated to me was small and simple, but adequate. It did not have in it much more than a desk, a computer, three chairs, an empty filing cabinet and a large palm-like plant in a pot on the floor in the corner of the room. There were only two pictures on the wall: one, a portrait of Ali and Sadiq, and one of a fleet of their lorries. These I could see from my window, as I was looking down on the loading and unloading bays behind the factory. While working for the Al Saadha-Wasel Trading Company, this was my office for at least four days of the week: I was there from Saturdays through to Wednesdays, but on Mondays I sometimes returned to my office at JBNC. I didn't really have anything in particular to do there; I just needed some variety in my working life and to communicate sometimes with westerners. I didn't see any at Al Saadha-Wasel. Most of the employees seemed to be from the Indian subcontinent. In the canteen at lunchtime many of them communicated in their own languages, and at times I did feel a little isolated. Though I did see Ali and Sadiq on most days, I think that they went home for lunch each day.

Nightclubbing

*J*as wasn't a regular night clubber back home in the UK, but he agreed to go to a club on our third Thursday evening in Dubai. He said that it might be a good way to check out the local talent and possibly to meet other expats in order to 'widen our social circle'. Both Jas and I had meant to ask some of the chaps at the office if they could recommend anywhere in particular to go, but we had forgotten to do so. We went to a Lebanese restaurant for dinner. This was located on the ground floor of the Al Khaleej shopping centre on Al Mankhool Road. The food was excellent, and so was the service. It was a reasonably priced restaurant, yet it had an up-market feel to it. There was a pleasant mix of clientele ranging from Emirati and Indian families to western expats like us. We took a set main-meal menu which included various kebabs (skewered meat that had been cooked over a grill), *tabbouleh*, a mix of chopped parsley, tomato and crushed wheat in olive oil and lemon juice, *dolmathes*, vine leaves stuffed with a rice mixture, *hummus*, the dip made from chick peas and sesame seeds, and a range of fresh bread. And we washed it all down with a cocktail made of various fresh exotic fruits. It felt like really healthy eating, which made the meal even more enjoyable. After we had finished our meal and our table had been cleared the waiter returned with two plates of *Esh asaraya* (which translates as 'bread of the harem', but which is actually a sweet kind of cheesecake with a cream topping). 'We didn't order any desert,' Jas said immediately, but the waiter replied, 'No, no sir, these are on the house.' Now where on earth does that ever happen in the UK? The pudding was delicious, and especially so since it was free I suspect.

When we left the restaurant just before ten o' clock we still had no idea of our final destination. Jas suggested that we take a stroll around the block to 'walk off the meal'. We could then stop a taxi with a driver who looked like he might know where to go for a good night out. 'After all,' Jas had said, 'taxi drivers must be taking people to clubs every evening, and then taking them home at the end of each night. They must know which are the popular places, and they probably hear what their customers have to say about the various places.' For once, I was prepared to give Jas some credit for this suggestion. I had feared that we would end up back home early with nothing better to do than watch an old movie on Channel 33 (not even knowing at the time that Thursday nights were saved for Indian language films).

After twenty minutes or so of walking I suggested to Jas that we start looking for a taxi. We stopped and got into the first one that we saw. The driver was a middle-aged Indian. 'Maybe not the best choice of driver,' Jas whispered in my ear, before saying more loudly to the driver, 'Do you know any good nightclubs in Dubai?'

'Nightclubs where lots of girls go,' I added quickly.

'I think I know where you want to go,' the driver said. 'The Storm Club. Many beautiful girls there. Lots of choice. You definitely have a good time there and you certain to score.'

'Is it far away?' Jas asked.

'Only five or ten minutes, depending on the traffic.'

'Then please take us to the Storm Club,' Jas said eagerly. I had never seen Jas trying to pull a girl and hoped that he would be more of a help than a hindrance. I thought this because girls often go out in pairs and like to be 'pulled' by a pair of boys so that neither of them ends up alone. From a girl's point of view I would have thought that Jas was a quite good-looking chap, it was just that he sometimes came across as a stuck-up pompous twat. Sometimes, Jas just didn't know how to keep a conversation flowing. He could start boring a person to tears without picking up on any of the signals they gave off that were intended to tell him so.

We soon turned off the main road into a residential road with a distinct lack of street lighting. It was almost pitch black. On our left I could see what looked like some sort of sports stadium. Then, we turned a corner and again there was proper street lighting. We pulled up behind a long queue of taxis. 'Storm Club ahead,' the driver announced. People were still getting out from at least two or three taxis in front of us, and by the time we had paid our fare and got out of ours, another two taxis had arrived and pulled up behind our taxi. This was obviously a popular nightspot, thank goodness. Then I noticed that Jas and I were the only men in the street. Jas noticed too and commented on the fact. 'Either this is a very good thing,' I said, 'or perhaps it is a bad thing, because maybe its ladies night or something.' It looked like we were on some kind of industrial estate and the nightclub was hidden behind a long wall. There was just one door in it with a small sign above saying 'The Storm Club'. Two doormen stood chatting by the door. As we approached, one of the doormen said, 'Okay gents?' and gestured that we should proceed. We each paid our fifty dirhams entry charge at a little ticket booth before going indoors into the main building.

We came initially to a large room with a bar at either end. It could have been any large pub in England. There were not many seats and most people were standing in pairs or small groups around the edges of the room. This large room led to several other rooms. I could see that one of them had a deejay and a large dance floor. There were already a handful of people dancing to the latest European and American club hits. There were also signs indicating that there was a restaurant on the upper floor. 'Shall we circulate before we get the drinks in?' Jas suggested. I agreed. We walked around the club, trying to look cool and confident. As we did so we checked out the talent, and there was plenty of it. In fact for every one male, there were at least three females. 'There's plenty of tasty crumpet,' I couldn't help myself remarking.

'Sure is,' replied Jas cheerily. 'I wasn't expecting anything like this amount of choice. The taxi driver was certainly right. We're bound to pull here tonight.'

It wasn't only the fact that the females far outnumbered the males that delighted us, it was also the great variety of girls. They ranged in age from late teens to well into the upper forties, and they seemed to come from every continent. There were many oriental looking girls, many blonde, Slavic looking types and many black-haired Middle Eastern types, quite a few black girls, presumably from Africa, a handful of Indian looking girls, and also a few from western countries, possibly from America, Western Europe or Australia. In their own ways, they all looked gorgeous. Some girls were dressed as if they had just come from the office, some were wearing formal, almost flashy evening wear, some were wearing trendy nightclubbing gear, some were wearing casual things like short, tight tee shirts and jeans, while others looked like they were just about to start a strip show. Those falling into the latter category wore things like boob tubes, stiletto shoes and hot pants or very tiny mini skirts, and with the way they did their make up, many looked very sluttish. But to me, at that moment in time, it was all wonderful. There was a girl to suit every taste and every mood.

After we had walked around the whole club taking in all the sights and sounds, Jas and I each got a beer at one of the bars. Jas spotted an unused table that was surrounded by four chairs and suggested we sit down. We had a good view of the door leading from the entrance, and so could 'check out' all the talent as it arrived. By about midnight, a lot more men had arrived, making the male/female ratio in the club about 50/50. The men arrived on their own, in pairs or small groups. Like the women, the men also looked as if they came from every corner of the globe (except no Africans) and they were of all ages. In the UK, it would be unusual to see male teenagers socialising in the same nightclub as white haired men who could easily be sixty or seventy years old. They would have different tastes in music and want different things from their venue. Obviously, in Dubai, men of all ages and nationalities enjoyed, or at least came, for the same thing. But what was that? The chance to get out of their homes and meet friends, or the chance to drink alcohol in a public place, or was it just one of the few places in Dubai where men and women could meet? I fancied that it could possibly be a mixture of all three things that brought men, and possibly also women, to the Storm Club.

By about one o' clock, Jas and I were still occupying our table. We had each drunk four pints. No one had taken the two vacant chairs at our table. Jas commented on this. 'Maybe one of us has b.o.' he had jested. But soon after that our luck changed. Two girls fought their way through the crowds and when they got close to our table they stopped. The prettier one smiled and winked at Jas, then asked, 'Do you mind if we join you?'

'Please do,' replied Jas.

'I'm Ming,' continued the prettier girl, 'and this is ZhuSha.'

'I'm Jas and that's Nick.'

'Are you from the UK?' Ming asked.

'Yes, from England, or London to be precise,' Jas continued. The conversation continued for a while without ZhuSha or myself participating.

'I've always wanted to go to London,' was Ming's response, obviously trying to flirt with Jas.

'It's a great place. You really should go over one day.'

'I'd go sooner if I knew someone there. I really do believe that you can enjoy a place better when you're on holiday if you have a guide who really knows the place.'

'I'd show you around if I was in town. I know all the hot places,' replied Jas enthusiastically. I gave a little yawn, and tried to gesture to Jas that he was being corny, but both he and Ming pretended not to notice. They continued chatting, and Ming was soon telling Jas about China, the country from where she and ZhuSha had come. Ming was an extremely attractive girl. Like Chinese in general, she was not very tall, but she had gorgeous eyes, a delicate nose and seductive lips. When she smiled, she exposed a perfect set of brilliant white teeth. She had long, black hair, which shone brightly in the club's spotlights. Her slim limbs were smooth and golden. They contrasted nicely with her tight fitting white dress.

I decided that it was time to get to know my girl. As I began talking to ZhuSha I studied her in more detail. She was not bad looking, but I didn't fancy her. She had narrower eyes, a large nose and was slightly on the plump side for my taste. Her skin was oily and rather pimply. Despite not fancying ZhuSha, I thought that I would be civil and make conversation with her. It was hard communicating with her. I tried various topics of conversation, but all I could get her to say were mainly yes's and no's, and the occasional short sentence. I was not sure if this was because she didn't like me, or because she found the topics of conversation I picked dull, or simply because her English was very poor. She was smiling at me sweetly enough, so after some time I considered that her lack of communication was due to her lack of fluency in the English Language. I began talking to her in some sort of 'pidgin English', talking very slowly and trying to use only simple words, and leaving out words that lengthened a sentence in the hope that she might understand me better. After some twenty minutes of this I had lost all interest in trying. Jas had noticed the difficulty I was having trying to converse with ZhuSha, but he still abandoned me to dance with Ming. All evening I had been suggesting that we hit the dance floor, but he had refused saying that he couldn't dance and that he didn't like dancing. But as soon as little Miss Sexy Eyes asked him, he was off and bugger everyone else.

I finished my beer and decided to get another. I offered ZhuSha a drink but she declined. This was my chance to get away from her and hopefully to find a nicer girl, one that might be girlfriend material, or at least bonking material. I wasn't after a one-night stand. That's not my style. I took as long as possible getting to the bar, placing my order there and returning from it. ZhuSha must have taken the hint for when I returned to our table she was gone. Instead, two other couples occupied our seats. I went into the main dancing hall. It was now packed and everyone was dancing enthusiastically with considerable energy. The music was loud, the temperature hot and a little sweat dripped from my brow. I walked through the dancers hoping to catch a glimpse of Jas and Ming. As I went, I did a few movements as if I was doing a sort of dance, hoping that I might look cool and attract some girl's eye. It must have worked because as I passed a tall, beautiful blonde I felt a tap on my shoulder, and when I turned around it was her asking me for a dance.

The girl danced graciously. She was one of the smartly dressed women. She wore a cream jacket and trousers that looked well cut and quite expensive. I'm no expert on clothes but I believe I have the ability to tell an M&S number from a Giorgio Armani, Versace or Valentino. She had a chunky, but very tasteful gold necklace around her neck and a matching bangle on her wrist. As she waved her hands above her head, the stones in her rings sparkled. One of them looked like a rather large diamond. I was pleased that I might have 'pulled' a professional lady, someone who like me was successful in the world of business. She tried talking to me a few times but I couldn't really hear what she said because the music was far too loud. All that I caught was that her name was Natalie or Natalya or something like that.

After a while the woman with whom I was dancing gestured that she was ready for a drink. She took my hand in hers and led me through the crowd towards the bar. On the way to the bar, we bumped into Jas and Ming. 'We're going to head off mate,' Jas said. 'I see you've pulled. Nice one mate. So you'll be okay here on your own?'

'No problem,' I replied.

'Okay, Nick, I'll catch up with you in the morning then.' Before I could ask if they were going to our home or hers they had turned and left me and my blonde companion. At the bar, I ordered a large vodka with orange for her and another beer for me. I was now feeling more than halfway to being completely plastered, sloshed or stoned. It is not a condition I like being in. I like to have full control over my body's movements, I like to be conscious of everything around me and I like to have full control over what I say and do. This would have to be my last beer if I didn't want to embarrass myself. Natalya, as I later confirmed her name to be, knew how to down 'em however. I must have bought her at least four or five double vodkas in quick succession. I hoped that she would be worth this investment. I always thought that buying girls drinks must be some sort of investment; if men were not to get something in return, why on earth would they do it?

Natalya was from Russia. She had a sexy little accent and big pale grey eyes (the colour described by her). From what I can remember, our conversation took the usual, rather boring route of where are you from? What do you do? What are your hobbies? Tell me about your family, etc. etc. But Natalya was doing most of the asking, and me most of the answering. The conversation reminded me of the one I had had with Alira in my hotel room, only Natalya was definitely in a different league. She gave off the aura of success and class. Eventually, Natalya asked, 'So Nick, would you like me to come back with you to your place?'

'Well to be honest,' I replied, 'I usually prefer to take things a bit slower. I think that it's better in the longer term. Then you can't accuse me later of taking advantage of you or anything like that.'

'I wouldn't do that,' Natalya replied.

'You say that now. But you're under the influence of drink. I'm under the influence of drink. Who know's how we will feel in the morning?'

'Believe me, you won't regret asking me back to yours. Come on Nick, enjoy yourself. You want me, I want to go with you, what's the problem?'

I wasn't thinking straight. I was easily persuaded. 'Okay,' I said. 'If you insist, and if you're sure it's what you want to do then, sure, come back to my place. But I do share my home with a friend.'

'A man or a girl?' Natalya asked.

'A man.'

'No problem. I don't mind. Where do you live?'

'Jumeirah.'

'You have an apartment in Jumeirah?'

'No, a villa actually.'

'Lucky you.'

'Yeah, lucky me.'

'Is one thousand alright?'

'One thousand?'

'A thousand dirhams. And I'll stay all night and please you however you want.'

'You're a prostitute?' I almost shouted, being very surprised by the turn of events.

'Of course. You knew that, didn't you?'

'No I bloody didn't. You don't look like a prostitute at all. You look nice.'

'I *am* nice. And I could be very nice to you.'

'I'm sorry, but you've been wasting your time. I didn't understand the situation.' Natalya turned sharply around and left me abruptly. I'm sure that I heard her calling me a 'wanker' under her breath. I was pissed off now. How come I 'got off' with the whore while Jas got the pretty little Chinese girl? I didn't think he had it in him to pull so quickly. Perhaps I had underestimated him. He was certainly one up on me tonight. I sat at the bar, not drinking, but contemplating the meaning of life or something philosophical like that. Shortly after 2 am, the music stopped and the lights were turned up. 'Time to go,' the barman said looking me straight in the eye.

'I'm off,' I replied. 'Good night.' I got up and made my way to the exit. When I entered the big room by the entrance door I spotted to my great surprise Jas slouched on the floor. A couple of men with American accents had stopped to see if he was all right. When he saw me, Jas said, 'Ah, Nick. There you are! I hope you had a good night. As you can see I didn't get very far! That Ming, you see, was a fucking hooker.'

'The girl you saw me with was one too,' I replied, trying to offer some comfort to Jas.

'They're *all* hookers here!' exclaimed one of the two men who had stopped to check that Jas was all right, 'not that tonight I could find one that I wanted.'

Learning some truths

On the following Saturday morning I went with Jas to the JBNC office. I had a few papers to pick up before going on to the Al Saadha-Wasel office. When Mike saw me at my desk he beckoned for me to go over to his office. I went in and sat down. Mike drank coffee, but he also had a cup waiting for me. What a thoughtful boss, I thought. 'Are you settling in okay?' he began. I nodded, and he continued, 'I hope you had a good weekend?'

'An interesting one,' I replied. 'We went to the Storm Club on Thursday night. It was full of prostitutes. I was quite surprised to be honest.'

'It's a big problem in Dubai. Virtually all of the nightclubs are full of them. The only exceptions, I understand, are a couple of rave-type venues that serve mainly students and teenagers. I'm not keen on Haley going out nightclubbing in Dubai, but sometimes I have to give in, otherwise I feel as if I'm keeping her locked up as a prisoner in her own home. Life is good in Dubai, but it can also be stressful when you don't have your family and close friends around you, and when you've already been to all the usual places and attractions many times over. I read in the *Gulf News* recently that a government official had estimated that there could be four thousand prostitutes working in Dubai.'

'Amazing,' I interrupted.

'It's a paradise for the hookers. The city is full of foreign workers, many of whom are miles from home and who have not seen their families or girlfriends for many months. Think about it. Over three quarters of the workforce are male expatriates, and of those a large proportion are on single person visas. Not the westerners, of course, except for the oil rig workers, but most of the Asians, Filipinos, and even Arab workers from places like Egypt and Lebanon come to the UAE without their families. It's not really surprising that many of them are tempted to use the services of the "working ladies".'

'So are there any bars or places where one can meet girls who are not doing business?' I asked.

'Sure. Of course there are. There are many British, American, Canadian and Australian girls working as teachers and nurses, that kind of thing. They like to hang out at places like the Boston Bar, which is at the Jumeira Rotana Hotel, just round the corner from your villa really, or the *Irish Village*, which is just over the Al Garhoud Bridge and behind the Dubai Creek Golf and Yacht Club. The *Irish Village* is really just a big pub, but it is designed to look from the outside like a long row of traditional Irish cottages. And outside is a large, very pleasant patio area where you can drink and eat good food at reasonable prices. So, don't worry, there are places you can meet some decent western girls. Anyway, enough of all that. How are things going down at Al Saadha-Wasel?'

'I think we're making good progress,' I began. 'And we're on schedule for the listing in early April.'

'Good. Good,' replied Mike. 'And you're getting on okay with Ali Al Saadha?'

'No problems as far as I'm aware.'

'I have had dealings with him before,' continued Mike, 'and I did find him a bit strange. Wasn't sure how to take him sometimes. Well I'm glad to hear that you're getting on with him all right. Do your best to keep him sweet. There could be some more business coming our way from them later next year. So what are you working on this week?' I spent the next ten minutes giving Mike a detailed breakdown of everything I intended to do and achieve in the coming week. He seemed pleased with what he heard.

I then left the JBNC office and went over to my other (temporary) office at the Al Saadha-Wasel factory. Shortly after arriving, there was a knock on my door and then Ali promptly entered. 'Ah, Mr. Nick, you *are* in this morning,' he said.

'Yes, I had to stop by at JBNC to pick up some papers,' I hastily replied.

'And you had a good weekend I hope?'

'Yes thank you. I went out with one of my colleagues, who I also house-share with, and we explored a few of Dubai's delights.'

'There are many of those. Dubai is a wonderful city,' Ali replied, glowing with pride.

'Yes, I'm sure I will love it here,' was all I could think to say. I couldn't discuss the Storm Club with Ali. Would he know what was going on there, I wondered, and if so, what might be his opinion on the situation. I couldn't initiate a conversation on a topic such as prostitution as I might offend my host, and he might think that I was criticising his country, of which he was obviously very proud. 'Thanks for the report you dropped off last Wednesday,' Ali said. 'A most comprehensive report. You are to be congratulated. And everything else is going to plan?'

'Yes sir.'

'Good. Now tell me, have you got anything planned for this coming Thursday evening?'

'Not at the moment,' I replied.

'Well, how would you like to come to a wedding party? My nephew is getting married and there will be celebrations in the evening.'

'I would be most pleased to attend, thank you.'

'Okay. I'll send my driver for you at about eight. He will pick you up from your home.'

'Is there anything in particular I should wear or bring?' I then asked in slight panic as Ali had already started to turn to leave the office.

'Wear something like you wear to work. That will be fine.' Ali replied as he left my office. I felt that a lot of questions remained unanswered. Where was the party going to be held? What sort of food, if any, would be provided? Would there be any sort of entertainment? Would there be any westerners apart from myself? What sort of gift would the marrying couple want or expect? One thing was certain: the whole thing would be a fascinating experience. I was a little surprised by Ali's invitation. I saw him virtually every day, but only for very short periods. We tended to talk about business, though not in any great detail, and other topics of conversation were at a quite superficial level. I also met up with Sadiq each day. He monitored what I was doing much more closely, and we had frequent and detailed discussions about objectives, strategies and tactics. He was a confident young man. He was probably the Emirati equivalent of Jas or myself. He made it clear that he was successful and that he enjoyed his life. Having lived in America, he was probably less conventional than other Emiratis. Occasionally, he stopped by my office wearing western clothes, casual things like tee shirts and jeans, but only designer labels. He mentioned that he did things like diving, fishing and playing squash. He hinted that he mixed with company of the opposite gender, but gave no indication that he wished to socialise with me.

Finding Shannon

*A*fter mentioning to Jas that Mike had recommended a couple of bars where 'working girls' were *not* to be found, we agreed to visit the *Boston Bar* given that it was the closest to our home. As I now possessed my nice red Nissan Patrol, but Jas was only collecting his Land Cruiser the following weekend, and given that I wasn't intending to drink much, I offered to drive. We found the Rotana Hotel without any problem. The drive involved making only two turns. First, we drove to the end of our road, then we turned right onto the Jumeirah Beach Road, the street that runs for several miles along the coast. The sea, out to the left, glistened in the moonlight. On our right, we passed three shopping malls, which were located almost side-by-side. Then we passed the Jumeirah Mosque, before reaching the Al Dhiyafa roundabout where we turned right onto Al Dhiyafa Road. The hotel is the first building one comes to.

I turned into the car park, which was located behind the hotel. I drove around, but it was full. We had to wait five minutes until someone vacated a space, and even then I had to be quick to beat two other waiting cars to it. 'At least this place looks popular,' said Jas, trying, as usual, to be as positive as possible. He was studying his map as I pulled into the parking space. 'Interesting,' he said pointing at the name sign at the top of the hotel. 'We live in Jumeirah spelt with an 'h' on the end, the hotel is called the Jumeira Rotana, without an 'h' on the end, and the map says we are in Satwa, not Jumeirah. What do you make of all that then, Missssterrrr Nick?' He was mimicking how I had told him Ali and Sadiq addressed me: using 'Mister' before my Christian name and emphasising and lengthening the 's' and rolling the 'r' with a growl. In fact, I had already noticed that two of the shopping centres on the 'beach road' spelt 'Jumeirah' differently: the Jumeira Centre left off the 'h', but the Jumeirah Plaza had it. Did noticing such a detail make me as sad as Jas, I wondered, or did it just prove that we were both smart? In response to Jas's question, I just replied,

'Straaange.' In fact, I noticed in the coming weeks that there was no consistency in spellings anywhere in Dubai, not in the newspapers, not in government documents and not on the streets. For example, some signs along the Trade Centre Road spelt 'centre' the British way (ending in 're'), while others spelt it the American way (ending 'er').

We went into the hotel lobby and followed the signs for the Boston Bar, which was located on the first floor. It was supposed to be an American bar, but when we entered it, it was just like a typical English pub. It was quite crowded. A few groups of males obviously preferred standing, as there were still a few spare seats. Over ninety per cent of the people looked like westerners, and most were aged in their twenties or thirties. The male/female split was about 60/40, which I considered reasonable given that Dubai had a strongly male dominated workforce and population. We went to the bar and ordered two bottles of Budweiser from a pleasant English girl, who was possibly a student in the day. We then went and sat at a table. Several minutes later an American man approached us and asked, 'Are you participating in the quiz tonight?'

'We didn't know about it,' Jas replied.

'It's not too late to enter. I'll just take your names and table number, and then you can give your team a name. The prize for the winning team is a meal with drinks at the hotel's Bella Vista restaurant. But, ideally, you should have a team of five or six people.'

'Slight problem,' said Jas. 'We're here alone tonight.'

'I'll see what I can do for you,' replied the American before moving on to the next table. About ten minutes later, three girls approached our table: one with short black hair, one with light brown hair with blonde streaks and one with long, strawberry blonde hair. 'We understand that you are looking to make up a team for the quiz,' said the black-haired girl. 'Will we do?'

'That'd be great,' I answered promptly before Jas could offer a reply. 'Take a seat ladies. I'm Nick and this is Jas.'

'I'm Sinead,' said the back-haired girl.

'I'm Shannon,' followed the girl with the blonde streaks.

'And I'm Rebecca,' said the freckle faced girl with the long reddish blonde hair. We all exchanged a handshake, which was a bit strange really. I'm not sure who initiated that. All of the girls spoke with an Irish accent. We soon found out that this was their second year in Dubai and that they were all teachers in the same primary school. They had each come to Dubai straight from university. So, I worked out quickly in my head that they were probably about twenty-three years old. They would have got their bachelor degrees at twenty-one, a teaching qualification then took one year to complete and then they had already worked in Dubai for one year. Twenty-three was a good age for a twenty-seven year old, I thought, as long as the twenty-three year old is not too immature and too keen to keep living the student lifestyle.

The girls were good company, especially Sinead and Shannon. They were both very outgoing and quite funny. They really kept the conversation flowing, and we avoided serious subjects like work, money and love. We found out, however, that Sinead had a fiancé who was back at home in Ireland (although Shannon immediately revealed that it was a stormy on-off relationship) and that Shannon and Rebecca were both unattached. Both had not had a boyfriend since arriving in Dubai. 'The men in Dubai want one thing only,' Shannon said. 'None of them want to be in a stable relationship. Don't get me wrong, I'm not looking for anything serious, but I've had enough of one night stands and casual flings.' This girl clearly shared my own view on relationships. She was pretty, clever and apparently easy-going too.

Each of the girls was pretty, but each in her own completely different way. Sinead was possibly the most attractive however. She had pale ivory skin, a very slim figure and large black eyes surrounded by long black eyelashes. Her skin colour indicated that she was not one of the sun worshippers. Shannon, in contrast, was quite tanned. She had a fuller figure, which was most pleasing to the eye. Her face was pleasantly round, which fit with her overall appearance. Her eyes were as large as Sinead's, but they were blue. And lastly, there was Rebecca. She, like Sinead, was pale skinned, but she was very tall and very slim. She was a good deal taller than either Sinead or Shannon. She could easily have been a model and yet she didn't have the looks that most men immediately go for. Rebecca didn't seem to take much care over her appearance. Her hair, for example, was messily tied back with an elastic band and her clothes looked a bit creased. She was also quite quiet. I guessed that she was either just a little shy when meeting new people or perhaps she was generally a more reserved person. Given the bubbly and extrovert personalities of Sinead and Shannon, perhaps Rebecca just found it hard to get a word in. I noticed, however, that Rebecca was studying both Jas and me in great detail. I could feel her staring eyes focused on me for lengths of time that were longer than most people would generally consider polite. Occasionally, my eyes met her deep green eyes, and she turned down the intensity of her gaze, but she did not look away.

Sinead and Shannon told jokes and funny stories about life in Dubai and anecdotes about people they knew. They commented on topical items from the news, about celebrities and the like. And they gave reviews of films they had recently seen or CDs they had recently bought. Everything they said was interesting, light-hearted and amusing. Sinead and Shannon obviously liked to laugh and it was clear that they knew how to have fun and enjoy themselves. Rebecca seemed a bit like a 'hanger on', benefiting from the good vibes created by the other two girls. I wondered what Rebecca brought to the friendship between the girls. Maybe she was a good listener and supportive if they had problems.

Jas did not notice that the girls were skilfully steering the conversation around mundane and unoriginal topics and he started talking about JBNC and our jobs. Sinead, especially, did not look very impressed. I don't know what she thought we did for a living but she made it clear that she didn't really like men that could be classified as 'yuppie city types', especially those from London. 'Life should not just be about making money,' she said. 'Those yuppies working in the city should recognise this. There are more important things,' she continued, speaking with passion, but aggressively like a politician. 'And when those flash gits come over to Dublin from London for their long weekends and stand in our pubs slagging off and making fun of the Irish, I sometimes have to hold myself back from punching their lights out. D'you know what I mean?'

'We're not all like that,' I interrupted. 'Not that I consider myself a yuppie or a flash git, mind you. I'm just speaking as a man from London who happened to work in the city. I like to be stereotyped as a 'city yuppie' as much as I guess you like to be stereotyped as Irish girls.'

'And what is *your* stereotype of Irish girls?' Sinead retorted, now somewhat red in the face with rage.

'*I* have no preconceptions of Irish girls,' I began.

'But some English people think they're simple, living in the countryside, milking cows and the like and getting drunk on Guinness every night,' Jas continued.

'But not us. We're not so ignorant!' I interrupted promptly, trying to diffuse the situation. Shannon grasped Sinead's wrist tightly and whispered, 'Calm down, love.' There was a brief period of calm, and just as I thought we might become 'friends' again, Rebecca uttered her first words since our introductions. 'So, you're rich, are you?' she asked in a teasing manner.

'We're doing all right thank you very much. We both own flats in London, I'm getting a new Land Cruiser at the weekend and...' Jas began, but I stopped him talking before he had finished what he was going to say by kicking out at his ankles under the table, and by saying, 'Give it a rest Jas, yeah?' He still didn't seem to get it. These Irish girls, or at least Sinead, hated and resented men like us: young men who were successful, confident and wealthy, but my thoughts went along the lines of 'it's not our bloody fault we got ourselves an education and now work bloody hard. We're just getting what we deserve'. I said nothing further on the subject however, and waited for someone to change the direction of the conversation. No one had to make the effort at that particular moment, because the American quizmaster appeared on a small stage by the side of the bar and announced that the quiz was about to begin.

Each team was given a piece of paper on which to write their answers. Sinead offered to do the writing for our team. We answered questions on history, geography, entertainment, current affairs, sports and leisure, people, science and nature, and art and literature. Between us we made a good team. The girls were particularly good at questions on art and literature, entertainment and people, Jas was good at sport and current affairs and I was quite strong at geography and history. We all had fun proving, as a group, how clever we were. When 'Mister Quizmaster' had finished asking all his questions he came round to each team to collect their answer sheet. During the quiz I had studied the girls casually, trying to clarify what I thought about each of them. Jas's description of the English stereotypical view of Irish girls proved to be two-thirds correct. These girls could not be considered 'simple' as they were clever, educated and witty, but Shannon and Rebecca *did* both live in the countryside before going to university, and all three of them *did* drink a lot. In fact, they drank like fish, and even after several pints of beer and Guinness, they seemed to be totally unaffected by the alcohol. Jas and I drank much less. Jas and I bought one round each, but otherwise the girls bought their own drinks. At one point Shannon said, 'Actually, boys, you're lucky to see us here tonight. We normally go only to the bars that give us girls free alcohol.'

'Girls get given free alcohol?' I repeated, surprised by the fact.

'Yeah. On a Monday night we can each get two free drinks at the Capitol Hotel, on a Wednesday night we can get two free drinks at the Astoria in Bur Dubai, and on a Thursday afternoon we can get unlimited free drinks at the Plaza Hotel, just up the road, from one o' clock to six o' clock. By the time we leave there to go somewhere else for our Thursday night, we're usually completely wrecked.'

'How can a hotel make any money giving away free drinks all afternoon?' Jas asked.

'I expect the policy attracts many women, and that probably attracts many men, who probably end up paying double for their drinks,' I suggested.

'No,' replied Shannon. 'Not many men do come to the Plaza. Usually not more than half a dozen or so. And they typically stay seated around the edges seemingly intimidated by the large number of girls in one place at the same time. They're probably right to be cautious. We'd eat them alive.'

'It's a mystery how they make their money,' Sinead continued, 'and, to be honest, we don't really care. We just hope that they keep giving the stuff away.'

'And you can drink anything you want?' Jas asked.

'Yes. Beer, wine, shorts, whatever,' Sinead replied.

'Whoever said Dubai was a great place must have been right,' Shannon added enthusiastically.

I decided that of the three girls I liked Shannon the best. Sinead was engaged and so wasn't free, but her character would have been far too fiery for me anyway. Rebecca was too quiet, lanky and uninteresting. But Shannon was pretty, clever, jolly and fun to be with. I decided to make it clear how I felt. 'Shannon, what a beautiful name,' I began, in a rather corny fashion.

'My family is from just outside Limerick city, which lies on the Shannon river. It's a popular name round our way. Like "Smith" in England, except that's a surname of course.'

'Interesting,' I said, trying to sound like I really meant it (not that I didn't really think so). Shannon and I then drifted into a private conversation. Sinead was forced to talk to Jas because Rebecca was no longer sitting next to her, and Rebecca was left staring into space looking quite miserable and pissed off. I did feel sorry for her. It can't be nice having two prettier friends who always pull and leave you sitting alone with no one to speak to. I kept Shannon engaged in conversation, however, hoping that I might be able to turn on the charm and make her like me. Then, at the end of the evening, if I thought I had succeeded in this, I would ask her if she wanted to see me again.

An hour or so after the quiz had finished 'Mister Quizmaster' appeared back on the stage. 'Er Hum,' he said speaking into the microphone. 'Ladies and gentlemen, I now have the results of the quiz.

In third place with twenty-five correct answers out of forty-five it is the team from Emirates Bank International. In second place with twenty-eight correct answers it is the "Jumeirah Dream Team", consisting of six lovely housewives from Jumeirah. And in first place, with thirty-four correct answers we have the "Strangers Unite" team, so called because they were strangers until they met here tonight. So the winners of our free meal are Sinead, Shannon, Rebecca, Nick and Jas. Well done to them, and I hope they will be back next week to defend their title as this week's winners, and I hope to see all the other teams next week too. Good night, thanks for coming, and I hope you all had a good time.' Mister Quizmaster then came over to our table and gave us our meal voucher. He explained that we could use it on any day we wanted in the next thirty days, but that we all had to go together. I was a little relieved that I wouldn't now have to ask Shannon out on this evening, because she would have to see me again anyway if she wanted her free meal. Sinead looked at the voucher and said, 'So guys, will you be coming for your meal?'

'Of course,' replied Jas.

'Well, we have a netball tournament on Wednesday evening and on Friday we're going diving on the East coast. We won't be back 'til late, so how are you fixed for Thursday evening?'

'Unfortunately, I have a commitment,' I answered, remembering my wedding invitation.

'Surely, you can get out of *that*?' Jas replied.

'It would be rather rude. You see I've been invited to my boss's nephew's wedding,' I explained to the girls.

'No problem,' said Shannon. 'We can easily postpone it until the following weekend. Shall I give you my mobile number and then we can make arrangements early next week perhaps?' I got just what I wanted: Shannon's phone number and a firm commitment to another meeting. I hoped that she wasn't offended that I wanted to go to an Emirati's wedding rather than have a 'date' with her, but to be honest I was quite looking forward to going to the wedding. I was flattered to have been invited and I thought it would be a very interesting experience.

The wedding party

At eight o' clock sharp on the night of the wedding party I was ready and waiting to be collected by Ali's driver. He was, of course, late. He arrived at about twenty minutes past eight. He then drove us further out of town and into the desert. Fifteen minutes after leaving my home we were on a sandy track with no street lighting and no sign of any buildings—residential or industrial. The driver did not speak much. I think that his English was not very good. Eventually, I could see lights in the distance, and then as we came closer, two large tents some fifty or sixty feet apart, each similar to those that might be used by a smaller travelling circus in the UK. Ali's driver pulled up alongside dozens of other four wheel drives. He led me to one of the tents. I was feeling a little nervous, having no idea of what to expect inside. Here I was, smartly dressed in a casual cream coloured suit holding only a crystal vase that was my present for the bride and groom to be. I hadn't a clue what to buy so had telephoned Sheba, my 'administration support assistant' at JBNC. She had suggested something 'crystal' or 'fine bone china', but as I was about to enter one of the tents, I felt that my offering might be somewhat inadequate.

At the entrance to the tent, Ali's driver spoke in Arabic to a man dressed in a white dishdasha. The other man then beckoned that I follow him and he said, 'Please.... Come.' I followed him. Inside the tent there were many torches providing light. Incense was being burnt for its fragrant odour and to keep away the insects and flies. Dozens of men sat in rows on the ground, which had large Persian style rugs on it in an attempt to keep the sand at bay. I could see no other western men, and no females. The men wore dishdashas, mostly white, but some had other colours such as pale yellow, mauve or turquoise. Many were elegantly embroidered. The heads of the men were all covered with plain white or red and white checked headscarves. I was the only man exposing my hair to others. I hoped that I would not cause offence to anyone. I was led to a space between two men of approximately the same age as me. As I approached they stood to introduce themselves and to exchange vigorous handshakes. The men were called Majid and Abdul. Abdul was a brother of Ali's nephew, the groom, and Majid was one of Abdul's cousins. As I was introduced to other people later in the night I realised that everyone was related to someone else somehow, within the bride and groom's two families, and even they had historic links I was told.

I sat between Majid and Abdul. Majid couldn't speak to me much because he did not know much English, but Abdul was fluent. Majid owned several shops throughout the Emirates and he also owned two residential blocks of rented apartments. Abdul, in contrast, was doing an MBA at the London Business School. I wondered whether he had been admitted on merit or whether he had 'bought' his place, but after a while of speaking to him, I realised that he was quite a clever chap and probably a very shrewd businessman. He, like his cousin, also had retail and property investments. Between the rows of men were rows of low tables, already full of food and drink. It was like one big barbecue. Looking out of the tent in the direction of the ladies' tent I could see men roasting what looked like whole sheep on big open flames. They were also cooking chicken. Men were eating the meat with rice or mafrooda, a flat bread originating from Persia. They ate with their hands, but used only the right hand to put food into their mouths.

Abdul invited me to eat straight away, which I did, as I was quite hungry. Generous portions of food were served on large platters. The meat and rice had been flavoured with a mix of herbs and spices, such as cardamom, coriander, cumin, ginger, turmeric and saffron. Lemon juice had also been squeezed on some of the meat. It was all delicious, even better than the barbecued meats served at Mike's barbie. I felt very self-conscious eating with my hands however. I couldn't do it as elegantly as the others. I was also not very comfortable sitting on the ground. I could see that many men adopted the same position. This involved keeping one leg on the ground with the knee pointing outwards and the other leg drawn up with the knee pointing up towards the sky. I could not maintain this position for long, and changed back and forth frequently between it and several other positions that I invented on my own that night. I just hoped that I did not cause offence to anyone by having the soles of my feet or my knees or any other part of my body pointing in the wrong direction. The food was washed down either with water or freshly squeezed fruit juices. I drank both.

'Where is the groom?' I asked Abdul. He waved casually into the distance and replied, 'Over there.'

'Will we get to see the bride and groom together?' I continued.

'No, not tonight. The wedding celebrations will go on for several days. When the marriage contract is signed, then the couple will be seen together.'

'So, are the couple married now, or not?'

'The wedding has begun, but there is not yet a marriage contract,' replied Abdul. It all seemed quite confusing. I wondered how I would get my wedding gift to the couple. I asked Abdul. 'Don't worry,' he said, 'I will make sure they get it.' I handed Abdul my wrapped box, not convinced that the couple would ever get my gift or know from whom it came. My second thought was that it was just as well I didn't spend more time picking the gift or more money on it. Abdul placed the box on the ground by his side. I could not see any other presents and was curious to know whether the marrying couple would get any, so I asked, 'Do the couple receive many gifts?'

'Oh yes,' replied Abdul. 'They have already received much gold, jewellery for the wife, expensive silks and rare treasures. And my brother will pay to the father-in-law a dowry of seventy thousand dirhams. Not bad, eh?'

'Mmmm,' I replied, not knowing what else to say. Then, out of the blue, Abdul asked, 'So, Mister Nick, are you a Christian?'

'Yes,' I replied.

'And you go to church?'

'Sometimes,' I replied, which was a little white lie; or a rather big one actually, as the only times I had been in a church except as a tourist were for my own christening and the wedding of a friend I had met at university.

'Good... Good,' Abdul began, 'then you know how close Christianity is to Islam?' I shrugged sheepishly, realising that if we were to have a conversation about religion, I would easily expose myself as someone who is not familiar with religion and someone who does not regularly go to church. 'You believe that Jesus was born to the Virgin Miriam, whom you call Mary, and so do we. You believe that Jesus performed miracles, like curing the sick. So do we. You believe in heaven and hell. We believe in something similar. Both religions share the same principles of compassion, honesty, justice and love. So, you see my friend, there is much in common between Christianity and Islam. You, however, believe in a holy trinity of God, his son Jesus, and the Holy Spirit, but we believe there is only God. There is no God but God and Mohammed was the messenger of God. That's what we believe. God's message to man is recorded in the Holy Qur'an, just as it was revealed to the prophet Mohammed, and it is the Qur'an that guides Muslims in every aspect of their lives today. True Muslims are good people, kind people and peaceful people. Many Muslims can't understand therefore, why there are Christians in the west who seem to hate Islam so much. Such Muslims believe that many westerners are ignorant and blind to the truth. What is your view, Mister Nick?'

'To be honest,' I began, 'it's not a subject I have given much thought to. Certainly there are people in the west who are misguided about Islam, just as there are Muslims who misunderstand Christians and people of the west.' Abdul seemed satisfied with my reply. 'All conflict and fighting is unnecessary,' he continued, 'and we are Sunni Muslims here in the United Arab Emirates. We are very tolerant of other beliefs and, in principle, we are opposed to fighting and wars. Since 1971, the year in which the UAE was founded, we have not been in any war. For example, ever since Iran invaded and occupied three of our islands in the Gulf many, many years ago, we have continued to believe that a peaceful solution can eventually be found. Tell me honestly, Mister Nick, what did your friends and family think when you told them you were coming out to the UAE to work?'

'My family were surprised, but supportive of my decision and I think my friends were envious,' I answered.

'I am an observant man, Mister Nick. Even at the London Business School I see that all nationalities, from Europe, America, Asia, Africa or wherever, they mix and get on. They talk to each other every day and even socialise off campus. But the Arabs, we are kept at arms length. We are forced to stick together and to only socialise with each other.'

'I had noticed such things myself when I was at university,' I replied, 'but I always assumed that that was the way the Arabs wanted it: that they liked to keep themselves to themselves.'

'Maybe. Maybe. Perhaps there really is misunderstanding caused by the existence of two so very different cultures.'

'Is it so different here in Dubai?' I said, 'I recognise and appreciate that I have been invited to this wedding party, but really, how many Emiratis here in Dubai want to socialise with westerners? How many would have a westerner come to their home?'

'I suppose you are right, Mister Nick, and it is a great shame,' Abdul concluded in a thoughtful manner. 'It really is a great shame.' I then felt a tap on my shoulder. I turned around. It was Ali. I stood up to shake his hand and he said, 'I'm glad you made it here all right, Mister Nick, and I hope that my nephew Abdul is looking after you well.'

'Yes thank you, Mister Ali, I'm having a great time,' I replied.

'Good. Okay, I'll see you again later, Mister Nick,' he said. I did not, however, see him again that night. Mr. Ali then began shouting loudly in Arabic to someone sitting a fair way down the row of men.

A few minutes later the two rows of men in the middle of the tent stood up and carried their tables to the edge of the tent. Soon after came the sound of much drumming. I stood up to see six musicians sitting at the edge of the area that had been cleared. I could not make out the instruments they had, but they soon joined in with the three drummers to create what I assumed to be traditional Arabic music. Then, from the other side of the tent entered a dozen or so girls, probably aged between about eight and thirteen. The girls wore long colourful robes with varied designs and patterns. They began dancing energetically to the music, rotating their small hips almost like belly dancers do, and quickly turning their heads so that their long black hair whipped around their heads violently. The men stopped talking. Most now stood and they were clapping along to the music and cheering. The music was loud and had a strong rhythm. Despite the fact that I had drunk no alcohol, the intense heat, the loud music, along with the strong smell of incense, had a hypnotic affect on me; I felt as if I was in some sort of trance. There was something quite erotic about the way the girls were moving. I don't know what came over me but I just wanted to go over and dance with the girls. Eventually, a number of men joined hands and formed a circle around the girls. They too danced to the music. It became hotter and hotter in the tent and everyone was perspiring quite a lot. Some men went outside to smoke shisha from the water pipes. Eventually, I could detect various fruity aromas floating in the air. And that's basically how the party continued until its conclusion. I never did get to find out which man was the groom and I didn't see a single adult female all night.

First Friday alone

Despite arriving home at some time after two in the morning, I still woke shortly after six. I may have been woken by the dawn 'call to prayer'. There was a mosque a couple of streets away from our villa. Five times a day the *muezzin* melodiously 'called' all the local Muslims to prayer. The *Adhan*, or 'call to prayer' is a verse that is said or sung in Arabic by the *muezzin*. Our local mosque transmitted the *Adhan* using loudspeakers at the top of its minaret, so it was easily heard from inside our home. I had already heard some westerners moaning about the 'call to prayer', but I liked it. It reminded me that I was in a foreign land, a strange and exotic land, and to be honest I found the melodious singing both soothing and uplifting. I continued lying in bed with my eyes closed and I thought about several different things: about the wedding, about things I had to do at work the coming week and about Shannon.

An hour or so later, when I heard Jas moving around, I too got up. He was already making breakfast. He offered to make me some and I gratefully accepted. 'So how was your wedding?' Jas asked.

'It was quite fun actually,' I replied. 'Not that I got to see the bride or groom. I barely saw Ali or Sadiq either.' I then told Jas all about the wedding and he listened intently. I made some freshly filtered coffee and its aroma wafted pleasantly out of the kitchen and into our lounge/dining room. Jas made a traditional British breakfast with eggs, bacon, sausages and toast. We ate together at our dining table in the lounge. From the table we had a lovely view of our garden through large French windows. I opened the doors a few inches to let a cool breeze drift into the room. 'It's a shame you don't play golf, Nick,' Jas then said. 'Maybe you should give it a go some time. You might enjoy it.'

'I'm sure that's possible. Maybe one day I will take some lessons.'

'Mike says that the golf course we're going to today is one of the best he has ever played on.'

'What time are you meeting him?' I asked.

'I'll be off in another half hour or so,' he replied, looking at his watch. 'And do you have any plans for today?'

'Not really. I'll just take it as it comes I think.'

'Hey, mate. Do you mind washing the dishes and pans so that I have time to take a shower and get ready without rushing?'

'No problem,' I replied, trying to sound as enthusiastic as possible.

'Cheers, mate. You're a real pal,' Jas said as he left the table. I stayed sat at the table for a while and looked out into the garden. The sun was shining and the sky was blue. It was the start of another glorious day in Dubai. Abdul had told me the previous evening that parts of England were having snow. The thought of everyone I knew freezing in the miserable British winter was somehow quite comforting. Then, from the corner of my eye, I thought I saw something quickly slithering through some sand in the garden. My first thought was that it was a snake. I got up and went closer to the open door but could not see anything. Jas was still in the bathroom. I went there and called through the door, 'Jas! I think that I just saw a snake in the garden. They do have snakes in the UAE, don't they?'

'Yes,' he called back. 'What colour was it and how long?'

'Brown. And about two feet long.'

'Only a tiddler then! Did it have a triangular shaped head?'

'I didn't have time to study the shape of its head,' I replied.

'If it did, it could have been a viper. They're poisonous, but I guess it's unlikely you saw one of those.' Jas then laughed out loud. I thought that it was not a matter to laugh about, as I was sure that he had not thought about the possibility of dangerous animals in our garden any more than I had until that time. I may not have read anything about dangerous animals in my guidebooks on Dubai, but that didn't mean that there were none, did it? I was not particularly worried, just curious to know the facts. I went and did the washing up.

Fifteen minutes later Jas appeared again and announced that he was leaving. After I had finished the washing up and put everything back in its proper place, I went and lay on the settee in our lounge. I turned on the radio and listened to one of the English speaking stations based in Dubai. I was relaxed and very comfortable. Again, my thoughts turned to Shannon. I really wanted to call her and tell her how I was feeling. I spent ages debating in my head whether or not I should call her. In the end I couldn't stop myself from making the call. I had already programmed her number into my mobile phone so I made the call quickly and easily. She answered on the third ring, but it was an awful line. 'Hello,' Shannon said.

'Hi. It's Nick. I just called to say....er...er...hi.' What a fool I was. I hadn't decided beforehand what I was going to say.

'Well hi then, Nick. Was there anything else you wanted to say?'

'No, not really.'

'Well, how did you enjoy your wedding last night?'

'It was good. Yes, I enjoyed it very much thank you. Not that I wouldn't rather have been having dinner with you. In fact, I would definitely have enjoyed myself more being with you.'

'Flattery will get you everywhere!' Shannon replied teasingly.

'No. Seriously. I really do like you.'

'Pardon.... What did you say?' was Shannon's response as the line began to crackle incessantly.

'I was just saying that I like you. Where are you? Why is the line so bad?'

'We're in the car. Sinead's driving us to Khor Fakkan. We're diving today.'

'Oh yes,' I said. 'Well have a good time. And I look forward to seeing you later in the week.'

'Likewise, Nick. Bye then. Take care,' she said.

'Bye,' I returned just in time before she hung up.

For the next couple of hours, I just continued lying on the settee and listening to the radio. As the morning passed, the temperature in the room got warmer and warmer. By eleven o' clock I could see that the sun was out at full strength. It looked beautiful outside, yet I didn't particularly feel like going out. After a while I felt a bit restless. I didn't feel like reading or watching TV, I certainly didn't want to do any work, I didn't want to stay at home all day, but then I didn't have enough energy to go out either. For a while I thought about walking over to the public beach, just a ten-minute walk away, and lazing around on the sand, perhaps under the shade of a palm tree if it got too hot. I realised by about midday that Fridays in Dubai could be as boring as Sundays in the UK, unless a plan of action was decided upon in advance and then successfully implemented on the day. Jas had the right idea, I concluded. He was probably having a great time going around his golf course with Mike, and here I was being indecisive and not having a particularly great time.

I made myself a cup of tea, and I ate a few biscuits as I drank it. I decided that I would go for a walk. I would explore more of Dubai. I had already walked, with Jas, down the Jumeirah Beach Road in the direction of the shopping malls, so I decided to go in the other direction, towards the Jumeirah Beach Hotel. This is the hotel, shaped like a breaking wave, that Jas and I had had a beer at on our first Friday in Dubai. I didn't know how far away the hotel was, or whether I would walk that far, but I had also heard about a sailing club in the area that I thought I might check out. I was wearing shorts and a tee shirt. I put on my sandals and grabbed my sunglasses, but decided not to wear a hat. About twenty minutes later I was walking up the Jumeirah Beach Road past the Jumeirah Beach Park. I stopped to read the notices by the entrance kiosk to find out what the park had to offer. Apparently, it had a long sandy beach patrolled by lifeguards, a desert garden 'forming an oasis of colourful flowers and lawns', a children's play area, volleyball courts, restaurants and barbecue areas. All this came for an entry fee of five dirhams, less than one UK pound. As I stood by the park's entrance, two families, each with young children, went in. I continued walking up the beach road, past mainly older-style villas. Every now and then there was a small food store between the villas, but as it was a Friday, they were all closed. At times, the pavement turned from tidy paving stones to sandy track. I saw a sign for the 'Jumeirah Sailing Club' and went to have a look. There were a couple of dozen boats on dry land behind a high wire fence and a gate locked with padlocks, a small club house in the distance by a small harbour, but no signs of life. This was not the sailing club I was looking out for, so I continued walking. The road was quite busy with traffic in both directions, but I was the only person walking.

I eventually came to the Jumeirah Beach Hotel, and then to the small beach, which that 'naughty' taxi driver had brought Jas and me to on our first Friday in Dubai. At this point the road turned to the left, so I went to the left and then took the first turning on the right so that I was still walking parallel to the coast. This road was set back further, however, so that I could no longer see the sea. The area was very green, and behind the hedges and trees I caught a glimpse of a few large villas. This road didn't seem to be going anywhere so I wasn't sure what to do. Should I turn around and go back home, or keep going, and then possibly take a bus or taxi home if I went too far? The sun was quite strong for a day in mid December, and I was by now quite hot and thirsty. I decided, however, to keep walking in the same direction, thus going further and further from home. This road had no pavement and I walked in the road. Cars passed me without slowing down and it was at times a bit scary. After a while, I saw Dubai College, one of the British curriculum schools, on my left hand side. I had read that it was a popular school and was surprised that it was located so far out of town in an area where there seemed to be so few homes. I crossed the street to have a look at the school and its grounds, but couldn't really see more close up than from a distance.

I guess I was sort of loitering for a moment or two, and a big navy blue BMW X5 pulled up at the kerb. The vehicle had dark tinted windows and I could not see the driver inside. Then the nearside window came smoothly down all the way, and I could see inside a local man, of about my age, dressed in his white dishdasha. 'Are you alright?' he asked. 'Has your car broken down, or something?'

'No, I'm alright, thank you,' I replied.

'Can I give you a lift somewhere?' the man then offered.

'I'm okay, thank you. I was just out walking.'

'Where are you going?'

'In the direction of the sailing club.'

'Which one?' he asked.

'Al Mina,' I replied.

'Jump in,' the man said. 'It is not far. I will take you. No problem. Come, jump in.' I somehow felt it would be rude not to accept the offer, so climbed into the big 4x4. The vehicle was pleasantly cool inside as the air conditioning was on at full strength. The leather seats were more comfortable than those most people have in their homes. 'It's in the other direction,' the man said looking over his shoulder. At this point, the road was a dual carriageway with a steeply sloped central reservation of stones, rocks and sand. I hoped that the man was not going to attempt to drive across the reservation, as it didn't look like a safe thing to do. Furthermore, there was a proper space for U turns not so far ahead. But the driver did cross over the central reservation and at quite a fast speed. I felt a moment of fear, then a moment of exhilaration as my stomach turned in the way that it might on a roller coaster. I did my best not to look concerned, and the driver drove on with confidence, as if he did that kind of thing every day. He asked me a few questions like how long I had been in Dubai and where I worked, but offered no information about himself. In less than two minutes he stopped and pointing to his right said, 'That's the Al Mina Sailing Club. Take care now.' I thanked him and got out of his lovely X5.

Being offered lifts by locals was something that happened to me quite regularly after this time. I enjoyed walking, but the locals don't walk anywhere. They don't understand the joy or benefits of walking, and when seeing someone like myself on foot, they feel the need to offer 'help'. I was offered lifts by single men, groups of men, and even men who had their wives and children with them. Most of them seemed to enjoy the experience of meeting a stranger and 'practicing' their spoken English. To me, this was one indicator of many that I could eventually identify that showed the kind-hearted nature of the local Arabs. Although I did during my time in Dubai accept several lifts, I never thought it a dangerous thing to do. I always felt safe, and my 'hosts' were always polite and respectful.

I went into the grounds of the sailing club. A number of people were sailing dinghies or windsurfing in the area behind the breakwater. Over on my left, on a small sandy beach, a group of teenagers were having a barbecue. I went into the clubhouse, which had a bar and dining area. I must have stood out as a stranger, because conversations stopped, and people stopped doing what they were doing as they 'checked me out'. I looked around doing the same I suppose. There were families, couples and groups of men or women of all ages. There were only white faces however, or at least white faces with tans. I was promptly approached by Sarah, a bubbly blonde from England who was probably about my age.

'You haven't been here before, have you?' she asked.

'No,' I replied.

'I'm Sarah. I'm on the club's entertainment committee.'

'I'm Nick.'

'Were you thinking of joining the club? Have you sailed before?'

'Yes, but only a few times, with friends,' I answered. 'I'm new in Dubai and just thought I'd drop by to see what the club had to offer.'

'Do you plan to own a boat?' Sarah then asked.

'I hadn't really thought about it yet,' I replied. 'Do you hire out boats at all?'

'We do,' said Sarah, 'but we don't have enough, and unless you book at least a week in advance, you're unlikely to get one. It's really best to own your own boat. You can keep it here for a very small annual charge and it will be fairly safe. Only now and again does something go missing. On our notice board by the entrance where you came in, you will find several members advertising boats for sale. Perhaps, take a look and see if anything takes your fancy. Would you like me to show you around the club?'

'That would be nice,' I replied.

Sarah went behind the bar and got me a very brief information pack about the club. She then walked me around the clubhouse and the grounds outside. She didn't really show me anything that I had not already seen on my own. She kept suggesting that I buy a boat, for that way, she claimed, I would really enjoy being a member of the club. I interpreted her message as, 'If you don't buy your own boat, then we don't really want you as a member of the club.' I didn't really like her attitude, given that the club's advertisements I had seen clearly stated that boats were available for hire by the day or half day. At the end of my five-minute tour, I thanked Sarah and told her I'd think about what to do. However, at this stage of my time in Dubai I had no intention of buying a boat. Perhaps, I'd consider it when I settled in a bit more and if I couldn't find something better to do at the weekends. After I left the club, I walked to the Metropolitan Beach Hotel, which was located 'next door', from where I got a taxi to take me back home. When I got there, Jas had still not returned from his day of golf with Mike.

Discovering pyramids in Dubai

*T*he next morning, while I was at work at Al Saadha-Wasel, I received a call from Abdul, brother of the groom at the wedding to which Ali invited me. 'Hello, Mister Nick. How are you?' he began. 'It's Abdul.'

'Hello, Mister Abdul. How nice to hear from you again,' I replied.

'Did you enjoy my brother's wedding in the end?' asked Abdul.

'It was a magnificent party,' I answered with as much enthusiasm as possible.

'Well I was just wondering Mister Nick whether you played tennis, and if so, whether you might like to meet up for a game some time?'

'Yes I do and yes I would,' I replied. 'That would be great.'

'How about Monday evening then?' Abdul suggested.

'That would be fine,' I confirmed. We made arrangements to meet at the entrance of the *Pharaohs' Club* in the *Pyramids* at six o' clock. Abdul gave me directions on how to find the club. He said that the club was not difficult to find, as it was on a well-known site known as 'Wafi City', right opposite the Wafi shopping mall. He said that he would bring racquets and balls; all that I needed to bring was myself, suitably dressed.

On the Monday evening I arrived at Wafi City some thirty minutes early, so I took the opportunity to walk around and see what was there. After I had parked the car, I went into the mall. It was much like any other, only with more designer names and up-market boutique-style shops. There were not many people about, just a few small groups of women dressed in their long, black abbayas. As they were probably Emirati women, they also wore black headscarves. I even passed one old woman who also wore a gold coloured mask that covered her eyebrows, nose and mouth. It made her look quite fierce, like a bird of prey with a big powerful beak. It is possible that this woman was not an Emirati. All of the women walked around at a leisurely pace, as if they had all of the time in the world. Some held bags displaying designer names. Others brought their maids to do the carrying.

Outside, I caught a glimpse of the Pyramids building. The building was designed in an ancient Egyptian style, and on either side of the grand entrance there was a tall obelisk complete with detailed hieroglyphic carvings and two giant statues of pharaohs. In fact, the exterior of the whole building was covered in ornate carvings. And rising high into the sky from the top of the building was a pyramid. It was all very impressive. I peered briefly inside the entrance. I could see that in addition to the Pharaohs' Health and Leisure Club, there were also bars and restaurants in the building. As I was still early for my meeting with Abdul, I did not stay in the Pyramids building but instead continued to walk through the car park. In the distance I could see *Planet Hollywood*, a branch of the international restaurant chain that was supported (before the company declared itself bankrupt) by several Hollywood movie stars like Arnold Schwarzenegger, Sylvestor Stallone, Bruce Willis and Demi Moore. The building had a huge globe by its side with the 'Planet Hollywood' name on it. It was, in fact, a big version of the company's logo. I had once been to Planet Hollywood in London. It was nice enough, but that type of fast food is not really my thing.

At six o' clock I was waiting by the Pharaohs' Club entrance. Abdul entered, not a minute early or a minute late. I couldn't help remarking to Abdul that he had been the first punctual local that I had come across. He just laughed and said, 'You're right. Most of us are not very good timekeepers.' No sooner had I made the comment, I regretted it. It was, perhaps, a bit rude, and after all, I didn't really know Abdul that well. At the reception counter, Abdul signed me in, and we were each given a locker key. We then went into the club. All the staff we passed greeted us politely, addressing us each as 'Sir'. Abdul was wearing his dishdasha, and I my office clothes, so we went to the changing rooms to change into our sports wear. The design of the whole place was impressive. The detail of the architecture was enough to make me feel as if I was transported back in time to ancient Egypt. Outside the two changing areas were a couple of sinks in front of one big mirror, and everything else one might need. There were small piles of cloth flannels, hairdryers, and bottles of eau de cologne and body lotion, so that after showering we could smell nice and have smooth, baby soft skin.

There were a couple of other locals in our changing area. I was surprised by what I saw when they changed from their dishdashas into gym wear. They were very good looking young men and very toned. They were obviously regulars at the gym. They could easily have been Italian or Greek, with their smooth brown skins and short black hair. One of the two men spoke a couple of times to Abdul in Arabic, and all three of the locals laughed together. Abdul did not translate to me what had been said. Instead, he spoke to me about trivial things like the weather. When we were changed, Abdul led me through the club. We passed a steam room, a big, circular Jacuzzi, a tall climbing wall (the only indoor one in Dubai) and two workout rooms. He told me that one of them was only for ladies at certain times of the day. Then we went outside and saw a massive swimming pool, beautifully landscaped with palm trees and sun loungers all around. A group of women were in the pool taking an exercise class in the water, accompanied by music. An instructor shouted instructions and demonstrated the required movements from outside the pool. We passed one of the poolside bars and then came to the 'lazy river'. This was a moving channel of water, which if you sat or lay in a rubber ring or dinghy, transported you slowly around in a big meandering circle. A few children were playing in the 'river', some with rings, some without. 'The children love it here,' Abdul commented. 'I sometimes bring my younger brothers or nephews.'

Eventually, we came to the six tennis courts. They were beautiful, full size courts. 'Shall we just have a "knock around" for a bit?' suggested Abdul. I agreed. I could tell that he was a competent player. After a while he suggested we start playing some proper games. I thought that I was a fairly good player, but he was far better. We played two whole sets, and I won only one game. By the time we finished our games, floodlights lit the court, and no one was playing on any of the other courts. Abdul thanked me for playing with him, and praised the way I had played. He asked if I would like to join him for dinner. I was famished after all the running around, so gratefully accepted his offer.

After we had showered, rubbed creams into our bodies and sprayed ourselves with eau de cologne, we got dressed and went to one of the restaurants above the Pharaohs' club. Abdul was now wearing western clothes: a casual sports top and slacks. It was still warm so we sat outside, with a view down on the main swimming pool, which was now deserted. A waitress came with the menus and asked for our drinks order. I was not sure what to ask for. Would I offend Abdul if I drank alcohol? 'Um. Ah. Now let me think,' I said.

'I'll have a large Budweiser then,' Abdul said to the waiter. He caught me looking a bit surprised for a split second.

'Make that two,' I added. The waitress turned and went to the bar.

'Its not a problem for us to drink alcohol in restaurants or bars, as long as we're not in traditional dress,' said Abdul, trying to address my look of surprise.

'Oh, I see,' I replied.

'I think that most young men in Dubai drink alcohol sometimes,' Abdul continued. 'The difference between us and English men, is that we tend not to drink so much as to get ourselves drunk.'

'Very wise,' was all I could think to say.

'Do you drink much alcohol Mister Nick?'

'I wouldn't have said so.'

'I see that it is very common among students in London. Even among postgraduate students.'

'Yes, that is the student culture in England,' I confirmed.

'I think I'll have a steak,' Abdul said, still looking down at his menu. 'Have you decided what you're going to have Mister Nick?'

'I thought I'd be healthy and have something light, like the Chicken Caesar salad.'

'Good choice. I've had it before. It's very good here.'

'Yes, I already noticed that everything being eaten by other people looks good. Thank you Mister Abdul for bringing me here.' There was a brief pause. Enough time for me to reflect on what I'd just said. It made me laugh inside. It just wasn't what friends said to each other back home, at least not in such a way. 'So, Mister Nick, how long do you think you'll stay in Dubai?' asked Abdul.

'It's a little too early to say. I'll have to see how the job goes, but certainly I do like Dubai very much.'

'Its funny. Some foreigners don't like Dubai that much. They stay maybe one year or two, then go back home. Others love it. They stay twenty years or more and wish they could stay for ever.'

'I'm not sure that I would like living as "the foreigner" in any place for too long,' I said.

'But in a place like London, at least a quarter of the population are regarded by the English as "foreigners". It doesn't seem to bother most of them.'

'Maybe. Maybe not. There is a lot of underlying racial tension in a lot of British towns where there are high proportions of foreigners.'

'Ah. You mean places like Burnley and Oldham?'

'No, that's not really what I had in mind. All I meant to say is that to an outsider, London can seem a very cosmopolitan place where all nationalities and people with different ethnic or religious backgrounds live together in harmony. But in fact, many of the ethnic minorities *prefer* to lead very insular lives. They speak their own languages, are keen to maintain their own customs and in many cases, even want their children to go to separate schools.'

'Just like the British behave in Dubai,' replied Abdul.

'But is it by choice? Do we British know *how* we could integrate ourselves without converting to Islam and with the existing language barrier?'

'Oh, I think if you're honest Mister Nick, the British in Dubai have things just the way they prefer them. You can do more or less as you please here. You can go where you like, wear what you like, eat and drink what you like, even believe in whatever religion you like. You have many luxuries available to you, like this place where we are now, and like the many golf, sailing and diving clubs. And most British families have maids or nannies. They wouldn't have those if they were at home, would they? And you still get paid quite high salaries. More than many locals, you know, and all tax-free. It's not a bad deal really, is it Mister Nick?'

'I never said that it was, or even intended to imply as such,' I replied. I felt that our conversation had gone somewhat off course. I felt as if I had been wrongly accused of criticising someone or something. Luckily, the waitress returned with our drinks. She then took our food orders. 'You see Mister Nick, I invited you here tonight, to treat you as I would like to be treated in London. I wanted to be the good host.'

'And it is much appreciated Mister Abdul,' I replied.

'You don't have to call me "mister". I know that it is our custom, not yours. You can call me just "Abdul". No problem.'

'As you say Abdul,' I answered, realising that this evening might easily turn into something of a chore. I felt like I was walking on eggshells, always being cautious not to do or say the wrong thing. It was quite tiring really. Our conversation continued in the same semi-aggressive tone, though Abdul didn't seem to notice. He seemed to think that he was just having a normal conversation with a friend. I wondered, however, if these were the types of conversations he usually had with his Emirati friends. Every topic had to have a good or bad, a right or wrong, and everyone had to agree on everything.

Eventually our food came, and it was worth waiting for. It was very tasty. As I ate, I noticed that the moon high above was 'upside down'. It shone brightly, but it was obvious that we were seeing it differently than people do in the UK. As we ate, the conversation got a bit more light-hearted. We discussed countries we had been to, our hobbies, our favourite foods, that kind of thing. I glanced down towards the swimming pool and was surprised to see Sadiq, dressed in his dishdasha, with two western girls, one either side of him. He had his arms around them, and, as they walked, he kissed each of them on the neck. He led them through a door on the far side of the pool area.

'That was Sadiq, Ali's partner, wasn't it?' Abdul asked.

'Yes, I think so,' I replied.

'He's the kind of man who's been spoiled by western culture. You know where that door leads to Mister Nick? It leads to the Wafi apartments.'

'Oh,' I said.

'It's a surprise that man has any time for his business. He's often drunk and he loves the ladies, as you just saw.'

'Two at the same time? Maybe they are just friends,' I suggested.

'Don't be naïve Mister Nick. Either he picked them up in one of the bars, or maybe even in the shopping mall, or maybe they are prostitutes. That man is a disgrace to our people, our country and our culture.' I remained silent. 'Do you think Mister Nick, that Emirati men behaved in this way before they were exposed to western culture? Western films and television with its sex and swearing. And western women, with a complete lack of morality. Sex, drugs and alcohol to excess. That's what *your* culture has encouraged among many of our young men.'

'Its not *my* culture, Abdul. I don't get drunk, do drugs or go with prostitutes.'

'But it's the behaviour encouraged by *your* culture.' Again, I decided to remain silent. 'You know, Mister Nick, Sadiq has two wives and several children,' Abdul continued. 'What if he brings them AIDs? Does he think about such things? I think not. He is a very, very irresponsible man. But Mister Nick, I tell you, Allah sees all, and come judgement day, Sadiq will get what he deserves.' I continued to remain silent. I decided that I would not see Abdul again, but after this evening, he never called me again either. We did, however, meet again by chance several months later.

As I drove home from the *Pyramids*, my mobile rang. I pulled up at the curb on a quiet road to answer it. To my surprise it was Shannon. 'Hi, its Shannon,' she said.

'What a surprise,' I answered. 'How did you get my number?'

'I saved it into my mobile that day you called me, when we were on the way to Khor Fakkan.'

'Well, its good to hear from you.'

'Nick, the girls and I were wondering how you and Jas were fixed for this Thursday evening. Could we possibly go for our dinner on this day? You know that Ramadan starts on Friday, so there won't be the usual atmosphere in most pubs and restaurants from then on for the next month?'

'I'm free on Thursday. Look, I'll be home in about ten minutes. I'll check with Jas that he has nothing planned and then I'll call you straight back.' Jas was free and happy to claim our complimentary meal on the coming Thursday evening, so the date was confirmed with Shannon.

Last night before Ramadan

*J*as and I agreed to meet the girls at the Boston Bar. When we arrived, they were already there. They seemed happy to see us, but then they looked as if they had already had a few beers. 'Been to the Plaza this afternoon?' asked Jas.

'Well as it happens, yes we have,' answered Sinead.

'I wouldn't have guessed,' replied Jas.

'We had to have one big, last fling before Ramadan,' said Shannon jokingly.

'What are you drinking chaps? I'll get them,' offered Sinead.

'A beer would be great,' Jas replied.

'Same for me. Ta,' I added. I was impressed. It wasn't very often at all that a girl bought me a drink. I was further taken aback that it was Sinead who offered. I thought that she hated our guts. Well maybe she didn't, or at least not as much as I had thought. 'Come, take a seat,' said Shannon. 'So what have you been up to this last week?'

'Mainly working I'm afraid,' I replied, 'but I did have an evening out at the Pyramids. That was quite cool. I also played tennis at the Pharaohs' Club. Have you been there?'

'We've been to the Pyramids for drinks, but we haven't been to the leisure club,' replied Shannon.

'Well if you ever get the chance, I can highly recommend it,' I continued.

'Isn't it supposed to be the best health and leisure club in Dubai?' asked Rebecca, finally contributing to the conversation. 'I've heard it's very expensive.'

'You're not wrong there,' I answered. 'I picked up a leaflet. Membership costs seven thousand dirhams a year.'

'Bloody hell. We would have to work for six weeks to pay that,' said Shannon.

'Now you've told them what we're worth,' joked Rebecca.

'Yes, school teachers are not very well paid out here,' said

Shannon. 'We could get more in Ireland. The only financial benefits of working here are that we get free accommodation and the pay is tax-free. But I love it here. I love the fine weather and the whole social scene. It beats rural Irish life any day!'

'We get roughly the same pay as we would have done in London,' I said, 'but the exact take-home pay depends a lot on the exchange rate. At the moment, with the pound strengthening against the dollar we are slightly worse off.'

'Why is that?' asked Rebecca.

'It's because the dirham is pegged to the American dollar. The UAE government keeps the dirham at about three dollars and sixty-seven cents. That effectively means that the cost of buying pounds with dirhams is determined by the pound/dollar exchange rate.'

'Oh, I see,' said Rebecca.

'It must be the same for you when you buy Euros,' continued Jas.

'Yes. The exchange rate always fluctuates, but I never understood why.'

'But as you said Shannon,' continued Jas, 'the real financial benefit of working here is the tax-free salary and the accommodation allowance.' Sinead returned with our drinks. She said a toast, we all raised our glasses, and then we each gulped down some nice cold beer. We spent about twenty minutes engaged in pleasant conversation before Shannon suggested that we go up to the Bella Vista restaurant so that we wouldn't be late for our reservation.

The Bella Vista restaurant was described on its menu as a 'global dining restaurant'. There was pretty much something to suit every taste. We each ordered our food, and a bottle of red and white wine. It was great that the drinks were on the house. Everyone was in a relaxed mood, obviously eager to enjoy themselves. Sinead and Jas were doing their best to avoid upsetting the other. Even Rebecca seemed to be a little more involved in the conversation. After we had eaten our starters, main courses and desserts, Sinead suggested that we have a game of 'truth or dare' so that we 'might get to know each other better'. Everyone agreed enthusiastically. 'Right,' said Sinead, 'I'll start as the game was my idea, and the first to play is Jas. So Jas, truth or dare?' He thought for a moment and then said, 'Truth.'

'Okay Jas, at what age did you lose your virginity, and to whom?' Sinead asked.

'Er. Em. I was about nineteen and it was with a girl called Louise, at university.'

'And whose idea was it?' prompted Sinead, obviously wanting more details.

'It was hers, actually. After a party.'

'Okay Jas,' said Sinead, 'now you can ask someone "truth or dare?"'

'Your turn Shannon,' declared Jas. 'Truth or dare?'

'Dare please.' Jas thought for a moment. 'Right. I'm going to order you a pint of lager, which you then have to drink completely in one minute.'

'Oh Jas! I've had enough already! Must I?'

'You asked for the dare! Now your turn to perform!' When a waitress passed, Jas asked for one pint of lager. When it arrived he pushed it across the table, right in front of Shannon. 'Right, here I go,' said Shannon. 'Get your watches ready. And if you have to carry me home it will be your own faults.' She opened her mouth and the beer quickly disappeared, though some dripped down her chin and on to her chest. She was making good progress with the beer, but after thirty seconds or so, she began to choke a bit. As her face moved away from the glass, she sprayed Rebecca and Jas with beer from her mouth. 'Ahhhhhh!' exclaimed Jas loudly. Shannon paused for a moment, and then began drinking again. 'Times up!' declared Jas after the minute had passed. Shannon hadn't yet finished the beer and she kept drinking. Ten seconds later she did finish, and she thumped the glass down on the table and murmured, 'That was nice!'

'Right,' shouted Shannon, causing a few heads in the restaurant to turn, 'now your go Nick. Truth or dare?'

'I'll have a dare please,' I replied.

'I want you, Nick, to go to the toilet and stay in there for two minutes. But not the men's toilet. I want you to go into the ladies'.'

'Oh no! I can't do that. We'll get thrown out of here.'

'Off you go Nick,' urged Sinead. I got up and went over to the toilets. I didn't hesitate. I went straight into the ladies. A middle-aged woman was washing her hands at the sink. She looked at me in surprise and said, 'This is the ladies.' I didn't reply but went straight into one of the cubicles and locked the door. I could hear the woman muttering to herself. I looked at my watch and waited for a good three minutes before leaving, to ensure that I couldn't be accused of not staying in for long enough. When I emerged from the cubicle, luckily there were no other ladies in the room. I returned to our table to a round of applause. 'Right, your turn Rebecca,' I said. 'Truth or dare?'

'Truth,' she replied.

'What's the worst thing you have ever done in your life?'

'When I was ten,' began Rebecca, 'I led a five year old boy in our village away from his home and left him in a field by a stream. As I walked away, he began to cry and begged that I not leave him alone. He just sat on the grass with his head buried between his arms. He did not know how to get home. He just sat there crying for ages. I watched him from a distance, from under a tree, just in case he fell into the stream or something. Then, after a couple of hours, I returned to his home and told his older sister, who was about my age, where her brother was.'

'That was awful of you!' said Sinead. 'We'd better be careful not to cross you I can see.'

'I'm very ashamed of myself now,' replied Rebecca blushing, 'and I don't think I ever did anything so cruel or wicked since that time.'

'Good game this,' said Jas. 'Isn't it?' Everyone agreed.

'For that one Nick,' said Rebecca, 'I'm going to throw the game back at you. Truth or dare?'

'I guess I had better have a truth this time,' I replied.

'If you were marooned on a desert island, which of us three girls would you want with you and why?' I could feel my cheeks beginning to blush, and yet I recognised straight away that Rebecca had done me a favour. I could now declare my feelings for Shannon. 'It would have to be Shannon,' I answered, 'because she's beautiful, fun to be with and she's obviously very smart. So, after a few weeks of fun, she'd work out how to get us off the island.'

'What a sweetie,' said Shannon. She then leant across the table and gave me a long, sensual kiss on the lips. I put my arms around her shoulders in an attempt to make the kiss last as long as possible. As she finally pulled herself back into her seat I heard Rebecca say to her, 'See, I told you he liked you.'

We continued playing the game for a while. The worst thing that happened to me was a dare that came from Sinead. She wanted Jas and me to kiss 'with tongues'. We couldn't bring ourselves to do it however, and pretended to do it behind clasped hands. That brought the game to an end, as the girls seemed to lose interest once we failed to perform one of their dares. At the end of the evening, I told Shannon that I wanted to see her again. She suggested that we could go to the Jumeirah beach park the next day, but added that she might have to bring Rebecca along. Sinead would not come, as she would be preparing for her flight back to Ireland later in the afternoon. Sinead, Shannon explained, wanted to spend Christmas with her fiancé, but her fiancé didn't want to come to Dubai. I said that I might have to invite Jas, depending on his plans for the day. 'Then we'll have a nice foursome,' Shannon joked. However, I didn't really like the idea of forcing Jas and Rebecca together. I didn't know how Rebecca felt about Jas, but I knew that Jas didn't fancy Rebecca.

Sunbathing in December

Just after ten the next morning I called Shannon on her mobile. She said that Rebecca did want to come to the beach with us. I told Shannon that Jas was out playing golf, although he was really staying at home to catch up on some office work. He had told me that when he finished his work he planned to relax in the garden with a good book. In truth, I think he was not that keen to see Rebecca again.

I met Shannon and Rebecca at the park entrance at midday. I paid the five dirhams entrance charge for myself and for each of the two girls. 'Aren't we waiting for Jas?' Rebecca asked as we went through the turnstile and into the park.

'He had already made plans to play golf,' I lied. Rebecca looked a little disappointed. Shannon had obviously not mentioned that Jas was not coming. I hoped that she would not have a 'sour face' all day, but she then smiled and said, 'Never mind. I'm sure we can all have fun without him.' I felt pretty contented having two good-looking girls with me, who were walking one on either side of me. We walked past the shops and restaurants, past some of the gardens and the barbecue area, and eventually, through a gap in the line of palm trees that ran along the beach we could see the sea. It was a deep blue colour, glistening brightly under the sun. A moment later we could see the sandy beach. The scene was straight out of a holiday brochure. It was beautiful. The sand was whitish-gold in colour, and it was perfectly clean. In the distance, the sea, also, looked clear. The row of palm trees behind the beach provided the perfect tropical backdrop. I flicked off my sandals and carried them. The sand was warm and soft to my bare feet. The beach was not very crowded, but there were still quite a lot of people. There were families, couples and groups of younger people, like us. Some people were sunbathing, some were walking around, some were swimming, children were chasing each other around on the beach, and a group of men played with a boomerang. The beach was quite long, perhaps half a kilometre in each direction, but bodies on the beach were fairly evenly spread. In front of the entrance to the beach, perched high on a timber-framed tower was a lifeguard.

'Where do you want to go?' asked Shannon. 'Sun or shade?'

'I think it would be a shame not to get some sun,' I replied. 'If that's alright with both of you.'

'No problem with me,' said Rebecca, 'and I know that Shannon is dying to top up her tan a bit.' Shannon looked up at the lifeguard and waved. He waved back. 'When we girls come to the beach alone we tend to stay fairly close to the lifeguard because when we get bothered by groups of men he comes down and gets rid of them. So, this one knows us,' Shannon explained.

'Do you get a lot of bother from men?' I asked.

'Unfortunately, yes,' replied Shannon. 'Men, especially the low class, unskilled, Asian workers, think that any single girls on the beach are fair game for them to enjoy as they please. They come and stand so close to you that you fall under their shadow. Or they come and sit or squat on the sand nearby to you. Then, mostly, they just stare. They stare and stare, and don't take their eyes off you. It's an awful feeling when that happens. Only very occasionally will one of them try to talk to you. I feel a little guilty when I have to tell them to 'piss off', but they really are a pain those sort of men. They don't come to enjoy the beach, sea or sun at all. They come only to look at almost naked girls while they themselves stay dressed in their gowns.' For a brief moment, I felt a pang of guilt, for I enjoy ogling at beautiful girls on the beach. What red-blooded man does not enjoy looking at beautiful women, especially when they're wearing far less than what they would normally be seen wearing in any other situation? Admittedly, I do my admiring from a distance and with discretion. I wondered how sinful my behaviour would be regarded by the girls, but I had no intention of asking. 'They should be given some girlie mags, and then maybe they wouldn't have to look at us,' Rebecca said thoughtfully.

'But they're illegal here,' responded Shannon. 'Hey, Nick, have you bought any British newspapers or magazines yet?'

'Yes,' I answered.

'And have you noticed the work of the censors? Any exposure of female flesh is covered in black ink. A fashion magazine I bought last month had a feature on swimwear. The one-piece swimwear was acceptable to the censors and all the pictures remained as they were, but all the bikinis were drawn over in black ink as one-piece swimming costumes. A real artist did that! I mean, can you imagine it, a room load of men turning every page of every newspaper and every magazine just looking for bare flesh to cover with black ink?'

'It does seem a bit over the top,' I answered.

'They're mad,' murmured Rebecca.

'But they allow sex galore on the satellite TV,' continued Shannon. 'I've seen many films on the television with quite explicit sex scenes. Why don't they edit those out?'

'And why don't they do something about annoying men on beaches and in shopping malls?' added Rebecca. 'Anyway, as we are with you today, Nick, we won't be having any men problems, as they prey only on the single girls.'

'Glad to be of service,' I replied.

The pace of our walk slowed. 'Will this do?' Shannon asked, pointing at an unoccupied piece of beach. 'Yes,' replied Rebecca and I together. We each took out our towels from our bags and spread them out on the sand. We then took off our clothes, each revealing our swimwear, which we already had on underneath our normal clothes. 'Damn,' exclaimed Shannon. 'I've chipped my nail on my zip.' Rebecca and I were already lying on our towels. To my surprise, I found that the girls had gone either side of me so that I was in the middle. That made me feel somehow important and very good inside. 'The sun is quite strong,' Rebecca declared. 'No way is it twenty degrees. More like twenty-five. I'd better get some sun cream on, or I'll be looking like a lobster again.'

'She can't handle the sun, our poor Rebecca,' joked Shannon. Rebecca began to rub cream onto her face, then onto her arms, then her front and legs. I always quite enjoy watching girls applying sun cream. There's something quite erotic about it, especially when they're massaging the lotion onto their legs or onto or near their breasts. I couldn't help noticing that Rebecca was looking particularly attractive today. Maybe Jas had been wrong to write her off so quickly. She had perfectly smooth skin, and the little freckles on her face, arms and chest were quite cute. Rebecca then turned onto her front and said, 'Shan, can you do my back?' Shannon was still standing, fidgeting with her fingers. 'I'm still sorting out my nail. Can't Nick do it?'

'Would you?' asked Rebecca, after turning round to face me.

'No problem,' I replied as I picked up the bottle. I began massaging the lotion into the top of Rebecca's shoulders and the back of her neck. She had her long hair tied up. I moved slowly down her back, rotating my hands in what I hoped would be a sensual way. As well as rubbing, I couldn't resist a bit of soft pinching. I then applied lotion to the back of Rebecca's arms and legs. As I rubbed cream into her firm thighs, absent of any cellulite, I couldn't help noticing her perfect little bum. Her lime green one-piece swimsuit was cut high on the thighs and revealed a lot of bum. I wondered whether or not I was expected to apply cream there too. I continued down the legs while I debated whether or not I had the bottle to do Rebecca's arse also. In the end, I couldn't resist, so I did it, but rather quickly and nervously. I had a bit too much cream left on my hands so moved back to Rebecca's shoulders to get rid of it there. As I began massaging there, she suddenly murmured, 'Ahhhh, that's really nice. We'll have to bring you to the beach every time we go.'

'Oi,' bleated Shannon as she flicked one of my ears. 'Are you just applying sun lotion, or giving a full body massage down there?' Rebecca promptly turned herself over. She did it too quickly and without giving any warning. My head was in the wrong position and ended up in her crotch. I couldn't miss the slight swelling of pubic hair under her swimming costume. I blushed, Rebecca blushed and Shannon just laughed. I was glad, however, that Shannon had showed signs of jealousy. That suggested that perhaps she did care for me, if only a little. But then again, perhaps she was just teasing Rebecca and me.

A moment later, we were all stretched out on our backs soaking up the sun's warmth. 'I can't believe it,' I said. 'It's just two days before Christmas and look at us here, sunbathing in this heat.'

'It really is wonderful here,' replied Shannon. 'The weather is probably the best thing about Dubai. Well, at least until May. Then it gets a bit unbearable when the humidity picks up and the temperatures hit high forties every day. But then we look forward to our summer holidays, and by the time we get back to Dubai in September its already getting better again.'

'What are you doing on Christmas Day?' I asked.

'Rebecca and I were just going to go out for a quiet meal. We've got a table booked at the Radisson. You're welcome to join us if you like, but we'd have to check if they have any places left.'

'I'd love to join you if you really don't mind,' I replied, hoping for confirmation from Rebecca. But she just lay on her towel, not saying a word. She was probably still getting over my sensational massage! Shannon, however, got straight onto her mobile and booked me a place. I was conscious that she didn't mention Jas, and for some reason neither did I. However, I immediately felt guilty that I hadn't waited to speak to him before booking my own Christmas dinner. But then I consoled myself with the argument that if I got a place, then so could he, if he booked later that day.

We lay on our towels for a couple of hours, not talking very much, before Shannon suggested we go for a swim. Rebecca and I agreed, and we all made our way to the water's edge. I put one foot in to test the temperature. It seemed quite cold. I wasn't sure if that was because the sea was cold, or that it just felt cold because I was hot after soaking in the sun's heat for a couple of hours. While I was still debating whether to go in or not, Shannon and Rebecca went straight in. It was obvious that they loved water as much as fish. 'Come on in, it's lovely,' cried Shannon. I hesitated for a moment. 'Come on, don't be a wimp!' Rebecca then shouted. That did upset me, so I dived right into that cold, but beautifully clear, clean water. A few minutes later I no longer felt cold, but pleasantly refreshed. Shannon and Rebecca were good, strong swimmers. They swam fast and confidently, above and below the water. I was not as good, and struggled to keep up with them. The sea was salty and felt good on the skin. The afternoon sun, still strong, kept the air warm. Other swimmers we passed seemed to be enjoying themselves. I concluded that swimming in the Arabian Gulf in December was indeed a very enjoyable experience.

As we left the sea to return to our spot on the beach, we met Mike and Stella who were walking along the water's edge, the sea splashing around their ankles. They were still wearing their swimwear but were carrying their bags. I did the introductions. 'We were just going for hotdogs and drinks,' said Stella.

'That sounds like a good idea,' replied Shannon.

'Please do join us,' answered Stella.

'Okay, you go ahead,' I said, 'and we'll follow in a few minutes.'

'We'll be at the beachside café,' replied Mike. He then gave me a wink and a big grin as he nodded at Shannon and Rebecca, who were both at that moment looking the other way. As we returned to our things, I walked behind Shannon, enjoying the view all the way. She had a nice walk. She was wearing a bikini that had thin vertical stripes of pink, turquoise, orange and white. She looked beautiful in it, especially when it was wet and left little to the imagination. When we returned to our things, Shannon picked up her towel from the sand, shook it vigorously for a few seconds and then began to dry herself with it. She then held it around her body while she changed into a pink tankini top and matching shorts. I was covered in salt and sand, and didn't feel particularly comfortable. As I had noticed some showers by the entrance to the beach, I decided to make use of them. I picked up my towel, bag and shoes, and told the girls that I would meet them at the beach entrance. Unfortunately, the water from the shower was not temperature adjustable and was far colder than I had bargained for. In the end, I only washed the sand from the lower half of my legs and my feet. By the time I was dressed in my normal clothes, Shannon and Rebecca were already there waiting for me. I could see Mike and Stella in the café at the top of the stairs. As I looked up, Stella waved. We all waved back at her. 'She seems like a nice lady,' Shannon said.

'Yes, she is,' I replied. 'And she does a mean barbie too.'

When we got to the café, I ordered three hot dogs and three large coca colas for Shannon, Rebecca and myself. As I was waiting for the food to be prepared I could see the girls and Stella deep in conversation. I wondered what they were talking about. Not me I hoped. When I eventually got over to them, they were talking about Sting, the singer. Apparently, all four of them had been to his gig in Dubai the previous month, and they were saying how good it was. 'We're really lucky here,' said Mike. 'Every year, more and more big-name pop stars come to Dubai. But there's also increasing variety in the entertainment. Earlier this year, we even went to an opera and a ballet. Both were very good, very professional. The emirate has also become an international centre for major sporting events. There's the Dubai Tennis Open, the 'Desert Classic' for golfers, the Dubai World Cup, that's horse racing, the International Rally, that's motor racing, the Dubai Rugby Sevens, and em...'

'You like sports then, do you Mike?' Shannon asked.

'I'm a golfer me, to play and to watch,' replied Mike. 'But Stella and I have also been to the tennis and the horse racing. The World Cup, Nick, is rather like your Ascot. The ladies get dressed up in their best frocks and extravagant hats. They have brass bands playing music, and there's champagne and strawberries galore. Last year we even found ourselves just a few feet away from Sheikh Maktoum Bin Rashid al-Maktoum.'

'The whole thing sounds great,' said Shannon. 'We've not been yet.'

'What's really great though,' continued Mike, 'is that every event seems to attract the world's best. Everyone wants to come to Dubai. At the Desert Classic I've seen Nick Faldo, Seve Ballesteros, Ian Woosnan and Colin Montgomerie, and at the Tennis Open we've seen people like Boris Becker, Greg Rusedski, Jonas Bjorkman, Martina Hingis and Serena Williams.'

'So what do you do for leisure and pleasure?' Stella asked Rebecca.

'Oh, we just go out for quiet drinks really,' answered Rebecca. 'But we play netball and hockey at school, and we've been diving a few times.'

'You enjoy diving then?' prompted Stella, trying to encourage Rebecca to talk more.

'Oh yes. It's lovely when the sea is nice and warm,' replied Rebecca. 'But when you go down deep, the visibility is not as good as you might think. Sometimes you can hardly see anything. But a couple of times off Khor Fakkan we've seen some really beautiful fish. All shapes, sizes and colours. One was bright orange with white stripes.'

'Ramadan must be a bit of a drag if you enjoy going out and drinking,' said Mike. I wasn't sure if he meant it as a statement or a question, but Shannon answered. 'We survived through it last year, so we'll cope,' she said. 'We're not complete alcoholics, you know.'

I was still to discover the joys of Ramadan. Ramadan is the time when God revealed the Qur'an to the prophet Mohammed. It occurs during the ninth month of the Islamic calendar, which, because of differences with our calendar, causes Ramadan to occur about two weeks earlier each year. During the month of Ramadan, Muslims are supposed to focus on their spiritual growth and development, and between the hours of sunrise and sunset they should not eat, drink or smoke. This self-denial is an expression of faith and a method of self-purification. Fasting is supposed to develop strength, patience, knowledge and self-awareness. The fasting Muslim will, for example, gain a true sympathy for those who go hungry.

Ramadan impacted upon my life in more ways than I expected. Ali and Sadiq, at the Al Saadha-Wasel Trading Company, greatly reduced their working hours. I understood and appreciated that fasting might cause them to slow somewhat both mentally and physically, but I could get no sense from them at all during the month of Ramadan. If I had a query, the response was either 'you can decide' or 'we can discuss that tomorrow'. But tomorrow never came. The firm's workers, regardless of whether they were Muslim or not, were expected not to eat or drink during the working day. The poor workers on the factory shop floor, working in hot conditions, were denied even water. Sadiq told me that I should bring in a packed lunch during Ramadan, and eat it discreetly in my office. Lunchtime was often my only opportunity for social interaction during the working day, and during Ramadan I was deprived of even that. Needless to say, it was not a joyous time for me.

Outside, the streets were largely deserted during the day. Most shops, and all restaurants, stayed closed during the day and opened only at about seven in the evening. There were no business lunches therefore. That, for many, also meant a Christmas dinner with no alcohol. As it happens, the Radisson got special permission to serve liquor during the hours in which they served their Christmas dinners, so I was not one of the many who had to go without on Christmas Day. It did strike me as severe, however, that if a family was at the beach, then even the children would be expected to go without their usual ice creams and cold drinks. Not that I'm criticising, mind you. It's their country and it's their religion, and I didn't think it unfair for them to expect us expatriates to restrain ourselves to some small extent for just one month of the year. From what I had already seen, the expats were allowed to please themselves completely at all other times of the year.

Mike said that Haley, his eldest daughter, often compared Dubai to Cancun because it offered as much 'fun in the sun'. That's a place in Mexico where they had once had a lively family holiday, and which in some ways might be compared to the European holiday resorts of Ibiza, Ayia Napa in Cyprus or Faliraki in Rhodes, which all attract a largely young clientele. The evening entertainment in these places, especially for the British, but also for young people from several other North European countries, tends to focus on heavy drinking in the many bars and nightclubs. Haley had told her father that Dubai provided 'top sounds' played by top visiting US and European DJs, a lively party atmosphere at most venues and relatively cheap booze, but without the drunkenness, drugs and lewd behaviour which, unfortunately, are associated with Ibiza, Ayia Napa and Faliraki.

After about an hour of good conversation, Mike and Stella decided to go home. Stella's last words were, 'Nick, now you be sure to bring Shannon and Rebecca to our next barbie.' I offered to make Shannon and Rebecca a light meal at my place, but they said they had to get back home as they had things to do. I didn't ask them what it was they had to do, even though I knew that their pupils were already on holiday from school. Shannon drove me home in her rather clapped out Hyundai Accent. When she pulled up outside my villa, I invited them in. 'Come in for just a quick coffee,' I said, but again Shannon declined my offer. However, Rebecca looked like she could have been persuaded otherwise. Maybe she was nosey and wanted to check out my home, or maybe she was hoping to run into Jas. I'm not sure, but I didn't invite them in again. Shannon then said, 'Go in and see if Jas is there, and if so, whether he wants to join us for Christmas dinner. I could then make the arrangements right here on my mobile, and you will then both know it's done.' I did as Shannon suggested. Jas was in, he wanted to come and Shannon reserved him a seat at our table.

Christmas Day

Christmas Day, falling on a Sunday, was a normal working day at Al Saadha-Wasel. Nevertheless, Ali had told me that I need not come to work on this day. I thought that this was really nice of him, and it showed the importance he placed on religion, even when it was not his religion. I had agreed with Shannon that we would all meet up at the Radisson at midday. I offered to drive Jas and me to the hotel, and before we left I consulted a map so that I knew where the hotel was. It was, in fact, located just beyond the Al Mina sailing club where there were several hotels almost side-by-side along the beach. The Radisson was the furthest away from the sailing club, and therefore also the furthest away from the centre of Dubai. Beyond the Radisson was a power station and then the DUBAL aluminium plant, one of the biggest in the world, and then the Jebel Ali Port. I thought that being adjacent to an industrial zone, the hotel might not be as nice as some of the others, but when we arrived, I was pleasantly surprised. The grounds around the hotel were pleasantly landscaped, and it was only just possible to make out a number of chimneys in the distance. As we arrived fifteen minutes early, Jas suggested we go into the hotel and have a look around.

In the entrance lobby was the reception counter of course, and right in the middle of the lobby a large Christmas tree, at least fifty feet tall and very elaborately decorated. 'I wonder how they got that here,' said Jas.

'The same way they get everything else here', is what I wanted to reply in a sarcastic tone, but as it was Christmas Day I just smiled and said, 'I wonder too.' There was a big restaurant at the back of the entrance lobby, and it was obvious that that is where we would be having our Christmas dinner. Some people had already started. Most were middle aged and very smartly dressed. There were couples eating alone and also several groups, both same-sex and mixed gender. The number of women with blonde hair suggested to me that many of them might be from Scandinavia, given that the Radisson was part of the SAS (Scandinavian Airlines System) Group. If I was right, I can conclude that Scandinavian women age very graciously. It must be all that fresh fish they eat and the fresh air they breathe. The food was being served buffet style, and apparently with great choice. I tried to see what people were eating, but most had obviously only just started. Some were having soup, others plates of cold meat or fish. Before we knew it, we were in the hotel's garden. It was splendidly landscaped with plenty of palm trees and other plants to provide patches of shade above the lush, green grass. The sun was shining, and, believe it or not, there were actually a few people sunbathing on deckchairs around the swimming pool and down on the beach. I experienced another of those moments of self-satisfaction. What luck to be enjoying Christmas in the warmth, and in a nice five star hotel with all the cooking and washing up done for you, and without having to put up with distant relatives who are often hard work to survive the day with. I would have liked my mother and father to be there with me, but my father had not been very well and was unable to undertake the long flight from England.

'It's twelve o' clock,' said Jas. 'We'd better go and see if they're here.' We turned and went back into the lobby area. At that moment Shannon and Rebecca came through the main entrance. Shannon gave a little wave high above her head, which I returned. When we reached each other we exchanged hugs and kisses and Christmas greetings. I gave three kisses on the cheeks to Rebecca but Shannon's was on the lips, quite slow and firm. I didn't notice what Jas did. 'Have you been here long?' asked Rebecca.

'We got here about fifteen minutes ago,' replied Jas. 'And you?'

'Just got here,' answered Shannon. 'We're very punctual us two.' Then after a brief pause she added, 'So, are you hungry then?'

'Always for a Christmas dinner,' I replied with enthusiasm.

'It does look good,' murmured Rebecca, almost to herself. When we got to the restaurant entrance Shannon said to the waiter, 'Table for four booked under the name of Connolly.' The waiter glanced down at his book, and then looked up, smiled and said, 'Follow me please.' I gave Shannon a little squeeze on the arm and said, 'Is that your surname then? Connolly, I mean.'

'Yes. Shannon Connolly, that's my name.'

'Oh,' I said, for no particular reason.

'Any problem with that?' Shannon asked, with a big grin on her face.

'No, not at all. Shannon Connolly is a very nice name. Your parents should be complimented on their good taste.' Shannon continued smiling as she gave my arm a firm pinch. We had a nice table in the corner of the restaurant area. As we took our seats, the waiter unfolded our napkins and placed them on our laps. 'Can I get you any drinks?' he asked.

'Shall we have wine?' Shannon asked.

'That sounds good,' replied Jas.

'Red or white?' prompted the waiter.

'White perhaps,' answered Jas. 'Unless anyone would prefer red. I think white wine goes best with turkey.'

'Make it a litre of house white then,' I said. 'And a bottle of still water please.'

There were crackers on the table. We pulled them making big bangs and then put the paper hats on to help get into the festive spirit. The girls whispered to each other and then they reached under the table for their handbags. They each took out two little wrapped packages from their bag. 'Merry Christmas,' they said as they handed us the delicately wrapped packages. I felt my face going red with embarrassment. Neither Jas nor I had brought any presents for them. I opened Rebecca's present. It was a little furry animal, or perhaps a monster. 'It's for your car,' said Rebecca.

'Thank you very much,' I said as I leaned over the table to give her a kiss on the cheek. Then I opened Shannon's present. It was a metal wind chime. 'And that's for your home. Hang it on your veranda and it will bring you positive chi energy.'

'That's to do with Feng Shui, isn't it?' I asked with curiosity.

'That's right,' answered Shannon. 'This six rodded wind chime is used to attract good luck and good fortune to your home. It will bring you happiness and prosperity.'

'You believe in all this Feng Shui stuff, do you?'

'Yes, to some extent,' replied Shannon. 'I do believe that the way our homes are organised and decorated can influence our minds, bodies and spirits. I am not a very spiritual person, but perhaps I have started down the road to enlightenment.'

'I see,' is all I could think to say. I'm not particularly into this sort of thing. I did my best to keep a straight face so that Shannon would think I was taking it all seriously. I then thought about it for a moment. Maybe I should keep an open mind and give the chimes a go. What would I have to lose? So long as Shannon didn't think that she could come to my home and change everything to comply with Feng Shui rules. I looked to see what Jas had been given. He received a small bottle of aftershave and a silver bangle. Jas and Rebecca got up and Jas said, 'We're off to get our starters.' I was surprised. Did this mean that Jas was prepared to give Rebecca a go? Shannon saw me looking at Jas's presents. 'The good luck bangle was from me,' she said. She then stood and said, 'Shall we go for our starters too?'

There was a big selection of starters, which included three different soups, cold meats, seafood and salads. Shannon and I took the venison soup. I picked it because I had never tried venison before. We also took some freshly baked bread to have with our soup. When we got back to our table, Rebecca and Jas were already eating their prawn and seafood salads. I thought it was a bit rude of them not to have waited until we returned to the table. Rebecca looked curiously at our soup, and asked, 'What's that?'

'The venison,' replied Shannon.

'Oh, you're having Santa's reindeer,' giggled Rebecca in response. I gave her a look of disgust. I do hate people that make remarks about food that might put you off what you're just about to eat. She didn't take the hint however. 'Good job you've had your Christmas presents already, or else they might not have been delivered!' she continued, seemingly resulting in much amusement for herself. 'But they are such cute little things, aren't they? Just think of Bambi.'

'That's enough I think, Rebecca,' said Shannon, before I had the chance to say something to Rebecca about her mercury filled fish that had been swimming around in and eating sewage all of their lives. Jas remained quiet. I couldn't read the expression on his face. I couldn't say what he was thinking. Maybe he regretted coming out with us on Christmas Day. But then, he didn't really have an alternative. It was either a day with us or a day alone in front of the telly, or perhaps in the garden or at the beach. The soup was delicious. It was very rich and creamy and full of flavour, but I don't know how to describe the flavour or what it might be compared with. As we ate our starters, Shannon told stories, or rather details of the latest gossip and scandals, involving other teachers who lived on their school campus. Shannon was an entertaining storyteller, but as Jas and I didn't know any of the people mentioned, the stories didn't interest us for very long.

After the waiter had collected our empty plates and bowls, we all went together to get our main courses. As we approached the main serving table, one of the staff cutting and serving the meat asked, 'Scandinavian or traditional dinner?'

'What's Scandinavian?' asked Jas.

'Julshinka,' replied the meat cutter. 'Specially prepared whole ham, very tasty ham, with pickled herring, liver pate, meatballs, smoked sausages, cabbage, beetroot salad and potato au gratin. Also cod fish in cream sauce.'

'And traditional?' said Jas, as he scratched his head pretending to consider the choice.

'Turkey or goose. With all the usual trimmings.'

'I think I'll have the turkey then,' replied Jas. 'I'll be traditional.' I had a bit of turkey and a bit of goose, and I think that the girls copied me. To accompany our meat were bacon wrapped sausages, stuffing, lots of different vegetables, perfectly roasted potatoes and freshly made cranberry sauce, of course. When we got back to our table, the waiter gave us each a complimentary glass of mulled wine. That was a nice touch. The food was so tasty that we all went for a second helping. But by the time I had eaten that, I didn't really have any room for my Christmas pudding. But I forced myself, and that too was delicious. We all had the Christmas pudding except Rebecca, who had a rice pudding with sugar and cinnamon topping. 'I don't really like Christmas pudding,' she explained. I wanted to tell her that her rice pudding looked like puke, but I just about managed to control myself from saying anything that could escalate into an argument. As she was near to finishing her rice pudding, Rebecca suddenly stopped eating. In fact, she bit into something she didn't expect to find in her pudding and spat it back into her bowl. 'Oh my God! What is that in my pudding?' she shrieked.

'Only a beetle,' replied Jas calmly. I wanted to pat that man on the back for helping to get back at Rebecca for her reindeer comments. Just then a waiter passed. He obviously noticed the commotion at our table, but he looked pleased. He had a broad grin on this face. 'Ah, you got the almond, you lucky, lucky lady,' he said. 'You know what that means, Miss? In every Christmas rice pudding the Swedish put just one almond. The person who finds it will be the next to marry.' Rebecca was now very pleased with herself. 'Did you hear that?' she said to Shannon. I heard Jas mumbling something under his breath that sounded like 'not very likely'.

By the end of our meal, we were all very full, and the alcohol had made us all relaxed and happy. The conversation flowed easily and we were chatting like life-long friends. Eventually Jas suggested that we take a walk outside. We all agreed, but ended up lying on sun loungers around the hotel swimming pool. The sun was still quite strong and there was a refreshing breeze coming up from the sea. We must have stayed there for at least a couple of hours, stretched out comfortably with our eyes closed and without speaking to each other. We stayed there until some mist built up, which came rolling in from the sea, and which reduced the sun's warming effect. 'Time to go?' Shannon suggested.

'You'll come back to ours?' I replied, perhaps a little too eagerly.

'I've got a headache,' said Rebecca. 'I want to go home.' I shrugged my shoulders and said to Shannon, 'You're still welcome, my dear.' Shannon offered to drive Rebecca back to their flat and then to drive back down to our villa. So, I drove Jas and me back home and then waited eagerly for Shannon's arrival. She could have done both trips in about thirty minutes I estimated, so I was a little disappointed that she didn't come for over one hour and thirty minutes. When she did arrive, she was holding a video and a bottle of red wine. 'Have you heard of Ali G?' she asked. Neither Jas nor I had. 'He's the latest big hit on the telly back home, but I'm not going to say anything more or else I might spoil it for you.' The three of us watched the video and drank the wine that Shannon had brought. We all laughed out loud uncontrollably. However, it took me quite a while to work out the joke properly. It was a fun way to end a rather strange Christmas Day, a Christmas Day with no family around, and a Christmas Day with no chance of snow, just sun, blue skies and sunbathing.

At about ten o' clock, Jas got up and left, saying that he had some things to do in his room. Shannon and I were lying in parallel on our three-seater settee. I was pressed up along the back of the settee, and she lay in front of me with her head resting on my left arm, which was stretched out along the sofa's arm. The last thing that Jas said before he left the room was, 'I'll say "good night" now, as I won't be coming back out from my room again. So you don't need to worry, you have the place all to yourselves.' And as he said that, he winked. His comment made me feel rather uncomfortable because I felt that it might make Shannon feel uncomfortable. After all, he was suggesting that we could get up to some hanky-panky, but I had no idea if that was something Shannon wanted or not. After Jas had left the room we continued watching the television in an awkward silence.

As the minutes passed, my heartbeat quickened. I was in something of a dilemma. If I made a move and it wasn't what Shannon wanted, she might have thought that I had only invited her back to my place for sex, but if I didn't make a move and she was expecting me to, then she might have thought that I was a pussy. Which was the worse scenario? I couldn't decide. As Shannon watched the television I was watching her. First, I looked at her head, which was resting so peacefully on my arm. She had a lovely shaped head. It was nice and round, and her face, which I couldn't at this moment see, was sweet and innocent. My heart could melt in those big blue eyes. Occasionally, strands of her hair ended up in my nose. Shannon's blonde hair looked clean, strong and healthy, and, with a hint of a smell of hairspray or something, it smelt pleasant too. My eyes moved down her body. Her upper breast flopped out in front of her, seemingly begging to be cupped in my hands. Looking down on her from above left little to the imagination as her top sagged free from her body. Her lower breast was snugly pressed into the sofa. In fact, I too was feeling warm and snug. Our two bodies had become one, pressed together so tightly, with me wedged between Shannon and the back of the sofa.

My eyes then moved down Shannon's smooth, brown thighs, and then further down below the knee. She had taken off her shoes, and her toes were gently twitching, perhaps dancing to some music that only they could hear. They were well cared for feet. Her toe nails were clean, perfectly shaped and painted pink, the same shade of pink as her fingernails. The sight and smell of Shannon, along with the increased warmth from within my own body, eventually began to turn me on. I casually ran my right hand up and down her upper thigh, gently massaging that soft, silky skin. She didn't react. After a few minutes, my hand began to wander higher and higher up her thigh, and up beneath her skirt. Suddenly, her head rose from my arm and she turned to look at me. 'Good gracious me,' she began in a posh English accent rather than her usual Irish one, 'Nick Williams, don't you know that it's Christmas Day and I'm a good Catholic girl. I can't do things like that today!'

'Sorry,' I blurted out sheepishly.

'No problem. Just another time eh?' she replied giggling a little as she gave one of my cheeks a gentle pinch. Rather than being an embarrassing moment, I was actually quite relieved, because at least I now knew where our relationship stood. She had, after all, made it perfectly clear that she was willing to have sex with me and that I could expect it at some other time. Hopefully, it would be some time soon, was what I was thinking at that precise moment in time.

New Year

*F*rom Christmas Day until the 7th January, when Shannon started teaching again, we saw each other almost every day. On the days I was working, Shannon either came round to my home in the evenings or we went out somewhere, but at the two weekends during this period we spent the whole days, and nights, together. Shannon also slept over at my place on the night of New Year's Eve, and she stayed all of New Year's Day. She did remark on a couple of occasions that Rebecca was not happy that she had lost the company of her best friend. Shannon did not feel guilty, however, as she said that there were many other girls left on campus that Rebecca could visit or do things with. If she chose not to due to her own stubbornness, then that was her own fault and problem.

The only time that I saw Rebecca during that fortnight was for one day at the beach and for our New Year celebration at Da Vinci's, the Italian restaurant of the Airport Hotel. The hotel has a slightly confusing name given that it is not actually located at the airport, just quite near to it. Jas made up a foursome on that evening, but he told me before the event that it would be the last time he would socialise with Rebecca as he found her dreadfully boring and immature. As it happens, we all enjoyed ourselves that night. Again, the hotel got special permission to serve alcohol, and that certainly helped the atmosphere on the dance floor, which got very full after everyone had finished their meals. The highlight of any New Year's celebration for me is the singing of, and dancing to, *Auld Lang Syne*. I always find that a touching moment, and it often brings a tear to my eye. I once celebrated New Year at Trafalgar Square. That was an incredible night in London. I was only nineteen or twenty at the time, and what made that evening for me was that after midnight I got to snog at least twenty different girls, all strangers to me, but including many really good lookers. My friends and I got so carried away, that we missed the last train home. We didn't get back to our university hall of residence until about five in the morning. The night buses were running, but they were arriving full. I guess that there were just too many people out that night. We had to wait a couple of hours until one with unoccupied seats came.

At the Airport Hotel I kissed only Shannon and Rebecca after the singing of Auld Lang Syne. As far as I could see, not much kissing among strangers occurred, probably because a lot of the crowd were couples. Rebecca's kiss lasted a bit longer than it should have, given it was with her best friend's boyfriend. She even tried to flick her tongue into my mouth, but she didn't succeed as I kept my lips firmly closed tight. I don't know what her motive was. Was it to annoy Shannon, or to annoy me, or to test me, or to indicate her jealousy of what Shannon and I had together? I really don't know. I'm glad, however, that Shannon didn't notice what happened. When Rebecca tried to force apart my lips, I pushed her away, perhaps a little too hard, and she almost ended up on her arse. If she had, that would have amused Jas, I'm sure. Anyway, Rebecca looked surprised that I had acted as I did, and that made me feel a little better about the whole incident. I decided at that moment, however, that I would avoid contact with Rebecca whenever possible. She was obviously trouble. She had an agenda known only to her, which was likely to bring only misery and sorrow to others.

It was during the night of New Year's Eve, or rather the morning of New Year's Day, that Shannon and I first made love. It was slow and sensual and beautiful. I really enjoyed it, and it seemed that Shannon did too, for we made love every night during the week that followed. I thought that Shannon and I were getting on really well, but after she returned to work on the seventh day of January, things changed considerably. For a few weeks, we saw each other just once a week, usually on a Thursday or Friday, but never on both days of the weekend. We didn't see each other at all during the working week. Shannon refused to visit me at home and she refused to go out anywhere on working days. She said that after teaching all day she was tired and still had marking and other work to do during the evenings. She added that the headmaster was also not keen on staff leaving the school campus during the evenings of working days, and those who did often did not get their contracts renewed the following year.

I believed that Shannon's reluctance to see me during the working week might have been encouraged by Sinead, who had turned 'anti-men'. A few days after the girls had started their new term at school, I had an evening out with Shannon, Sinead and Rebecca. We went to the

Irish Village, a pub designed along traditional Irish lines, which is located adjacent to the Tennis Stadium and Aviation Club. From the exterior, the pub is designed to look like a terrace of traditional Irish cottages. Outside, is a large patio area with tables and chairs. We sat outside, and had our dinner there too. The menu was typical of that which might be found in a British pub. I had the cottage pie. It was relatively cheap and good quality. The bar staff and waiters looked like British or Irish students, so it really did feel like being back at home.

Anyway, soon after our food was served, I found out that Sinead had broken off her engagement. Or rather, her fiancé had broken off their engagement. Apparently, he had found a new girlfriend, but he didn't bother to tell Sinead. She had flown all the way back to Dublin to spend Christmas and New Year with him, but they met only once, and that was so that he could tell her she was dumped. Putting myself in her shoes, I could see that what had happened to her was truly horrible, but was it really necessary for her to sit there with a sour face looking as if she was about to explode with anger? Hadn't she already had several days to discuss the matter with Shannon and Rebecca to her heart's content? Why did I have to have my evening spoilt?

After half an hour of saying nothing, Sinead started mumbling quietly about how men were all bastards. 'Never trust them,' she said looking straight at Shannon. 'Men are completely unreliable. They say one thing and then do another. I should have listened to all of my friends. When I got offered the job out here they said to me, "Take the job or stay with your man, but you can't have both. Long distance relationships just can't stand the course of time." *I* should have dumped him back then. At least I would have been able to enjoy myself properly this last year and a half. *I* could have been pulling, instead of playing the stupid faithful fiancée.' I was not going to let myself be drawn into an argument, even though she was directing her comments at Shannon. Picking a fight with me is probably just what she wanted to get rid of some of her pent-up anger. Later on in the evening, Sinead said that she was going to become more like a man. She would shag around if that was what she wanted to do, and she would never again show commitment or get drawn into another serious relationship. I wanted to tell her that she had just been unlucky with her engagement, and that acting like a slapper wouldn't be any more satisfying in the longer term. I decided, however, to stay silent. I decided that Sinead would not be receptive to a man's comment on anything at that particular moment in time.

For some reason that I can't explain, by the start of the New Year both Jas and I still hadn't got round to applying for our alcohol permits. Without these permits we were unable to buy alcohol at any retail store in Dubai. However, one evening Jas came home from work and said that someone had told him about a place where we could legally buy alcohol without a permit. Apparently, we had to go to Ajman, one of the seven emirates of the UAE. This was a thirty to forty minute drive away from Dubai. All we had to do, according to Jas's source, was follow the coast road from Sharjah in a north-easterly direction. Sharjah is Dubai's neighbouring emirate to the north. We would eventually reach the Kempinski Hotel, and at this point the road would turn to the right running alongside Ajman creek. First we would see a couple of restaurants and then a long wall with no signs on it. There would be two gaps in the wall, one for vehicles to enter and one to leave the 'special place'. The entrance, apparently, was the gap to the right. This 'special place' was, according to our source, known among expatriates as the 'hole in the wall'. This was not because of the wall that ran alongside the street, but because behind the wall was a long brick building. Every couple of metres along this building was a small window (hole), perhaps eight or ten in all, through which orders were given and then the merchandise handed out.

Once Jas told me about the 'hole in the wall', I wanted to go there immediately, not because I was desperate for alcohol, but more because I wanted to see first hand this curious place. We decided to go one evening after work, and after we had eaten. Jas offered to drive, and it was only the second or third time I had been in his Land Cruiser. I have to admit that it was very nice. Jas had paid for all the upgrades and extras. This was travelling in luxury. We got to the Kempinski Hotel without any problems. It had been a pleasant drive, especially along the coastal road from Sharjah. The white sandy beaches seemed to go on for miles. Rows of palm trees separated the beach from the road in most places. The sun was beginning to set and there was nobody on the beach, but many people were strolling along the road. They all seemed to be local Arabs or Asians. There were no white expatriates to be seen outside. The atmosphere of Ajman was so different to that of Dubai. Ajman seemed so quiet and relaxed, the buildings looked so much older and there were no high-rise buildings. The main beach road was a bit bumpy, and many of the side roads looked like sandy tracks, with most not having pavements. It was like going back twenty or thirty years in time.

After we were forced to turn right at the Kempinski Hotel, we immediately saw the restaurants that we were advised to look out for, and then a few seconds later we came to the blank wall. All the land to the right of the road was open space covered in sand. There were groups of Asian men huddled together deep in conversation, mostly standing around their old cars. Close to the entrance of the 'hole in the wall' were two parked police cars, each with two officers inside. They seemed to look at us with great interest as we drove in behind the wall. 'I hope they don't stop us on the way out,' Jas said immediately.

'Why should they?' I asked. 'We're not doing anything wrong. Are we?'

'Not to my knowledge,' Jas replied. 'But who knows?' The car park had about a dozen vehicles in it, mostly big four-wheel drives. Surprisingly, most of the occupants looked like Arabs. There was a small crowd of people around each window. There was no orderly queuing, just a lot of pushing and shoving. Most of the customers looked like labourers from the Indian subcontinent, who presumably had come on foot, but there were also a few white dishdashas to be seen among the crowds. I saw only one other pair of white faces, and they looked East European, probably Russians. Somehow, they looked like mafia guys. They were stocky and looked a bit rough, but they were clearly wearing expensive clothes, and each man wore a chunky gold chain around his neck, and more gold in the form of rings, bracelets and earrings.

When we got to the window, I was surprised by the choice. They seemed to stock everything. The bottles were all lined on shelves behind the servers and there were many stacks of canned drinks around the room. It looked more like a warehouse than a shop in that big, dimly lit room. The man serving us, who looked like an Indian, was not keen to show us things, however. Jas was asking questions about different types of wine and the man kept saying, 'Tell me what you want and I get it. What you want?' Jas was not happy. He wanted to know where his Chardonnay, or whatever, came from. In the end, however, we each bought a few bottles of wine, both red and white, and a case of beer each. The prices we paid were roughly the same we would have paid at a supermarket back in the UK. 'People will think we're having a party,' Jas laughed as we struggled to carry all our purchases back to his car.

'Maybe we should have a house warming party,' I replied.

As we left the 'hole in the wall' the two police cars were still parked outside, but their occupants showed no interest in us at all. We continued driving alongside the creek. Above the water of the creek was a wall on which a dozen or so South Asian labourers in scruffy clothes were squatting like a row of toads. Their knees were bent right up under their chins, and they were balancing on their feet without their bums touching the wall. It was obviously their favoured way of sitting. Each of the men was drinking from a can of Heineken, Fosters, or whatever. The whole scene was the funniest thing I had seen since arriving in the UAE. One of the men turned to look at us. His red eyes and jerky movements indicated that he had drunk quite a bit, but he just smiled at me and gave a nod of the head. I wondered how often one of the 'squatting toads' ended up falling into the creek.

A few days later, when I was at work at Al Saadha-Wasel, I mentioned my trip to Ajman to Sadiq. He looked at me in horror. 'Never do that again,' he said. 'To get back to Dubai from Ajman you must pass through Sharjah, but Sharjah is completely dry. Alcohol is not permitted. If you had an accident in your car, or if the police stopped you for any reason, and then saw the alcohol in your car, you would be in big trouble. Believe me, my friend, you mustn't take that risk again. If you want to consume alcohol at home, get the proper permit and buy from the official outlets.' I thanked Sadiq for his advice.

Winter

January and February were quite cool months. Day temperatures averaged between twelve and fifteen degrees. The evenings were cooler. The days felt like spring or autumn time in the UK. But the change in weather after sunbathing and swimming in the sea in December came as a bit of a surprise. It was no longer sunny enough to sunbathe, and in the evenings it was a bit too cool to sit outside comfortably. In fact, that night with Shannon and the girls at the Irish Village was the last evening that I spent outdoors. On some days, it was very windy, and the wind could be quite chilly. But we had to wait only until early March to get warmer, more pleasant weather again. So, it was a short and hardly severe winter. I think that I noticed rain falling on only two or three days. I didn't miss the rain at all.

Jas and I joined the Pharaohs' Club at Wafi City. We went to the gym and worked out every other day. Afterwards, we would relax in the steam room or Jacuzzi. And after that we sometimes had a meal at one of the restaurants, or just a drink in the bar. I find that working out and keeping fit is good for both one's physical and mental health. Working out regularly made me feel healthier, fitter, sharper in mind and generally more contented with my life. And doing it in the luxury of the Pharaohs' Club made the whole experience that much more satisfying. After a while, Jas and I bought tennis racquets, and we played tennis now and again. Thankfully, I didn't bump into Abdul at the club until several months later, as he was back in London doing his MBA. When we did eventually meet, I suggested we have a drink at the bar. He seemed pleased that I did, and we had a pleasant couple of hours together. He really was a very pleasant chap, and I had to conclude that maybe I misjudged him after our previous meeting.

During the weeks that followed that night at the Irish Village, on many occasions, when I was at home in the evenings with nothing in particular to do or occupy my mind, I wondered if Sinead had dragged Shannon out to some pub or club in order to pull men. My mind became obsessed with this idea. I couldn't keep my thoughts bottled up, so I discussed my situation and fears with Jas. He admitted straight away that he thought Shannon and I had a strange relationship, but he had assumed that that was the way we both wanted it. He just assumed we both wanted a more casual and open relationship. When I told Jas about Shannon's reasons for not seeing me during the week he said, 'It seems rather unlikely to me that they're not allowed to leave the school campus in their own time, when they're not working. In fact, it sounds like a load of bollocks to me. Didn't they tell us about all their nights out around town whenever free drinks were available?'

Once Jas had reminded me about that, my mind got carried away. I began to want to know what Shannon was doing during every minute of every day. I called her two or three times a day to track her movements. During the evenings she always said that she was at home or somewhere on the school campus, but I often heard background noise that could easily have been a pub, restaurant or other public place. I couldn't work out what was happening to my relationship with Shannon. Our one day together each week was always pleasant enough. During these days, we went shopping, to the beach, or for drives or walks, and in the evenings we went to restaurants, bars or the cinema. And at some point during the day or evening we always made love. I began to think that perhaps I was just a handy shag, just a person who was prepared to provide a reliable service for her. At first, I believed that Shannon wanted a sexual relationship but that she didn't want a normal boyfriend-girlfriend relationship. Later, however, my mind began to think all sorts of different things. I lay in bed one night, and one thought that passed through my head was that perhaps Shannon was some sort of nymphomaniac. Perhaps she had several different men on the go, and perhaps she saw each of them just once a week. I became obsessed with trying to catch Shannon 'in the act' with another man.

I couldn't remember which bars it was that the girls said they visited that first time we met them at the Boston Bar. One evening I asked Jas if he could remember. He could only remember the Plaza Hotel, but their 'ladies' day' was on a Thursday afternoon, and as I often saw Shannon on a Thursday, it was not the obvious hotel to target. I needed to know which hotels gave girls free drinks during the week. Jas suggested I buy the *What's On* magazine. That was a good idea. The magazine, which comes out monthly, has a comprehensive listing of everything happening in Dubai on each day of the month. I was surprised how many bars ran 'free drinks for the girls' promotions. The promotions didn't run during Ramadan, of course, but promotions were listed for the end of January. I made a list of them all: the names of the bars and the days, or dates, and times at which females could get free drinks. There were at least two or three bars I could have visited each day of the week, but I visited only one bar on any one evening. All of the bars that serve alcohol are located in hotels.

I became something of a detective. I would visit bars, hide in shadows and peep around corners. When I got home, I described my capers to Jas, who thought I was mad. 'Don't you think you're taking this a bit far?' he asked one night. 'Why don't you just ask her if she has another man in her life? And if you don't trust her, then why don't you just dump her?'

'Because I like her,' I explained. 'I really like her, but I just find her behaviour a bit strange. I must know the truth.' So, I didn't change my behaviour. Every other night I went to a hotel that was giving away free booze to women, and I just waited, hoping that I might catch her in the act, which would then release me from the stress and anxiety I was at that time suffering with. At times, I considered that I might have had it all dreadfully wrong. But, unfortunately, those positive thoughts never lasted long.

On a Wednesday evening early in February, I went to the Astoria Hotel in Bur Dubai. The Astoria is located on Al Faheidi Street, the main road running through the area that specialises in the sale of textiles and cheap electronic goods. It's a busy road, especially during the evenings, when the road is full of cars and the pavements full of people, but it is in a down-market area. Although the area is bright and colourful, thanks largely to the big, multi-coloured shop signs and illuminated advertising, it is still a bit drab and dirty. As I drove into the area I considered for a moment whether the girls really would come to such a place. The hotel car park was full, and it took me about twenty minutes to find somewhere else to park the car. There are no big car parks in the area and the spaces in the street were all taken. It occurred to me that the hotel was a long way from where the girls lived. A taxi would have been quite expensive, and finding one to go back home may not be easy. Would they really travel so far for a couple of free drinks? But perhaps one of the girls had driven, despite the parking problems. Was I searching for an excuse to go home and not to go into the hotel, or did I really think that the odds of finding the girls at the Astoria were slim? Upon further reflection on the situation, I did indeed feel that my lack of enthusiasm resulted from the fact that I didn't really expect to see the girls at the Astoria on this occasion, but, also, I wasn't much in the mood for detective work this evening.

As I walked into the hotel lobby, I was greeted with a big surprise. I saw someone that I would never have expected to see there. I froze for a moment, and then retreated backwards a bit, hoping that I would not be seen. Walking towards the lift were Mike, and Inga, his sexy, Danish personal assistant. She looked tall and elegant, in her fur coat, designer trousers and high-heeled shoes. Mike had his arm around Inga's shoulder. They were deep in conversation, both seemingly laughing now and then. When a lift arrived, they got into it. As the lift doors closed behind them, I walked across the hotel lobby and I watched the light above the doors moving, which indicated which floor the lift was passing. The light stopped next to the number six. They had got out at the sixth floor. I went immediately to the reception desk and asked, 'What's on the sixth floor?'

'Only the rooms of the hotel's guests,' was the reply. I was shocked. Mike and Inga were certainly not at the hotel for a business meeting or indeed any other legitimate reason. Mike was such a nice guy. He came across so straight and honest. How could he be having an affair with his p.a.? His wife was so nice! I went outside to see if Mike's car was in the hotel car park, but it wasn't. I returned into the hotel, and went to the bar where the ladies were getting their free drinks. It was full of girls. Some looked pleased to see me enter, but there was nothing there to interest me. The women looked mainly like poor market traders from Eastern Europe, or like prostitutes. I could not see Shannon, so I left without even buying a drink. I went straight back home and told Jas about Mike and Inga. 'Are you sure it was them?' he asked. 'You couldn't have been mistaken?'

'That would have been rather difficult,' I replied. 'They are both quite distinctive.'

'Well, my respect for our boss will never be quite the same again,' said Jas.

'And how will we able to look Stella in the eye the next time we see her,' I added thoughtfully. 'Indeed, would telling her what I saw be the right thing to do? That her husband is having it off with his beautiful p.a.'

'If I were you mate, I would stay well out of it,' said Jas. 'You might not be thanked for telling the truth, and you might just be messing up everyone's life needlessly.'

'But if Stella saw Shannon with another man, I would hope, no, I would *expect* her to tell me about it. Wouldn't *you* want to know if *your* partner was being unfaithful?'

'Yes, but remember Nick that you've only known Shannon for two months, and it has not even been a very serious relationship. Mike and Stella must have been married for twenty years. They have three children. Honestly Nick, don't say anything to anyone. It'll just blow up in your face.'

'Not even to Mike, to tell him what a complete and utter bastard wanker he's being?'

'Just try to forget what you saw,' was Jas's final word on the matter. Jas has no feelings; that's his problem in my opinion. He thinks he's clever, always being calm and positive, but it's only because he's cold and probably never cared deeply for anyone. I said something along those lines to him, and did manage to get a reaction from him. 'Well, mate,' he answered in a sarcastic tone, '*I've* never had the girlfriend problems that you seem to be having with your current girlfriend.' That comment had the effect of a thumping punch to my heart. It hurt me, but I knew that I deserved it.

End of the world?

During February, my workload at Al Saadha-Wasel got heavier and heavier. The company's planned flotation date was fast approaching, being in early April. I seemed to be doing all the work, and got little help or support from Ali or Sadiq. Whenever I approached them for something, the answer always seemed to be either 'tomorrow' or worse still 'tomorrow inshallah'. One afternoon, I was working in my room, all alone, busily tapping on my computer's keyboard. Suddenly, I noticed the room getting darker and darker. I spun round on my chair to look out of the window. The sky had turned a dark shade of grey and it had reduced the amount of light coming from the sky. Over a period of fifteen minutes or so, I noticed that my room was getting darker and darker. The wind had picked up and I could hear it whistling around the building. A piece of plastic, or something, swirled around in the sky. Eventually, I got up and turned the light on. A few minutes later there was a tapping noise on the window. At first, I assumed it was hailstones, but then I remembered that it was too warm outside for hailstones. I turned to look out of the window, but all I could now see was my own reflection. It was so dark now that I could no longer see the loading bays or any of the lorries. The room seemed to get cold but there was sweat on my forehead. I could no longer tell if the psssssing noise was the wind outside or the building's air conditioning system. Then, the building seemed to be swaying. For a moment, I wondered if this could be the end of the world approaching.

I was scared and ran out of my office. Everyone else was already in the corridor. They all looked scared, or at least a little apprehensive. They seemed to be waiting for someone to tell them what was happening, or what they should do. I went straight to Ali's office. His door was open, and Sadiq and several of the other senior managers were in there with him. 'What's happening?' I asked.

'We don't know,' replied Ali. 'We've never experienced anything like this before. Yes, we've had storms, but the sky has never turned completely black like at night.' I looked out of the window, and it looked like an eclipse of the sun. I could see lights shining through the windows of the offices on the other side of the loading area, but none of the streetlights had come on. There was no sun, no moon, no stars, no hint of light in the sky at all. Sadiq said that he was going down to take a look outside. He advised everyone not to use the lifts. I followed him down the stairs and through the reception area. When we got outside, the sky was starting to lighten again, and the wind had disappeared. The ground was dry, so my theory of hailstones tapping against my office window was obviously incorrect. Sadiq and I stood there frozen in amazement. We did not speak. Ten minutes later the sky was back to normal, a hazy white sky with just a hint of the sun's rays shining through.

After work, when I got into my Nissan Patrol, I could not see through the windscreen. It was covered in a light layer of sand. My windscreen wipers shifted it immediately, but I decided to wash the car on my way home. I went through one of the automatic drive-through machines. It cost twenty-five dirhams, about the same as in the UK. But in the UAE, when you leave the drive-through washer, you are not finished, as you are in the UK. Usually, three or four men finish the job by hand. They polish the outside of your car with chamois leather, they apply wheel shine to the tyres, they dust and polish the car's interior, and they vacuum clean the seats, floors and boot. When they've finished, most cars look as if they're new and like they've just come straight from the showroom. When I got home and watched the TV news, they explained the day's phenomenon as a sand storm.

On the fourteenth day of February, Shannon and I went to an expensive restaurant to celebrate Valentine's Day. I bought her a bottle of perfume and she bought me a shirt and tie from the Ralph Lauren Polo shop. I was quite impressed with what she had chosen for me. I would wear that shirt and tie with pride when giving briefings to the press, analysts and brokers on the day that Al Saadha-Wasel floated. I enjoyed my Valentine's Day with Shannon. In fact, I always enjoyed my time with Shannon, but I still continued visiting hotels and bars in the evenings looking for her. Shannon soon noticed that I was out a lot in the evenings. She started calling in the evenings, to our home phone, and not my mobile, presumably so that she could tell if I was at home or not. Jas was usually at home during the week and he answered the phone, but he told me that he never offered Shannon any explanation as to where I was and that she never asked for one. The frequency of her calls increased each week that passed, and she rarely caught me at home. And if she did, the call was usually short and the conversation not very interesting. Knowing that I was going out at nights a lot didn't make Shannon want to see me any more frequently. Still, I did derive some satisfaction from knowing that she cared enough about me to check up on me so often. In my view, however, this did not mean that *she* was being faithful.

On the last Friday of February Shannon spent the day at my villa. We spent a lot of the day reading newspapers and magazines, just happy to be in each other's company. Towards the end of the evening Shannon asked if I would like to go away with her one weekend. She suggested that we could go somewhere one Wednesday evening, and then return on the Friday. I asked her where she would like to go. She suggested Oman, and I agreed. We went straight onto my computer to book a hotel. We booked a room at the Grand Hyatt in Muscat, the capital of Oman, for the second weekend ahead. I wanted to go the next weekend, but Shannon reminded me that we each had to get a visa first, so it was safer to book for a fortnight ahead, just in case there was any problem or delay.

Road trip to Oman

Shannon got to my place at 4.30 pm on the Wednesday we set off for Oman. I had to leave work earlier than usual. It was a difficult thing to do given the large amount of work I had at that time, but I convinced myself that I needed a short break to maintain my workflow in the longer term. I had already packed my things and loaded them into my Patrol, so once Shannon arrived, we were away within minutes. It was a clear, bright afternoon, warm but not too hot, just ideal for driving. We sped out of Dubai, along a dual carriageway, which had two lanes each way, but there were few other vehicles on the road. As we drove through the desert, the colour of the sand changed several times, from various shades of yellow through to a dark shade of reddish-orange. On a fairly steep hill to our left, a few four wheel drive vehicles were bravely 'dune bashing'. And in the distance to our right, a few camels were wandering about seemingly without a care in the world. At times, the desert gave way to areas with some degree of vegetation, which ranged from smatterings of green grass with small shrubs bearing yellow blooms to large orchards of date palm.

As we approached the town of Hatta, sand became less dominant in the landscape as there was more stone and rock. The road ran alongside steep rocky hills. As we passed a low, flat area, a road sign stated 'Wadi'. This is an area that is in danger of flooding during times of heavy rainfall. On this day, the ground was completely dry because there had been hardly any rain this winter. In 1996, however, there had been heavy rainfall throughout January and February, and many areas of the Emirates became flooded, including several towns. We passed through Hatta, which looked like a pleasant place, and on towards the Hajar mountains. They stood tall and dark in the distance.

Within ten minutes we had reached the Omani border. The checkpoint was not very busy. The officials checked and stamped our passports, and then made a brief check of our car, both externally and internally. They asked to look inside our bags, but showed little interest to see what was inside. Fifteen minutes later we were driving in Oman. The road took us through the Hajar Mountains, which were less spectacular than I had hoped for when seeing them from the distance. Eventually, the road turned to the right, and we were on the coastal plain known as 'Al Batinah'. We were now on the coastal road that would take us all the way to Muscat. At times, we had magnificent views of the Gulf of Oman. Shannon had her eyes closed. I was disappointed that she was missing the great views, and also disappointed that she didn't want to talk to me. Conversation would have helped relieve the boredom which was beginning to set in. Instead, I listened to the radio.

As we approached Muscat, there were more and more roundabouts to negotiate. I did my best not to take a wrong turning. It was almost 8.30 pm, so I decided to head straight to our hotel. First, I followed signs for 'Shatti Al Qurm', the area in which the Grand Hyatt is located, and as we entered the area, there were signs for the Hyatt. Shannon still had her eyes closed, so I gave her a gentle nudge on the arm and said, 'We're almost there now.' She opened her eyes quickly. 'Sorry for dozing off,' she replied. 'I had a rather hard week at work. You wouldn't believe what we have to do.'

'No problem,' I answered generously.

The hotel lobby was magnificently and ornately decorated in bright shades of cream, yellow and gold. It was almost too bright for the eyes. In the centre of the lobby was a life-sized statue of a man riding a horse. The man had his right hand held high above his head, and resting on it was a falcon. Surrounding the statue were a number of palm trees rising high up towards the high glass dome, that was the roof. We checked into the hotel quickly, and went straight to our room. Our bags were light, so I carried both Shannon's and mine up to the room. As we walked down corridors with real marble floors, I noticed that there seemed to be paintings, sculptures and other artwork on every wall and in every free bit of floor space. It was like walking through an art gallery. I read later, in the hotel guide in my room, that over one million dollars of contemporary art had been purchased for the hotel in the United States. Nevertheless, the feel and atmosphere of the whole hotel was very Arabian.

When we flung back the door to our room, we were pleasantly surprised by what we saw. It was a very generous size; it had a gigantic double bed, two big armchairs, a big writing desk with chair and plenty of wardrobe space. The satellite television had thirty free channels, there was a PlayStation for those who like to play games, and there were no fewer than three telephones in the room. When I followed Shannon into the bathroom, I was even more amazed. It was bigger than most hotel rooms these days. It had a bath and a separate walk-in shower, probably big enough for the entire English football team. There was a bidet, of course, but I have to confess that I have never used one and didn't use that one either. The idea just doesn't appeal to me. The floor and walls of the bathroom, like so much of the hotel, were marble, and all the decoration was very modern and tasteful.

I went to the mini bar and took out the champagne. 'Anyone for champagne?' I asked.

'Are we celebrating something?' Shannon replied.

'Do we need something to celebrate?' was my response.

'I guess not,' concluded Shannon. 'Go on then. Let's spoil ourselves!' I opened the champagne and poured us each a glass. We went out to sit on the balcony. I also took the complimentary bowl of fresh fruit. Our room was on the side of the hotel and so looked down on the tennis courts. But this also meant that instead of just looking out towards the sea, we could look up along the entire beach, which gave us a wonderful view of the whole bay. It was already dark but there was a near full moon, which shone brightly to reveal a smooth sea. There was only the gentlest of breezes, which was pleasant and refreshing after sitting in the stale air of my car for four hours. Shannon leant forward across the little round table on our balcony and gave me a long, soft kiss on the lips. 'Isn't this just paradise?' she said. 'Thank you for bringing me here.' She then gave me another kiss, this time with her mouth still containing some champagne. A small amount passed into my mouth, which tasted even better than that from my own glass.

At about 9.30 pm, we went down to the hotel's 'Marjan Restaurant', which was located on the beachfront. We ate some tasty oriental food while looking out at the great ocean in front of us. When we had finished our meal, we decided to take a stroll down the small promenade, which ran around the bay. It was down on the promenade that Shannon spotted a sign that said 'Free Tai Chi lessons here every morning at 8.30 am'.

'We must try that!' she said excitedly whilst pointing at the sign. I knew then that I wasn't going to get a lie-in in the mornings. I had never tried Tai Chi before, but I had occasionally thought that it might be worth a try to help reduce my stress levels and improve my health. At 8.30 am the next morning we were down on the beachfront, ready for our session of Tai Chi. Three other couples were already there, obviously waiting for the instructor. We all said 'good morning' to each other. One of the couples was from the Far East, perhaps from China, one was from India and the last one from America. Sam, the American man, said, 'I'm sure Lee will be along shortly. He is very good. This is our fifth day at the hotel, and we have been down here every morning.'

'That's good,' I replied, looking around at us all. We had nothing in common in terms of age or physical size and apparent physical fitness. We were, however, all wearing a selection of sports wear: vests or tee shirts, shorts or tracksuit bottoms and footwear, mostly bearing the names of well-known western brands.

Lee arrived, wearing a black suit and black, flat-bottomed shoes. He was a short, slightly built man, probably aged in his late forties or not far beyond fifty. 'Good morning,' he said. 'Okay, everyone, just let your body relax. Let your weight sink to the centre of the earth. And breathe deep and evenly. That's it. Just like me.' Lee stood with his legs shoulder-width apart and his arms just hung by his side. He looked completely relaxed and yet somehow he commanded respect through some inner strength that was apparent to all.

'That's it. Breathe slow and deep,' continued Lee. 'And soong yi-dien. Soong yi-dien. That's it, really loosen those joints.' Then, Lee bent his knees and rotated his wrists. 'Okay, bend those knees, but don't let them go further than your toes. And keep your back straight, keep your chin tucked in, and your bum too! And keep breathing. Keep breathing, nice and slow.' Lee then performed a series of simple movements. 'Copy me,' he said. These required small movements of the legs and the slow, circular arm movements that most people are familiar with from seeing them on TV. Watching other people doing it, you would think that it was easy, but it was actually quite difficult, and tiring. 'That's it,' said Lee, 'copy me and feel that meditation in motion.' Huh, I didn't feel relaxed, just tired. 'Come on you!' said Lee, looking at me. 'Concentrate. You must concentrate!' Lee's movements radiated internal strength, while mine made me look like a sad loser. I was doing my best however. I just needed more practice. And I got it the next morning. In my opinion, Shannon hadn't been much better than me, but she obviously thought she had. 'You'll get it tomorrow,' she said. 'Just keep working at it and you'll get there. And you'll be so glad once you feel the chi energy.'

'Did you?' I asked. 'Feel the chi energy?'

'Probably not. But I'm getting there,' replied Shannon. 'I've only tried Tai Chi a few times before, you know. Like anything else, it takes a lot of practice and commitment.'

'Well we aren't going to get there with two sessions, are we?' I answered a bit sarcastically, as we made our way back to our room in order to shower and change clothes for breakfast.

We didn't leave our hotel until it was time to drive back to Dubai on Friday afternoon. We ate a lot, slept a lot, read a bit, sunbathed by the outdoor swimming pool, swam in the indoor pool, went sailing single-handed in small *Topper* dinghies, went to the sauna and steam rooms, and had a massage each. Shannon even pampered herself with a facial and body treatment. And on the Thursday night we went to the hotel's Copacabana Nightclub, where we drank and danced the night away. It was a busy weekend, but a fun and relaxing one too.

Shannon's birthday

The 23rd of March was Shannon's twenty-fourth birthday. A few days before her birthday, Shannon told me that her parents had sent her some money so that she could buy a present of her choice. She said that with it she intended to buy herself some jewellery from the Gold Souk. She asked me if I would like to go with her to help pick something. I hadn't yet been to the Gold Souk, and having been told by several people that it is one of the tourist 'must sees' I agreed to go with her.

After Shannon had finished work, she drove down to my place. I had left work early, and went home to make some spaghetti bolognese. We ate it together quickly, and by about six-thirty we were on our way to the gold souk. It was only a ten minute drive away, and I offered to drive. We drove down the Jumeirah Beach Road in the direction of Port Rashid. Then, as we went around a complex roundabout, which had several roads leading into, and even through it, a taxi entered the roundabout at great speed, forcing me to brake hard and almost stop. The driver should have given way and waited until we passed before entering the roundabout. I flashed my lights and sounded my horn, but he continued driving, waving at me from inside his car. I was furious. His reckless driving had almost caused a serious accident, and Shannon was complaining of seat belt burn. I put my foot back on the accelerator, pressing it almost as far as it would go. I overtook the taxi, pulled in front of it, slowed down and then stopped, forcing it also to stop. I got out of my car and walked back to the taxi. The taxi driver got out too. He had no passengers. 'Is there a problem?' he asked.

'Yes, there's a bloody problem,' I answered. 'You just came onto that roundabout without looking and at too fast a speed, causing me to brake suddenly and heavily, and thus causing injury to my girlfriend.' The taxi driver stepped forward and looked at Shannon still sitting inside my car. 'Your good lady all right,' said the taxi driver. 'No problem. My driving okay,' he continued, as he shrugged his shoulders.

'No it wasn't,' I insisted. 'And I'm going to take down your number and report you to the police.'

'There's no need for that mister,' pleaded the taxi driver. 'Please be reasonable.'

'You should be taken off the road,' I continued. 'You're a menace to the general public. You should be sent back to India or Pakistan, or wherever it is you're from, before you kill someone.' I then took out a pen from the inside pocket of my jacket. I opened my wallet and found an old shop receipt on which I intended to write the taxi's registration number. As I started to write, the taxi driver tried to grab the pen from my hand. 'You don't have to do this,' he said. My response was to push him away violently. He was a middle-aged man of slight build, and it seemed that he lost his balance and fell over. I continued writing down his car number. He sobbed a little and didn't get up. I looked down over him and said, 'You had better slow your driving right down and keep your mind on the job.' I then turned and walked back to my car. I got in and drove away. Shannon turned in her seat and looked back. 'You didn't hurt him, did you?' she asked. 'He's only just getting up off the ground now.'

'Let's hope that I did,' I replied smugly. 'He hurt you and maybe now I've hurt him.'

'But everyone drives like him in Dubai,' continued Shannon. 'Was it fair to pick on him when *everyone* in this city seems to be a dreadful driver? I'm petrified on the roads most of the time, but I just slow down myself and drive with extra caution. That's all we can do if the police don't do anything, isn't it?'

'Well maybe it's time the police did do something about it. Did you know that almost a person a day dies on the streets of Dubai? In my opinion, the awful driving is one of the worst things about this city. It even scares me.' I never did get around to passing on the taxi driver's details to the police, but in truth I probably never really intended to. I just wanted to scare the driver a bit, and hope that he might improve his driving.

We drove through the Al Shindagha Tunnel, which runs under the mouth of Dubai Creek, and we came out facing the Hyatt Regency Hotel, where Jas and I had attended Maureen's 'culture awareness' course. I left the dual carriageway by doing a U turn, in order to head back in the direction from which we had just come. Moments later, I was on Al Khor Street, which runs parallel to the dual carriageway that leads to and from the tunnel. Shannon advised me that the gold souk started further down Al Khor Street and that I had better take the first parking space that I saw. The road was busy and we were moving along at a snail's pace. All the parking spaces on the road seemed to be taken. Then, as luck would have it, I spotted the white reverse lights of a small van. I stopped, and waited until it had reversed out from where it was parked. I then drove forward into the space, which was a nice big one that lay at right angles to the road.

'That was lucky,' remarked Shannon. 'Last time I was down here, it took us twenty minutes to park. And even the car park was full.' We were perfectly located for the Gold Souk. It started at the other side of the road. We walked down a side street to get to the main part of the souk. Two shops out of three were already jewellers. The shop windows were crammed with gold, in the form of necklaces, bracelets and bangles, rings and earrings. The gold sparked and shone under the window display lights. We stopped to look at each window display we passed. 'What are you looking for?' I asked Shannon.

'I thought maybe a little bracelet,' she replied. I had not yet bought her a birthday present. 'You could also pick something from me,' I suggested, thinking that it would save me having to think of something to buy.

'A box of chocolates would do,' she replied jokingly.

'Well if you see anything you like, just speak out,' I continued. 'Don't end up saying you weren't offered.' We then entered the pedestrianised part of the Gold Souk. There was a big, continuous canopy overhead. Every shop was now a jeweller; windows of gold continued for as far as the eye could see. We continued to stop at each window display. The powerful lights created a lot of heat, and it was rather hot standing in front of the windows. Men passed, selling bottles of cold water that stood precariously on trays balanced on one hand. The whole place was a hive of activity. There were many people looking in the shop windows, and just as many inside the shops. The majority looked like western tourists. They just had that touristy look about them. Many were sunburnt, and they carried maps and cameras, that type of thing. And there were traders rushing about, carrying boxes in their arms or pulling carts with many boxes. What was in the boxes I don't know, but the men all seemed to be in a great hurry.

'Do you see anything you like?' I asked Shannon.

'Perhaps,' she answered. 'I'm trying to remember what I see and where I see it.'

'That'll be tricky,' was my response. 'There are so many shops.' In fact, Dubai's gold souk claims to be the largest retail gold market in the world. Eventually, we started going into some of the shops. The shop owners and sales staff all appeared to be from the Indian subcontinent or from a Middle Eastern country. The first thing they wanted to know was 'were we paying with cash or a credit card?' The second thing they wanted to know, if one replied 'cash', was 'dollars or dirhams?' And the third question was 'how much are you looking to spend?' I thought that the question they should really have asked first is 'what are you looking for?' Anyway, those are the questions we were asked in every shop. I learnt that Shannon was hoping to get a gold bracelet for under five hundred dirhams, as the present from her parents. She looked at many different bracelets in many different shops, but they all looked pretty similar to me.

In one shop, Shannon asked to see a tray of rings. She tried on a few, flashing them under my eyes, but I didn't know what stones were in them, or how much they cost. 'Perhaps you would like a ring from me for your birthday?' I suggested.

'I think these ones might be a bit too expensive,' she replied.

'No. No,' replied the salesman. 'We will do you a very good deal. We have the best quality workmanship and the best prices. No need to worry.'

'How much is this one I'm wearing?' Shannon then asked the salesman. He looked at the price on his tray and answered, 'One thousand, eight hundred dirhams.'

'See,' Shannon said, turning to me.

'Is this your wife?' the salesman asked me.

'No, girlfriend,' I replied.

'Well she looks like a very special lady who deserves a ring such as this. Buy it for her and maybe she will become your wife one day.' I didn't respond. I didn't really like his sales strategy. He was putting pressure on me, and potentially making me look mean. I left the shop at the earliest opportunity, telling Shannon that I didn't like anything else she showed me. But the sales tactics were the same in every other shop. My girlfriend was special. She deserved their rings. I must show my affection for her by buying their rings. Blah, blah, blah. It wasn't that I didn't want to buy Shannon a ring. I just wanted her to be able to take her time and pick something she really liked, without her or me feeling pressured by the salesmen.

Shannon bought a gold bracelet within an hour, and before we had passed even half of the shops in the main part of the souk. She paid six hundred dirhams for it, which was one hundred more than she originally intended to spend. Still, Shannon thought that she got a bargain. 'This would cost at least fifty per cent more back home,' she insisted. When we got to the end of the canopied, pedestrianised section of the souk, we turned back looking at the shops on the opposite side of the wide path, which we had so far ignored. It seemed that we were now looking at rings, especially rings with diamonds in them. 'Diamonds are a girl's best friend,' Shannon sung jokingly in one shop. 'And they are so cheap here.'

'Are you sure they're kosher?' I asked.

'Everyone is saying that we'll get a certificate of authenticity, which is approved by the government. So, I guess they must be okay,' she replied, obviously hoping that she had convinced me, and perhaps even herself. In one shop, Shannon showed me a ring with a central diamond surrounded by eight dark sapphire stones. 'This is nice,' she said to me, followed by 'How much?' to the salesman.

'Nine hundred dirhams,' he replied.

'And I can barely see the diamond,' I whispered in Shannon's ear. 'If you want a diamond, at least get one you can see.' That was a big mistake. A diamond that looked of reasonable size to me, a half-carat stone as it happens, cost upwards of three thousand dirhams (about five hundred UK pounds). And that's about what I ended up paying.

As we walked back towards the car, it was clear that Shannon couldn't believe her luck. And reflecting on what I had just done, I couldn't believe it either. It reminded me of a story a friend once told me. He was a very careful person with money, the sort of person who compares prices in the supermarket. But one day he went with some friends to a casino, and came out eight hundred pounds poorer. The next morning he couldn't believe that he had gambled and lost eight hundred pounds, but he put it down to the use of chips. 'Playing with chips, you just forget it is real money,' he had said. Well that's how I felt in Dubai. Dirhams just didn't feel like pounds. I felt most of the time as if I was on holiday in Dubai, and when one is on holiday, one just spends, spends, spends. That is normal for most people, I think, as they are eager to ensure that they really do enjoy themselves while on holiday.

It was now just after ten o' clock, and the shops were turning off their lights and locking up for the night. When we got to Al Khor Street, there were noticeably fewer people walking about, but the road was full of cars, still crawling along as earlier in the evening. Then, I saw my car, blocked in by one of those big American saloons of the type we don't see in the UK. The car was parked across the back of both my car and the one next to me. 'What the hell!' I couldn't help blurting out. 'Where is the driver of this thing?' I stepped out into the road and looked in both directions. I couldn't see an obvious driver.

Shannon and I got into my Patrol and I sounded the horn a few times, but nobody came. After being in the heat of the gold souk, we both now felt a bit cold. Shannon suggested that I turn on the car's heater, which I did.

We waited and waited, but nobody came to move the car. I later decided to wait in the road in case a police car passed. I could then ask for help. Whilst standing in the road, I considered whether I should dial 999 on my mobile, in order to report the matter directly to the police. Probably not, I thought, as it wasn't exactly an emergency situation. It was, however, dreadfully inconvenient, and most inconsiderate on the part of whoever had left the car blocking us in. It seemed as if we were waiting there for ages. I was cold and yet my blood was boiling. I looked at my watch. It was ten past eleven. There were now fewer cars on the road, and no police cars passed. 'Never a policeman when you need one,' I said to Shannon when I returned to the car. 'What shall we do?'

'What can we do?' she asked.

'Leave the car here and get a taxi back to my place,' I replied. 'And I'll have to come back down here in the morning before work.'

'Whatever you think.'

'We could be here until two or three in the morning. Who knows?' was my response.

'Hold on a minute,' Shannon suddenly said. 'What do we have here?' Walking up the road towards us were three boys, probably aged between eighteen and twenty. Baby faces in white dishdashas taking big strides and swaying their shoulders like men. Sure enough, they got into the car that was obstructing us, without so much as even looking at us, let alone an apology. They were off before I had a chance to go over and talk to them. Not that I really wanted to after my argument with the taxi driver earlier in the evening.

Shannon celebrated her birthday by having a party in the flat that she shared with Sinead and Rebecca on the school campus. It was the first time that I had been invited to her flat or the school campus. It was a loud, student-like affair with plenty of drinking and dancing. Thirty or forty people squeezed into the flat, and into the open space behind it, which was definitely more than the architect had ever intended or imagined possible. It seemed that I was the only non-teacher there, but that didn't particularly bother me. However, with Shannon having to look after her guests, I did at times feel a bit neglected. Nobody really made the effort to talk to me, but there again, to be honest, I didn't really make any effort to talk to others either.

New boy

O*ne* evening, while we were eating our evening meal at home, Jas mentioned that a new consultant was starting work at JBNC the next day. He didn't know any further details. I was keen not to be the last employee to meet the 'new boy', or perhaps girl, so I called in at the JBNC office just after lunchtime on the premise that I needed to pick up some important files. And there he was, standing next to my desk talking to Jas. When Jas saw me, he broke his conversation with Baron, and turning to me, he said, 'Here comes Nick. We came over together from London last November. And we're currently sharing a villa.'

'Pleased to meet you,' I said, extending my arm for a handshake. 'Nick. Nick Williams.'

'Baron Washington,' replied the 'new boy' with an American accent. 'And likewise, pleased to meet you.' Baron was a very attractive man. I can say that as a one hundred per cent heterosexual man. He was tall and very muscular, as if he worked out very regularly, and while he had gentle facial features, he also had that 'don't mess with me' hard look about him at the same time. He was well groomed: he wore a smart black suit, his shoes looked brand new and his hair was cut close to the head. He was the first black professional male I had come across in Dubai. I wondered, just for a moment, whether his experience in Dubai would be any different to mine. For example, would Ali and Sadiq be happy with a black consultant? There's no reason, of course, why they shouldn't be, but who knows what beliefs and preconceptions they might have. I could tell, however, that the female staff in the office were pleased to see Baron. They all sat in front of their computers with big grins on their faces. They nudged each other and whispered to each other behind hands that covered their mouths.

You could tell that Baron knew he was attractive to the ladies. He just carried his body about with such confidence. And he had a big smile that exposed a perfect set of very white teeth. 'Where are you from?' I asked.

'From New York,' he replied. 'I was there for four years. Before that I was in Philadelphia.'

'Well, welcome to Dubai,' I continued. 'I'm sure you'll love it. It's a great place. Really wild and crazy.'

'That's what I've heard,' he replied.

'We'll have to get together at the weekend, and we'll take you out somewhere,' I suggested with enthusiasm. 'Jas and I now know all the hot spots to visit.'

'Well, actually, I've already got commitments on both days,' he replied, 'what with flat hunting and trying to find a car and all. And I'm meeting up with an old friend on Thursday evening, but on Friday I have accepted an invitation to go grinding.'

'Grinding?' said Jas questioningly.

'You know. The Grind on MTV,' replied Baron.

'Oh yes,' I responded, as I was familiar with the programme.

'Sexy babes dancing in their bikinis in and around hotel swimming pools,' whispered Baron, trying to put on a sexy accent.

'And they do that here?' Jas asked.

'Yeah. Not MTV, of course, but the Marine Club has 'borrowed' the idea. My friend says that they often get lots of the Emirates cabin crew down there, and they're hot. On Friday nights my friend is the deejay there, but during the day he is a university lecturer.'

'But we live very close to the Marine Beach Club,' replied Jas, 'and we go there fairly regularly. I've never heard of this grind thing.'

'I'm sure it was the Marine Club that my friend mentioned,' insisted Baron.

'It's probably up at the Dubai *International* Marine Club,' I suggested. 'You know, Jas, the one next door to the Al Mina Sailing Club.'

'Probably,' repeated Jas.

'Well lads,' said Baron, 'if you haven't been there before, then maybe it's time you gave it a try.'

'We might just do that Baron,' replied Jas, looking and sounding enthusiastic. I suddenly felt rather silly. I had just been boasting that Jas and I knew all the hot spots, all the best places to go to in Dubai, and now it was the 'new boy' who was taking us out.

We agreed that we would meet Baron at the Dubai International Marine Club. Jas found out during the week that the club was usually referred to as the 'DIMC'. We set off for the DIMC without having eaten our evening meal. 'We'll get something there,' Jas had said with confidence. Jas had been out all day, playing golf, as usual, with Mike and his other new friends. I had waited for Jas to return so that we could eat together, but he returned far later than I had expected. I had spent the day alone at home. I just pottered about the villa, moving with little energy or direction. I had read a little, washed and ironed my clothes, and I even did a bit of cleaning in the kitchen, lounge and bathroom. Shannon had visited me at home the day before and had remarked that 'the place could do with a dusting'. It was Shannon's comment that had spurred me into action. Although both Jas and I are clean people, and like cleanliness, we didn't, in truth, do all that much cleaning. Jas sometimes joked that we should get a cleaner who could visit the property once a week. I sometimes thought that he actually meant it, but I wasn't in favour of the idea. First, I didn't particularly want a stranger in our home. Second, I thought it was a waste of money. And third, I was, on principle, against the idea of having a 'servant'. Or perhaps, in truth, it was really more to do with what other people would think of me if I employed a servant. I'm sure, for example, that Shannon would have disapproved of the idea.

We reached the DIMC by going through the grounds of the Le Meridien hotel. We headed in the direction of the beach by walking down a path that passed through some beautiful gardens. As we approached the DIMC, we could hear music and the sound of many people having fun. We walked into a giant gazebo. The bar was there, and crowds of people were queuing for drinks. We went out through the other side of the gazebo into the swimming pool area. The deejay was set up here. He stood behind his console, occasionally doing some dance moves to the music. The music was slow and mellow, yet people were still dancing to it at various locations around the swimming pool. The crowd was young and beautiful, but disappointingly, there were no more than a dozen girls in bikinis or other swimwear, and there was no one actually in the pool. We were now at the end of March, and the air and water temperatures were easily high enough for swimming, even at night. This was a sophisticated crowd. They were really pleasing to the eye. They were well dressed, well spoken and well groomed. There were no rowdy teenagers. This was ClubMed for the professional. This is what a millionaire's private beach party might be like. This was pure hedonism.

'I smell a barbecue somewhere,' said Jas enthusiastically.

'The smell seems to be coming from over there,' I replied, as I pointed to a second gazebo located towards the back of the club's grounds, furthest away from the sea.

'Let's take a look,' suggested Jas. We took the long way around the pool, thereby passing the sexy babes in swimwear. A number of men stood serving food from behind a long table, but there was no bar here. 'Let's get our drinks first,' I said. 'Then we can bring them back here and get some food.' Jas nodded in agreement.

'Have you seen Baron yet?' he asked.

'No,' I replied. 'Maybe he's not here yet.' We then went back to the gazebo which had the bar. There was still a big crowd waiting to be served. As we stood in the crowd I heard Baron's unmistakable voice behind me. 'I'm generally known as *the* baron,' he was saying to some girl, 'but you can just call me Baron.' In response, she just giggled. By the look in her eyes, I would say that she was ready to jump into his bed the moment he asked. Baron was wearing a white vest, white tracksuit bottoms and a white baseball cap. He had several gold chains around his neck. He looked more like a rapper than a management consultant. I was envious of him. He so easily fitted into both worlds: he could change his image to be the smart, rich professional and he could also be the cool, trendy man about town. Baron then saw us. 'Hi guys!' he shouted out as he gave a little wave. The girl looked at him as if to say 'you know those two?' Baron didn't come over to us, and we didn't go over to him. I didn't want to cramp his style, and get blamed if he didn't manage to 'get off' with his girl.

We got our drinks, and then we got our food. We had grilled chicken and mutton pieces, salad, Arabic bread and hummus, of course. It was all washed down with nice, cold Australian beer. We shared a table with three Dutch ladies. We talked to each other a bit, and they were pleasant enough, but they were a bit old for us. They were probably in their late thirties or early forties. They might have been mothers let out for a night out alone without their families. One of them, who was quite attractive for her age, enjoyed teasing Jas. 'Would you like to be my toy boy?' she asked him more than once. Jas just laughed in an embarrassed way. After we had finished our food, we left the ladies, and strolled around the grounds. As we approached the place where the deejay was set up, we could see that Baron was there, surrounded by several girls, and busy chatting to the deejay. As we passed he turned and said, 'I hope you are enjoying yourselves, gentlemen.'

'We are,' replied Jas.

'I can't believe that you guys didn't know about this gig,' continued Baron. 'It must be one of Dubai's best kept secrets.'

'That's how we keep it exclusive,' joked the deejay.

'Pompous ass,' I muttered under my breath as we continued walking on.

'Who?' asked Jas.

'That Baron. Thinks he's "Mister It".'

'Well, maybe he has reason to think that. Just look how the ladies are attracted to him. Like bees to the honey pot.'

'More like flies to the shit,' I answered sarcastically.

'And Mike says he's pretty good at his job too. He came with an impressive track record, apparently, and glowing testimonials from many of the big wigs across the pond.'

'Come on, let's show him that we know how to have a good time too,' I said.

'Sure thing,' replied Jas. But a couple of guys out at a pub or club never do seem to have as good a time as those in larger groups. What could we do? Stand around drinking, watching those having a better time than ourselves? Sit on the grass and smoke shisha, like many others were now doing? But we could do that at home in our garden. Perhaps we could dance together like a couple of gays? Or, if we were feeling really brave, we could just go up to some girls and start dancing with them? But nobody seemed to be doing that kind of thing. There didn't seem to be any 'pulling' going on. Within groups of people, everyone seemed to already know everyone else. What Jas and I needed was a bigger circle of friends. Friends with appeal, friends with pulling power, friends like, dare I say it, Baron. And that's why, in the weeks that followed, I did my best to become one of Baron's friends. Jas and I followed him to pubs, clubs and parties, always benefiting from his popularity and social success. We gained many new friends, both male and female, during those weeks, but we knew that we were living in Baron's shadow. Or at least I did; I'm not sure that Jas thought about such things.

Jas and I danced in the vicinity of the girls who were wearing swimwear. When Baron later glanced over at us, I gave him a confident nod and wink, implying that we had got acquainted with the girls. But we hadn't. We didn't exchange one word with them. They seemed to be happy just dancing alone and attracting the admiration of many men from the distance. Baron probably knew that I was bluffing; that we were not dancing with the girls, just dancing near to them, but by then I didn't really care what he thought. Jas and I had still enjoyed our evening, and in the future, we were to go 'grinding' almost every other weekend.

Another barbecue

O n the day I had gone to the JBNC office to 'check out' Baron, Mike invited me to another barbecue at his villa. 'You may not have invited me to your house warming party,' he joked, 'but I'll still invite you to my parties. And I'll even invite your girlfriend.'

'We haven't had a house warming yet,' I replied. 'We just haven't had the time to organise one. Both Jas and I have been working at home many evenings, and we're not completely settled in yet. I even have a few boxes that I shipped over from England, which I haven't yet got around to opening.'

'Hard life,' answered Mike with a big grin on his face.

I invited Shannon to Mike's barbecue. She said that she would have liked to go, as she liked Stella and Mike, but she already other plans. 'What other plans?' I asked. 'Couldn't you change them?'

'No, unfortunately I can't,' was her reply. She didn't explain what her plans were. I was quite disappointed. I wondered if there was any point in having a girlfriend that didn't seem to want to be a part of my life. I had, by now, stopped visiting hotels and bars in the hope of catching Shannon with another man. As the flotation of Al Saadha-Wasel came closer, I didn't have either the time or energy to go out in the evenings. I was at home working on most evenings. And if I wasn't working, I either sat in front of the television like a cabbage or slept.

Because I spent so little time at the JBNC office, it was easy for me not to think about Mike and Inga. But now that I was going to his home again, the image of the couple going into the hotel lift kept reappearing in my mind. I really feared that while at the barbie I might accidentally say the wrong thing to Stella, or even to Mike and Inga. Something that I didn't intend might just slip out of my mouth, especially if I drank any quantity of alcohol. I didn't like, or in any way approve, of what Mike was doing, but I didn't feel that it was my place to confront him about it. And I certainly didn't want to get involved by saying anything to Stella about her husband's affair. So, I wasn't really looking forward to the prospect of going to Mike's home again, first because I was going as a sad single person again, and second, because of what I knew about Mike and Inga. I just hoped that, like last time, Inga would not be at the barbie.

Jas and I got to Mike's villa at about eight thirty in the evening. Upon entering his garden, we saw that the set up was much the same as the last time we had visited for a barbie. There seemed to be fewer people this time, but still there was a pleasant atmosphere. When Stella saw us, she rushed over immediately. 'Pleased you could make it,' she said, as Jas and I exchanged kisses with her in the air to each side of the head, 'but where is your girlfriend Nick?'

'Unfortunately, she couldn't make it tonight,' I replied.

'And do you have a girlfriend yet, Jas?' she then asked.

'No, not yet,' answered Jas. 'Still looking for the right one.'

'That's right,' Stella continued. 'No need to rush. You take your time and find the right one.' Jas saw the couple from Kentucky, with whom he had enjoyed talking so much at the previous barbie, and excused himself from Stella's and my company. Stella led me straight to the food table. 'I've made more of your favourite hummus,' she said.

'What a treat,' I replied, sounding a bit like an excited child.

'Tuck in,' she said. 'There's plenty here and nobody seems to be eating very much tonight.'

'Oh, I will', I replied. 'It all looks so tasty.' I looked around and could not see Inga. Thank goodness for that I thought. I didn't see Mike either, however. 'Where's Mike?' I asked.

'He's around somewhere,' she replied, looking around. 'He must be in the house.' As I filled my plate, I put a piece of grilled chicken in my mouth. 'Mmm. That's gorgeous,' I said.

'What a shame that Shannon couldn't come,' Stella then continued. 'She seemed like such a nice girl. Do you see much of her?'

'Not as much as I would like to. She's always so busy.'

'With what?'

'That's a good question. I don't really know. School work I think.'

'I guess that people in Dubai are worked quite hard. Just look at Mike,' she said. 'He sometimes doesn't get home from meetings or whatever until after midnight.' I wanted the ground to open up and take me away. The conversation was going exactly in the direction I didn't want it to. 'Are you finding the work more demanding over here?' Stella then asked.

'I work long hours here, and often at home in the evenings,' I replied, 'but I did too in England. I guess that's just the nature of our work.'

'Well, mind you don't overdo it. Don't let them take advantage of you.'

'Oh no, I wouldn't let them do that. But at least they do pay us reasonably well for our effort.'

'You might think that way now,' continued Stella, 'but money isn't everything. Just you wait until you have a family. They will be sitting at home waiting for you to come home from work and all too often you won't come. Your children will have to go to bed without being able to say 'good night' to their daddy. They will be sad and lonely, and you will be tired, stressed and lonely too.'

'But you and Mike are okay, aren't you?' I prompted.

'Sure. In a couple of months, we will have been married for twenty-one years. We've been through everything together, the good times and the bad. We're soul mates. But he hasn't looked that well lately. He always seems preoccupied with something these days. There's always something on his mind, something troubling him possibly. He comes home late and he is too tired to talk. He just keeps things bottled up these days. He never used to do that. You don't know, Nick, if he's having any particular problem at work?' There was a brief period of silence as I decided how to respond to the question. I could have replied, 'Well I think the problem is that he is screwing his p.a.,' but instead I took the coward's way out, and actually said, 'I wouldn't know really. I'm rarely at the office. I'm still at Al Saadha-Wasel.'

'Of course you are,' she replied. 'Silly me! Maybe I should speak to Jas later?' I did my best to save Jas from that torture by saying, 'I'm pretty sure there will be nothing he could tell you. If there was, I'm sure that he would have already mentioned it to me.' No sooner had the words left my mouth, I thought that Stella might easily have thought my response rather strange. I wondered whether I had come across as someone with something to hide. Then, out of nowhere, Stella suddenly said, 'Well, I hope, Nick, that your relationship with Shannon, or with whomever else you choose, can be just like my relationship with Mike.' It probably is, I thought. Your partner is unfaithful and, quite possibly, so is mine. I said nothing.

Suddenly, Mike appeared. 'Good to see you here again,' he said, giving me a hard slap on the back.

'Wouldn't miss one of your barbies for the world,' I replied.

'And we look forward to coming to one of yours one day,' he said teasingly.

'Well, if you didn't work him so hard, hubby, then maybe he would feel like organising one,' said Stella, leaping to my defence.

'He's young and strong and fit. His sharp mind can cope with anything that I could throw at it,' replied Mike.

'I've just been telling Nick how I wished you would take things a little easier,' said Stella. 'All those meetings at night, are they really necessary?'

'If they weren't necessary, love, I wouldn't be doing them, would I?' was Mike's response. Mike didn't look very happy any more. Now it was his turn to feel uncomfortable with the direction the conversation had taken. 'Business men have business meetings,' Mike continued. 'That's business!'

'At the Astoria,' I blurted out. I don't know why I said it. It just came out. Luckily, Stella didn't hear me, and I'm not sure whether Mike did or not. If he did, he didn't respond. Maybe he would do that on Saturday morning by giving me my dismissal papers! Anyway, luckily, Stella changed the topic of conversation. She started telling me about the shopping festival that was starting in the city the next week. Mike used the opportunity to slip away. Some time later, Stella's next-door neighbours joined us, and that gave Stella the opportunity to move on to attend to some of her other guests. I was left talking to the next-door neighbours. The couple, John and Jo, originally from Newcastle in England, had lived in Dubai for eight years. They were probably just a few years older than Jas and I, and they had a sweet little daughter, aged four. John worked in the oil industry. He said that it was a good life, except that he had to spend whole months away from home. Jo had a part-time job in an office. They both loved the Dubai lifestyle and they believed that it provided the perfect environment in which to bring up their daughter. Their little girl would start school in the coming September, and as far as John and Jo were concerned, the private schools in Dubai were better than any state school in Newcastle.

Some time later, Haley appeared. She grabbed my wrist, and pulled me away from John and Jo. 'Sorry John and Jo,' Haley said, 'Nick's needed elsewhere.' She led me into the house, and then into the living room. We stood together in the middle of the room. 'I was wondering if you would be coming,' she began.

'Well, I'm here,' I replied.

'You never rang me Nick,' she said. 'Didn't you want to see me again?'

'I told you last time,' I answered, trying to sound kind and sympathetic, 'that I am too old for you. You need to find a boy closer your own age.'

148

'But they're all so immature.'

'They can't all be,' I replied.

'They are! I need a real man, like you. I've always been attracted to older men.' Haley's arms rose as she tried to embrace me. I took a step backwards to prevent her from doing so.

'Don't you like me? Don't you find me attractive?' she continued.

'Of course I do, but that is not the point. People of my age are expected to act in certain ways.'

'We could keep our relationship secret. No one need know about it. I wouldn't tell a soul if that's what you wanted.' I couldn't help thinking about Haley's father again. It looked like Haley had inherited some of her father's personality traits: the willingness and ability to deceive and be secretive. These were not things that I admired. In fact, I prefer people who are honest and open, the type of people you can read like a book, even if they don't want you to. 'Anyway, I have a girlfriend,' I said, 'and I believe in staying faithful.'

'Well, where is she then?'

'She couldn't make it tonight.'

'She's not a very good girlfriend then, is she?' I didn't reply. Perhaps, I thought, Haley's statement might be proved correct one day soon. Stella came into the living room. 'Oh, there you are!' she said, looking at Haley.

'Yes, here I am,' replied Haley, as she left the room and went upstairs. I didn't see her again for a couple of hours, so presumably she had gone up to her bedroom.

The shopping festival

Dubai is an impressive city at any time of the year, but during the shopping festival it becomes something of a real-life Disney World. During the days before the start of the festival I had noticed men up ladders and in trees all over the place. But I couldn't have imagined the end result that was revealed on the first day of the shopping festival. Lights, decorations and flags from around the world lined all of the main streets in the city centre. Lights were placed in the branches of trees, so that from a distance, they revealed the shape and outline of the trees. I've heard that the Blackpool illuminations are good, but I bet they couldn't compare with Dubai's. That is very much the culture in Dubai. Whatever is done in Dubai, it has to be the tallest, longest, widest, most impressive, most technologically advanced. Second best is not in their vocabulary. And of course, the city is rich. They can afford to build the tallest, most impressive buildings, the widest, newest roads, the smartest airport, and the largest man-made harbour and marina.

Dubai's shopping festival lasted the whole month of April. The shopping festival concept was actually 'invented' by Singapore however. It was introduced in 1994 as an annual event, to revitalise what was then a flagging retail sector. Three thousand retailers in Singapore agreed to participate in deep price cuts and special promotions in order to attract the international customer. But the shopping festival, as offered by Singapore and Dubai, is not only about shopping. It is about attracting tourists who will come and spend, and thereby benefiting many sectors of the economy, most obviously the airlines, hotels, restaurants and taxi drivers. But the tourists will also buy manufactured goods, many of which might have been domestically produced.

Tourists come from all over the world for Dubai's Shopping Festivals, not only to enjoy the shopping, but also to enjoy the good weather, the fine hotels, the long, clean, sandy beaches and the 'special' attractions. The festival planners at the Department for Tourism attempt to satisfy the needs and desires of every visitor, and they work with airlines and hotels to provide special packages, and they provide a daily non-stop programme of entertainment and leisure activities. This includes street performers, recruited from around the world, sporting events, like the Dubai World Cup, the horse race with the largest prize money in the world, participation 'sports', ranging from a chess competition to bungee jumping over the creek, various types of show, ranging from performing dolphins to performances by international pop stars, a daily fireworks display, and 'one-off' events like organising the world's biggest breakfast in order to get into the Guinness Book of Records. This involved fourteen thousand people gathering at Creekside Park one morning to eat Kellogg's breakfast cereals with milk.

April was an exciting month to be in Dubai, but not if you don't like crowds. The hotels were all full, and the shops seemed incredibly busy, each night of the month having the same excitement and bustle of the first day of the January sales at London's Oxford Street. Driving became even more of a nightmare than usual. Dubai has no metro, train or tram system, and the buses are used mainly by the poorer workers. The tourists, therefore, rely on either taxis or rented cars. Too many seem to opt for the latter option, and they cause traffic jams at all times of the day. What was normally a twenty-minute journey would take one hour to complete during the shopping festival, and then finding a parking space usually took another ten or twenty minutes, often taking you far from where you really wanted to be. And the wide, multi-lane roads with many other roads leading to and from them confused the tourists, as did the long dual carriageways that force you to do U turns all the time. They frequently got lost and, when not in the traffic jams in the city centre, many couldn't cope with the fast, aggressive driving outside the centre. Consequently, there were even more crashes and accidents on the roads than usual.

I had little time to enjoy the first ten days of the shopping festival, because I was busy seeing to the final preparations for Al Saadha-Wasel's flotation. All I had time to enjoy really, were the street decorations and lights as I drove between home and work. On several days, as I drove home, I was caught in a traffic jam going over the Al Maktoum Bridge. But I didn't mind. It was actually a pleasure to be there and have time to look and enjoy everything. The bridge was covered in lights and decorations. The row of palm trees in the middle of the dual carriageway shone brightly like Christmas trees. I always seemed to be crossing the bridge during the firework display, which was held daily at Creekside Park, over to my left. The displays lasted a good thirty minutes. Every night, the fireworks seemed different, and somehow more impressive. And, as I looked to my right, I could see all of Dubai lit up, with the sky above glowing, and colourful reflections shimmering on the water of the creek.

Finally, the day of Al Saadha-Wasel's flotation arrived. It was a great success. We had priced the shares high, but they still rose another five per cent on the day of issue. So Ali and Sadiq were happy, the investors were happy, the analysts were happy, the brokers were happy and so were the media, covering another success story in Dubai. Although I was at the analyst, broker and media briefings, I stayed in the background, allowing Ali and Sadiq to do all the talking. They were praised and admired for building up a successful company and for seeing through its successful flotation. My considerable contribution to the success of the flotation went unnoticed in the public eye, although Ali and Sadiq thanked me sincerely in private. Ali even asked me whether I would like a new Mercedes as a 'thank you'. I insisted that such a generous gift was not necessary, and I never got one, but I have no doubt that had I said 'okay' then I would have. I did think, however, that asking someone if they wanted a present was a strange thing to do. In my opinion, presents should just be given or not given. The media seemed to want to cover the story as 'another local success' and that's probably why my face did not fit with that theme. I did, however, briefly sneak into the picture on the Channel 33 news. Shannon saw me on the television, and she was very pleased that I was wearing her valentine's shirt and tie.

Throughout the rest of the shopping festival I worked at my desk in the JBNC office. It was good to be back there, working with Jas, Baron, Mike and the others. I felt a sense of belonging there. There were people I could rely on to help me with my work, and people to talk to over lunch. On my first day back at the office, Mike invited me into his office. He congratulated me on a job well done at Al Saadha-Wasel. He then apologised that my next assignment was not going to be of the type that I usually specialise in. 'We need you to go to the Deira National Bank to help them with their human resource strategy,' Mike explained. 'They just had a bollocking off the government for not employing enough nationals. The increasing participation of nationals in the workforce is a government priority at the moment. It was a key component within the Dubai Strategic Development Plan for 1996 to 2000, and is again included in the current plan. Dubai, you see, has high youth unemployment, yet young people are increasingly educated, and it has a relatively high birth rate and slowing economic growth. The economy can no longer afford to support a large and inefficient public sector and the generous levels of social welfare traditionally offered. That's why the government wants more nationals working in the private sector, for companies like the Deira National Bank.'

'The government has a problem, however,' Mike continued, 'because of a glaring mismatch between the needs and requirements of companies and the expectations of the young nationals. Employers complain that the nationals lack skills, qualifications, experience and motivation, while the applicants complain that the salaries are too low and the working hours too long. In contrast, the foreigners currently doing the jobs are cheaper, more highly skilled and qualified, and they work harder and better. But the government is targeting certain sectors, banking being one of them, and they have set minimum targets relating to the proportion of nationals in each company's workforce. Did you realise, Nick, that the percentage of national labour in the entire private sector is less than two per cent? It's incredible, isn't it? The locals only want to work in the public sector, which they perceive as offering higher salaries and better working conditions. Your brief then, is quite a complex one. You will help the DNB, the Deira National Bank, to develop a human resource strategy that increases the proportion of nationals in their workforce, but without significantly increasing total labour costs or sacrificing operational performance and profitability. You will also need to develop strategies that will result in an increase in the number of nationals applying for positions with the bank. That's part of the problem you see. The nationals don't really want to work for banks.'

'How long will I be at the DNB?' I asked.

'Nine months initially,' replied Mike. 'You will be a key link between the HR and finance functions of the bank. You might have to help decide which jobs in the bank to nationalise, the pay and conditions to be offered for those jobs, the training programmes to be offered, and then you'll have to prepare budgets and detailed forecasts relating to the outcomes of such actions.'

'Sounds like quite a challenge,' I said.

'It certainly is. But you would not be wrong, however, to focus more generally on the ways in which the bank could be more efficient and profitable, while remembering to incorporate the HR objectives wherever possible.' I spent the next three weeks doing research and making preparations for this assignment. This was a complicated assignment, but less demanding on my time than the Al Saadha-Wasel job, at least at this stage. This allowed me to enjoy the activities of the shopping festival in the evenings. On several occasions I called Shannon and asked her if she would come out with me. To my surprise, she said 'yes' each time. I'm not sure if she agreed because she felt she owed me after I had given her a diamond ring for her birthday or whether she was just keen to go out and enjoy the fun of the shopping festival. In truth, she could have done the latter with Sinead and Rebecca.

One evening, we went to Al Rigga Street to see the dolphin show, which we both enjoyed. Al Rigga Street was very much at the centre of the street entertainment. There were shows to watch, street markets, with stalls selling produce from around the world, and even a small funfair. The road is a long dual carriageway, but it is not one on which cars drive fast. It is lined throughout with palm trees, on both sides of the street. The central reservation has bushes and plants. During the festival, the road was decorated with lights, banners and flags. The whole place had a Mediterranean feel to it. The road had many restaurants and cafes, with people sitting out on the pavements. There was something to suit every taste, from Middle Eastern food through to Chinese, Indian, Italian and Mexican. There were also several international fast food chains, such as KFC, Pizza Hut and McDonald's. Shannon and I ate at the *Automatic Restaurant*, a popular chain serving Lebanese food. I ordered a plate of Shish Taouk (grilled chicken pieces), which had become one of my favourite dishes, while Shannon ordered a mixed grill. We ate it with pitta bread, salad, and hummus. It was a tasty, healthy and refreshing meal to eat, especially during the very warm evenings that we were then having. Most westerners were not comfortable wearing more than tee shirts and shorts, or light dresses for the ladies. Apart from the heat, it was becoming more humid too. The cold, freshly squeezed fruit juices that we had with our food were most welcome to quench our thirst and replace our lost fluids.

After we had eaten, we walked slowly up and down Al Rigga Street, watching the street performers and looking at the street stalls. We passed, but didn't go into the Al Ghurair shopping mall, which was the first one to be built in Dubai, some twenty years or so ago. Now, Dubai has over thirty shopping malls. Then, we wandered along some of the side streets, until we came out on Al Muraqqabat Road, which runs parallel to Al Rigga Street. This road also had street entertainers, market stalls and yet another small funfair. Both children and adults screamed as they flew through the air in little aeroplanes, competing to be heard over the loud pop music blaring out from below. The big wheel, with its flashing lights, was as tall as the blocks of apartments that surrounded the open space on which the funfair had been set up. I wondered how on earth the people living in those apartments could survive the month, with such noise continuing well beyond midnight every night of the week. In addition, the apartments seemed to be directly under the flight path of aeroplanes coming in to land at the airport. Every four or five minutes another plane roared overhead. As a tourist, it was interesting to look at the names of the airlines and the logos on the planes' tails and to speculate where they might have come from. But how could the residents sleep through such noise? Could they sleep at all? Could they even hear their own televisions or radios?

Shannon bought a couple of the official shopping festival raffle tickets at a kiosk. She handed one to me. 'Good luck,' she said. 'You never know, it might be your turn to win.'

'What am I going to win?' I asked, with a big grin on my face.

'Oh, I don't know. Perhaps a car, or maybe a million bucks,' she replied. 'But somebody at school did win a holiday to Thailand a couple of days ago.' Dubai had gone raffle crazy. The festival organizers had their 'official raffle', but it seemed that every shopping mall and every big company also had their own too. Each day it was possible to win prizes like BMW or Lexus cars, Nissan Patrols or Land Cruisers, holidays, money, a kilo of gold and even 'your own weight in gold'. With Islam not permitting gambling to occur in Dubai, the raffle was the closest that both residents and tourists could come to having a flutter. Even at the horse races, the 'punters' do not bet on the races. Instead they buy, or receive complimentary raffle tickets in lieu of their entry charge. I checked in a newspaper two days later to see whether my number had come up, but I hadn't won anything.

A few nights later, a group of us went to the big funfair that was located between the Wafi City and Creekside Park. The group consisted of me, Shannon, Jas, Baron, Sinead, Rebecca and another two female teachers from Shannon's school. Shannon had driven the girls there, and Jas the boys. The fair had all the usual rides and games like dodgem cars, carousels, waltzers, helter skelters, a ghost train, a big wheel, rifle shooting to win big soft toys and throwing rings around jars to win a goldfish. But many of the rides seemed taller, scarier and more technologically advanced than those I was familiar with from my childhood. These included rides that tossed and turned you at speed in every direction some fifty feet or so high, a reverse bungee that fired you high into the air, and one in which you fell from a great height at great speed whilst strapped into a chair. The girls seemed the keener to try the 'scary' rides, and they coerced us boys into joining them. Some of those rides were not my idea of fun, and by the time I came off the waltzer, I was ready to be sick. I managed to hold it in, but I didn't feel that good at all. When we had been on all the rides that we wanted to go on, Sinead suggested that we walk over to Wafi City and have a drink at the Pyramids. Everyone agreed, but Shannon noticed that we had lost Rebecca and Baron in the crowds. We walked a circuit of the fair, looking for them, but without success. 'They'll have to take taxis home,' Sinead declared without sympathy or concern. We walked over to the Pyramids, and that made me feel better again. By the time we got there, I was ready to enjoy a nice cold beer.

The next morning at the office, Jas and I had already been working for nearly an hour, and there was still no sign of Baron. 'Perhaps we should give him a ring,' suggested Jas. 'To make sure he's okay.'

'Maybe we should,' I answered, feeling a little guilty that we had left the fair without him. As Jas picked up the phone to make the call, Baron walked in. 'Here comes the baron,' said Jas loudly. I didn't respond because I didn't much care for his use of the 'the' before Baron's name. I felt that it was only serving to boost Baron's already large ego. 'Did you get home alright?' Jas asked.

'Yeah. No problem man,' replied Baron. 'Where did you get to?'

'We lost you in the crowds,' answered Jas. 'We did walk around trying to find you, but without success. So, we went for a drink at the Pyramids.'

'No problem, my friends,' said Baron. 'I was with the lovely Rebecca, who stayed over at my place last night.'

'You sly old fox,' said Jas, with obvious envy, even though he could have had Rebecca if he had chosen to.

'So, you had sex with her?' I asked, in order to understand what exactly had gone on between Baron and Rebecca.

'Yeah man. And it was very nice,' he replied.

'You don't waste much time, do you?' commented Jas.

'How many have you bedded now?' I asked.

'She's the third since I arrived in Dubai,' he answered. 'I just love the ladies you see, and I love sex. I just can't get enough of it.'

Lunch talk

O n the ground floor of the building in which the JBNC office is located is a restaurant called *Aroma*. At lunchtime it serves an international buffet. You can eat as much as you like for thirty dirhams, which is about five UK pounds. Jas said that while I was working at Al Saadha-Wasel, he had lunch there once or twice a week. Jas went down with Baron, and I said I would meet them at the restaurant, as I wanted to finish off what I was working on before lunch. When I got downstairs, the restaurant was quite full, but Jas and Baron hadn't saved me a seat at their table. One man and woman sat at a table for six. I asked if I might join them, and they seemed pleased to have some new company. They introduced themselves as Seb and Maggie, and they too worked at offices in the same building as me. They were having one of those 'isn't Dubai great?' conversations.

'I've been here for twelve years now,' said Maggie, 'and there's no way I want to go back to Scotland. My husband talks about it sometimes, but I say "what for?" Life is much better here in Dubai. My husband's company pays for our villa, we pay no tax here, and every month we send a couple of grand to our bank account in the Channel Islands. We could afford to retire by the time we're both fifty! But it's not really for the financial benefits that I want to stay in Dubai. The quality of life is better here. The weather is great, the beaches are great and there are many things for the children to do. They belong to clubs, play sports and go to the cinema once a fortnight. My son goes go-karting twice a week and he goes sailing every week, while my daughter goes riding and has violin lessons. We'd never be able to give them all that in the UK. And we are confident that they're getting a good education here. If they choose to go to university, they'll be able to, either in the UK or over here.'

'Yes, I'm sure it's a splendid place in which to grow up,' replied Seb. 'But how do you think your children will cope when eventually you do have to go home? You can't stay here forever, after all. Once

157

you stop working, they won't want you here. It seems to me that Dubai can never be called "home" until the day we are allowed to buy property, and have the right to live in it forever.'

'That day will come very soon,' said Maggie. 'My husband told me that the government is planning to let expatriates buy all those apartments they're building up at the new marina.'

'It will be good if that is the case,' replied Seb. 'Even I would be tempted if the price was right, and if the contracts looked legally sound.'

'I'm sure that the government will give the expats what they need and want for their peace of mind,' was Maggie's response. Then she continued, 'I am a Christian, but I really can see the benefits of Islam in this part of the world. I mean where else in the world is there so little crime, and so few social problems? I have never once heard of a street mugging or any violent incident on the streets. A woman can walk about on the streets, even late at night, and feel perfectly safe. At home, I leave my doors and windows open without worry of intruders or burglars. And people drive to shops, and then go inside leaving their cars unlocked with the engines left running so that the air conditioning keeps working. Have you ever heard of anyone driving away in such a car? People in this country know right from wrong, and either because they're religious or because they're afraid of the strict punishments if they are caught breaking the law, they remain peaceful and law abiding.'

'But Islam doesn't really respect women. Does it?' Seb asked.

'I feel very respected here, much more so than I would feel in Scotland. Women don't usually have to queue for service in banks or public organisations, like the utility companies, while men often have to wait in line for considerable periods of time. Women get their own sections in the buses. There are always seats available at the front of buses for women, while men stand huddled together behind. In shops, the sales staff definitely show extra respect for women. You're addressed 'Madam' and they're attentive to your needs. And in Dubai, unlike in most other countries, men don't take advantage of women by committing crimes against them. So, Seb, no I don't agree with what you just said. But I have to get back to work now, so we'll have to continue this conversation another time.' Maggie said 'good bye' and left me with Seb.

'She obviously doesn't read a newspaper,' said Seb to me. 'If she did, then she would know that what she just said represents just one narrow viewpoint of the lives of women in Dubai. I can give you several examples, which I have read about during the last few weeks, all in the *Gulf News*. First, a local couple were driving along the eastern coastal road one Friday, somewhere near Fujairah, when they started to have an argument. The husband stopped the car. Witnesses saw the couple standing outside, shouting at each other and pushing each other around a bit. But nobody saw what happened next. The husband picked up a rock and smashed it over his wife's head. She later died in hospital. Now, Nick, you tell me what punishment you think the man got for this crime.' I thought that the punishment must have been lenient to support the argument that Seb was trying to put forward, so I answered, 'Five years in prison.'

'No,' replied Seb. 'He received no punishment at all. The judge felt that the husband had been unduly provoked, and therefore was not responsible for what had happened. Now compare that with this next case. A young wife went to her local store to buy some bread and other basic foodstuffs. She left her husband at home smoking. He was unemployed, he was user of drugs, and on that morning he was drunk, as he had consumed a whole bottle of whisky. It is believed that the husband probably dropped a lit cigarette. It might have set fire to his chair or the rug on the floor beneath him and then spread before he could leave the house. Perhaps he had fallen asleep or was unconscious. The wife returned to her house to see it on fire, with all of the neighbours outside it throwing buckets of water into the flames. The husband's family claimed that the wife had started the fire, although the statements of several people who had seen her going to and coming from the shop would have made that almost impossible to achieve. Now, Nick, what punishment do you think this lady got?'

'I haven't a clue Seb,' I replied. 'You tell me.'

'She got life in jail. Now let me tell you one last story. A French Muslim was in Dubai on a business trip. She worked for a big multi-national and she was a senior executive. After work one evening she went to a bar for a drink. She got chatting to three Arab men. She said that they were very charming and very polite. When the woman said she was going back to her hotel, the men offered to give her a lift. She accepted. But they did not take her straight back to her hotel. First, they drove to some wasteland, where they each took it in turn to rape her. Later, they did drop her off outside her hotel. She got straight into a taxi, went to the nearest police station, and reported the assault. A doctor examined the woman and confirmed that she was badly bruised in her genital area and upper legs, and that the semen of three different men was inside her. The three men were found. What punishment do you think they got?'

'I really don't know,' I answered. 'Two years each?'

'No. The men weren't punished at all. The judge held that the sex had been consensual and that the woman had asked them to 'give it to her rough'. But that's not all. Wait for it. The woman was charged with adultery. Because she was a foreign national, she was not stoned or anything like that, but she did get a prison sentence of thirty days followed by immediate deportation.'

'I must admit,' I said, 'I haven't noticed such stories in the *Gulf News* myself. I'm surprised that they're allowed to report such stories.'

'The media are pretty much allowed to write what they like,' replied Seb, 'as long as they don't criticise the sheikhs or the government. Anyway, these were the sorts of things I was thinking about when I said that Islam doesn't respect women.'

'It's a strange religion, which has a strange affect on the local culture,' I continued, 'and yet so many aspects of it seem very positive. Maggie gave us some examples. Basically, it just goes to prove that there is nowhere in this world that is perfect for everyone. But do you like it here Seb?'

'Sure, I've been here for seven years,' he replied. 'I love it here. It's like being permanently on holiday. And it's the best place in the world for sex. Forget Amsterdam, forget Bangkok, this is the place! I treat myself a couple of times a week. I've had, at last count, thirty-two different nationalities, and tried more positions than in the Kama Sutra.'

'You go to the clubs then?' I asked.

'No. Clubs are not my scene. I live in Deira, in an apartment not far from Al Rigga Street. Usually there are some girls out on the streets later at night, but sometimes I go to one of the local bars. Mind you, it seems to be all Chinese girls at the moment. And they're not as good as the East Europeans. Those girls from Ukraine or Latvia, or wherever, really make you believe that they're enjoying it. And they're cheap too. The doorman at my apartments, an Indian chap, says that he treats himself every weekend, and that he refuses to pay above fifty dirhams. I don't know if he's telling the truth, because I always have to pay at least a hundred, but that might just be the minimum going rate price for a white face I guess.'

This man was beginning to disgust me. He was grossly overweight, he hadn't combed his hair or shaved that morning, and he just looked dirty and sweaty. I would have bet that he didn't have any close relatives and that there would be no one in the world that would have noticed or cared if he dropped dead right there and then. How sad. It seemed that this man from New Zealand lived and worked solely to treat himself to a prostitute twice a week. They must be really desperate to go with a man like that, I thought. I said no more to Seb, and when the conversation dried up, he decided to go back to work. I saw Mohammed in the distance, just about to sit down, and I waved him over.

Mohammed had come into the restaurant just to have a milkshake. He sat opposite me and said, 'Hello Mister Nick.' He didn't look very happy however. I commented on this, and asked him if he was all right. 'It's my daughter's birthday today,' he explained, 'and I am just a bit sad that I can't be there to enjoy it with her.'

'You have a daughter?' I asked in surprise.

'Yes, I'm married,' he replied. 'My daughter is three today and I also have a son aged seven.'

'Where are they?' I asked.

'They are in India. We have a small house in Trivandrum.'

'Can't they come and live here?'

'No. JBNC won't sponsor their visas and I couldn't afford to bring them over. I originally came here to earn some money. I intended to stay no longer than five years, and I've already been here for nine. Most of what I earn I send back to them, but it is not enough for them to live well, and it doesn't leave enough for me either. I share a flat here with three other men. It's horrible. There is not enough space for any of us, and one of the others has to sleep in the living room. That way, when we split the rent, it works out a bit cheaper. But to be honest, Mister Nick, I'm just getting disillusioned with the whole country and the state of things over here for Indians. You know what my job title is, Mister Nick?'

'No, actually I don't,' I replied. I knew that he performed a lot of the office duties; he saw to things like the employees' visas, work permits and medical insurance. He was also the company's driver. It was Mohammed who had originally met Jas and me at the airport when we first arrived in Dubai. 'My contract calls me "office boy",' he said in disgust. 'I am thirty-five years old and I have a degree in management from the University of Kerala. How can I be called "a boy"? Is it not degrading to call a man of my age "boy"?'

'Sorry. I didn't know,' I said.

'There's no point in being sorry, Mister Nick. That's the way things are out here, and no one can change that; at least no one but the locals themselves. I am here only for the money. I make five times more here than I would make at home, but I am not happy here. All

Indians are here only because we have to be. We don't like it here, but we need to be here to support our families. Only, perhaps, a few doctors or businessmen, who are able to lead lives similar to those of the westerners, are happy here. But we do have a choice. I do accept that no one is forcing us to be here. So, perhaps, I should not complain, and instead just be grateful that I have a better life here than I could have in my own country. But, Mister Nick, think about it, the things that make your life in Dubai good are at the expense of the Asian. Most western families have some sort of servant; maybe a cook, cleaner or nanny, but none of them are usually paid very much. Think, when you go and get your car washed. Those men who vacuum and polish afterwards, they are paid only four hundred dirhams a month. And rich people in their Mercedes and Land Cruisers do nothing but complain if one little speck of dirt remains anywhere on the car, inside or out. But do most of them leave a tip? No they don't!'

'I guess that I didn't really understand the situation,' I replied. 'If we pay for a service in the UK, many people no longer feel obliged to then tip as well. Restaurants are the main exception. But I guess that we have the minimum wage, and things like that, so it's not fair to compare. But I never would have guessed that there are workers in Dubai earning the equivalent of less than twenty UK pounds a week. After all, the cost of living in Dubai is fairly comparable with that of the UK, but Dubai, I would have thought, was a far richer country and could have afforded to pay higher wages.'

'I'm not criticising the westerner, Mister Nick. Most of you are in Dubai for the same reasons we Indians are here. The only difference is that you are able to enjoy yourselves while you are here. But how are you to know how the rest of us live? You can't know, unless someone tells you. But, Mister Nick, you realise that you are one of the few in the office who would call me over to share your table for lunch.'

'I see some things,' I continued. 'But it's easier not to think about them. I see, for example, construction workers going to work in the mornings, in the back of trucks that are used in the UK to transport sheep and cattle. Those trucks are so crowded, that it seems that the workers are piled in on top of one another. I can see that they are treated with no respect and dignity. I'm really not sure at times how I feel about it all, whether I can live in a place with such inequality. You may not feel equal to me Mohammed, but believe me, I do not feel in any way equal to the local. And I have had to work surrounded by them for the last four months.'

Going off-road

Shannon asked me if I had yet been off-road in my Nissan Patrol. When I answered 'no', she said, 'Well what's the point of having a four wheel drive then?'

'I plan to go off-road. I just haven't got around to it yet,' I replied.

'Well, the reason I asked is that some of the lads at school said there's a glorious beach just past Jebel Ali. But to get to it you must go off-road for a kilometre or so. Do you think you could handle that?'

'I don't see why not,' I answered, trying to sound confident. But I wasn't feeling confident. I wasn't really sure how off-road driving would be different from normal road driving, in terms of what the driver has to do differently. I'd heard stories of people getting stuck in the desert, but I figured that at this place Shannon spoke about there would probably be other people nearby who would give us help if necessary. We agreed to go on the next Friday.

I picked up Shannon from her flat after a late breakfast. It was about eleven-thirty by the time I reached Shannon's place. She was already waiting for me when I arrived, already packed with her things, and eager to experience the thrill of driving on sand. She jumped into my Patrol before I had the chance to leave it. She gave me a kiss on the cheek and said, 'Good morning, lover.'

'Hi there,' I replied. 'Sorry if I kept you waiting.'

'It's already quite hot, isn't it?' she said. 'I heard on the radio it's supposed to reach thirty-three degrees today.'

'Perfect for a day at the beach,' I replied. 'Anyway, I hope you know where we're going.'

'I checked last night with the lads. They said we should go past Jebel Ali, and just after we pass a little settlement called Bandaq, we should turn right, off the road, and just keep going until we reach the coast.'

We sped off up the Sheikh Zayed Road. I maintained a steady speed of 120 kph, which was the official speed limit. The road was not very busy, but several cars overtook me, obviously doing well above the speed limit. I was surprised given that there were many speed cameras. But these speeding drivers just seemed to ignore them. I did notice one flash, so I decided not to break the law. Driving on a day like this was such a pleasure. The sky was clear and blue, and the sand looked dry, but bright. It was obviously hot outside, but with the air conditioning on, we were nice and cool inside the car. The occasional camel could be seen in the distance, grazing on the shrubs that grew in the sand. After we passed the Jebel Ali Port, the road narrowed from three to two lanes each way. The road was fairly straight, and it had a lovely smooth surface. It was easy to drive on, and it felt that we were just gliding along on it. We soon reached Bandaq, which seemed to consist of a row of apartment blocks with shops on the ground floor, a few small villas on the parallel road behind, and a couple of mosques.

When we had passed all the buildings of the settlement, I cautiously left the road. We drove on the sand with no difficulty, but we did seem to be on some sort of track. I tried to drive as gently and smoothly as possible, selecting the low 4WD gear ratio and avoiding over-revving the engine. In the distance, I could see that the track parted to form two different tracks. 'Which one?' I asked Shannon. 'Left or right?'

'I don't know,' she replied. 'You choose.' I decided to turn off to the left. I had to make a quick decision because I wanted to avoid having to stop, start or brake heavily; all things that I perceived could give me difficulties driving on the sand. As we continued to drive, the track became fainter and fainter, and the sand seemed to be getting softer and deeper. I was becoming concerned, but I didn't say anything to Shannon. 'This is cool, isn't it?' she said, full of enthusiasm.

'Mmm,' I replied, not revealing my true feelings of worry and concern. I maintained my slow, constant speed, but I wondered whether it was best to keep the steering wheel straight or to gently turn it from side to side. I looked in my rear view mirror. I could still see the buildings of Bandaq. That filled me with confidence. But ahead of me there was only sand, and some trees in the distance. We were now driving up a sand dune, which seemed to be getting steeper. Then, suddenly we were at the top. We could now see the sea, and the beach, and it did indeed look gorgeous. But I didn't have time to admire the view. We were at the top of a steep hill that led all the way down to the beach. I panicked and braked suddenly. I could feel the tyres digging into the sand. I knew that we had to drive down the hill head-on, to avoid rolling the vehicle, but that looked like a scary prospect. It would be like going down on a roller coaster.

'Go on Nick, you can do it,' said Shannon, trying to offer me encouragement. She now realised that I was nervous about driving this last bit. 'It's very steep,' I pointed out.

'Just keep the car straight, and we'll be okay,' she replied. 'Look, there are a couple of other cars down there. They obviously got down there alright.'

'They may have come another way,' I observed. The way the vehicle was balanced on the mound of sand on which I had stopped made it impossible to turn around and go back in the direction from which we had come. 'Okay. Hold on,' I said. I put the car into gear, released the handbrake and then the clutch gradually, and then put my foot on the accelerator. The wheels spun, but we did not move forward. I lowered my foot further on the accelerator. The engine revved up, but we still didn't move. I took my foot off the accelerator and reapplied the handbrake. 'I think we may be stuck,' I declared.

'Have another go,' suggested Shannon. I did, and it just felt that we were sinking deeper into the sand. 'We'll have to walk down to the beach and ask those other people for help or advice on what to do,' Shannon continued.

'Bloody great,' was all that I could think to say. Now I knew why I was in no hurry to go off-road driving. It's nothing but hassle. Maybe it was excitement for Shannon. But for me it was hassle. I just wanted a quiet day on the beach. As we started walking down the sand dune, the two vehicles on the beach drove off out of sight, and then did not return. 'That's it. Now we're on our own,' I said.

'Maybe we should try to push or lift the vehicle out of the sand,' suggested Shannon.

'I think it's too heavy for us two,' I replied. 'I think it would be better to try to dig the sand away from in front of each tyre. Try to make a sort of ramp, on which we can drive out.' We tried this, but the sand was warm and dry. As we removed some sand, more just fell into its place.

'I think we'll have to walk back to Bandaq and get help there,' I eventually suggested. I locked up the vehicle, and we set off back across the sand dune. It was not easy walking on the sand. With each step, one sort of sank into it. It was really hot now. The sun was shining down on us brightly. I was perspiring heavily and wished that we had brought some water with us. It took us about thirty minutes to get back to the main road. 'I think we should try to stop someone in a four-wheel drive vehicle,' I suggested. 'Hopefully they'll be able to tow us away from where we're stuck.'

We waited on the main highway, trying to wave down drivers in four-wheel drives. We only tried to stop westerners, however, and only those who looked like they might be the types to stop and help. In the first hour, we must have tried to wave down four or five vehicles, but none of them stopped. I don't know whether they thought we were hitchhiking or whether they realised we were in trouble. Unfortunately, being a Friday, the shops were all closed, so we couldn't ask for help there. Also, there was no one out on foot to ask for help. We tried to wave down several more vehicles, but no one stopped. 'I'm sorry I suggested this trip,' said Shannon.

'So am I,' I answered snappily. I was now so hot, and my clothes were completely wet with my perspiration, that I was in quite a bad mood.

Eventually, after what seemed like at least two or three hours, a vehicle, which we had not attempted to wave down, stopped. A boy of about eighteen years of age looked out of the passenger window of the Land Cruiser and asked, 'Are you all right?'

'Actually we're stuck in the sand dunes back there,' I answered, gesturing back towards the coast.

'Would you like some help?' the boy asked.

'If you could help us, that would be very kind of you,' I replied.

'Jump in then,' said the boy, gesturing with his head to the rear door. We jumped into the Land Cruiser. It was a top specification model, just like Jas's. The driver also looked about eighteen, or perhaps twenty years of age. They were local boys, but spoke good English. 'You were trying to get down to the beach?' the driver asked.

'Yes,' I replied.

'That's quite tricky,' he continued. 'But not so difficult if you know the best way to go.' I gave the driver directions to my vehicle. When we got there, the driver reversed his vehicle to my car's rear. He got out some towing rope and fastened it to the two vehicles. 'Release your handbrake and leave your gear in neutral,' the driver said. 'I will then try to pull you away from the ridge. Then, I will come to the front of your vehicle and turn you right around. Okay?'

'Thank you very much,' I replied. Ten minutes later, my Patrol was free of the sand and facing the right way for the main road. I shook hands with the boys and thanked them for their help. 'No problem,' they replied. They then drove back across the sand with confidence and great speed. When they reached the main road, they waited in their vehicle for a while, possibly to make sure we got off the sand all right.

As we too approached the main road, they sounded their horn and each gave us a wave out of their window, before continuing on their journey. 'What nice lads,' I said. 'See, we tried to ask expatriates for help and they ignored us. But these local boys, who we did not try to ask for help, stopped and gave it to us.'

'Praise to Islam,' replied Shannon. I then drove back to my place, and we spent the rest of the day lounging about in my garden.

Mad May

*A*fter that off-road trip, I didn't see Shannon for a couple of weeks. She did not call me and I did not call her. I guess I remained a bit annoyed with her for suggesting the trip that got us stuck in the sand dunes near Bandaq. On the first day of May, I started work proper for the Deira National Bank. Its head office was located in Bani Yas Square, in the heart of Deira. Bani Yas Square was the original centre of Dubai, where the first shops were located. Now it was surrounded by small, independent retailers selling mainly textiles or electrical items, several older hotels, used mainly by traders from the countries of the old Soviet Union, or from Africa, and apartment blocks, which generally looked old and run-down.

By international standards, the Deira National Bank (DNB) was a very small bank, but with eighteen branches and over a thousand employees, it was actually the third largest in the UAE. On my first day, I reported to Jane Ellison, who was the Head of Human Resources. She was a smart lady, probably in her late forties and she originally came from Manchester. We discussed my brief. Basically, she only repeated what Mike had already told me. She advised me that some of the bank's directors were very concerned that employing more nationals would lead to increased costs, reduced profits, reduced standards of customer service and reduced operational performance. My task was to develop solutions that would satisfy the bank and the nationals who took up employment with the bank, and which would have a positive effect on profitability and performance. Jane assured me that this was going to be no easy task.

My working pattern was much the same at the DNB as it had been at Al Saadha-Wasel, that is to say I worked Saturday to Wednesday at the DNB's premises, and occasionally had a half-day at the JBNC office. But most of the senior managers at DNB also worked on Thursday mornings, and they soon made it clear that they expected to see me there too. So, I also worked a half-day on most Thursdays. The bank's head office is in a built up area of the city. They did not offer me a parking space anywhere, so I had to park in a public car park each day on the other side of the square. It was a good five-minute walk to cross the square, and as the days got hotter and hotter, the walk got more unpleasant. It was not very pleasant arriving at work feeling hot and sweaty, and with damp clothes, only to walk into air-conditioned rooms that were noticeably on the chilly side.

The journey to work to get to Bani Yas Square took considerably longer than to get to the Al Saadha-Wasel office, which was located off a road heading out of town. Sometimes, the journey to work took over forty minutes, as the traffic often slowed to a snail's pace shortly before reaching Bani Yas Square. The journeys home were only slightly better. The afternoon traffic in Dubai is always slightly lighter than the morning traffic, because the office workers' journeys home are more spread out. Some people work split shifts, typically with a break between one o' clock and four or five o' clock, while others leave at any time between four and six. To make matters worse still, there were road works on Al Maktoum Road, a street I had to go along to get to the car park. The road works started at a big junction. Each morning, different lanes of the road were closed, and it was chaos.

On one particular morning, the traffic lights at the junction were not working, and several policemen on foot were controlling the traffic. As I approached the junction, I needed to make a left turn, and, as traffic in Dubai drives on the right, this meant that I had to cut across the lanes of traffic coming in the opposite direction of both the road I was on and the road I wanted to be on, the Al Maktoum Road. It was a bright, already hot morning, and the traffic had been even busier than usual. I was already late for work. As I approached the junction, the traffic was chaos, as usual. Every driver seemed to be trying to change lanes, and despite the presence of the policemen, the cars in the middle of the junction were in gridlock, unable to move.

As I was about to enter the junction there was one policeman right in front of me, seemingly indicating that I should continue. However, I saw a second policeman in the centre of the junction who seemed to be telling me to wait. The road ahead looked blocked, so I waited. The policeman nearest me tapped on my windscreen, and made a hand movement that indicated I should continue moving ahead. So, I did, but no sooner did I start to move forward I saw the other policeman standing in the middle of the junction looking very angry with me. I continued to the centre of the junction, and made my left turn into Al Maktoum Street. As I turned, this second policeman gave up his position at the centre of the junction, and walked towards me. He indicated that I should pull over. I pulled over at the kerb and wound down my window. 'Turn your engine off and put on your hazard lights,' the policeman said. I did as I was asked. I was now blocking one of the three lanes going in my direction, and causing even more chaos and congestion behind me. Angry drivers started sounding their horns. 'Get out of the car,' the policeman then demanded. Again I did as I was asked. 'Can I see your driving licence and car registration?' he continued. I leant back into the car and got them out of the glove compartment. The policeman took them from me and looked at them. He then said something into his radio, in Arabic. There was a pause of a minute or so, and then a reply came back over the radio. 'What were you doing?' the policeman asked me.

'What do you mean?' I replied.

'Did you not see me telling you to wait?'

'Well yes, but...'

'Then why did you enter the junction?' he asked. 'Don't you respect policemen in England?' I thought that he was trying to make a point of the fact that he recognised from my accent that I was English. 'Yes, but the other policeman was telling me to go on,' I continued.

'No he wasn't.'

'He was,' I insisted.

'But I was telling you to wait.' With that he took out a pad from his inside jacket pocket and started writing. He then tore off the sheet he had been writing on, and handed it to me. 'Five hundred dirham fine,' he said smugly.

'What for?' I asked.

'Failure to comply with a traffic policeman's instructions.' He then started walking around my car, looking at it in great detail. He looked at all my lights, and crouched down to inspect my tyres. 'Car is dirty,' he finally said.

'Yes, it's surprising how dirty they get with the sand blowing around,' I replied.

'You must wash it,' the policeman continued.

'I do. I did. Only three or four days ago.'

'Not enough,' said the policemen. He started writing in his pad again and then handed me a second sheet. 'What is this?' I asked.

'Second five hundred dirham fine for dirty car,' he replied.

'You've got to be kidding,' I laughed.

'You may go now. Pay fines at traffic department office within seven days.' And then the policeman just strode off and returned to his position at the centre of the junction. When I got to my DNB office, Jane entered soon after. I apologised for being late and told her what had happened to me. She just shrugged her shoulders and said, 'These things just happen out here. But I'm sure similar things happen in the UK too.'

'I just got over a hundred and sixty pounds worth of fines and I did nothing wrong,' I replied. 'And that would never happen in the UK!' Jane left my office quickly without saying anything more. Jas was working out at the airport now, and he was loving it. And Baron was enjoying himself at a small tech firm, located in the Internet City. I wondered why it was that I got the bum assignment. Was it because I had mentioned the Astoria Hotel at Mike's barbie, thus indicating that I knew about him and Inga, and now he wanted to punish me?

I eventually tired of waiting for Shannon to call me, so I called her. 'I was wondering whether you would ever want to see me again after last time,' she joked.

'Of course I do,' I replied. We then chatted for a while, about nothing of any great interest, and then I asked when I was going to see her again. She responded by telling me how busy she was, and she then recited details about a great number of her 'chores'.

'Okay, okay, I've got the message,' I finally said.

'I'll call you,' were her last words to me. I waited, day after day, but Shannon did not call me. I did not call her either. 'Two can play that game' is what I thought. Instead, I started visiting hotel bars again in the evenings, in an attempt to see if I could catch Shannon cheating on me.

One evening, towards the end of May, I went to the Capitol Hotel. One of its bars was giving away free alcohol to women. I entered the bar, and it was pretty full. Whilst standing still, not far from the entrance, I scanned the place quickly, but did not see Shannon or any of her friends. I decided that I would stay for a beer, so I made my way over to the bar. As I went towards the bar, a group of girls sat over to my left started giving me wolf whistles. 'Come on over 'ere darlin',' one of them called out in a working-class London accent. I glanced over. There were about half a dozen girls, aged in the low twenties, and, despite it not being very late, they already seemed quite intoxicated. It was only to be expected I considered if bars such as these were going to give girls free booze every night. I ignored those girls and placed my order at the bar.

When I got my drink, I began to walk around the bar, which was actually quite large. Then, sitting in a dark corner, I saw her! Shannon was there with Sinead and Shannon, and a group of other people that included both females and males. Shannon sat next to a young man with spiky blond hair. He had a hand on her lap and was talking away, while she just sat there listening. Occasionally, she said something, something which usually got a laugh out of him. I watched them, through the crowds, for quite a while. No one saw me. As I watched, my anger built and built inside me. Suddenly, I could no longer stop myself from storming over to the corner where Shannon sat. 'Hello darling,' I shouted out. 'I thought you weren't allowed off campus during the week. And who is this lover boy?'

'Don't tell me this is diamond man,' said the spiky-haired blond. He then laughed out loud as he removed his hand from Shannon's leg. 'That's right, you jerk. You take your hand off my girlfriend,' I shouted loudly.

'Take it easy, old chap,' the young man replied as he rose to his feet.

'Sit down, Mark,' pleaded Shannon. And then I let Mark have it. I threw my beer into his face. It was a brilliant feeling. He looked like a sad, half-drowned rat in the gutter. He clenched his fists and thrust forward towards me, but his male friends got hold of him and held him back. 'He's not worth it,' I heard one of the group saying to Mark. I saw tears in Shannon's eyes. 'You can keep her if you want her,' I said as I turned and walked away. 'I don't want her, the two-timing bitch.' As I continued walking out of the bar, I heard Shannon call after me, 'You've got it all wrong, Nick. We only came out tonight because it was Mark's birthday.' I did not turn around again, but kept walking out of the bar. Once outside in the street, I felt much better, as if a heavy weight had been taken off my shoulders.

Enjoying the single life again

I did not see or speak to Shannon for several weeks after that incident at the Capitol Hotel. I didn't miss her very much either. I kept myself busy, with work for the DNB, by working out and relaxing at the Pharaohs' Club, and by having regular nights out with Jas, Baron and other male colleagues from JBNC. I tried not to think about the last thing I heard Shannon say at the Capitol Hotel, about it only being Mark's birthday. I realised that, perhaps, Shannon had not been cheating on me, and if she hadn't, then I had acted very unreasonably.

One morning, as Jas and I were eating breakfast at home, he suddenly pointed to an Etisilat phone bill on the table, which I knew had been lying there for at least a couple of weeks. 'One of us had better see to that,' said Jas.

'I'll go after work,' I offered. I thought that it was only fair given that Jas had gone to pay all of the previous utility bills. I had simply paid my half of each bill to him afterwards. 'You know where to go?' Jas enquired.

'No, not really,' I replied.

'Their office is on the first floor in the Al Khaleej Centre,' said Jas. 'You know, on Al Mankhool Road, opposite the Spinneys supermarket. We passed it when we walked to Al Faheidi Street on our first day in Dubai. There's a McDonald's on the ground floor.'

'Oh yes. I know where you mean now. Consider the job done,' I said, confirming my intention to pay the bill that afternoon.

I left work at five-thirty that afternoon. I drove to the Al Khaleej Centre and found the Etisilat office without any problem. Etisilat is the state's national telecom company. I was pleased to find on arrival, that they stayed open until eight o' clock. There was a long row of counters, perhaps fifteen in all, but a sign above the desks indicated that only the last three were handling bill payments. It was not clear what the staff at all the other counters were doing. Presumably, they were handling things such as new accounts, account closures, and connection problems. There was a long queue leading to the bill payment counters. At least twenty men were in front of me. I joined the queue, hoping that it might not take too long to get to the counter. However, after about fifteen minutes I had seen only three or four people leave the bill payments counter. It was annoying to see that staff elsewhere in the office sat idle with nothing to do. This was not a good example of management, I thought. I then realised that women did not have to queue. As a woman entered the office, the doorman ushered her to the front of the queue in which I was standing. That was one reason why we were making such slow progress. Another reason I soon noticed was that many of the men in the queue were not holding just one telephone bill; instead, they held many! They were obviously settling the bills of businesses, seemingly including some very big ones.

An hour later, there were only four people in front of me. I noticed that most of the staff in the office seemed to be moving in slow motion. The ones on the bill payment counters seemed completely oblivious to the long queue in front of them. One of them, a young man, even stopped working in order to talk on the phone. By his laid-back posture, the tone of his voice and his constant laughing, I would have guessed that it was a social not a work-related call. All of the employees seemed to be nationals, except the doorman, who was a middle-aged Asian man dressed in a smart uniform that could easily have been a policeman's. I wondered if that could have been the main reason that the whole place seemed so inefficient. The staff looked so bored and uninterested, and there was no sign of any supervisor or manager monitoring what was going on.

When it was my turn to be served, I found myself face to face with the young man who had been on the telephone. I wanted to say something to him about it, but I managed to restrain myself from that course of action. Still, he was a miserable sod, this young man. He snatched the bill from my hand without so much as a smile or greeting, or even eye contact. 'I can't go through that again,' I began, in what I thought was a pleasantly reasonable tone. 'Can't I set up a direct debit or something to settle future bills?'

'No, we don't do direct debits,' replied mister miserable.

'Then perhaps I could send a cheque somewhere?' I continued.

'You must pay here,' mister miserable snapped.

'You mean that the only way I can settle my phone bill is by queuing here for over an hour every month.'

'Correct,' the man snapped again.

'And I thought this was a modern country,' I said sarcastically. 'I thought you were supposed to be smart and progressive.' Someone tapped me on the shoulder. I looked around. It was an older man, of Middle Eastern appearance, who was the next person in the queue. He held a finger in front of his lips, indicating, I thought, that it might be best for me to shut up. I smiled at the man and took his advice. When I got home, I moaned to Jas about the queue and the bad customer service. 'It's always the same,' he replied.

'And you never even mentioned it to me,' I said.

'What would have been the point?' was his response. Again, I had evidence that this was a really top guy. He must have already paid five bills, and he did so without any fuss and without making any comment about the hassle involved. Sometimes I wished that I could have been more like Jas; the ability to stay calm and just take everything in my stride would have been a really nice quality to possess.

One of my favourite nights out was always to the DIMC for 'the grind'. I just loved the atmosphere out there. It was always so peaceful and relaxing, just what one needed before starting a new working week. I usually went with Jas and Baron, and sometimes a few other chaps from the JBNC office came as well. During the previous few weeks we all had to hear constant stories from Baron about his problems with Rebecca. A few days after she had stayed over at his place she had called him declaring her love for him. He avoided seeing her, but she called him every night at home. When he stopped answering the phone at home, she started calling him at work during the day. We were all surprised that she had been able to track him down to the small tech firm where he was working. She even waited outside the office one afternoon until he had finished work. He apologised to her, apparently, and said that what had happened between them was a mistake.

Rebecca was now going around town telling anyone who would listen that Baron was a user, who deliberately got her drunk and then took advantage of her. But that was not all. Baron had received abusive and threatening letters from her in the post, and one morning he set off for work to find his car covered in spray cream with the word 'wanker' written across the roof. 'This is fatal attraction all over again,' was one of Baron's favourite lines. I think that somehow he got some perverted sense of satisfaction from the whole situation. On this particular night at 'the grind', Baron gave us an update on the 'Rebecca saga', by telling us all that had happened during the previous week. 'Let's just hope that she never follows me here,' he laughed, 'because that really would cramp my style.'

On each occasion we went 'grinding' we were getting closer to summer. Now that it was June, it was very warm, even at night. If there was any wind, it was warm not cool. The warmer it got, the less the girls wore, which was great. On one night, almost half of the girls were wearing bikinis or swimwear, and many people danced, or swam, in the pool. We boys were all wearing our swimming shorts. I felt reasonably pleased with my body, and I walked about the place with confidence. My body was quite well toned as a result of my regular workouts at the gym of the Pharaohs' club, and its golden colour must have added to its attraction. I felt the gaze of many female eyes upon me, and now that I was single again, I felt free to enjoy myself.

I got talking to a group of girls who were nurses at the American Hospital in Dubai. They were mostly British however, though some were obviously from America or Canada and Australia or New Zealand. One girl said she was from South Africa. So, basically, this little group of beauties were from every English speaking country around the world. And it seemed that they knew how to have fun and enjoy themselves. They were dancing, chatting, swimming and drinking, but without actually getting drunk. Baron walked past this group of girls and me at some point during the evening and he gave me a sly smile. 'Nurses,' I said softly in his ear.

'Well, you know what they say about nurses?' he replied. 'Get on in there!' But he carried on walking, and a while later I saw him with his own group of girls, though on average, mine were nicer! Jas and some of the other lads were chatting within a large mixed gender group on the opposite side of the pool from where I was. That's what us guys from JBNC were like at 'the grind'; we didn't go around holding hands all evening, instead we each went off and did our own thing. But if one of us couldn't find anyone of interest to pursue, then it was okay to link up again with one of the gang.

I found myself talking to Michelle, a big-busted brunette from somewhere in South Wales, more than any of the other girls. She was pleasant enough but she was not exactly my type. She could have been good looking but she spoilt herself with two facial piercings. She had a ring through one of her eyebrows and a stud earring on top of her mouth, between the upper lip and nose. She also had at least two tattoos. I must be a bit old fashioned and traditional because I do not like girls with either piercings that are not in the ear or tattoos, and both, unfortunately, seemed to be highly fashionable at the time. Nevertheless, I tried to disregard what I did not like about Michelle, and concentrated on the rest, which was pretty good. She was tall, slim, well tanned and she had a pretty face with a fine bone structure and nice eyes, nose and mouth. An attractive face is important to me. It is, after all, what you have to see close up when you're kissing (I often like to kiss with my eyes open, as do many men) and when you wake up first thing in the morning (if you have been that lucky). She had an extrovert personality and plenty to say, although most of what she had to say didn't particularly demonstrate a high level of intelligence or education. But none of this was of great concern to me. I didn't want to marry the girl after all, just have some fun. At the end of the night, Michelle wrote her phone number on a little scrap of paper, and invited me to call her some time. As it happens, I mislaid that little piece of paper so I never did call her. I wasn't too concerned however, as my attitude at the time was that there were plenty more fish in the sea. I didn't ever see Michelle again at 'the grind', or indeed anywhere else.

A few nights later, Jas came home from work and announced that he was going out again as he had, as he put it, 'a hot date'. He didn't tell me much about her, except that her name was Heidi, she was German, she was attractive, she was about our age and she worked for Deutsche Bank. He had several dates with her that week and the next, but he didn't bring her home. 'Why don't you bring Heidi back here?' I asked Jas one night.

'Because she is quality and I don't want any misunderstandings,' was his reply.

'Fair enough,' was mine. But one evening, at about six-thirty, Jas did return home from work with Heidi. He introduced Heidi and me to each other. 'Pleased to meet you at last,' I said.

'Likewise,' she replied, in a very soft German accent. She was dressed in a smart business suit. I assumed that she had come straight from work. She bore an uncanny resemblance to Claudia Schiffer, the German supermodel. 'You don't have a sister called Claudia?' I asked jovially.

'No,' she answered. 'But a lot of people do ask me that.'

'We're not stopping long,' said Jas. 'We've got a seven-thirty reservation at the Chinese restaurant at the Metropolitan Hotel.'

'No problem,' I replied.

'Would you like tea or coffee?' Jas asked Heidi. 'Or you could have a beer.'

'Tea would be nice,' she answered. 'With milk and two sugars.'

'I'll go and make them,' I offered. 'Are you having tea as well?' I asked Jas.

'Yes please,' he replied. 'That'll be great if you don't mind making them.' I went to the kitchen and made the tea. Ten minutes later I returned to the living room to find Jas and Heidi sitting snugly together on the settee. It was rather hot and humid in the room. Sunil, the lettings negotiator, had not been entirely truthful about the effectiveness of our air conditioning units. Even with all of them on, our thermometer usually showed a temperature above twenty-five degrees.

I served the tea, and sat on one of the two armchairs. 'It's a nice place you've got here,' said Heidi.

'We thought so until this hot weather came along,' replied Jas.

'But it must be nice to have so much space and a nice garden like that,' Heidi continued. 'I live in an apartment. It's not really as nice.'

'So, what do you do for a living?' I asked Heidi.

'I work as an analyst for Deutsche Bank,' she replied.

'I didn't know they were in Dubai,' was my response.

'We only have a small office. We offer banking services only to a handful of high-worth people, mainly German nationals. But we're looking into the possibility of launching a Gulf-based investment fund, and that's what I'm working on.'

'I worked on the flotation of the Al Saadha-Wasel Trading Company,' I said.

'How interesting. Well, actually, that is the type of company we have been looking at.'

'So what do you think are the prospects for the Dubai stock market?'

'In the long term it should do well, but in the short term it will be greatly influenced by the global economy and global stock market levels. It could also suffer if political instability in the region increased. Another war involving Iraq or a big terrorist attack could result in a major setback for the local stock market.'

'Yes, it seems like a bit of a risky investment to me.'

'All stock market investing is risky. Its just a matter of degree of risk,' continued Heidi. 'For many Middle Eastern investors the Dubai market is considerably less risky than their own domestic market.'

'Yes, I suppose so,' I added, in agreement. Jas was staying silent, allowing me to chat freely with Heidi, which I thought was very gentlemanly of him.

'What are you up to tonight?' Heidi then asked me.

'Just relaxing in front of the tele,' I replied.

'You could join us for dinner,' she said, and then turning to Jas, 'That would be alright wouldn't it?'

'Sure mate,' said Jas. 'You're welcome to join us if you fancy some Chinese.' I thought about it for a moment. I really wanted to go, to get out of our hot, humid home, but I thought it wouldn't be very fair on Jas for me to play the gooseberry. 'It's very kind of you both to invite me along for dinner,' I replied, 'but I think I'll take a rain check on this occasion. I'm a bit tired really, but I do look forward to going out with you on another day.'

'You're sure that you can't be tempted?' asked Jas.

'No thanks,' I stubbornly insisted.

At about eleven o' clock, as I was getting ready for bed, there was suddenly a knock on the door. My first thought was that Jas had forgotten his front door key. I quickly put on my dressing gown, and then made my way to the front door. I opened it to reveal two policemen standing there. 'Mister Nicholas Williams?' one of them asked.

'That's me,' I replied.

'Would you please come with us to the police station to help us with our enquiries?'

'What's this all about?' I asked. 'Can't it wait until tomorrow?'

'Better to get it over with now,' replied one of the policemen. 'Go and get dressed.' I went into my bedroom to get dressed while the policemen waited outside in the hallway. When I was ready, they drove me to a police station, which was not far from the Gold Souk, I think. Once inside the police station, I was led into an interview room. We all sat down, and one of the policemen, the older, more senior one I assumed, took out a pen and pad of paper from a drawer under the table. He then opened the covers of the folder he had been carrying, revealing sheets of handwritten and typed Arabic. 'Mister Nicholas,' began the policeman with the pen and pad, 'we have had a complaint from a taxi driver that on the evening of the nineteenth of March earlier this year you overtook him and then stopped, forcing him to also stop on the Al Khaleej Road just before reaching the Al Shindagha Tunnel from the Bur Dubai Side. He then claims that you got out of your vehicle, verbally abused and physically assaulted him causing actual bodily harm.' For a moment I was speechless, although I knew immediately what he was talking about; it was the incident that occurred on the evening I had taken Shannon to the Gold Souk. 'That was three months ago, ' I inappropriately blurted out. 'When did the taxi driver make this complaint?'

'That does not matter,' replied the policeman. 'These are very serious allegations. If we receive a complaint about an assault, which results in injury to the body, we *will* investigate the matter. Always!'

'Do you confess to the charge of physical assault?' asked the second, younger policeman.

'No I don't,' I replied. 'The whole incident has been described out of context.'

'Then tell us your version Mister Nicholas,' said the older policeman, who got ready to write notes as I spoke.

'On the evening in question I drove from my home in Jumeirah to the Gold Souk area. I had a passenger, who was my girlfriend at the time.'

'What was her name?'

'Shannon...er...er...Connolly, that's it. Shannon Connolly. She's a teacher at the Jebel Ali British School, and she lives on campus.'

'Carry on with what happened on the night in question.'

'We drove past Port Rashid and came to the roundabout which has several roads leading into it.'

'The Al Saqr Roundabout?'

'I don't know its name. Anyway, it's the one immediately before the Al Shindagha Tunnel.'

'Carry on.'

'I was just going along at a normal speed, the same as all the vehicles in front and behind me, when suddenly the taxi in question came in front of me at great speed from one of the roads on my right.'

'Did you go through a red traffic light?'

'No. Definitely not. But maybe the taxi driver did.'

'So what happened when he came in front of you?'

'I had to do an emergency stop to avoid hitting him. And that caused injury and considerable pain to Shannon. You know, burn from the seatbelt.'

'So what did you do?'

'I flashed my headlight and sounded my horn.'

'Why?'

'I don't know. Perhaps to let the taxi driver see how dangerously close behind him I was.'

'Then what happened?'

'I could see the taxi driver waving his arms about. I thought that perhaps he was doing a rude hand gesture. I thought that was inappropriate and decided that I needed to speak to him. So, I overtook him, and then as you said earlier, I forced him to stop behind me. I only wanted to talk to him, and actually, my main objective was to take down his car registration number so that *I* could report *him* to the police.'

'And did you report him to the police?'

'No, in the end I didn't.'

'No, you couldn't after you had physically assaulted and injured the old man.'

'I didn't assault him. He tried to assault me. He just went for me when I started writing down his number. He told me to stop writing, and when I didn't, he tried to force me to stop.'

'So how did he get his injuries?'

'What injuries? I didn't see any injuries. As far as I am concerned, I didn't give him any injuries.'

'So how did he get them then?'

'I don't know. All I know is that he came for me, we had a bit of a push and shove, and he ended up falling down. I didn't punch him or kick him, or anything like that!'

'Well, your record of events is quite different from the details provided by the complainant. Who are we to believe?'

'You can believe who you want. But I'm telling the truth,' I said, almost shouting now as my anger reached boiling point.

'Calm down, Mister Nicholas,' said the older policeman. 'Just calm right down. Now put yourself in our position. Would you believe the man who comes to the police station of his own accord to make a statement or the one who does not, even though he says he wanted to?'

'Where is the taxi driver now?' I asked. 'Bring him here now and then let him try to tell his lies to my face.'

'That will not be possible,' replied the older policeman, as he continued busily making notes in his pad. 'He has returned to Pakistan.'

'When is he coming back?' I asked. The older policeman shrugged his shoulders and said, 'Perhaps never.'

'Then what is the point of all this? Why am I here?'

'We are investigating a complaint, as we already told you!'

'If you want to know the truth, then speak to Shannon,' I blurted out without thinking. The moment I mentioned Shannon's name I regretted it. Would her testimony exonerate or crucify me? I remembered then that Shannon seemed to have thought on that evening that I was rather too hard on the taxi driver. And after what happened at the Capitol Hotel, she might be in no mood to do me any favours. 'Indeed we might interview Miss Sharon Connolly,' replied the older policemen.

'No, not Sharon Connolly,' I corrected him. 'Her name is

181

Shannon. No r, but two n's in the middle. *Shannon* Connolly.'

'Okay. I've got it down correctly now,' said the older policeman. The two policemen then spent a couple of minutes talking to each other in Arabic. They then went to the door, and the younger one said, 'Please come.'

They led me to a cell, with nothing in it but a concrete shelf to sit or lie on. The cell didn't even have a window. 'Wait in here,' said the younger policeman. 'We go to speak with the Chief.' And then the door to the cell was closed. It was horrible in there; it was dark, hot, smelly and dirty. The only things that I could hear were a few voices in the distance, speaking in Arabic, and the faint sound of vehicles passing on the street outside. I wondered how long I was going to be in the cell. I looked at my watch. It was twenty past one in the morning. Many thoughts went through my head. Would they, for example, be going to get Shannon in the middle of the night? If not, did that mean I was staying until morning? Would Jas realise that I wasn't at home? If he did, what would he do? What if I wasn't released in the morning, how would I explain my absence at the DNB? I sat upright, determined for some reason not to fall asleep.

Eventually, I heard footsteps in the corridor outside, coming in my direction. I glanced at my watch. It was now quarter to four in the morning. The cell door opened and the same two policemen who had collected me from my home and then interviewed me were stood there. The older one entered the cell while the younger one stayed by the door. The older one came and stood right over me. He looked very serious. 'You are very lucky, Mister Nicholas. The Chief, on this occasion, has decided not to take the matter any further than a warning. I think, Mister Nicholas, however, that perhaps you have a bit of a temper. You must learn to keep that under control. Remember that we now have your details on our files, and if you get into any kind of trouble in the future, the penalty next time will be much more severe.'

'Understood, Sir. Thank you, Sir,' I replied, trying to sound humbled. The policeman responded with a small smile, and then said, 'Come, we will take you back home now.'

Saying sorry

*O*n the following Friday, Jas didn't go to play golf as he normally did; instead he went with Heidi to the beach. I stayed at home and sat reading under the trees in our garden. When Jas and Heidi came back late in the afternoon, she went into our kitchen and prepared vegetable and potato salads, which we all ate with frankfurter sausages and mustard. It was a refreshing and tasty meal to eat on a hot day. After we had finished eating, Jas announced that he and Heidi were going to the Uptown Cocktail Bar at the Jumeirah Beach Hotel for 'sundowners'. He invited me to join them, and I gratefully accepted the invitation.

Jas drove us to the hotel, and upon arrival, we took one of the lifts up to the twenty-fourth floor. We went to the bar and studied the cocktails list. The mature Filipino bartender, in his pristine white shirt and black bow tie, waited patiently for our order. 'I think I'll have a Pina Colada,' Heidi said to the bartender, and then to us, 'That's one of my favourites. And you can't usually go wrong with those.'

'I'll have the same please, barman,' said Jas.

'Me too,' I added.

'So, three Pina Coladas in total,' confirmed the bartender. 'Please take a seat and I'll bring them over to you.'

'Do you want to stay inside or go out?' Jas asked.

'It seems silly coming to this bar and not going outside,' replied Heidi. 'What do you think, Nick?'

'Outside is fine by me,' I replied. The inside of the bar was much like any other, except it had floor to ceiling windows, which, being on the twenty-fourth floor, obviously offered attractive views. However, all the seats by the windows were already taken. We stepped outside onto the terrace. It was still a bit humid, but it was no longer as hot as it had been during the day. We took a table at the edge of the terrace, so that we were right up against the railing that surrounded it. We had a spectacular view, looking up the coast in a north-easterly direction.

A few people were still on the beach below. We could see all of Jumeirah, including the Jumeirah Sailing Club, the Beach Park, Safa Park, the shopping malls on the Beach Road, and we could even work out exactly where our villa was. If we looked over to our right, we could see the skyscrapers that lined the Sheikh Zayed Road. 'The city looks so big and impressive from up here,' said Heidi.

'Yes, when you look at the city from up here, you're reminded just how big it is,' I agreed. 'And we're really only looking at one tiny part of it.'

'It puts me in a holiday mood being up here,' said Jas. 'Looking down at all those villas, all painted white, with their flat roofs and palm filled gardens. You know that you're somewhere tropical.'

The bartender came out with our drinks and two bowls of complimentary snacks, one filled with mixed nuts and the other with salty biscuits. We thanked him, and he then advised us that the 'happy hour' was finishing in ten minutes and that if we ordered our next drinks there and then, they would be half price. 'That sounds like an offer too good to miss,' replied Jas. We passed around the drinks list. Jas ordered a *Tequila Sunrise*, I ordered a *Hurricane Carolyne*, although I didn't really have time to take in all that was in it, and Heidi, to my surprise, ordered a *Screaming Orgasm*. 'What's in *that*?' asked Jas, as the bartender left us.

'Kahlua, that's coffee liquor I think, Irish cream, amaretto and vodka,' she replied. We sipped our Pina Coladas. For me they had the perfect mix of rum, pineapple juice and coconut cream. They were cool and refreshing, but not too sweet. As I glanced around the terrace trying to soak in the relaxing atmosphere, which I was sure was having a therapeutic benefit on my stress levels, I saw Shannon, Sinead and Rebecca coming out from the bar, each holding a cocktail. They took a table on the other side of the terrace. None of them had seen me, but I suddenly felt very uncomfortable. What should I do? What course of action would minimize the risk of another scene? With Sinead there to stoke the fire, I might not get off lightly. Jas also saw what I had seen. He looked at me and shrugged his shoulders. 'Is everything alright?' asked Heidi.

'My ex-girlfriend is over there,' I replied. 'And we didn't really finish on good terms. My fault really.'

'You want to go and clear things up?' said Heidi. I wasn't sure if she said it as a question or a suggestion. 'I think that I should,' I replied.

I got up slowly and made my way over to their table. 'Good luck,' Jas called after me. As I approached their table, Rebecca saw me first.

She obviously told the others. Sinead was already facing my direction, and I could see the look of hatred on her face. Shannon turned around to look at me. I could not read the expression on her face. 'Please, Shannon, may I have a quick word with you inside?' I said.

'Tell him to piss off,' said Sinead, but Shannon rose to her feet and replied, 'A quick word only.' I led her into the bar. We remained standing quite close to the terrace door. 'I want to apologise for my behaviour at the Capitol,' I began. 'I know that I was completely out of order.'

'Yes you were,' replied Shannon. 'You made yourself look like a fool and you made me look like a fool. And all over nothing. We were only having a night out to celebrate a colleague's birthday. I really have nothing more I want to say to you.'

'Do you accept my apology?' I asked.

'Yes, all right,' she replied. 'If it will make you feel any better.'

'I don't usually behave like that,' I continued. 'Not with any previous girlfriends, and never in a public place like that. Living in Dubai has changed me. I can't explain really, but I feel somehow insecure. I feel like I have to be enjoying myself every minute of the day because I perceive that is what everyone else is doing.'

'That's silly,' replied Shannon sympathetically. 'I understand that you don't have the support of your close friends and family over here, and it often feels that there are more hours in the day than you know what to do with, but trust me Nick, we are all in the same boat. That's why everyone has to convince themselves and everyone around them that they're having a good time and enjoying life in Dubai. It's a defence mechanism.'

'I suppose,' I said, 'Anyway, I'm really sorry for what happened. Maybe I'll see you around one day.'

'Maybe,' she replied. And then we went back outside and parted.

When I returned to my table, my *Hurricane Carolyne* was waiting for me. I took a sip. It was rather too sweet for my taste. 'Cor, that's sweet,' I said.

'Everything okay?' enquired Jas.

'Yes, everything is fine,' I replied. Heidi was looking at the drinks list. 'It would be sweet,' she said. 'Its made with dark rum, light rum, Malibu, orange juice and cranberry juice.'

'I didn't think,' I replied, 'but it's nice enough'. All I wanted at that moment was to leave that terrace, and leave the memory of 'that night' at the Capitol Hotel well behind me. Jas realised this, and as soon as we had all finished our drinks, he suggested that we leave. The sun had just set over the ocean, painting the sky a pretty shade of reddish-orange, which was reflected on the ripples of the sea. The street lights had come on, and from the terrace Jumeirah looked like a criss-cross of orange and white lights.

The next morning when I stepped out of the house, it was like having a hair dryer blow hot air onto my face. There was a strong wind, and it was surprisingly warm. My Patrol was covered in condensation, caused by the humidity. When I got into the car, its thermometer indicated that the temperature was thirty-two degrees. This was the summer in Dubai that all expats dreaded. It was only on the beach that one didn't notice the heat and humidity. I thought that this was very strange, but it was true: on the beach, the climate seemed just perfect. When I got to work, I went to see Jane to discuss a few matters. She told me that she had fixed up a few interviews for me with young nationals who were already working for the bank. She said that it should be useful for me to ascertain their original motivations for joining the bank, to discover whether they thought their expectations and personal objectives had been fulfilled, what they thought was good and bad about working for the bank and any other relevant issues. The nationals had been asked to speak freely and they were assured that I would keep anything they said confidential. 'I doubt that it will make any difference however,' said Jane. 'I think they'll probably just tell you whatever they believe you want to hear. They're a very diplomatic people. Maybe one or two will have a bit of a whinge. We'll see. But I thought it was worth a try.'

My first interview was with a young lady called Miriam. She was a credit control supervisor. We met in my office. I wondered whether or not I should close the office door; close it in order to maintain Miriam's privacy and encourage her to talk, or not close it, because she was a female, and I was a male, a western male at that, and in her culture it was unusual for a female to be alone with a non-family male. I decided that the best thing to do was to ask her what she wanted. 'You can close it,' replied Miriam. We exchanged greetings, and Miriam offered a hand for shaking. 'I am very pleased to meet you,' I began. 'Jane, I hope, briefed you on what I am doing for the Deira National Bank.'

'Yes, I understand,' she replied.

'The bank wants to devise new ways of attracting nationals into the bank and we want to learn about your experiences and feelings,' I continued. 'Not only do we want to recruit more nationals, we want them to be satisfied, to grow and develop with the company, and of course to serve the company well.'

'I understand.'

'Perhaps you want to start by telling me something about yourself, perhaps about your education, why you chose to work for the bank, what you think about your job and the bank as an employer in general.'

'I am from Al Ain. That is where my family live,' Miriam began. 'I went to school in Al Ain and then to the UAE University, where I got a bachelor's degree in Business Administration. I enjoyed the accounting and finance parts of my programme and thought that maybe a career in banking would suit me. So, I applied to join the Graduate Training Programme, and I was offered a position. I had hoped to be working in Al Ain. I was told that was possible when I applied for the job, but I have been based here in Dubai for two years now. I travel from Al Ain every day, and that is probably the thing that makes me most unhappy. Not unhappy exactly, just tired. It makes me very tired. I end up spending most of the weekend sleeping!'

'It is a long way to travel each day,' I agreed. 'How long does it take you?'

'Usually, about one and a quarter hours each way,' replied Miriam. 'But it can take a bit longer if the traffic is bad, like during the shopping festival.'

'But otherwise, how do you find your job and working for the bank?' I continued.

'I enjoy the work. It is not too difficult, but it takes a lot of concentration and it can be quite stressful at times. The problem is that the people here don't really understand the concept of credit. More than a quarter of our loan book is in arrears, and possibly ten per cent will be written off as bad debts this year. The locals are the worst. They borrow, borrow, borrow, but they do not repay. And the bank does not resort to court action because many of the judges still believe that our business goes against Islamic principles. I was, however, very pleased to be made a supervisor after one year. I am the youngest supervisor in the department.'

'You obviously worked well, and showed senior management that you could do the job.'

'Yes. I worked very hard. I wanted the management to be pleased with me.'

'And where do you see yourself in, say, five years' time?'

'I hope that I will be the manager of the whole department,' she giggled.

187

'And why not?' I added by way of encouragement.

'Only I hope that I can transfer to the Al Ain office, or that my family move to Dubai.'

'Is it a possibility that your family could do that?'

'It's possible, but not very likely.'

'Is there anything else you can tell me?' I asked.

'Not really,' answered Miriam. 'Everything is good. I am happy here. If it would be helpful, I could go to the UAE University and give a talk to the students to tell them more about working in a bank. I think that many of them do not apply for jobs with banks because they fear that they will end up in a branch, working as a teller.'

'That's a good idea,' I said encouragingly. 'You could, perhaps, visit all of the universities as the ambassador of the Deira National Bank.' Miriam smiled. She seemed like a very nice person. She was friendly, bright, hard working, determined, well mannered, and she spoke very good English, except that she did that rolling of the 'r', which all of the locals seemed to do. She was, of course, wrapped in her black abbaya, so I couldn't see much of her. All I could see was her face, and that was very attractive. She was obviously quite slim. I wondered when and how her family would marry her off. Would she have any say on the matter? What if she fell in love? Worse still, what would happen if she fell in love with a westerner? I had heard many stories, even met a few local men who had married western women, and often non-Muslim women at that, but never heard of a local woman marrying a western man. I really did find the local women mysterious and intriguing.

My second interview was with a twenty-five year old man called Nasser. He had graduated from the Higher Colleges of Technology, and he was married with two children, both boys, which he told me with great pride and obvious self-satisfaction. He was already a manager in the credit card division. He was a pleasant young man, very out-going and friendly, and he too spoke excellent English, but he didn't really want to talk about what we were supposed to be talking about. He made statements such as, 'My aim is to develop innovative solutions to make DNB's credit card the most desired and successful in the Emirates, in order to help ensure a solid future for the bank both in the Emirates and, hopefully, throughout the Gulf region in terms of increasing market share, increasing its number of branches and geographical coverage, diversification into the full range of financial services through organic growth and possibly horizontal or vertical integration, increasing customer satisfaction through improved and unrivalled standards of customer service, all to increase overall profitability and return to the shareholder.' That sounded like it all came straight from his business degree, but obviously his heart was in the right place. And he had a clear vision for the bank, which even some of its directors may not have had. But did this mean that Nasser would be suitable as a director? Who knows? Maybe yes, maybe no. One day, perhaps Nasser would gain a position on the Board of Directors.

I didn't have to ask Nasser any questions. He just talked and talked. 'I love this bank and I love my job,' he said at one point. 'But I do not work for money. I could get three or four times more working for my father's company. If a person enjoys banking then this is okay, but if the person doesn't really enjoy the job and doesn't need the money, then it's a problem. Do you understand me, Mister Nick?'

'Yes, I think so,' I replied.

'Many of my friends think I am silly working so hard and such long hours every day. They ask me, "Nasser, are you mad? Why do you do it?" and I tell them, "It keeps me alive, it provides me with challenge and interest in my life", but they don't understand. Many of them come from rich families. They don't *need* to work. They will only work if the job is easy, if it has a very good title, which must include 'director' or at least 'manager', if the working hours are not too long, and preferably flexible, and if there are many subordinates to delegate to. Of course, the bank does not want to employ them on those conditions, and that is why the bank still does not employ many nationals. And, of course, the others hate us: the Indians, Pakistanis, Filipinos, even the Egyptians and Lebanese. They see us nationals joining the bank, taking the best jobs and getting fast promotions, and they are envious. Many will do anything to help us fail in our positions. This is hassle many nationals also do not want.'

'I never thought of that, I must admit,' I said.

'But I am a positive person,' Nasser continued. 'I am happy and content with my life, and I thank Allah in my prayers five times a day. Allah has made this country great and I have everything I could possibly wish for: good health, a good wife, two beautiful boys, my parents and other relatives, a nice home, a job I enjoy and all the material things that I could wish for or need. When I was married, we received from the state, a piece of land on which to build a home and also money towards building it. We have free education, free health care, free utility services and we pay no taxes on our income.'

'Indeed, you are very lucky,' I replied. 'As a foreigner in this country, it really does seem to me that nationals have everything they could need or reasonably desire.'

'We are lucky that Allah gave us Sheikh Zayed as the country's president, as he has led it wisely since its foundation in 1971,' said Nasser. 'And Sheikh Maktoum too, as the ruler of Dubai. They have both used the wealth generated from our oil and gas resources to benefit the people of this country. They did not build big, luxurious palaces for themselves or spend it all on jewels or frivolous things like that. Instead they invested it in building the country's infrastructure: its roads, schools, universities, hospitals, electricity generation and water desalination plants, telecommunications and housing. In under thirty years, they turned the UAE from an underdeveloped nation of nomads in the desert to one of the world's richest, most modern and most dynamic countries.'

'That was rapid progress,' I agreed.

'Just look at all the big international companies that are rushing into the country to set up in the development zones that are being established,' Nasser continued. 'All that is Sheikh Zayed's vision.'

'I do understand why nationals seem to respect the Sheikh almost like God,' I said, rather foolishly I immediately recognized.

'No, not like God,' Nasser corrected me. 'Only God is like God. But we have deep respect for our Sheikhs as our wise and faithful rulers who have brought us peace, prosperity and respect.'

'That came out wrong,' I said, trying to defend my silly comment. 'I only meant to comment on the great respect you display for your Sheikhs by having their pictures on the walls of every shop, bank and office. And the way your media reports every day on where the Sheikhs have been, what they have done or who has visited them.'

'That is our tradition,' replied Nasser. 'You have your Queen's portrait on your coins and banknotes, and on your postage stamps. That is your tradition. We have ours.'

I spent the rest of the day interviewing a number of other young nationals working for the bank. I found what they had to say both fascinating and useful. When I had finished work, I was not in the mood for driving straight home, so I decided to stroll down to the creek, which was only a five-minute walk away. The walk to the creek wasn't particularly pleasant in the hot and humid conditions, but I really did feel that I needed to stretch my legs, and I didn't feel like going to the gym for a workout. In fact, since the hot and humid weather started, I generally felt rather tired and lethargic in the evenings and thus abandoned my routine of regular visits to the gym.

And that, I suspect, led me on to the spiral of increasing tiredness and lethargy. As any regular gym goer might confirm, working out usually makes one feel fitter, more alive and energetic, and less, not more tired.

I walked to Beniyas Road, the dual carriageway that runs alongside the creek on the Deira side of the city. To get to the creek's edge I had to take the pedestrian subway that passed under the road. It was busy, with people bustling hurriedly in all directions. In the middle of the subway sat an old woman, perhaps aged sixty or seventy with a girl, probably aged less than one as she was not yet walking. Perhaps the child was her grandchild or great grandchild. The woman held her hand out at the people passing by, but she looked at the ground. This was the first beggar I had noticed in Dubai. I wondered where she had come from and why she was begging. As I walked towards the old woman, it seemed that every third or fourth person that passed her, put their hands in their pockets and gave her some coins. There were two things that struck me as curious about the 'transactions'. First, most of the givers looked like the poorest type of workers that one sees in Dubai. Their clothes were old and torn, and their shoes had holes in them. If people gave to this woman so readily, she could probably make in a day what those poor workers made in a month. And second, the woman showed no sign of gratitude or recognition each time she received some money. As I came up on the other side of the road, I could not stop thinking about what I had just seen. And then, suddenly, I got it. In England, the person who gives to a beggar expects thanks, or at least a nod of the head or a glance of recognition. In England, the giver gives not for the beggar but for themselves. The giver feels self-satisfaction that they have been generous and done something good. In Dubai, however, the giver does not even attempt to gain eye contact with the recipient. They do not want or expect thanks or gratitude. They are simply fulfilling their obligation as a good Muslim, for one of the five pillars of Islam, the 'rules' that all Muslims follow, is to give alms to the needy. It was now clear to me that those poor workers believed that the beggar was even more needy than they themselves for the coins that were given. Having worked all this out by myself, I could not stop thinking about the concept of charity and its role in religion. It led me to think about and evaluate my own beliefs and behaviour, not only with regard to charity, but also every other aspect of my life as a member of the human race who wished to be considered 'good'.

I looked down on the abra landing stages. The wooden boats were arriving and leaving, with passengers hurriedly rushing on and off. I watched the busy activity for a while, debating whether or not I too should cross the creek, just for the ride, and to come straight back. I decided, in the end, to leave it until another day. Instead, I continued walking down the creek side and past the big wooden dhows that were tied up there. Two dhows were sailing down the creek, probably heading for destinations further up the Arabian Gulf, or perhaps they were going to India, Pakistan or East Africa. A flock of seagulls followed overhead, even though the boats had no fish, or indeed anything else to eat; instead, they were likely to be carrying car tyres or electrical goods such as televisions or washing machines.

I walked past a number of modern, but very distinctive and remarkable modern buildings. First, I passed the Inter-Continental Hotel, one of Dubai's older hotels, but still one of the few to command a position right on the creek side. Then I came to the Etisilat Tower, with its giant globe at the top, which is particularly striking when illuminated at night. Moments later I passed the Sheraton Hotel, the offices of the Department of Economic Development and the headquarters of the National Bank of Dubai. This tall, thin building is shaped like the letter 'D'. Its bronze coloured windows sparkled in the sun and reflected all the activity on the creek below. Then, finally, I came to the offices of the Dubai Chamber of Commerce and Industry. This is a triangular-shaped building composed solely of blue glass. Each building I passed had a unique design. They were made with different materials, including bricks, concrete, steel and glass, creating buildings of all shapes and sizes, and using many different colours. It would have been paradise for any student of modern architecture. Dubai proved that modern architecture didn't have to mean boring, repetitive or unoriginal. After admiring the buildings for a while, I walked back to the car park where my car was, and then drove home.

Stood up

A few days later I got home from work and Jas was already in the kitchen fixing us both some dinner. 'Have a nice day?' he asked.

'Yes, a nice hot one,' I replied.

'You know, Sheba had to go home for something at lunchtime. She said that the thermometer on her balcony was showing fifty-three degrees. But I've just been listening to the radio and they reported that today's high was forty-eight degrees.'

'Haven't you noticed,' I said, 'that the official temperature never goes above forty-nine degrees? There must be some rule or something that if the temperature reaches fifty degrees then all workers are entitled to stop work. That would explain it!'

'Maybe that's it!' agreed Jas.

'Do you remember what we're supposed to be doing tonight?' I asked Jas.

'No.'

'Baron was supposed to be taking us to see one of his favourite bands at the Country Club. *Seven Shades of Grey* I think they were called.'

'But we haven't got tickets.'

'Baron said we'd get them on the door,' I replied. 'He said that as they're not a really big band, there's no way the gig would be sold out.'

'To be honest, Nick,' said Jas, 'I'm not really in the mood for it tonight. And Baron hasn't been in touch, has he?'

'I'll give him a ring,' I replied. 'I'd go if he's still up for it.' I checked my *What's On* guide to make sure that I had the right date. My memory had served me well. The gig was that night, and the doors opened at eight. *Seven Shades of Grey* weren't likely to get on until nine or nine-thirty however, because there was a support band on stage first. I thought, therefore, that it probably wouldn't matter to Baron if we got to the Country Club a bit late. I dialled Baron's number and waited for him to pick up the receiver, but he did not. 'No answer,' I said, more to myself than to Jas.

'Maybe he's still not home from work,' suggested Jas. 'Or perhaps he's in the shower getting ready.' I decided to go and have a shower myself, and then I dressed in only a tee shirt, shorts and sandals. I tried phoning Baron a second time, but again there was no reply. 'I think I'll just call round at Baron's home and see what's happening,' I said. 'Are you sure that you can't be tempted to a night out?' I hoped that whilst I had taken my shower Jas had changed his mind about staying in, but 'No thanks mate,' was his final reply. So, I left him at home alone.

I drove to Baron's apartment, and parked in one of the spaces under the building, which was built on stilts. The parking spaces were supposed to be for residents only, but I told myself that as I was only going to be there for five minutes, it wasn't a very serious offence. I took the lift up to Baron's apartment and knocked on the door. I waited for a while, and was just about to knock again when I heard Baron call out 'I'm coming' from inside the apartment. He opened the door wearing only a pair of boxer shorts. 'Hi there Nick, what are you doing here?' he said.

'Have you forgotten?' I replied. 'We were supposed to be going to see one of *your* favourite bands tonight.'

'Oh lord!' said Baron. 'Is that tonight? I thought it was next week.'

'I've just checked the *What's On* guide, and it's definitely tonight,' I continued. 'So are you still up for it or what?' Suddenly, I heard a female voice from behind Baron. 'Who's that?' she asked. I thought that I recognised the voice, and then I saw who it was. Standing behind Baron, barefoot and seemingly wearing only a silk dressing gown was Shannon. 'You bitch!' I shouted at her. 'What are you doing here?' Baron pushed me further out into the corridor, and pulled the door almost shut behind him. 'You bastard!' I said to Baron. 'What are you doing with my girlfriend? Or do you normally like to have a go after your mates?'

'I was under the impression that you two had finished,' replied Baron. 'At least, that's what Shannon told me.'

'But we had made up,' I explained. 'We were on the verge of getting back together.'

'Then what is she doing here?' asked Baron. That was a good point, for which I had no answer. 'It's just another name to add to your list, isn't it?' I continued. 'But why did you have to pick her?'

'Believe me Nick,' said Baron, 'it was she who did all the chasing.'

'*She* chased you, even after she saw how you treated Rebecca? Incredible!'

'Women are!' said Baron. 'But don't stress yourself bud, there are plenty more fish in the sea.'

'I don't want the other fish in the sea,' I replied. 'I wanted Shannon.'

'Then how come you were collecting phone numbers at the grind?' said Baron. 'Don't be a hypocrite, man!'

'If you're talking about Michelle,' I replied, 'I was just talking to her and I never called her.'

'Whatever,' said Baron, suddenly seeming very bored with our conversation. 'Look, Nick, just go home and cool off. You and Shannon were obviously not meant to be. So, just move on with your life.' I didn't say anything more. I just turned and walked down the corridor, back to the lifts.

I was no longer in the mood to go and see *Seven Shades of Grey*, or to return home, so I drove down to the creek. I stopped on the Bur Dubai side, opposite the Dubai Chamber of Commerce and Industry. Despite the heat and humidity, there were plenty of people about. There were young people, old people, single people, couples and families all walking along the promenade. People were jogging, children were playing football or riding bicycles, and a big group of people were even doing fitness exercises together. Much of this activity occurred on the grassed areas that lay between the road and the promenade.

I just strolled along the promenade, admiring the creek and the floodlit buildings on the opposite side. The globe on top of the Etisilat Tower looked like a hundred stars shining in the sky in the shape of a circle. I watched all the people I passed. Everyone seemed happy and content with their lives, even the other single people that walked or sat alone. Why then did I feel that there was something missing in my life? I stopped at a café on the promenade and ordered a couple of shawarmas, one chicken and one lamb. I washed them down with a freshly made fruit juice and a small bottle of still mineral water. Most of the people at the café seemed to be Arab nationals. Many of the men smoked shisha. The scent created in the air was sweet and pleasant. I was tempted to order a water pipe for myself, but I finally decided against it. Instead, I just sat there for a while, watching the world go by. Occasionally, the sound of people talking and laughing was drowned out by the noisy engine of an abra as it passed on the creek.

Summer alone

August is the month when half of Dubai's population seems to pack up and go elsewhere. Many of the expatriates return home during the month, and many of the locals decide to go anywhere where the temperature might be a few degrees lower than Dubai. Some go to other countries in the Middle East, while others prefer destinations in the Far East, Europe or North America. Many seem to go to London, Paris, Australia or the United States. A large number have second homes or relatives in these countries, while the others stay in five star hotels or rent apartments. Some areas of Dubai can seem like a ghost town during August, especially during the day. The roads become quiet, with traffic jams unknown, and many shopkeepers and restaurateurs don't bother to open during the day.

Jane Ellison, at the Deira National Bank, asked me if I would wait until September before taking any leave. I didn't feel that I was in any position not to comply with her request, so I agreed. Jas, however, went back to England for the last three weeks of August. Mike and his family went back to the States, and even Baron, who had come out to the UAE well after Jas and me, went back home for a couple of weeks. I hadn't, however, seen or spoken to Baron since the evening I found Shannon at his apartment. August was quite a lonely month for me. During the times that I had gone to pubs, clubs and parties with Baron, I thought that I had built up a large social circle. But night after night I called those people listed in my address book, and found that they were either out of the country, or too busy or too tired to see me. Some said they were busy doing work-related things while others said they had prior arrangements, not just for that night or the next, but for every night of the week. No one, however, invited me out. It quickly became clear to me that I had many acquaintances in Dubai, but very few friends.

It was torture sitting around at home in the heat, with mainly repeats and cheap American programmes being shown on the television. It was not much more pleasant being outdoors. Sometimes, the humidity was so high, that one felt wet the moment one stepped outside. The windows at home would be covered in condensation, and so would the car outside. I started reading a lot. That offered me some distraction from my suffering, but only for short periods of time. Weekends, which I normally looked forward to all through the working week, became something I dreaded. From June onwards, I usually went either to the beach or to the Pharaohs' Club at the weekends. At either location, I usually lay on a deckchair reading under a tree. The heat and humidity were more bearable at these locations. It was slightly cooler at the beach, where one sometimes got a breeze, but at the club I had access to quality food and both soft and alcoholic beverages. So, my choice of destination depended primarily on the exact weather conditions on any particular day, and whether or not I wanted to eat or drink. When visiting either place, I also swam. I liked swimming in the sea. The sea has no boundaries and I could swim out far, feeling free. Also, I found that the salty water had a positive effect on my skin, rather than the chlorined water of the swimming pool. But the pool was temperature controlled, while the sea was about the same temperature as a warm bath. It was not refreshing at all!

The beaches in Dubai are particularly interesting places. They attract such a diversity of people, all acting and enjoying themselves in very different ways. Europeans walked about in the skimpiest of swimwear trying to be sexy or fashionable, and with the intention of getting as much tan as possible. Arab women, and other Muslim females, in contrast, often stayed fully clothed. They stayed sheltered from the sun under parasols or trees. Occasionally, these women ventured into the sea, but still fully clothed. Their husbands, however, wore traditional western swimming trunks or shorts, and their children usually wore swimwear too.

Labourers from the Indian subcontinent usually swam in the underwear they wore all day. They usually stripped down from their normal clothes by the water's edge and then just rushed into the sea. The labourers liked to swim, sit, lie or stand close to wherever there were females, and particularly white females. Western girls wearing G-string knickers were unlikely to get any peace away from such men. If girls were dressed provocatively, then the lifeguards usually did not intervene, but for 'respectable' girls like Shannon, they would usher the men away and threaten to expel them from the beach if they returned to bother the girls. It seemed to me, however, that many of the females in G-string swimwear enjoyed the attention they got from the men, even if it was from poor Asian labourers. Topless sunbathing was not very common, although some girls did go without bikini tops. It was strange seeing such girls on the same stretch of beach as women who stayed fully clothed. Men and children often played games like beach volleyball or football, or they threw Frisbees or boomerangs around. Families often brought a portable barbecue onto the beach, although this was not allowed at the beach parks.

On one occasion, I was walking along the beach at the Jumeirah Beach Park when I saw a dead shark lying in the sand. To me, it looked undoubtedly like a shark. It had a streamlined body with a pointed snout, round, black, lifeless eyes, a row of distinctive gill slits, two dorsal fins, with the first one being considerably larger and of the shape made famous in the *Jaws* films, and a tailfin with a longer upper lobe. It was about two feet long; small enough to swim up close to the shore among the bathers, but probably big enough to bite a chunk out of someone's leg. I thought that I had better report my sighting to the lifeguard, so I walked back to the lifeguard tower. The Filipino lifeguard came down when he saw that I wanted to talk to him. 'I think there's a dead shark on the beach,' I began.

'Yes, I've already reported it,' the lifeguard replied. 'Someone should come along soon to take it away.'

'It is a shark then?' I asked with curiosity.

'Yes, I think it's a reef shark,' replied the lifeguard.

'Are there many sharks in these waters?' I continued.

'Yes. There are at least ten different species of shark in the Arabian Gulf. Just up the coast in Sharjah they land and process tonnes of shark every year. They catch them mainly for their fins. You know, the Japanese will pay one hundred dollars for a good bowl of shark fin soup, so it's big business. But even if you go to small harbours all around the UAE you can often see rows of shark fins hanging out to dry.'

'But are they dangerous?' I asked.

'Most of the varieties in the Gulf are not thought to be dangerous to man,' the lifeguard replied, 'but the Tiger Shark has been known to attack swimmers, surfers or divers. However, there has been no record of any shark attack in the UAE for at least thirty years.'

'And before that?'

'Rumour has it that in the olden days, the men that dived for pearls were occasionally the victims of shark attacks. But, really, the sharks are probably making swimming safer for you. They feed on the sea snakes, poisonous jellyfish and stingrays.'

'I see,' I replied, although I was not wholly convinced about the benefits of having sharks swimming nearby.

Then, suddenly, the lifeguard rushed to the water's edge and started energetically blowing on his whistle. He started jumping up and down, and gestured with his arms to four Indian men who were swimming far out from the beach that they should come in closer. 'Fools,' he said to me. 'Why must they swim so far out?' Then he continued blowing his whistle and waving his arms around. I must confess that even though I am not a particularly strong swimmer, I do enjoy swimming far out from the beach. Sometimes, when I was out there, I thought that I heard the lifeguard's whistle, but with the wind carrying sounds away and the waves obscuring my view of the beach, it was hard enough to see the lifeguard at all let alone work out if he was blowing his whistle at me.

I must admit, that on this day, the sea did look very choppy further out. It was a hot day, but the wind was quite strong. The lifeguard looked through his binoculars at the men. 'They're taking no notice of me', he replied. He was quite worked up, but it made him look quite comical. He was such a small man. He was muscular and looked strong enough, but when we stood side by side he came up only to the level of my shoulders. I wondered how he would cope with rescuing a big European or American man in rough seas. The lifeguard was probably quite a good catch for a Filipino girl, however, with his toned bronze body, long black hair and sexy red shorts. He returned to the water's edge and blew his whistle. Then, he looked through his binoculars again. I walked off down the beach a little way and then spread out my towel on the sand. I sat on my towel, watching the lifeguard and wondering why he was getting so excited.

A moment later, the lifeguard was in the sea, swimming quickly to where the four men had been swimming. Now I could see only three. The lifeguard swam through the waves, with his red plastic buoyancy aid trailing along behind him on a towline. I stood up to see better what was happening. I could no longer see the missing swimmer or the lifeguard, only the red buoyancy aid bobbing up and down on the surface of the sea. Then, eventually the red blob of the buoyancy aid looked like it was coming closer to the shore again. The lifeguard was pulling the swimmer through the water on his back. When they got to the shoreline, the lifeguard dragged the man a few metres up onto the sand. He turned the man onto his side. The man spluttered and water came from his mouth. The lifeguard stood over the man, just watching, but not saying anything. A crowd had gathered around. 'Please leave us,' the lifeguard pleaded, but the crowd was slow to disperse. I returned to my towel, which was just nearby, so I was happy that I wouldn't miss any more of the action while not obviously seeming nosey.

The rescued swimmer looked as if he was recovering. He eventually sat up. His friends looked more anxious and worried than he did. 'What happened?' asked the lifeguard.

'I don't know,' replied the man. 'I was swimming okay, and then I just froze, and found myself being pulled under the water. It seemed as if there was some kind of undercurrent pulling me down.'

'Did you not hear my whistle and see me indicating to you to swim closer to the beach?' continued the lifeguard.

'No,' replied the man. I noticed that at no time did the man either thank or apologise to the lifeguard, who had potentially risked his own life to make the rescue. The lifeguard said he needed to record the details of the incident, and he wrote down on some paper the man's name, address, nationality and employer.

On working day evenings, when I could no longer bear being in the hot, stuffy villa on my own with nothing decent to watch on the television, I did what many residents in Dubai seemed to do: I went to a shopping mall. Shopping malls offered a temperature-controlled environment. Their air conditioning systems provided a coolness that many people couldn't achieve in their homes. It was obvious that many people went to the malls just to walk around or sit in the seating provided and that they had no intention of actually buying anything. At the end of each night, large numbers of people left the shopping malls carrying no shopping bags at all.

One of my favourite malls was the *City Centre* mall in Deira. That was the largest shopping centre in Dubai. It had over three hundred shops, including many of the big international chains, such as Debenhams, JC Penney, IKEA, Woolworths (the South African chain, not the British one) and Carrefour, the French hypermarket chain. The branch of Carrefour at *City Centre* was the largest food store in the Emirates. It was very popular and always very busy, too busy in my opinion. In fact, when in Oman, Shannon and I had got talking to an Omani man at the hotel who had for several years driven to Dubai once a month to do all of his main food shopping at Carrefour. He then had to drive back to Oman at two hundred kilometres an hour, so that he got home before his frozen food had defrosted too much.

In addition to its shops, *City Centre* also had a multi screen cinema, a food court and a hotel, which had restaurants and bars available to the 'shoppers'. I went to the cinema quite a few times. In Dubai, there was no stigma attached to going to the cinema alone. It was a common occurrence, especially among expatriate men living and working in the country without their families. I enjoyed going to the cinema, but I generally found the shops in Dubai boring. They seemed to lack the variety that one found in other countries. They all seemed to be selling the same things: clothes, bags, perfume, jewellery or electrical goods. There is, in my opinion, only so much perfume one can buy, and one really only needs one watch, camera or mobile phone!

I passed a lot of my time in the malls just sitting and watching the people around me. It was fun watching the tourists rushing about, hoping not to miss any 'bargains'. Then there were the families from the Indian subcontinent, who just walked around all night, passing me every twenty or thirty minutes during their circular tours of the mall. And there were locals, of course, moving about slowly and elegantly, the men in their white dishdashas and the women in their black abbayas. Some went as couples, or families accompanied by their children and a nanny, but it was also common to see single-gender groups of locals of all ages. Groups of young local males often stood about ogling the female tourists and occasionally they would try to 'chat them up'. I found it fascinating to watch the local women however. They may have been wrapped from head to toe, but their femininity could not be hidden. The shapely female form of the girls was still obvious, and the lack of visible skin made them no less alluring. It seemed that a pretty face with nice eyes and lips, a couple of hands and forearms of smooth, olive skin, and the hint of long, slim, shapely legs was enough to set the imagination running wild. I thought that western girls could learn a thing or two from the locals; for example, that it was not necessary to wear boob tubes and hot pants or micro skirts to look sexy or seductive. I understood, however, why many local men preferred their wives and sisters to stay at home, rather than them going out and attracting the attention of men who might lead them astray.

'Treating myself'

*O*n the Thursday evening after Jas had left to return to England for his summer break, I decided to pay a visit to the Storm Club. I don't know whether it was because I hadn't had sex for over three months and felt the need to release myself or whether it was just because I was bored with walking around shopping malls. Anyway, I had a shower, splashed on some aftershave and dressed in some smart, but lightweight clothes. I didn't go to the club with the intention of leaving with a girl, but I thought it might be a possibility. Rather, I just wanted to go somewhere lively and with loud music, where I could get merrily sloshed. For this reason I went to the club by taxi. I knew that things didn't get lively until after midnight, so I left my home at eleven, even though it only took twenty minutes to get there.

Once inside the club, it didn't take long for the girls to start swarming around me. They could obviously smell the money in my wallet. I chatted to some, but I didn't buy them any drinks despite their asking, and I hoped that my casual attitude made it clear that I was not there to do business. The girls didn't stay around me for long once I refused to open my wallet for their benefit. I bought myself several beers, however, and suddenly the world seemed a better place. Whenever I went to the bar to get a drink, I lost my seat and then had to find another. At twelve-thirty, I returned from the bar to the seating area to find no spare seats. So, I had to stand. I walked around, mingling among the crowds, and as I passed around the edge of the dance floor, I watched the dancers waving their arms about over their heads. Everyone seemed to be at the club for some specific reason. Some men came simply to get out of the house and have some fun, some came to socialise with their mates, some came to get drunk, and some, of course, came for sex. And why were the women there? Money, money, money and that's all. Why was I there? I didn't know.

Maybe I was the one person who had no clear reason for being there.

By a quarter to two, fifteen minutes before closing time, the girls who were left in the club were increasingly worried that they were not going to get any business that night. They were busy approaching any man that they felt might possibly become a customer. I had drunk at least seven or eight pints and my mind was not thinking clearly at all. In fact, I doubt that I was able to walk in a straight line at that point in the evening. A stunningly beautiful Russian girl approached me and introduced herself as Galina. 'Would you like to have some fun tonight?' she asked.

'I don't know yet,' I replied teasingly.

'Your satisfaction is guaranteed,' continued Galina.

'How could I turn down an offer like that then?' I answered. 'How come a beautiful girl like you has not been taken yet?'

'Nobody wanted to pay my price,' replied Galina.

'You're expensive then?' I asked.

'If you want the best, you must be prepared to pay the best,' she answered.

'How much then?' I asked, more out of curiosity than as the start of the bargaining process.

'One thousand dirhams for the night,' said Galina.

'That *is* expensive,' I replied. I then casually looked away, in the direction of some other girls who were loitering close by.

'Don't play games,' pleaded Galina. 'How much do you want to pay then?'

'Five hundred,' I replied, not fully realising that I was striking a bargain that I was neither mentally or physically ready for.

'Okay,' she replied, and that was that. We took a taxi back to my villa. My home seemed to impress her. 'It's so nice in Jumeirah,' she said. By the time we got there, I was so tired that I would have paid Galina the five hundred dirhams just to leave me alone so that I could go to bed and then sleep, but she insisted that I fix us some drinks. She wanted a vodka with orange juice. I pretended to have the same, but my glass didn't have any vodka in it, only orange juice. When I took the drinks into the lounge, Galina was sitting comfortably on the settee. 'I'm hungry,' she said, as I passed her drink to her. 'Have you got anything to eat? Some nuts or biscuits would do.'

'I think we've got some little salty snacks,' I replied. 'Will they do?'

'That would be really nice,' she answered. I returned to the kitchen to find them. When I got back to the lounge, Galina had already drunk half of her drink. I must have looked a little surprised for she said, 'Sorry for not waiting for you. I was so thirsty.'

'Can I get you another before I sit down?' I asked. Galina nodded, gulped down the remainder of her drink and then handed me the empty glass. I went straight back to the kitchen to prepare her another drink. After I had given Galina her second drink, I sat on one of the armchairs. We chatted for a while, but I really can't remember what about. I remember my head feeling heavier and heavier, and it got harder and harder to keep my eyes open.

I woke at eleven-thirty the next morning on the settee in the lounge. I had obviously slept there. Had we not made it to the bedroom then? I couldn't remember. 'Galina, are you there?' I called out. I assumed that she was either in the bathroom, or perhaps in the kitchen getting something to eat, but there was no reply. 'Galina, are you there?' I repeated, a bit louder this time. Again, there was no reply. Eventually, I managed to get to my feet, and I walked around the villa. Galina had gone and everything looked normal. I returned to the lounge. The air in the room seemed stale and damp, and the smell of Galina's cigarettes lingered. I opened the french windows. The breeze that blew in was rather too warm to be refreshing, but it was better than having stale, motionless air in the room. I sat in the garden for a while, and then made some toast and tea for my breakfast, even though it was now well past midday. I felt pretty strange the whole day. I had no energy to do anything and I had a funny feeling in my stomach. I put it down to the excessive alcohol I had consumed the previous evening. I spent most of the day sleeping in the shade provided by the trees in our garden.

At some point later in the afternoon, it occurred to me that I hadn't paid Galina, or at least I didn't remember paying her. I went indoors to look for my wallet. I looked for it in the pockets of the trousers I had been wearing the previous evening, and I looked all around the house in all the usual places I normally put it down. It soon became clear to me that Galina must have taken it. I had paid the taxi driver, so I must have had the wallet with me when I came into the house. I tried to remember how much money I had in it, and concluded that it was probably over two thousand dirhams. She also had all of my credit and debit cards, my driving licence and my health insurance card. But what could I do? I could hardly go to the police and tell them that a prostitute I had taken into my home had robbed me. I would probably end up being arrested myself! I decided that I would just have to inform all of the relevant organisations that I had 'lost' my wallet, and request replacement cards. I feared, however, that getting a replacement driving licence in the UAE might be no easy task. Later in the evening it occurred to me that I could keep going to the Storm Club until I saw Galina there again. I later decided that with dozens of other nightclubs and bars she might also patronize, it might be a long time before I saw her again. And if I did see her, what could I do if she denied stealing my wallet?

The following day I was back at work at the Deira National Bank, and once I had notified those necessary about my 'lost' cards, I forgot all about my incident with Galina. I immersed myself in my work to distract me from the deficiencies in my life. In the evenings, I preferred to go out, rather than staying indoors, staring at the walls or watching boring television programmes. Most often I went for a walk along the beach or around some shopping mall, but sometimes I went to a bar for a drink. I didn't really enjoy going to pubs on my own, however, as I didn't particularly enjoy the superficial and forced conversations that I always ended up having with other people there on their own. Later in the week I discovered that Galina had also found and taken my 'emergency' cash, which I kept hidden under my clothes in a chest of drawers. I think that I had kept three or four thousand dirhams there. She had removed the cash without disturbing my clothes or moving anything else around in the room. It was as if she knew the money was there, but nobody did know about the money, not even Jas. Eventually, the weekend came, bringing another two days to be spent by the pool or at the beach. Despite the fact that I had seen less of Jas since he started dating Heidi, I remember going to bed on the Friday evening thinking about him and looking forward to his return the next weekend.

In the middle of the night, I was woken by some banging noises. I tried to ignore them and continue sleeping, but without success. I soon realised that there were people moving around outside my villa. They spoke to each other in Arabic. Then there was some more banging, and I realised that it was on my front door. I put on my dressing gown and went to see what all the commotion was about. I opened the door to see two policemen standing there. In the background were another two, one with an Alsatian dog. The man without the dog looked like he had been waiting by the back garden door. 'Come with us,' said one of the policemen in front of me.

'Why?' I asked. 'What's this all about?'

'Come,' is all that the policeman said again.

'Can I get dressed?' I asked.

'Quick,' he replied. I returned to my bedroom and the two policemen followed me. They watched me getting dressed. When I was dressed, one of the policemen said, 'Now give us your passport.' I got it out of my wardrobe and handed it to him. 'Now, stand facing wall, with hands on wall above head,' the policeman continued. I did as instructed. I felt my left arm being pulled back down behind my back and then handcuffed, and then the same thing happened to my right arm. My wrists were fastened tightly behind my back. Then I was pushed from behind towards the front door, and all the way into the back of a van. I heard my front door close behind me. Once inside the van, a black hood was placed over my head. I was in complete darkness and could no longer see anything. I knew that two of the policeman rode in the back of the van with me as they continued speaking in Arabic. I also knew that one of them was the dog handler, because I could hear the dog's heavy breathing. The journey didn't seem to take very long, perhaps ten minutes. I was bundled out of the van, still blindfolded, and pushed along into a building. I had no idea where I was. Eventually, the hood was pulled from my head, and I found myself alone in a concrete walled cell. The big iron door slammed shut behind me immediately the hood was removed from my head.

What did I do?

There was nothing in the cell at all, not even something to sit on. The cell had no window, but one bulb in the ceiling provided some dim light. I sat on the floor. I was very uncomfortable as I was still handcuffed. I began to speculate why I was in jail again. I guessed that probably the taxi driver who had complained about me had returned to the country. That was the only thing I could think of, except Jas and I not paying our municipality tax. All expatriates were supposed to pay a local tax equivalent to five per cent of their annual residential rent. We once received in the post a letter requesting the payment. I didn't know anything about the tax so I asked Mike about it. 'Just ignore it,' he said, 'No one ever pays it and nobody ever gets chased for it.' We never did get a reminder that demanded payment, but maybe I was now chosen as the person who would provide a warning to all other expatriates to pay their taxes.

I was not wearing my watch, so I was unable to keep track of time. It seemed like I was in the cell for many hours before anyone came to talk to me. My arms had gone numb, I needed to go to the toilet, and I was hungry and thirsty. Eventually, a guard came and opened the door. 'Sabah al khair,' he said, which I recognised as 'good morning', so I replied, 'Sabah al nur.' He beckoned that I should follow him. He led me down the corridor, which seemed to have about a dozen cells like the one I had been in. At the end of the corridor, we turned left and then entered the first room on our left. Two men were already there, sitting behind a table. They spoke to the guard in Arabic. The guard then removed my handcuffs. The older of the seated men, who seemed to be in charge, gestured that I should take a seat. As I did so, the guard who had brought me to the interrogation room left and shut the door behind him. 'Sabah al khair,' said the older man.

'Sabah al nur,' I replied. The man returned a small smile.

'Keef halek?' he continued. This I knew meant 'how are you?' I thought it would be best to stay polite, so I replied, 'Zayn, shukran,' which means 'fine, thanks'. The man then asked if I spoke Arabic. 'Tatakalam Arabiah?' he asked. I replied that I didn't. 'Ana la tet kalam al Arabiah,' I answered.

'But you just did!' he laughed. 'Then we have problem because my English not good. My colleague will translate what I ask.' And from that point on, the senior interrogator spoke only Arabic. He spoke, and then the junior officer translated his questions. I replied, and then the junior officer had to translate my answers. They started by asking me things such as my full name, my date and place of birth, my nationality, my religion, my employer's name and address and my home address. I was now desperate to go to the toilet. I didn't think I could hold it any longer.

'Please sir,' I asked. 'May I visit the toilet? And is there any chance of a glass of water?' Once my requests had been translated, the senior interrogator nodded in agreement. The junior officer led me to the toilet, which was at the end of the corridor. He waited outside. The toilet was not like a western one. It was more like a shower cubicle. There was no toilet seat, just a hole in the ground, and no sign of any paper, just a shower attachment. I did what I had to, and after washing my hands in a sink, returned to the corridor where the officer was waiting for me. We returned to the interrogation room. A plastic cup full of water was waiting for me on the table. I thanked them for it. 'Shukran,' I said, before drinking the water.

The senior officer then spoke at some length to the junior officer. Of course, I had no idea what was being said. 'The inspector says that you know why you're here,' said the junior officer, 'so can you please start telling us all about it?'

'I don't know why I'm here,' I insisted.

'Don't be stubborn, Mister Nicholas,' replied the detective. 'It will only make things worse.'

'Is this about the taxi driver?' I asked.

'You killed a taxi driver as well?'

'I haven't killed anyone.'

'But we think you have. In fact, we *know* you have.'

'Then please tell me, who am I supposed to have killed?'

'No, you tell us!' replied the detective.

'How can I tell you, if I don't know?' I pleaded.

'You will not leave here until you tell us!' was his reply. We carried on in this way for two or three hours, with the officer demanding that I start talking, and me answering that I didn't know what I was supposed to have done. I noticed that a clock on the wall showed the time as twenty past two. I began to feel very tired and weak. I hadn't slept in the cell. I tried to remember when I had last eaten anything. I had a bowl of cornflakes before I went to bed, but that meant I hadn't eaten anything for at least sixteen hours. The questioning continued, but we made no progress. The inspector began to lose his temper. He spoke to me sternly in Arabic and thumped on the table. 'I would help you sir,' I said, 'if I only knew what this was all about.'

Eventually, the inspector declared, 'We must go now for prayers. We will see you again later.' It seemed that the inspector could speak some English when he wanted to. The junior detective led me back to my cell. An hour or so later, the door opened, and a guard entered carrying a tray which he put on the floor. On the tray were a bowl containing rice, vegetables and meat mixed up, an orange and a plastic cup of water. The food wasn't very nice, but I was so hungry I ate it all. After having the orange, my hands were sticky. Not having access to any water, I had to wipe them on my shirt. I felt dirty and uncomfortable. It was incredibly hot in the cell, and there was no ventilation at all. I thought that if I had to spend another night in that cell, I might suffocate in my sleep due to the lack of oxygen. I lay on the floor and waited for the detectives to send for me again. I waited and waited, but no one came for me. Several hours later a guard returned with another tray. This time I received a vegetable curry, one slice of dry white bread with nothing on it and a glass of tea with sugar, but no milk. That is the way the Arabs drink their tea: sweet, but with no milk. The guard took away my lunch tray. 'Enjoy,' he said as he left my cell.

'Shukran,' I replied. An hour or so later the guard returned to collect my tray. 'May I please go to the toilet?' I asked. The guard nodded and gestured that I may leave the cell. There was a toilet a few cells down on the left. Only prisoners used this one. It was dirty and smelly, and the walls and floors were stained with faeces. Flies buzzed around my head merrily. I went to the sink afterwards to wash my hands, but no water came from the tap. The guard saw me standing at the sink, and said, 'Broken.' I was led back to my cell.

I spent a second night in the cell. The light was not turned off, however, but was left on all night. Despite being very tired, I was so hot and uncomfortable that I couldn't sleep much. As I lay on the floor, giant ants walked over me. I tossed and turned all night, trying to find a position that might be more comfortable, but I couldn't find one that I could bear for more than twenty minutes or so. In the morning, a guard brought me two pieces of bread with strawberry jam and a glass of tea, this time without milk or sugar. I wondered what the time was. I realised that I had made a big mistake not putting my watch on when I left home. It was really annoying not knowing the time. However, it might have been even more frustrating watching the minutes tick by. When the guard came to collect my tray, I asked him the time. He didn't understand me, and when I pointed at my wrist, he just walked out of the cell again.

Several hours later, I was taken to the same interrogation room that I had been questioned in the previous day, and it was the same two detectives waiting for me again. After we had exchanged greetings in Arabic, the inspector told me to sit down. 'I hope you have had enough time to think about your situation,' the junior detective began. 'The inspector will not have as much patience today.'

'Tell me who I'm accused of murdering and I'll tell you anything I know,' I offered, in an attempt to make some headway with the interrogation. The junior detective translated for the inspector what I had said. The inspector spoke a few sentences in Arabic to his assistant and then nodded his head. 'You are accused of murdering Miss Katerina Olegovna Bogdanova,' said the junior detective, 'and before you say anything, please know that we have much evidence to connect you with this woman.' I remained silent. I didn't know what evidence they could have to connect me with a woman that I had never heard of before. 'Well?' the detective said.

'To be honest, I don't recall having ever met a Katerina Ole... Whatever it was you just said.'

'That's very interesting, because she certainly knew you.'

'Can you tell me roughly how long ago I might have met her?' I asked.

'You certainly met her last weekend,' he replied, smiling.

'Is that when she was murdered?' I asked.

'You should know,' he replied.

'But I've already told you that I have never murdered anyone.'

'Mister Nicholas, please don't take us for fools. We have evidence.'

'I'm trying to think,' I pleaded. I tried to recall what I did the previous weekend. I had stayed at home the whole weekend, except for my visit to the Storm Club. That Katerina, whatever her name was, must have been someone I met at the Storm Club. 'The Storm Club,' I blurted out.

'You met Miss Katerina at the Storm Club?' said the detective, now looking pleased that we seemed to be making some progress.

'I don't recall meeting anyone by that name, but I spoke to many people,' I replied.

'What kind of people?'

'I spoke mainly to ladies. In fact, I spoke only to ladies. Quite a few as it happens. You see, all of my friends are out of the country at the moment.'

'That is very sad, but how did you know these ladies you spoke to?'

'I didn't know any of them. It was just casual chit-chat.'

'Chit-chat?' the detective repeated, raising one of his eyebrows.

'Yes, just talk about nothing really,' I said.

'Were you trying to proposition a woman for sex?'

'No. I just went there for a drink,' I said. 'I was feeling a bit down, and thought that a lively atmosphere might cheer me up a bit.'

'So, at what point in the evening did you meet Miss Katerina?'

'I already told you. I don't remember meeting a Miss Katerina.'

'But you did.'

'Maybe I did, but I don't remember because of the drink.'

'Maybe you killed her, but don't remember because of the drink.' I didn't reply. What could I say? 'Okay, Mister Nicholas,' the detective began. 'Tell us how Miss Katerina came to have one of your credit cards on her body when she was discovered. That was very careless of you!' I was now really confused. Had Galina given or sold one of my credit cards to this Miss Katerina? My mind was throwing around the few facts known to me, trying to fit together the pieces of the puzzle. 'Did you give Miss Katerina the credit card or did she steal it?' the detective asked.

'I didn't give it to her,' I replied.

'Then she stole it,' the detective concluded.

'Perhaps I lost it and then she found it,' I suggested.

'Perhaps. But is that the truth? I don't think so!'

There was a brief pause. The inspector started talking to his assistant. The junior detective replied, and a two-way conversation between the two of them then continued for several minutes. Then, the junior detective continued asking questions. His first one was a shocker: 'Why did you decide to dump Miss Katerina in a waste disposal bin?' he asked. 'You must have known that she would be found in such a place?'

'I didn't dump her anywhere!' I protested.

'You must have been very annoyed with her,' he continued. 'You must have really hated her to do what you did.'

'I didn't do anything to her,' I said.

'Perhaps you just don't remember doing it?' suggested the detective.

'My memory of that evening might be very hazy,' I began, 'but I would never kill anyone. I had no reason to kill her!'

'Maybe she didn't give you what you thought you were going to get? Maybe, instead, she stole your credit card!'

'No, that's not true,' I said.

'So you *did* have sexual intercourse with Miss Katerina?'

'No. No I didn't.'

'How do you know if you can't remember?'

'I just know,' I said. 'If I did meet this Miss Katerina, then it was only inside the club; I never saw her outside.'

'Mister Nicholas, I've already told you that we have evidence, so why do you keep insisting on telling us lies?' Then, he flipped open a folder that was on the table in front of me. Some photographs were inside. 'Take a look,' said the detective. 'It might jog your memory.' I looked down at the pictures. They showed Galina lying in a big open topped bin among household refuse that included chicken bones and rotting vegetables. Her throat looked like it had been cut. Her clothes were badly torn, revealing a body that was bruised, cut and covered in blood. I couldn't look any longer. I looked away. 'Take a good long look,' said the detective. 'See the result of what you did.' I looked again at the pictures. 'They're awful,' I said.

'It was an awful crime, don't you think?' replied the detective.

'Yes.'

'What would a person have to do to be punished like that?'

'I don't know,' I replied.

'What would someone have to do to you to make you want to do that to them?'

'Nothing could make me do something like that.'

'Why the mutilation of the body Mister Nicholas?'

'Mutilation?'

'The hands.'

'I don't know what you're talking about.'

'What did you do with her hands?'

'I really don't know what you're talking about,' I repeated. The detective turned to speak to the inspector. I was thankful for a pause in the questioning, as I needed time to think. I now knew that it was Galina they were talking about. Obviously, the police had traced me through my credit card that they found in Galina's possession. Maybe they also had a witness who had seen us together at the club. I couldn't decide what to say, or what to confess to. Even confessing to taking a prostitute home might be enough to keep me in big trouble, and rather than eliminating me as a suspect for the murder, the fact would probably be used to support the case *against* me.

'So, Mister Nicholas, is there anything you now want to tell us?' the detective said.

'I didn't kill her,' I replied.

'And you still maintain that you did not leave the club with Miss Katerina?'

'The woman in the photograph, I do recognise her,' I replied, 'but she introduced herself to me as Galina.'

'So you knew her as Miss Galina, not Miss Katerina, is that correct?'

'That's right.'

'So you did leave the Storm Club with the woman you knew as Miss Galina?'

'Yes.'

'And you took her back to your home?'

'No.'

'Then where did you go?'

'We just walked around outside the club for a bit,' I said. 'Then, because I was feeling tired, I decided to go home and I think Galina went back into the club.' I don't know why I started lying. I just panicked I guess. I didn't want to confess that I had taken Galina, a prostitute, back to my villa. 'How long were you outside the club walking, and where did you go?' asked the detective.

'We just walked around the block, which took ten or fifteen minutes I guess. We both just wanted to get a bit of fresh air really.'

'Did you want Miss Katerina? I shall call her Katerina, as that is the name in her passport. Okay? Did you want Miss Katerina to go to your home?'

'No.'

'Or did you want to take her anywhere else?'

'No.'

'Did Miss Katerina want to go to your home, or anywhere else with you?'

'No.'

'So, she did not try to do business with you even though she was a prostitute?'

'I didn't realise,' I replied.

'Mmm,' said the detective. 'I find that hard to believe, but even so, your version of events still does not fit with the information we already have.'

'Aren't I entitled to legal representation or anything?' I asked, partly out of panic, and partly to stall the questioning, which was starting to take a course I was having problems dealing with. 'So you now think that you need a lawyer?' the detective asked.

'I don't know. Do I need one?' I replied.

'You will have one without doubt when you really need one, when your case goes to court.' That last sentence really scared me. I hadn't had time to think that far ahead. Would I get justice in an Emirati court? Who would help me to ensure that I did get treated fairly and have a fair trial, if it came to that? I thought that perhaps Mike would be able to help me. 'Does my employer know I'm here?' I asked. The detective flicked through some papers in his file. 'Ah, yes,' he answered. 'We were contacted by a Mister Michael Tomlinson, who has now been informed of your situation.' There was then a brief pause before the detective spoke again. 'Mister Nicholas, I will tell you one thing. Your crime was a truly terrible crime, but if you confess your guilt now and show some repentance, it is quite likely that you would escape the death penalty. But if you continue to insist on your innocence, then the death penalty will be the likely outcome.'

'But I can't confess to something I didn't do,' I replied. The detective shrugged his shoulders. The inspector stood up and announced that they were going to prayers again. The junior detective walked me back to my cell.

I found that as my interrogation had lasted several hours, I had missed lunch. I was not given anything to eat until the evening. I could not wait that long for some liquid however. It was so hot and I felt that my body was dehydrating. I banged on the cell door. When the guard came, I asked for some water. He returned with a metal jug full of water and a plastic cup. I did not see the inspector or his assistant again on that day. I was not surprised as that is what had happened the previous day. I knew that the interrogation earlier that day had not gone well for me, and that the detectives were close to discovering as much of the truth as I knew. The problem for me was that they seemed to have more pieces of the puzzle than I did. I was slightly disappointed that I was not called back for further questioning that day only because I wanted to get it over with. I wanted to know what evidence they thought they had against me and I wanted to know what was going to happen to me.

Waiting for someone to help me

*T*he next morning, a guard opened my cell door and gave me a bar of soap, a small toothbrush, a small tube of toothpaste and a piece of cloth, which I later discovered was to be used as a towel. He spoke no English, but led me to the bathroom. It consisted of a room with four showers, all in a row with no dividing walls, and on the opposite side a row of sinks. Two other men were already showering when I arrived. They were both about my age, or perhaps a bit older, and they both looked like they were from the Indian subcontinent. Even though they were naked, I guessed from their overall appearance and manner that the one with the darker skin was a labourer while the lighter skinned man was some kind of professional, perhaps a businessman. We all avoided eye contact with each other, and didn't even acknowledge each other's presence. I had been so hot and sticky, it was a real pleasure to be able to wash and clean my teeth. The water from the showers came at only one temperature, and that was very warm, but not hot. The water was probably from the cold water supply, for in summer in the UAE, cold water taps usually deliver anything between lukewarm and hot water. I had no shampoo with which to wash my hair however, and nothing to shave with. Two guards watched the three of us. As each of the other two prisoners finished washing, showering and using the toilet facilities, they were led by one of the guards back to their cell. When I had finished using the facilities, I dressed again in the same clothes I had been wearing since taken from my home. I was then escorted back to my cell by both guards. As we walked back to my cell, I glanced down at the watch worn by one of the guards, and saw that it was not yet 6 am.

Breakfast was the same as the previous day: two pieces of bread with jam and a glass of tea. After I had eaten my breakfast, I waited to be taken for interrogation again, but no one came for me. Outside my cell, everything seemed silent. For lunch, I received a bowl of lentil soup and a bread roll. Then, all afternoon I continued waiting for something to happen. As the day went on, my cell got hotter and hotter. The cell had no means of ventilation and the air was stifling. I sweated profusely and sipped at my water regularly to prevent dehydration. Sitting or lying on the floor became incredibly uncomfortable so I stood frequently and 'walked' on the spot. The cell was too small to take more than four of five steps in any direction. My whole body felt stiff so I tried to do a few press-ups and sit-ups, but my lack of energy prevented me from doing more than about ten of each.

When a guard came with my evening meal, I asked if I could see the 'officer in charge'. I wanted to find out why I hadn't been questioned that day, whether I could make a phone call to Mike or the British Embassy in Dubai and whether I was going to get legal representation. The guard kept replying, 'Anna mush fahim,' which I knew meant 'I don't understand.' Communicating with the guards in the prison or police station, or wherever it was that I was being held, was very difficult as less than half of them spoke or understood any English, and the remainder were still quite weak. At least a couple of hours after I had finished my evening meal, my cell door opened and a guard took me to another room in which I hadn't been before. It contained only a table with one chair on either side of it. I was told in Arabic to 'sit down'. A few minutes later, Mike entered the room. He took the chair opposite me. The guard locked the door, but remained inside the room, standing in front of the door. It occurred to me that as he appeared to speak no English, I could say anything to Mike, but then it occurred to me that perhaps he was only pretending not to speak or understand English.

'I came as soon as I could,' said Mike. 'As soon as they would tell me where they were holding you.'

'And where am I?' I asked.

'This is Jumeirah police station,' replied Mike.

'Have they told you what I've been charged with?' I asked.

'They told me that you had murdered a Russian prostitute,' answered Mike.

'Oh, bloody hell,' I responded. 'It's all so very complicated.'

'What happened?' asked Mike. I replied in little more than a whisper and the guard did not object. His eyes stayed focused on us however, probably to make sure that Mike didn't give me anything or vice versa. Knowing about Mike and Inga made me feel that I could tell Mike the truth about my trip to the Storm Club. 'On the Thursday before last I went to the Storm Club, and I met a girl who called herself

Galina. We ended up going to my place. I was pretty much out of it. I had drunk quite a bit and for some reason I felt really tired. I'm pretty sure that I didn't do anything with Galina, but my memory of the whole evening after leaving the club is very fuzzy. I woke the next morning on the settee in my living room. Galina was gone, and she had taken my wallet, with my credit cards, driving licence, health card, the lot. The police have now told me that Galina, whose real name was Katerina, was murdered that night. It was a brutal murder apparently, with her body mutilated and her hands taken. They found one of my credit cards on her body, but not, as far as I know, my wallet or any of its other contents. The police say that they have more evidence linking me to the murder, but they have not told me what they have. What I've just told you is what I know or what the police have told me. I haven't admitted to taking Galina, or rather Katerina, to my villa however.'

'Why not?' asked Mike. 'I think it would be better to tell the truth.'

'I'll probably only get done for procuring prostitutes, or something like that,' I replied. 'And I don't really fancy a hundred lashings and five years inside for that either.'

'Yes, but murder?' said Mike. 'That is far more serious.'

'But how would confessing to taking a prostitute to my home help get me off the murder charge?'

'If they know you're lying about one thing, that may lead them to believe that you're lying about other things.'

'I suppose so,' I replied. 'But I didn't even use her services. I'll still be accused of something I didn't do. That's the annoying thing. All I remember was giving her a couple of vodkas with orange juice and chatting for a while.'

'Well, you do what you think is best,' said Mike. 'I did bring you some stuff to eat and some books and magazines to read, but they wouldn't let me bring them in to you. Are they treating you alright?'

'The cell is small and has no window or ventilation, and I have no bed, or even a mattress to sit or sleep on. The heat is unbearable. The food is pretty awful, but at least edible. The guards are okay, but I've only been questioned twice, for three or four fours each time. I've not yet seen a lawyer or been given any information about being getting one.'

'Have you been formally charged with the murder?' asked Mike.

'I don't think so,' I replied. 'I think that despite the evidence they say they've got, the investigation is still ongoing. I just hope that they are continuing to look for the real murderer.'

'I think that I need to contact the British embassy,' said Mike, 'and they should then send someone over here to help and advise you.'

'That would be very good of you, Mike,' I replied. If he had not offered to contact the British embassy, I would have asked him to do it anyway, but I was very glad that he had offered before I had needed to ask. I then asked Mike what was happening at work. He told me that he had told Jane, Head of Human Resources at the Deira National Bank, the truth: that I was in jail. Her response to Mike was that she was prepared to wait two or three weeks to see how my situation developed, before deciding how to proceed with the labour nationalisation project. We chatted a bit more about work-related news and gossip before Mike left. As he was leaving, I asked him the time. He looked at his watch, and answered, 'Ten minutes to ten.'

I was taken back to my cell. I stood for a while, facing the wall, with my legs wide apart and my arms up above my head, with my hands on the wall. The wall was warm, and the rough concrete uncomfortable for my hands, but I felt the need to stretch before later trying to sleep. I was very tired, and yet I knew that I would still not sleep well; the air was too hot, the floor was too hard and the light was left on all night. It must have been after midnight when my cell door opened. I had already been lying on the floor for about an hour with my eyes closed. The guard led me to the interrogation room. This time three men were waiting for me: the junior detective who had previously questioned me, and two new officers, who didn't look like a very friendly pair. The junior detective was as friendly as usual. We exchanged greetings in Arabic, but the other two did not join in.

'I hope you have had enough time to think,' began the detective. 'There is no point in wasting any more time with lies. The inspector is expecting me to get the whole truth tonight.'

'You mean my confession?' I asked sarcastically.

'If that is the truth,' replied the detective. 'Have you anything you want to say before I begin with my questions?'

'No,' I replied.

'Yesterday, you told us that you left the Storm Club with Miss Katerina in order to take a walk around the block. You said that you then saw Miss Katerina go back into the club before you took a taxi home.'

'No. I said that I thought she *may* have gone back into the club.'

'That is not what the Storm Club's CCTV shows.'

'Really?' I replied, wondering what it did show. The detective paused a while before continuing. 'It shows that you got into a taxi with Miss Katerina,' said the detective. 'So, Mister Nicholas, would you like to tell me where you two went in the taxi?'

'I suppose you already know,' I replied.

'So tell me.'

'We went back to my place.'

'To the villa in Jumeirah, which you share with a Mister Jasper Harrington?'

'Correct. But Jasper was, and still is, in England.'

'And you went straight there?'

'Yes.'

'For what purpose?'

'I don't know really. It's not the reason you think. I was tired and I wasn't thinking straight.'

'I'm not clear, Mister Nicholas, how you could take someone back to your home at two-thirty in the morning with no particular purpose in mind.'

'Maybe I was just a bit lonely. Maybe I wanted some company for a bit longer.'

'But you were so tired?'

'I was. That's true,' I replied. 'I can't explain my actions.'

'Okay,' said the detective, 'so now you admit that Miss Katerina went with you to your home. The taxi driver said that he dropped you off at about two-thirty. What happened then?'

'She drank two vodkas with orange juice. I drank just orange juice, but she thought I had the same as her. I knew that I had already consumed too much alcohol and I didn't want any more. She ate some little salty snack biscuits with her drinks. We chatted for a while. I think that I must have fallen asleep on the settee in my living room.'

'Did you engage in sexual intercourse with Miss Katerina?'

'No, I'm sure that I did not.'

'Did you go into your bedroom with Miss Katerina?'

'No, I didn't. But I found out a few days later that she had gone there on her own. I had some money hidden under my clothes in a drawer, which I kept for emergencies. That had gone.'

'How much?'

'About three or four thousand dirhams. She had also taken my wallet containing another two thousand dirhams, a number of credit and debit cards, my driving licence and my health insurance card.'

'Did you report this to the police?'

'No.'

'Why not?'

'I was embarrassed to.'

'Why?'

'Because I thought that the police would think what you are now thinking: that I had taken Katerina back to my villa for sex.'

'Yes, you're right, because even if you didn't end up having sex with Miss Katerina, it *must* have been your intention to do so when you left the Storm Club.'

'But it wasn't!'

'Whatever. That does not matter now,' said the detective. 'So what happened after you had your sleep?'

'I slept right through until the morning. I woke up on the settee in my living room still fully clothed. But Galina, I mean Katerina, had gone, and she had taken my wallet and the money from my bedroom.'

'Had she taken anything else?'

'Not that I am aware of.'

'If she took all these things that you claim, then why when she was found dead just several hours later, did she have just one of your credit cards?'

'I don't know. She took what I said and I reported it to my bank and credit card companies the next day. You can check.'

'You may have reported them stolen, but that does not mean they were stolen.'

'But they were. And I applied for a replacement driving licence and a new health insurance card. Why would I have done that?'

'I don't know.... yet.'

'I'm telling the truth. I've now told you everything I know.'

'You still haven't explained where, how and why you killed Miss Katerina.'

'That's because I didn't kill her.'

'We know, Mister Nicholas, that you didn't do it at your home because the forensic scientists have already told us that. So, you must have taken her somewhere else. Where did you take Miss Katerina?'

'I didn't take her anywhere.'

'Where did you take her?'

'I slept right through until the morning, when I found her already gone.'

'Mister Nicholas, you have already told us many lies. How do we know this is not another?'

'I promise, this is the truth.'

'This is not acceptable to us.'

'What can I do?' I asked. 'I've told you everything I can remember.'

'Why did you kill Miss Katerina?'

'I didn't.'

'How did you kill Miss Katerina?'

'I didn't.'

'Where did you kill Miss Katerina?'

'I didn't.'

'Why did you kill Miss Katerina?'

'I didn't.'

'How do you know that you did not kill Miss Katerina?'

'I just know.'

'But your memory of the evening is so unclear. Maybe you just don't remember the details?'

'I didn't kill Katerina. Yes, I was tired. Yes, my mind was a bit muddled. But I *would* remember murdering someone.'

'Tell us the truth!' The questioning continued like this for over an hour. The same questions were repeated over and over. Then, suddenly the detective said, 'Stand up, Mister Nicholas.' I hesitated for a moment. 'Stand up, Mister Nicholas,' the detective repeated. I rose to my feet. One of the other two officers came up behind me and placed a bag over my head so that I couldn't see anything. Then, my hands, back and legs were beaten with some kind of stick or baton. I very quickly fell to the ground. The beating did not last long but the pain was considerable. As I lay on the ground, the three men spoke to each other in Arabic, and even laughed a few times. A few minutes later, I was dragged back to my cell. The bag was removed from my head, and the cell door closed quickly behind me before I could see who had brought me back to the cell.

The following day I was not interrogated. I was not given a visit to the shower room and I was allowed only two trips to the lavatory the whole day. I received my three small meals, as usual, and a new jug of water. I spent most of the day trying to sleep, or at least rest. My body was still sore from the beating, yet there was little bruising or other evidence of it. The day passed very slowly. I was more bored than I had ever been in my life. Like any free person living in a developed country, I was not used to living in an environment without music, television or reading matter. I wondered how long it would take the British embassy to send someone to see me. I decided that I would not tell whoever they sent about my beating, because that would only complicate matters and maybe distract them from the bigger problem: that I was being accused of murder.

The consulate section of the British Embassy in Dubai sent

someone to see me the next day. He arrived a couple of hours after I had finished my breakfast. I met him in the same room in which I had seen Mike. He introduced himself as 'Adrian Shackleton'. He told me that he had come to see me in response to Mike's request. Mike had told him briefly about my situation, but Adrian also wanted to hear all of the relevant details from me. I told him exactly what I had told Mike. After Adrian had listened to all I had to say, he began to tell me about the services that could and could not be provided by the British consulate.

'First of all, Mister Williams,' began Adrian, 'or may I call you Nick?'

'Nick is fine,' I answered.

'First of all, Nick, let me tell you what I cannot do. I am not able to investigate the crime of which you are accused, I am not able to give you legal advice and I can't get you out of prison. I cannot get you any better treatment in prison than is given to UAE nationals. I can, however, help you get in touch with local lawyers or interpreters. I can communicate with local authorities or organisations on your behalf and I can arrange for messages to be sent to relatives or friends in the UK, or in the UAE if necessary.'

'I think that I would like legal representation,' I said.

'I can certainly put you in touch with some local lawyers,' continued Adrian, 'but their costs will have to be borne by you. Do you have the necessary funds in the UAE to settle such expenses?'

'Enough to get started with, I'm sure,' I replied.

'The lawyers out here are *very* expensive,' said Adrian, 'and it's often difficult to assess what they're doing to earn their money. This could be seen as a big case that requires a big fee. But don't assume that it will be easy to get a lawyer to take on your case. I have met other British nationals in prison who found it very difficult to find a lawyer that would represent them. And please be clear that the names of any lawyers I give to you are not in any way recommended or approved by either the British consulate or me.'

'So how do I go about selecting one?' I asked.

'I can tell you which lawyers have worked for other British nationals in the past,' Adrian began, 'but as none of them were up for murder, how helpful that would be to you I don't know. Of course, it might be easier to have a lawyer who can communicate well in English, but that might not be the lawyer who works hardest on your behalf to get the best outcome possible. To be honest, you're facing something of a lottery; you're not going to know how good any lawyer is until he's actually working for you, and the lawyers out here do generally have the reputation of charging too much and doing too little. How accurate that reputation is, I couldn't say, but I thought that it might be helpful to know.'

'I see,' I said, feeling great pessimism.

'How good a friend is Mike?' asked Adrian.

'He's my boss,' I replied.

'Only I don't know how much access you will have to a phone, so it might be better if Mike could make initial contact with the lawyers you're interested in. I do have a list of names and addresses with me now. I could leave you a copy, and perhaps fax one to Mike, or anyone else that you think might be able to help you.' Adrian suggested that I call Mike there and then, and he lent me his mobile phone to do so. Mike agreed to help, and he gave his fax number to Adrian, who wrote it down in a little notebook. Adrian then left, but before doing so he promised to visit me again the following week.

After lunch, I found myself back in the interrogation room with the inspector and his assistant, the detective who had actually questioned me in English on every occasion that I was interrogated. As usual, the interview started civilly, with handshakes and greetings in Arabic. 'How are you feeling?' asked the inspector. 'A little sore perhaps?'

'Yes,' I replied.

'What happened was out of our control, you understand,' said the inspector in reasonable English, although he claimed he couldn't speak it fluently. 'The officers who sat in on your last interview were from the special crime investigation unit. They wanted to come again today but we persuaded them not to. I do hope that we will not be proved wrong for doing that.'

'I intend to co-operate fully,' I replied. The junior detective then started asking questions, the same ones that ended the previous interrogation: Why did I kill Katerina? How did I kill Katerina? Where did I kill Katerina? Why did she have one of my credit cards? Where were my wallet and its other contents? What did I do with Katerina's hands? Why was my memory of the details of the night in question so poor? Wasn't it possible that I had killed Katerina but not remembered doing so? They seemed to be asking the same questions over and over, and I was giving the same answers. We must have continued in the same way for at least two hours. I could see that the inspector was getting more and more angry. I feared that he might call again for the 'special' officers to give me another beating, but there was nothing I could do to prevent it if that is what was going to happen, because I was telling them everything I knew. It eventually sunk in that they had nothing else against me. I was bolshier about this fact than perhaps I should have been.

'It seems to me,' I began, 'that the only evidence you have against me is that Katerina was at my home. You have even already told me that she was not murdered at my home. But you have nothing to directly connect me with her murder or the place where you found her body.'

'Don't be so sure Mister Nicholas,' replied the detective.

'The only thing that connects me with the murder scene is that Katerina had my credit card in her possession at the time she was murdered. And even that we don't know for sure. Somebody else, perhaps the real murderer, could have placed my credit card with the dead body, hoping that I would take the blame for the murder.'

'That is an interesting theory, Mister Nicholas,' replied the detective, 'but no judge would ever believe it.' That last comment brought me back down to reality. It seemed that the police didn't have to prove me guilty, instead I had to prove my innocence. I knew what I had to do, but I had no clue about how I could achieve it. The ultimate truth was that as I couldn't remember anything after having drinks with Katerina in my home, I could not be one hundred per cent certain that I was not in some way responsible for her death. My heart and soul told me that I did not kill Katerina, but how could I know it as a fact when I could remember nothing. I was beginning to lose hope. I think that the detectives could see it on my face, and they continued questioning me, repeating the same questions over and over, obviously hoping that I would eventually cave in with a confession.

Of course, I did not confess to murdering Katerina Bogdanova. I was not going to confess to something that I did not know I had actually done. Perhaps if I had been tortured or beaten again, they may have forced a confession from me, but it would not have been made of my own free will. Eventually, I was returned to my cell, tired and depressed. I could not see any way in which I would ever escape the situation in which I found myself, unless they actually found the real murderer. There was no evidence to suggest, however, that the police were even looking for another murderer of Katerina. It seemed to me that the police were quite content to pin the murder on me. It would be another successful result for them, which would maintain the near perfect clear-up rate for murder cases in the country.

The next two days were Thursday and Friday, the Emirati

weekend. I saw no one over the weekend except the guards who brought my meals and escorted me to the lavatory. On the Thursday morning I was allowed a quick shower before breakfast. The hours passed by very slowly. The air in the cell was stifling, as usual, and the high temperatures made me sweat a lot. I drank as much water as the guards would bring me. Even the tiles of the floor were uncomfortably warm. I tried not to let myself feel down, but it was a difficult task when I had nothing to divert my thoughts from my grave situation. I tried to think about my parents, my friends in London and beautiful, peaceful places that I had been to in my life, such as quiet English beaches.

Empty fridge

*I*got back to our villa at three-thirty in the afternoon on the first Friday in September. I did not expect Nick to meet me at the airport, but I was disappointed that he was not at home when I arrived. Before I left for my holiday I had written down for Nick my contact number in England in case of any emergency and my return flight details. Therefore, he should have been expecting me. If he wanted to go out, he could at least have left me a note saying where he was and what time he expected to be back. I could then have planned my meal arrangements. I had intended to have my evening meal with Nick, but by about five o' clock I wondered if I should try to make alternative arrangements with Heidi.

The villa was in a complete mess. Much of our furniture was not in its usual places and there was dirt and dust everywhere. It looked as if Nick had held a party in our villa the previous evening, which would have explained why the living room furniture was all over the place. He had, however, made little effort to clean up or get things 'back to normal' afterwards. I cursed Nick for sometimes being so inconsiderate. After my long flight, the last thing that I needed was to come back to a dirty house and an empty fridge. The fridge had virtually nothing in it except some mouldy bread and some milk that had soured. The food cupboards and freezer also had much less in them than was usual for Nick and I. There was barely enough to make a complete meal.

My bedroom looked as if someone had been in it. Things were not exactly as I had left them. I wondered whether it was Nick who had been in my room, or whether he had visitors in our home who had. In the eight months I had been sharing my home with Nick, I had never noticed that he had been in my room before. Perhaps he had needed to borrow something important. I unpacked my suitcase, and put some dirty clothes into the washing machine. I then rearranged the furniture in the living room, swept the floor and polished the coffee table, display cabinet, television and music centre units. I then called Heidi. She immediately suggested that we go out for dinner, and I had no hesitation in gratefully accepting the offer. Half an hour later, Heidi arrived. We had spoken on the phone every two or three days while I was in England. Some calls lasted over an hour. We seemed to be getting on very well together. When we came face-to-face again, she gave me a big kiss and hug, and her huge smile indicated how happy she was to see me again.

I told Heidi about the messy and dirty house that I had come back to and the kitchen without food. She expressed great surprise. 'Nick came across as a thoughtful and considerate person on the few occasions I met him,' she said.

'I am a bit surprised myself,' I replied. 'I thought at first he'd had a party because of the state of the living room, but then thinking about the mouldy bread and sour milk in the kitchen, I've come to the conclusion that perhaps Nick hasn't been here for a few days.'

'You'll find out once he shows up, I suppose,' said Heidi. 'Come on Jas, let's go for our dinner.' We went to our favourite Chinese restaurant at the Metropolitan Hotel on Sheikh Zayed Road. We had a lovely meal, throughout which we chatted enthusiastically, although we had little gossip to catch up on due to our recent and frequent telephone conversations. I was very glad to be back in Dubai as I was really enjoying my life at that time. I loved my home, my job, the Dubai lifestyle and I was falling in love with Heidi. The hot and humid weather didn't bother me at all. Everywhere one goes in Dubai is air conditioned, and somehow the heat and humidity are never as bad on the coast. If I felt like a walk, I simply walked along the path that ran alongside the beach. There was usually a breeze coming in off the sea, and although the air was sometimes quite warm, it was pleasant nonetheless.

When we had finished our meal, Heidi and I decided to have coffee back at my place. We got back at about ten o' clock. There was still no sign of Nick. 'I really do wonder where Nick is,' I said.

'Why don't you call him on his mobile,' Heidi suggested.

'If you don't mind, I think I will,' I replied. 'I can't take the suspense any longer.' Nick's number was stored in my mobile's memory, so the number was dialled in seconds. Then, to our surprise, we heard Nick's phone begin to ring. I left the phone ringing and we followed the sound to his bedroom. As we entered the room, the phone stopped ringing.

'That's strange,' I said.

'Maybe the battery's gone dead,' Heidi suggested. Nick's phone was on top of a chest of drawers. I picked it up and examined it. 'I think you are right,' I said. 'It seems to be dead.' We looked around the room. It was clean enough, but it was also rather messy. Several doors and drawers of the bedroom furniture weren't properly closed and I could see that none of his clothes were properly folded or hanging. It looked as if Nick had been searching for something but then gone out in a hurry before tidying up again. His bed was unmade. It had only a pillow and a sheet on it, which was probably used as a light blanket, but almost half of it hung down onto the floor. 'Something doesn't seem right,' I said. We went to the kitchen and I made the coffee. We drank it in the living room, while the MTV channel on my television provided the background music. 'You seem quite concerned about Nick,' Heidi finally declared, realising that I wasn't concentrating fully on our conversation.

'I am,' I replied. 'He's not always the most reliable person, but this is not really like him either.'

'Why don't you give Mike a call,' suggested Heidi. 'Maybe he knows something.' I did as Heidi suggested. Five minutes later I knew everything. After I had put the phone down, I repeated everything Mike had told me to Heidi. 'I'm shocked,' was all she said.

'Me too,' I added.

'But he couldn't have done it,' said Heidi. 'Could he?'

'I would have said never,' I replied. 'But Mike said that even Nick couldn't say for certain because his memory of the latter part of the night in question is completely blank.' We sat for a while in silence. Heidi ended up staying the night, even though it meant her having to get up and leave before six o' clock the next morning. She had to go home to shower and change before going to work. Like many other office workers in Dubai, she generally started work at about seven-thirty in the morning.

My assignment at the airport was virtually finished, but I had a few loose ends to tie up so the next morning that is where I went. I couldn't concentrate on my work duties that well because my mind kept wandering back to Nick and his situation. I left work a bit early so that I could call in at the JBNC office to see Mike. I told him that I wanted to go and see Nick, and he gave me the necessary directions. I decided to go home and have dinner before going to see Nick. As I ate my pasta, the telephone began to ring. I picked up the receiver. 'Hello, could I speak to Nick please?' the voice on the other end asked. I wasn't sure, but I thought it might be Nick's mother. I thought for a moment how to answer. 'Is that Jas?' the woman asked.

'Yes,' I replied. 'May I ask who you are?'

'I'm Nick's mother,' she replied.

'I thought so,' I said.

'Nick usually calls us at least once a fortnight,' said his mother, 'but as we hadn't heard from him for nearly a month I thought I'd phone this time.'

'Mrs. Williams,' I began. 'I'm afraid I've got some bad news to tell you. I only got back to Dubai from my holiday in England yesterday, so I don't yet know the details, but it seems that Nick is being held at a police station.'

'Why, what's he done?' interrupted Nick's mother.

'He's been accused of murder,' I replied.

'That's ridiculous,' responded his mother. 'Nick would never do that.'

'I was just having a quick bite to eat and then I was going over to see him.'

'He has denied the charge I assume?' his mother asked.

'Yes, I think so,' I replied.

'And does he have a lawyer?'

'I don't know.'

'And has anyone from the British embassy been to see him?'

'Yes, I think so.'

'Jas, would you please do me a favour?' asked Nick's mother. 'When you get back from the police station, would you please give me a call to update us with everything?' She then began to cry.

'Yes, of course I will,' I replied. I wanted to tell her not to worry and that everything would turn out fine in the end, but I didn't think it appropriate to perhaps give her false hope.

When I arrived at the police station and said whom I wanted to see, I was led to a room with just a table and two chairs in it. I was searched, and then told to sit down. I waited for at least half an hour before Nick entered the room. He looked pretty awful. He and his clothes looked dirty, and he moved slowly, like he was very weak. He was unshaven and his hair looked greasy and matted. He took the seat opposite me. 'Thanks for coming mate,' he said. 'You got back alright?'

'Arrived yesterday afternoon,' I replied. 'I was quite concerned about what had happened to you, so I called Mike last night, and only then found out.'

'So, you've spoken to Mike?' asked Nick.

'On the phone last night, and I dropped in at the office today,' I replied.

'Did he say anything to you about a lawyer?'

'He said that somebody had agreed to come and see you in the next couple of days.'

'I had hoped that Mike would return to see me and keep me updated. He came only last Monday.'

'He's very busy at work at the moment,' I said, trying to defend Mike.

'I guess so,' agreed Nick. 'Well I suppose you've heard everything?'

'Mike told me all that you told him,' I replied.

'What a mess I'm in, aren't I?' said Nick. The question didn't seem to require a response so I said nothing. 'I wish that I could remember *exactly* what happened that night,' continued Nick.

'Surely you don't think that you're somehow implicated?' I asked, in little more than a whisper, so that the guard still standing in the room near to the door could not hear.

'Of course I didn't murder the woman,' answered Nick. 'Why would I? What could she have done to me that would make me want to kill her?'

'And it couldn't have been an accident?' I asked, still whispering.

'Whose side are you on?' Nick grunted. 'You're beginning to sound like the bloody police.'

'Sorry mate,' was all I could think to say in response to that statement.

'I may have been drunk, and I may have been stupid to take a prostitute back to our place, and I may have been careless to let myself be robbed by her, but I am *not* a murderer. Nobody seems to believe me and nobody seems to want to help me.'

'I'm here for you mate,' I replied. 'If I can help you in any way, just say.'

'I'd be grateful if you could chase up the lawyer,' said Nick. 'At least then I might know where I stand: what my chances of getting out of here are. He might also be able to tell me what the police are up to. I don't even know if they're still investigating the case or looking for anyone else.'

'I'll certainly try to do that for you,' I confirmed. 'And I'll come back to see you before the end of the week.' Nick then asked about Heidi and my work at the airport. I could see that he was not really interested in what I had to say. His mind was far away, and given his situation, that was very understandable. After twenty minutes or so, the guard in the room said, 'Enough. Time to go.' He took Nick by the arm, and led him out of the room. Another guard came to escort me out of the building.

On the following Wednesday evening, Mike and I went to see Nick again. He seemed in better spirits, having met with his lawyer. Nick told us that his lawyer was called Khalifah Sultan Al Marzooqi, who was to be addressed simply as Mister Khalifah. He was, Nick estimated, about forty years of age. He had been a practicing lawyer for twelve years, but had never before taken a murder case. Nick hired Khalifah, however, because he seemed confident and keen to take the case. Nick said that the police were still questioning him for hours every day, although the detectives only repeated the same questions over and over. He said that the detectives looked as bored as he felt. I asked Nick if he had been mistreated. He answered 'No', but not very convincingly. He told us at length, however, about his uncomfortable cell and his monotonous daily routine. He described the tiny meals he was given and he told us the details about his trips to the shower room and lavatory. It's an awful thing to confess, but what Nick had to say was so depressing, that I think both Mike and I felt relieved when the guard ended our visit after twenty minutes.

Seeing daylight again

Thursday and Friday passed slowly. I was not interviewed and I did not see anyone. Most of the time I felt weak and hungry, and the heat was unbearable for all twenty-four hours of each day. There was little space for movement in my cell and nothing to occupy my mind. I used my meal times as the point of reference to estimate the time. The guards who brought my meals who spoke English would tell me the time. On Saturday morning, the guard who came to release me from my cell spoke only Arabic. I assumed that I was going for a shower, but I was rushed out of the cell before I could pick up my soap, toothbrush or the piece of cloth that was my towel. As we walked up the corridor the guard continued speaking to me in Arabic. 'Ana la tet kalam al Arabiah,' I said, so that he would know I didn't speak Arabic. The guard just shrugged his shoulders. It seemed to me much earlier than the usual shower time. I guessed that perhaps it was in the middle of the night. Before we reached the shower room, the guard stopped and ushered me into another room. It had nothing in it other than a dozen or so chairs in the middle of the room arranged in a circle back-to-back. Five men were already seated, including the two men of Indian appearance I had previously seen in the shower room. The lighter skinned one, the one that I thought could be a businessman, gave me a nod of recognition. I went and sat in the chair next to him. We all sat in silence waiting for something to happen. I speculated that perhaps we were all going to be punished or tortured for failing to co-operate with the detectives, or perhaps we were waiting to be examined by a doctor, or perhaps we were going to be taken to another prison. 'Do you know why we're here?' I whispered to the Indian looking businessman.

'I think we're probably going to be prepared for court,' he answered. Both of the two guards stared at me, so I decided to say nothing more. How could I be going to court I wondered, when I was not informed so in advance and when my lawyer seemed not to know about it?

232

A dark skinned man of South Asian appearance entered the room carrying an electric shaver. He plugged it into an electric socket and pulled one of the chairs closer to the wall. We then took it in turns to be tonsured. It was the first time in my life that I had no hair on my head. I had not shaved my beard since arriving at the police station. It was long, messy and uncomfortable. Sweating in the heat made my beard very itchy. The 'barber' touched my chin and asked, 'You want beard?'

'No,' I answered. He changed the attachment on his shaver and removed my beard. When all of the prisoners had been tonsured, a man with a camera entered the room. He took a photograph of each of us. When the photographer had finished taking our pictures, we were led to the shower room. As I entered the room, I was handed a blue shirt and matching trousers. They had been cleaned and pressed but they looked many years old. 'Change into these,' said the guard. The other prisoners were already wearing the blue jail suits. I had previously noticed this, but hadn't given much thought about why the other prisoners were wearing the blue suits while I was not. I had hoped that I was not issued with the prisoners' clothing because it was assumed that I would not be held in jail for long. It now seemed that perhaps this assumption might be wrong.

After we had finished showering, all six prisoners were expected to share one towel to dry ourselves. I decided to dry myself with the shirt I had been wearing for the last two weeks. A couple of the prisoners looked like they could be sick, and despite showering, they still looked somehow dirty. I thought it safer not to use the towel provided after these men had used it. I dressed in the blue clothes provided. The shirt was a little small. It was tight across my chest and the sleeves were an inch or so short. The trousers were okay, though perhaps slightly on the large side. Shortly after returning to my cell, breakfast arrived.

Half an hour or so after finishing breakfast, the guard who had taken me earlier in the morning to have my head and beard shaved, the one who spoke no English, opened my cell door. He indicated that I stand up. He then brought my wrists together in front of my body and handcuffed me. Shackles were then placed around my ankles. When I was cuffed on both hands and legs, the guard indicated that I follow him down the corridor. I could take only small steps with my legs shackled. We took a couple of turnings and then I could see daylight. The sun was still low in the sky, so I guessed that it was about seven o' clock given that sunrise occurred shortly after six. I then found myself standing in a yard. A wall, perhaps thirty feet high, surrounded the yard. The guard pointed at the wall that was part of the building from which I had just come. A couple of the other men that had been tonsured with me earlier were already waiting there. I went and stood with them. The guard then said something in Arabic, which I assumed to be something like 'wait here'. The other men who had been tonsured with me arrived during the next few minutes. When the Indian businessman saw me he said, 'Looks like I was correct about us going to court today.'

I took some deep breaths. It was good to breathe fresh air after two weeks in the cell. The sky was blue and bright, and the humidity in the morning was not yet high enough to be unpleasant. 'Have you been to court before?' asked the Indian businessman.

'No,' I replied.

'This will be my third appearance,' said the Indian. 'And I still don't know what's happening. I have not yet been found guilty, I'm not yet in a proper prison, but I am not released either.'

'Doesn't your lawyer tell you anything?' I asked.

'I don't have one,' replied the Indian. 'I couldn't find one that I could afford and the Indian embassy does not help at all. Not like yours.'

'The British embassy helps find a lawyer for British nationals who need one, but it does not pay any of the costs involved.'

'I bet it would if it had to,' replied the Indian. I knew that he was wrong but I couldn't be bothered to argue with him. I remained silent. 'The fetters around my ankles are far too tight,' complained the Indian. 'They're cutting into my skin already.'

'Mine are very tight too,' I added. A number of guards entered the yard and a couple approached us. 'Get into the truck,' one of them ordered. There were three trucks in the yard, but the one nearest to us had its back doors open. I climbed into the truck and was followed by the five other prisoners. The compartment in which we sat had no windows except small ones in the back doors. We could not see the driver or those at the front of the truck. We sat on a couple of benches facing each other. Two guards came into the back of the truck with us and shut the doors behind them. A few moments later we were moving. It soon became hot and sticky in the back of the truck. It felt as if there was a lack of air despite the fact that the truck's capacity was about sixteen people while we were only six prisoners and two guards. There was, of course, no air conditioning in the back of the truck and the one light bulb in the roof seemed to give off considerable heat.

The journey seemed to last only twenty minutes or so. Upon

arrival at the court, we were led to a small, narrow room that had no windows or ventilation. There were, perhaps, twenty men packed into the room like sardines in a can. The door to the room was kept permanently open, but three or four guards stood continuously in the doorway. Every five to ten minutes, a prisoner was led out of the room while another returned to it. Some men sat on the floor, while others stood. I was the only white prisoner. Two thirds looked like they originated from the Indian subcontinent while the remainder were of Arab appearance. The Arabs were all smoking. A guard had even given one of the prisoners a light. The smoke they produced was suffocating as it produced a fog in the room. I went up to the guards in the doorway and asked, 'Is my lawyer here? Does my lawyer know I'm here?' The guards muttered to each other in Arabic and shrugged their shoulders.

A couple of hours after arriving at the courthouse, it was my turn to face the judge. It was clear who the judge was, but there were several other men around me taking turns to speak to the judge. Everything was said in Arabic and there was no translation for me, so I didn't have a clue what was going on. There was no sign of Khalifah, my lawyer. I was in the courtroom no longer than five minutes. Then, I was dragged back to the holding room. No one told me what was said in the courtroom or what the outcome was. Midday passed and the heat was once again becoming unbearable. Since receiving breakfast at about six in the morning I had received nothing to eat or drink. The Arab prisoners passed a bottle of water around themselves. 'The locals get privileges,' whispered the Indian businessman in my ear. 'And the Yemeni guards also like Iraqis and Saudis. You see, Yemen supported the Iraqi invasion of Kuwait and many Yemeni have family in Saudi Arabia. That's how things are here. Your treatment may depend upon the diplomatic relations between your country and that of your guard.'

Some time in the mid afternoon, I and the five other prisoners from Jumeirah were loaded back into a truck. I was feeling weak and dehydrated. The skin on my shackled arms and legs had become scuffed. Both my wrists and ankles were fastened too tightly. I had an itch in the centre of my back, which, of course, I could not reach. That annoyed me throughout the whole journey back to the police station. When we arrived back at the Jumeirah police station, we were greeted by a policeman with an Alsatian dog. The dog examined each of us in turn. It was a lively thing that jumped up on us sniffing everywhere. I'm not the biggest dog lover and this dog made me feel quite nervous. I've never fully trusted dogs since the time I was at primary school, when I saw one jump up on a girl and bite out a big chunk of her cheek. I was glad when I was back in the relative safety of my cell. I was hot, tired and uncomfortable, but at least my arms and legs were set free again. I wasn't brought any food or water until the evening.

The next morning I asked the guard who brought my breakfast if I could have access to a telephone, so that I could contact Khalifah. 'No phone,' he answered. That was a long day. I saw only the guards who brought my meals and escorted me to the lavatory. I spent much of the day just lying spread out on the floor speculating what had happened in the court the previous day. I had to wait until the next day to find out. Khalifah arrived not long after I had finished my breakfast. He told me that I had been to a preliminary hearing, but that he had not been notified about it until the previous afternoon. He could not come to speak or interpret for me because he was already committed to being in another court defending another client. 'Don't worry,' said Khalifah, 'I have all the papers now and can tell you exactly what happened. It really wouldn't have made any difference to the outcome if I had been there. Basically, the judge gave the police permission to hold you for another thirty days while their investigation is on-going.'

'Thirty more days!' I shouted out. 'But they don't even have any real evidence against me.'

'That's probably why they need the thirty days,' replied Khalifah. 'To get some.'

'That won't be possible, unless they invent some,' was my response. Khalifah assured me that he was doing all he could to defend me, and that he had a contact in the police who was 'seeing to my interests'. And then he was off again, probably to visit another client or to go to another courthouse.

Breakfast the following morning seemed to come earlier than usual. Several minutes after I had finished eating it a guard entered my cell. 'Get up,' he said. 'You're being transferred to the Al Wathba central prison today.'

'Where's that?' I asked.

'Abu Dhabi,' the guard replied.

'Does my lawyer know that I am being transferred?' I enquired.

'He will be informed,' answered the guard. I was cuffed on both hands and legs, and then escorted to the yard where the trucks were parked. I was bundled straight into the back of a truck, identical to the one that had taken me to court three days earlier. The truck was already full of prisoners and more came after me. There must have been at least twenty of us in there, despite the truck being built for only about sixteen. The doors of the truck slammed shut without any guards riding in the back with us. The journey to Abu Dhabi took about a couple of hours. At times I thought that I would suffocate before we got there.

When we arrived at the Al Wathba prison, we were again examined in the arrival yard by an Alsatian dog. I could see that the prison was very large, with many blocks. We were led into a three-storied building and then to a room where we were photographed and fingerprinted. We were ordered to hand in all personal belongings. I had nothing to give. Then, we were each given one more blue jail suit in addition to the ones we wore, two blankets, a plastic cup and a plate. I had left my soap, toothbrush, toothpaste and towel in Jumeirah and wondered whether these items would be reissued to me. The guards then started calling out our names. I heard my name 'Nicholas Alexander' being called out. They used my first two names rather than my Christian and surname. The guard that called out my name and those of three other prisoners led us down a corridor. At its end, we turned left into another corridor. We passed many rooms that looked like small offices or interview rooms. Eventually we came to a round shaped hall. Around it were about twenty cells. We were led into a cell that can be described only as a concrete cage. Inside it were twelve mattresses spread out on the floor. Eight were already occupied, with men sitting or lying on them. There was no window and no ventilation in the room, and the smell of sweat and unwashed bodies was awful. We were allowed to pick our own mattress. I made a dash for one against the wall, between two of the men who looked slightly cleaner and more respectable than the others. The mattress was thin, lumpy and badly soiled. I decided that I would have to use one of my two blankets as a sheet as there was no way I wanted my body to come into contact with such filth. I sat on my mattress and said 'hi' to each of the men on either side of me.

Life outside

I found it hard to get my life into its usual routines once Nick went to jail. Our villa seemed too quiet and it only encouraged me to think about Nick, which wasn't good for my mood. I was conscious of using Heidi as much as possible to distract myself from my 'living alone' situation. At times, I wasn't certain whether I actually wanted to spend time with Heidi or just avoid time spent on my own. I was reminded that I had now spent nearly ten months in Dubai when I received a letter from our lettings agent reminding me that our tenancy expired in just over two months' time and enquiring whether we wanted to renew it. Mail is not delivered to private households in the Emirates so people either rent a post box at the central post office or have their mail delivered to their work addresses. I opted for the latter option. I had now finished working at the airport and was doing a bit of desk research for another client, which allowed me to work at the JBNC office.

The letter from the lettings agent distracted me from my work and made me feel somewhat anxious. I didn't know what was going to happen to Nick, and I was sure that he would not be willing to pay rent on a long-term basis if he was locked up in jail. And I couldn't afford to keep on the villa on my own. I wanted to blame Nick for putting me in this awkward predicament. If he didn't have such an awful temper and if he didn't have to keep testing and pushing at the boundaries of acceptable and expected behaviour, then he probably wouldn't have been in the mess he was in. I remembered the incidents Nick had with the taxi driver whom he allegedly attacked and the unpleasant way in which he confronted Shannon in a public place. I should have been more careful about who I decided to share a home with. I felt a bit depressed after visiting Nick with Mike the previous Wednesday evening, and I spent considerable time during the few days after considering how frequently it would appropriate for me to visit him in future. He wasn't a particularly close friend, rather just someone with whom I was thrown together by circumstance. In fact, I wasn't even sure that Nick liked me. It appeared to me at times that he had some sort of chip on his shoulder about me having gone to a public school and Cambridge. His mother, however, was calling me every other day for an update, and I did feel a bit guilty when I had nothing new to tell her. Now I would have to see Nick fairly promptly in order to discuss his view on what to do about our tenancy of the villa.

Mike called me into his office. 'Jas,' he began, 'did Nick ever talk to you about his project at the Deira National Bank?'

'A little,' I replied.

'Well, they now want us to replace Nick.'

'I see,' I said.

'I know that it's not really in your area of expertise or interest,' began Mike, 'but I've not really got anyone else I could ask to take over at the moment.'

'What about Baron?' I suggested.

'I don't think he'd be suitable,' replied Mike. 'So would you be prepared to give it a go?'

'It doesn't sound like I have much of a choice,' I replied.

'You always have a choice,' was Mike's response.

'It's okay,' I said. 'I'll do it. Just give me the details.'

In the afternoon, I noticed a crowd gathering in Mike's office. The crowd included managers, consultants, administrative workers and even Mohammed. They all seemed to be looking at Mike's TV in horror. I wondered what it was that they could be watching. I tried to continue working for a few minutes but then couldn't fight my curiosity. I got up and went over to Mike's office. 'What's happening?' I whispered in Mohammed's ear.

'There's been a plane crash in New York,' replied Mohammed. 'Into one of the towers of the World Trade Center. They're not sure what caused it yet, but it looks like it might have been the work of hijackers.' Mike switched the TV from the Bloomberg business channel to CNN. The picture showed the north tower of the World Trade Center in flames. Black smoke billowed up into the early morning sky. On the street below, hundreds of people were running away in panic from the burning building. The reporter's voiceover said, 'All we know at this time is that American Airlines flight 11, a Boeing 767, departed from Boston at 8.15 am for Los Angeles. It was carrying eighty-one passengers, two pilots and nine flight attendants. After becoming hijacked, the flight was diverted to New York. At 8.45 am the plane crashed into the north tower of the World Trade Center, tearing a gaping hole in the building and setting it afire. Who committed this act and why is not yet known.'

Everyone watched the television screen in silence. But worse was still to come. As we were watching pictures of the burning north tower, the reporter suddenly announced, 'It is not yet confirmed, but it is believed that a second hijacked plane is now headed towards this location.' Seconds later, we watched live as United Airlines flight 175 made impact with the World Trade Center's south tower. That too went up in flames. At 9.30 am local American time, President Bush, speaking in Florida, announced that the country had suffered an 'apparent terrorist attack'. At 9.45 am a third plane crashed into the Pentagon in Washington, and at 10.10 am a fourth plane crashed in a wooded area in Pennsylvania, south-east of Pittsburgh. A few minutes earlier, at five past ten local American time, we saw the south tower of the World Trade Center collapse.

'Oh my God,' Mike kept repeating. Some of the females were sobbing, with tears flowing from their eyes. Some of the Americans had relatives or friends who lived and worked in New York or Washington, and for them the news was especially hard to cope with. The pictures on the screen were horrific: buildings collapsing, debris falling down on people in the streets below, scenes of chaos in the streets with people running in panic while injured people lay waiting for help and unable to move, traffic in gridlock, a sky which had been bright and blue on a sunny morning turning dark grey. The reporter said, 'America is in chaos. This is the worst terrorist attack the United States has ever suffered. The FAA has halted all flight operations at US airports, the first time ever that air traffic nationwide has been halted. All bridges and tunnels leading into New York City have been closed. The White House, the State and Justice departments, The United Nations building, the World Bank and all other government buildings in Washington have been evacuated. Trading on Wall Street has stopped. The US military has been placed on high alert. President Bush has called the crashes a "national tragedy".'

'I don't know about all of you, but I can't watch anymore,' said Mike.

'Turn the TV off,' someone called out. Something like a group hug then occurred, which I guess was intended mainly to console the females and those Americans who might have been directly affected by having relatives or friends in the cities hit.

At the end of the working day, when most of the other employees had already gone home, Mike approached my desk. 'Jas, have you got any plans for dinner?' he asked.

'No,' I answered.

'Would you like to join me then?' he said. I accepted his invitation, and we agreed to dine at the Crowne Plaza hotel, which was just down the street, also on the Sheikh Zayed Road. We ended up in the *Western Steakhouse*, one of the hotel's restaurants. I had a good steak and washed it down with a cold beer. We talked about Nick, Mike's daughters, Heidi, events coming up in Dubai in forthcoming weeks and several work-related things, which was unusual for Mike as he didn't normally like to 'talk shop' outside work. Of course, we also talked about that day's events in America, which is now commonly referred to as '9/11'. 'Do you think it will affect us here in Dubai?' I asked Mike.

'Who knows?' was his reply. 'I mean, if the people responsible are Muslims who are anti-American, or even anti-Western, then we could well be a future target.'

'Who knows what the locals really think of us,' I said. 'We come to their country, take many of the best jobs and then tell them how things should be done. I'm sure many of them must resent us.'

'Probably,' agreed Mike. 'Although we're basically here to help them. We might also benefit from generous salaries and high standards of living, but us expatriates bring the knowledge and skills that they themselves do not have at this time. Give it another ten to fifteen years and there will no longer be a role for us. Labour nationalisation should be complete by then. But if there are future attacks against westerners, as there have been in Saudi Arabia, then many expatriates might decide to leave earlier. Have you thought about how long you would like to stay out here?'

'It's hard to say,' I replied. 'On different days I have a different opinion.'

When the evening felt like it was drawing to a close, I suggested we walk back to our office car park. 'Actually,' said Mike. 'I'm staying here at the moment. In the hotel.'

'Oh,' I replied.

'Stella found out about Inga and me and kicked me out of the house. I don't blame her really, but it's all over now. You knew about the two of us though, didn't you?'

'Well, actually...' I began.

'Oh, it's alright,' said Mike. 'Inga told me that Nick had seen us together at the Astoria Hotel one night. She had seen Nick watching us while trying to be inconspicuous. I figured that he'd probably have told you about it.'

'But as far as I know, he didn't breathe a word about it to anyone else. Not even to Baron.'

'I'm grateful to him, and you, for that. I had wondered how Stella got to find out about Inga and me, and for a while suspected Nick of telling her, but now I don't believe that he did. I still don't know, however, how she did find out.'

'So what's going to happen to you two?'

'Stella's saying that she's going to take the kids and return to the States alone, but I'm hoping that it won't come to that. I still love her and hope that with a little time she will be able to forgive me.'

Visits to Nick

The following evening I decided to visit Nick to update him about Mike and the previous day's events in America, and to discuss our tenancy of the villa. When I got to the Jumeirah police station, I was asked to take a seat in the entrance lobby. I must have waited for over an hour and nobody attended to me. I went back to the reception counter to find out why I wasn't being allowed to see Nick. 'Please wait a while,' replied the officer. Ten minutes later, another officer approached me. 'You are a friend of Nicholas Alexander?' he asked.

'Yes,' I answered. 'Although I know him as Nicholas Williams. I guess that Alexander is his middle name?' The man nodded.

'Yesterday he was transferred to Al Wathba central prison.'

'Where is that?' I asked.

'Abu Dhabi.'

'Is there any news on what's happening to his case?'

'He went to court last Saturday. I understand that he will be detained while we complete our inquiry.' I thanked the officer for updating me, and left.

Later that evening, Nick's mother called again. I told her what I had found out. 'Nicholas's father and I have decided to come out to Dubai,' she said. 'We feel that we must be there to support Nicholas. Do you think that it would be alright for us to stay in his room?'

'Well...er..' I began. I didn't know if she was asking whether Nick might object, or whether I had any objections. It was Nick's room, he paid for it and these were his parents, so I didn't feel that I had the right to try to put them off from coming, although I didn't particularly want to share my home with them. They would probably just sit around being sad and miserable, making me also miserable in the process. 'The tenancy ends in two months, however,' I added. 'And I guess that it will not be practical for us to renew it.'

'We can deal with that when the time comes,' she replied. 'Good.

Then we shall make the travel arrangements. We'll let you know as soon as something is sorted.'

I had agreed with Heidi earlier in the week that she would stay the weekend with me at my villa. She arrived several minutes after I had finished speaking to Nick's mother on the phone. I gave Heidi an update on all of the news. 'My poor love,' she said sympathetically as she ran her fingers through my hair. 'So when do you plan to see Nick next?'

'I'll have to find out where the prison is and what the visiting hours are,' I replied. 'Given that it's in Abu Dhabi, perhaps I'll go next Thursday.' Heidi screwed up her face, indicating that she wasn't particularly happy with my suggestion. I could understand why; a Thursday would, after all, be one day lost out of our precious weekend together. But then she surprised me and said, 'Perhaps I could come with you?'

'That would be nice if you wanted to,' I said. 'And we could always make a day of it. We could do a bit of sightseeing in Abu Dhabi afterwards and then perhaps have dinner there too.'

The following week went by very slowly. I started work at the Deira National Bank. I didn't enjoy it much and I wondered how Nick would feel about me taking over his assignment. Eventually, Thursday came. Heidi had slept over from Wednesday night so that we could make an early start for Abu Dhabi. It wasn't really necessary, however, because I found out that the visiting hours at the prison on a Thursday were from four to six in the afternoon. So, Heidi and I decided that we would visit the city of Abu Dhabi and do some sightseeing before visiting Nick, and then stay for dinner in the city after leaving him.

As we approached Abu Dhabi, but while we were still twenty miles or so from the city, a continuous line of palm trees, bushes and flowering shrubs began to run along each side of the road on which we travelled. The flowers provided splashes of colour in shades of white, pink, orange, red and purple. The greenery also extended into the distance. It was hard to believe that we were driving through a desert state. My first impressions of the city were that all the buildings were tall, modern, sleek and shiny. The roads were constructed in a grid network, so that they ran in parallel and crossed each other at right angles. It was immediately obvious why Abu Dhabi is known as the 'Manhattan of the Gulf'. The pace of life seemed slower in Abu Dhabi than in Dubai. People were not rushing about in the streets and the drivers drove slower. At junctions, some drivers actually gave way to us, a rare occurrence in Dubai. We drove up and down the long, straight shopping streets, which seemed to have many of the well-known international chains. We then went along the Corniche, the coastal boulevard that runs along one side of the city. On one side of the road were parks and gardens with fountains and recreational areas, while on the other side was the spectacular backdrop of the modern city with its high-rise buildings. We continued along the Corniche road and soon left the city centre behind us. The road now ran alongside the harbour's edge. Eventually, we took a turning to our right and drove on to the breakwater, going right to its end. We got out of the car to stretch our legs and to get cold drinks from the café. This was undoubtedly the best place, other than from a boat on the water, to admire the Abu Dhabi skyline.

When we had finished our drinks and felt refreshed, Heidi and I got back into the car and we drove to the Al Hosn Palace, also known as the 'White Fort'. This was the home of the former ruling family and it is the oldest building in Abu Dhabi. To be honest, it was not a very impressive building. We then visited the *Heritage Village*. This was an interesting living exhibition of the traditions and lifestyle of the indigenous peoples of the region. We learned much about the Bedouin tribes that lived with their camels in the UAE for hundreds of years and about the traditional industries of pearling and fishing. The exhibition reminded us that life stayed much the same in the region for many hundreds of years, right up until about fifty years or so ago when oil and gas were first discovered. It was easy to forget that the UAE was created only in 1971 and that forty years ago only a handful of tarmac roads existed, and the high-rise building was virtually unknown. It made all the more impressive what the UAE had achieved in thirty years: modern homes and offices, schools, universities, hospitals, reliable electricity and water supplies and a modern road network.

As Heidi and I left the *Heritage Village*, I couldn't help myself saying, 'This really is an incredible country.'

'That's probably why we're here, don't you think?' she replied.

'I didn't really mean from a personal perspective,' I responded. 'I was thinking about the progress made by the country in developing its infrastructure, its economic development, its provision of social welfare, free education, health care and utilities for its people, and a political stability that has avoided any serious domestic or international conflict. This country might be ruled by a dictatorship, but it's a bloody good one in my book. The rulers seem to really care for their people.'

'Maybe,' said Heidi.

'I mean, look at the UK,' I continued. 'We had plenty of oil and gas, but how did that ever benefit the people of the UK? Instead, we have high taxes and a high cost of living, increasing poverty and crime, and it seems that we have to get involved in every international conflict wherever in the world.'

'It's nearly four,' said Heidi. 'Shouldn't we start making our way to the prison?'

We got to the prison at about ten minutes after four. There was a long queue outside. 'Is this the queue for the visitors?' I asked the man in front of me. He didn't understand me and just shrugged his shoulders. I didn't want to be waiting in the wrong place, so I continued asking people further forward in the queue until at last an Indian man confirmed that it was the queue for visitors. The queue did not move for over twenty minutes, but then we made a considerable move forward. Another twenty minutes then passed before we moved forward again. It was obvious that the visitors were being admitted in batches. By five o' clock we had not moved more than halfway to the prison's entrance. 'If they stick rigidly to the visiting times,' I said, 'then I don't think we're going to get in today.' The temperature was still in the thirties and the sun was strong. There was no shade in which to shelter from it. We were hot and sticky, and stupidly had left our water in the car. 'Shall I get the water from your car?' Heidi offered.

'I don't know,' I replied. 'It would just be our luck that we would be let in while you were away and then you mightn't get in. What do you think?'

'I suppose you're right,' replied Heidi. 'It might be wiser to wait here.' At a quarter to six an English couple, probably aged in their early fifties, passed us having come out from the prison. The man looked at us. 'Are you waiting to visit someone?' he asked.

'Yes,' I answered.

'You won't get in now,' he said. 'If you want to make sure you get in on a Thursday, then you must start queuing before two, and on a Friday you must start queuing before six.'

'What time does visiting start on a Friday?' I asked.

'It starts at eight in the evening and goes on until eleven,' replied the man. 'But it's usually even busier on Fridays than Thursdays.'

'Thanks for the information,' I said. The man was right, we did not get to see Nick on that day. 'We'll have to come again next weekend,' I said. Heidi pulled a face that indicated she wasn't very happy about that.

We went, as planned, to have dinner in one of Abu Dhabi's hotels. We ended up at the Inter-Continental. As we were finishing our food, Heidi suddenly said, 'Nick, I've been thinking, and if you have to give up your villa, then perhaps we could find a new one together. That's if you want us to live together.'

'I would love it if we could live together,' I replied. 'But you could simply take over Nick's part of our current tenancy.'

'To be honest,' said Heidi, 'I would rather not move in to your current villa. It might hold bad memories for us in the future. I think that we should get a new home for the start of our lives together.'

'You're probably right,' I confirmed. I realised that I would now be hoping that Nick did not want to continue with our existing tenancy. I realised also that things might work out easier for me if Nick did not get released from prison before our current tenancy expired. I did not hope for this however. Of course I wanted him to be proved innocent and set free. But if he wasn't, I wondered what would happen to all of his possessions if we had to vacate the villa. Hopefully, his parents would deal with that if they were coming out to Dubai.

The next morning when I arrived at work, I went straight to Mike's office to tell him that Nick was now in Abu Dhabi and that we had tried without success to see him the previous day. The first thing that he said when he saw me was, 'Have you heard about his?' as he pointed at an Arabic newspaper on his desk, which had a picture of Nick on its front page.

'No,' I answered.

'One of yesterday's papers now claims that Nick was responsible for three murders in the country, including that of a national woman in Fujairah,'

'That's ridiculous,' I said. 'I don't believe that for one minute.'

'Yousef in the legal department brought the paper in and translated it for me.'

'And what does it say?' I asked.

'Apart from accusing Nick of two new murders in addition to the Russian prostitute, JBNC is mentioned several times. The writer asks whether American companies that don't vet their staff properly should be allowed to operate in the UAE. He further suggests that it is the increase in westerners and other foreigners in the UAE that is responsible for the spiralling crime rates. The whole article is basically anti-western. After 9/11, this really is the last thing that the company needed out here.'

'I can see that,' I agreed. Mike already knew that Nick had been moved to the Al Wathba prison as it was mentioned in the newspaper, as were the details of his preliminary court hearing.

A few days later, Heidi met me after work outside the offices of the Deira National Bank. We decided to have a drink in one of the many three star hotels nearby. When we walked into the bar we were surprised to find it full of locals, dressed in their white dishdashas. This was unusual, for while everyone knew that locals visited bars and drank alcohol, they were not permitted by law to do so in national dress. This bunch looked like they could have been a group of students. They were all aged between about eighteen and twenty-five. They were watching a TV that had on it images of the World Trade Center in flames, before showing one of its towers collapsing. The crowd were laughing and cheering, some throwing punches into the air. 'What's going on here?' I said to Heidi.

'I don't know,' she replied. 'But I don't like it. Let's get out of here.' We turned around to go, but a nasty looking young man with a long bushy beard, dressed in a dishdasha, blocked our path. 'America got what it deserved, don't you think?' he asked.

'No, I don't think that three thousand innocent people deserved to die,' Heidi bravely answered.

'That is no more than the number of Palestinians killed by Israel and the Jews in the last few years,' he replied.

'But two wrongs don't make a right,' was Heidi's final word on the matter as she pushed past the young man, taking me by the arm too.

'My God, what's happening to this place?' she said once we were outside. For me, however, the young man's words were thought provoking. 'If that man was right, I had no idea that so many Palestinians were being killed,' I said. 'Why is that do you suppose?'

'It could be because of the biased media coverage in our home countries or it could just be that you previously paid little attention to the facts because you had little interest in them.'

'A bit of each, I suspect, explains my ignorance of the facts regarding Palestine,' I agreed.

'You're not beginning to sympathise with the terrorists, I hope?' said Heidi in a teasing manner.

'Of course not,' I replied. 'But living in the Middle East, one is exposed to different perspectives on the region's conflicts and that I find interesting.'

Guilty and forgotten

Life in the Al Wathba prison was hard. Sharing my cell with eleven others made me feel claustrophobic. Other people surrounded me twenty-four hours a day. There was little space in the cell to move about, as there was only about three feet of floor space between each mattress. There was no place, other than the lavatories, to go for a moment alone. One couldn't even spend much time in those, as there was always a long queue to get into them. I didn't want to spend any more time in them than I had to because the dirt and smell in them made me feel sick. Often, little or no water flushed into the bowls, and many people's faeces were left to pile up in them until the guards allowed a prisoner to fetch buckets of water to pour into the toilets. The smell was unbearable. It could knock you out. About two hundred prisoners used three bathrooms. Quite often, the taps failed to deliver any water. The cells were dirty and dusty, and prisoners often had to go for days without washing themselves. Living in such unsanitary conditions, it was not surprising that many prisoners seemed to be sick or suffering from long-term health disorders, such as skin diseases and respiratory problems.

Communication was a problem for me because only two people in my cell spoke English: Emilio, a Filipino man of about the same age as me, and Ramesh, an older, rather reserved Indian man. The guards could not, or chose not to speak English. During my first two days in the Al Wathba prison, no one spoke a word to me. We received food and drink three times a day. Typically, we received a slice of bread and a glass of tea for breakfast, and then a meal with meat, usually served with rice, potatoes or bread, for lunch and dinner. Vegetable curries were also popular with the chefs. Sometimes, we got only a vegetable soup for our evening meal. Emilio told me that the meat served was usually camel, but we sometimes got chicken or mutton. The water we were given to drink was cloudy and it smelt foul. Sometimes, our meals were brought to our cell on two or three platters from which a number of prisoners had to eat with their hands. One had to eat fast to get one's fair share of the food. We didn't get enough to eat and I was permanently hungry.

The men in my cell originated from a range of countries including India, Pakistan, Sri Lanka, Afghanistan, Bangladesh, Iran and Egypt. On my third day in the prison, Emilio approached me. 'May I join you?' he asked.

'Yes, please do,' I replied. He sat on my mattress. 'What are you in for?' asked Emilio.

'I'm accused of murdering a prostitute,' I said. 'But I didn't do it. I'm innocent.'

'A lot of us are,' said Emilio. 'My employer accused me of embezzlement, but I didn't do it either. In fact, I think it was my employer who set me up.'

'What are the others in for?' I asked.

'Jatin, Saad, Ahmad, Khalid and Radhwan are, as far as I know, all in for theft,' replied Emilio. 'Ramesh was a businessman who wrote cheques that were not honoured by his bank. He owes his creditors over one hundred thousand dollars. Hisham, I think, was involved in a car accident while under the influence of alcohol, and Raza is accused of assaulting a work colleague. You're the only one in for murder.'

'I wish my lawyer would get my case moving,' I said, 'but I don't even know if he has been informed of my movement from Dubai to Abu Dhabi.'

'Possibly not,' said Emilio. 'But don't expect too much from your lawyer. The lawyers out here are happy to take your money, but they don't feel that they have to earn it. They'll take your money for doing nothing. Don't get taken for a ride, my friend.'

'What alternative choices do I have?' I replied. 'My lawyer is my only hope for getting out of here.'

'Maybe,' replied Emilio. 'But if you keep praying to God, he will see justice done. I will pray for you too.' I didn't tell Emilio that I wasn't religious, but I was still grateful that he was willing to pray for me. I figured that anything that might lead to proof of my innocence was worth a go. I was not ready, at this stage, to start praying for myself however.

I became depressed when day after day I received no visitors. I wondered what Khalifah was doing and why Jas hadn't been to see me. Jas must have found out that I had been transferred to Abu Dhabi by now, and Abu Dhabi wasn't *that* far from Dubai. Emilio told me that there was a telephone we could use in a corridor that led from the circular hall to the administrative block. He lent me one dirham to make a call. During the morning, when our cell was unlocked, I went to the phone. I had just dialled Khalifah's number when a man standing behind me reached over my shoulder and pressed some of the buttons on the phone, thus cutting me off. I turned around. I was facing two big East European looking men who I guessed might be Russian. 'Forty dirhams or ten dollars to use the phone,' one of them said.

'What?' I asked.

'If you want to use the phone, give us forty dirhams or ten dollars,' the man repeated.

'I have no money here at all,' I said. 'Only this one dirham that someone else lent me to make a call.'

'No money, no call,' the man said. 'Unless you have cigarettes?' I just walked back to my cell. I told Emilio what had happened. 'It's incredible,' he said, 'that the Russian mafia think they still go on making money while in prison, in an Emirati prison at that. And everyone is too scared to take them on. Of course, they leave the locals alone. They probably even give some of their earnings to the locals, or at least cigarettes.'

'Are there many locals in the prison?' I asked.

'Oh yes, in the other cells,' answered Emilio. 'They're usually in for things like being drunk, committing adultery or theft. Their lives are not as bad as ours. The guards give them cigarettes and bottled water to drink. They get more food and they are allowed more visitors. They send and receive letters every day, and sometimes they even get newspapers and magazines to read. And they never have to do any of the cleaning duties or anything like that.'

'You seem to know about everything,' I observed. 'How long have you been here?'

'I have been in here six years, and a court has never even declared me guilty,' Emilio replied. 'Hopefully, they will release me one day in the not too distant future.'

Eight days after I arrived at Al Wathba, Khalifah eventually showed up. We were allowed to meet in a private room. 'Sorry for not getting here sooner,' he began, 'but I have so many cases at the moment and I had nothing new to tell you anyway.'

'And have you now?' I asked.

'There's good news and bad news. Which do you want first?'

'The bad,' I replied.

'The local media is claiming that in addition to murdering Katerina

Olegovna, you also murdered two other people including a local woman.'

'That's ridiculous,' I said.

'You see, there has been a terrible act of terrorism in America. Over three thousand people were killed. There has been a great increase throughout the Middle East in all things anti-western and you, I'm afraid, fall into that category. It suits a lot of people to accuse a British man of three murders. But don't worry too much about this. I've checked some of the details with the police, and it would have been impossible for you to murder the woman in Fujairah because you were at work at the time the crime was committed. In fact, it occurred on the day of the Al Saadha-Wasel flotation, and your movements have been accounted for every minute and hour of that day. I'm sure that your innocence with regard to the other murder will be equally easy to prove.'

'And the good news?'

'I have it from a good contact in the Criminal Investigations Section of the police that they are still investigating the murder of Katerina Olegovna and that new information has come to light that may eventually prove your innocence. He was not willing to give me any details however. So have hope. We are all doing what we can to help you. And unless the police start to interview you about any murder other than that of Katerina, then don't worry about what the press are saying. I will keep you informed if there is any news.'

The next day, at about five o' clock, a guard came and told me that I had visitors. I was led to a small room, perhaps fifteen foot by fifteen foot. It was already crowded with visitors and prisoners. Most were standing. I immediately saw Jas and Heidi at the far side of the room. I thought that they saw me too so I gave them a wave, but they did not respond. I then pushed past a few people to get to them. 'Glad you came,' I said once we were face to face.

'We came last Thursday also,' said Jas, 'but after queuing for two hours we still didn't get in. Today we arrived at two. We queued outside until four-thirty before being allowed in to be searched and have our details logged. It all took quite a while. We had to give our full names, our dates of birth, our home addresses and the names and addresses of our sponsors. We got the impression that they were definitely trying to put us off from visiting again.'

'I'm sorry they put you through all that but I'm really grateful that you persevered,' I said. 'I really needed to see a couple of friendly faces.' I asked for the details about what had been written about me in the local press. Jas told me about that and more about the details of

9/11. I told them about my life in the prison but they didn't seem much interested. They seemed much more eager to discuss the tenancy of the villa. I don't know what they expected me to say. I didn't know what to say. I asked if I could have a few days to think about it, perhaps until after my parents had arrived. I also told them that Khalifah was hopeful that new evidence was coming to light that would prove my innocence. Jas and Heidi didn't look especially pleased for me. I don't know if I was being paranoid, but both Jas and Heidi seemed very cold towards me. It seemed as if they didn't really want to be there at all. I can't blame Jas really. I've never been especially nice to him or considered him a particularly close friend. Ours was more a friendship of convenience, and for him there was no longer any convenience. After twenty minutes, all of the visitors were asked to leave the visiting room. Jas and Heidi left without indicating whether they would be visiting me again. That made me rather sad.

I was cheered up the following morning when a guard brought me a letter. I immediately recognised the writing on the envelope as my mother's. The envelope was already open. Presumably, the prison officials had already read the letter. It was short but caring:

> *My dear Nicholas,*
> *Your father and I were very sad to hear from Jasper about what has happened to you. We hope that they are treating you well in prison. Please try to stay positive. We will be flying out to Dubai next week. Jasper said that we could stay in your room. I hope that is alright with you.*
> *You can be sure that we believe in your innocence and we will not leave Dubai until it's proven and you're released from prison. We have already contacted our local MP who plans to raise your case in Parliament to ensure that you get the full support of the relevant government departments, and we have also sought help from the 'Fair Trials Abroad' organisation. The 'Daily Mirror' has started a campaign of support for you and your story appeared on their front page a couple of days ago. The local television news also did a feature on your plight. Everyone is behind you and fighting to get you released.*
> *We will see you soon. Take care.*
> *Love and best wishes,*
> *Mum and Dad*

Later that day, a big Pakistani man decided to stand up to the two

Russians when they tried to prevent him from using the phone. Shortly after they started fighting, the guards pulled the three men apart and then took them away. When they reappeared the next day the injuries to all three men looked far worse than that caused by their original fighting. The Pakistani told his cellmates that he had received fifty lashings and a beating that involved kicking and punching by several officers to all parts of his body. Within hours, word of the beatings spread throughout the other cells. One of the Russians was beaten so harshly that he was unable to stand up straight. According to Emilio, the guards beat at least one prisoner every week for breaking some rule or other. He told me that some guards were corrupt and enjoyed being brutal. Prisoners with money were often forced to pay for privileges or to avoid punishments, and the guards sometimes raped young, good-looking men. During the coming weeks I saw plenty of evidence to support what Emilio had told me.

A few days later, Jas brought my mother and father to see me. It was good to see them, but I felt sorry for them for having to travel so far just to see me in such awful conditions. My father didn't look particularly strong. After only recently recovering from illness, I hoped that the stress and worry caused by me and my situation would not make him worse again. He said that they would hire a car and come to visit me every two or three days. They did this, and to be honest it helped me to remain sane. They visited Adrian at the British Consulate but concluded that he was a 'useless ass'. They also acted as the go-between for Khalifah and me. They passed messages between us regularly, although the big break-through that I was hoping for did not materialise quickly. During one visit, my mother asked me whether I would stay in Dubai if I were released from prison. I had already thought about that, and was able to tell her straight away that I would return to the UK. 'In that case,' she said, 'I would advise you to give up the villa and ship your things back to the UK.'

'Is Jas okay with that?' I asked.

'He said that if you decided not to renew the tenancy then he would rent a new villa with Heidi.'

'I see,' I said. 'In that case your suggestion sounds like the sensible course of action.'

'We will pack up all of your belongings and arrange the shipping,' said my mother, 'so you will have nothing to worry about. And we will rent a furnished apartment in Dubai until you're set free.'

'And if I'm not?' I whispered.

'You will be, Nicholas. You will be,' she replied.

November

When I had been in prison for ten weeks, Jas reminded me that it was exactly a year since we arrived in Dubai. I had never known a year pass so quickly. I had done so much during that year. A week later, Jas vacated our villa. He and Heidi moved to a villa in Al Satwa, which was slightly closer to the city centre. My mother and father rented a furnished apartment not far from Al Faheidi Street. All my personal belongings were on their way back to England. My mother said that I was beginning to look too thin. She brought food to the prison on most visits, but usually the guards stopped her from bringing it in to me. I did feel weak. The heat, and the lack of food, drink and exercise all worked against me. My arms and legs were covered in insect bites. I never really saw any insects in the cell, so suspected that they lived in our mattresses. I tried to wash my mattress every now and again, but I noticed that most of my cellmates didn't bother despite the fact that we spent almost twenty-four hours a day sitting or lying on them.

By the end of November, I was convinced that I was going to face the firing squad. I didn't share my thoughts with my parents because I didn't want them to know that I was losing hope. Inside, however, I wanted them to return home to England. I felt that they were wasting their time in Dubai. They would probably accomplish more for me in England. Then, on the last day in November, Khalifah visited me. When I walked in to the interview room he was smiling and looking confident, and I sensed that maybe he was bringing me some good news. 'Ah, Mister Nicholas,' he began. 'I am very happy to inform you that at last the police are making progress with your case. Yesterday, two Russian men were arrested for the murder of Katerina Olegovna. I don't yet know any of the details but it would seem that if the charges stick, then you will be off the hook.'

'That is wonderful news,' I said. 'Thank you, Mister Khalifah, for coming to tell me in person so quickly.'

'No problem,' he replied. 'You know, Mister Nick, I always knew that you were innocent and that the police would eventually prove it. The police here are very efficient you know. They solve virtually every murder case. It was only a matter of time until they solved this case.'

Nothing happened during the next few days. My mood changed daily. Some days I believed that I would be set free within days, while on other days I feared that something might go wrong and I would be kept in prison indefinitely, or worse still, put before the firing squad. I would rather have faced the firing squad than life in prison, but the firing squad is final. Once one is dead there are no second chances. Once I was dead it would no longer matter if one day it was discovered that I did not murder Katerina. It was about two weeks after Khalifah informed me of the arrest of the two Russians that he visited me again. His first words were, 'It's all over Mister Nick. It's all over.'

'What's happened?' I asked.

'The two Russians have been to court,' he replied. 'And the judge found them both guilty and sentenced them to death.'

'Do you know how it happened?' I asked.

'Apparently Miss Katerina worked for a Russian mafia gang. The gang is involved with drug trafficking, money laundering, prostitution, theft and fraud. Katerina was a prostitute, but at least once a week she was also expected to steal from a client. She usually did this after slipping a drug into her client's drink, which would quickly make them unconscious.'

'She probably did that to me when she sent me back to my kitchen to fetch her something to eat,' I observed. 'But maybe she even did it at the Storm Club. I was already feeling pretty lousy by the time I got home.'

'And that also explains why you can't remember anything about the latter part of your night with her. Anyway, she would have been particularly looking to take large amounts of cash, credit cards, your passport and other identification documents. Apparently, many cars were also stolen from clients and then shipped to countries of the old Soviet Union. Virtually none of the victims of theft reported the crimes because they were either too embarrassed to do so or feared that they themselves might face some punishment for going with a prostitute. But Katerina was greedy. The gang found out that she was keeping a lot of what she stole. She was supposed to give everything to the gang. That is why she was killed. It is assumed that she gave your wallet to the gang but kept back one of your credit cards for her own use. That is why when her body was found she had only one of your credit cards with her. The cutting off of her hands was apparently inspired by the use of the punishment for thieves in Saudi Arabia. Katerina's hands were shown to the other prostitutes as a warning not to keep stolen items. One of the girls tipped off the police with an anonymous telephone call, but she was eventually traced. She was persuaded to tell all, and it was proven with DNA evidence that the two men sentenced for Katerina's murder were personally responsible. So, you will soon be free Mister Nick.'

'When?' I asked.

'Soon. Please try and be patient,' replied Khalifah. 'Sometimes it takes a few days to sort these things out.'

It was ten days later that I was actually freed. No official of the police or prison gave me an apology or attempted to offer me any explanation or justification for why I was held for so long. But I didn't care about that too much, as I was just glad to be free. I went with my parents straight to a travel agent to buy our flight tickets home. We got a flight for the next evening. And the last thing that I did in Dubai was to visit the creek with my parents and cross it on an abra. After my weeks in prison it was wonderful to feel a breeze against my skin. It was even good to smell the salt from the water and the petrol from under the abra's deck. These were the smells of real life, of a free life. I wanted my last memory of Dubai to be a good one.